I0650595

UNDISCLOSED: THE COMPLETED SERIES

BOOKS 1-4

DEIIRA SMITH-COLLARD

This novel is dedicated to all the beautiful women who had the odds stacked against them, but never counted themselves out. These are the women who dive deep inside of themselves to find their light and shine brighter than people ever thought possible.

Keep shining!

COPYRIGHT © 2020

DeiIra Smith-Collard
Cover Design & Photography by
NubianFX Covers & Graphics
www.nubianfx.com

All rights reserved. No part of this book may be reproduced in
any form, except for the inclusion of brief quotations in a review,
without permission in writing from the author or publisher.
**This is a work of fiction. Names, characters, places,
and incidents are either products of the author's
imagination or are used in a fictional manner. Any
resemblance to actual events or locales or persons,
living or dead, is entirely coincidental.**

ACKNOWLEDGMENTS

I feel so honored and humbled as I'm writing my acknowledgements. For so long I thought I lost my voice and my desire to write. There were a million stories inside of me, screaming to get out but I was somehow, broken. Then one day I realized I had a God given gift and talent to create. I began writing and didn't stop. Now, I'm back and better than ever.

To my wonderful family, thank you for your endless support and encouragement.

Dana Pittman, thank you so much for motivating me and believing in me enough to light that fire under me. You push me to be a better writer, I'm in awe of your expertise.

Josie Sloan, thank you so much for always being here for me. I am blessed to have a friend like you. A friend that will rock with you through thick and thin, and who truly wants nothing better than the best for you.

To Lulu Botello, my fearless fuego warrior. You are bigger than life and inspire me everyday. Thank you for being a voice of honesty in my writing process and a constant motivation.

Lastly, but most importantly thank you to my readers. You all make this possible, without loyal readers my voice goes unheard. Thank you for the endless support. Enjoy this just as you did the last and the many more to come.

UNDISCLOSED: A TALE OF LOVE AND DECEIT

BOOK ONE SYNOPSIS

What happens when the past collides with the present?

Kyra escaped New Orleans burning bridges and harboring secrets. Determined to create her perfect life she finds her dream man. And now she lives a life of comfort and convenience as the wife of a high powered Texas attorney. But Kyra's perfect life is about to get turned upside down when her web of lies and deceit return in the form of Redd.

Lawrence "Redd" Richardson a hustler and man on a mission. Katrina and the FEDs devoured his life in New Orleans and he heads to Houston ready to shatter Kyra's life created with smoke and mirrors to get his life and enterprise back on track. To take back what's rightfully his.

There's just one problem: their undeniable attraction.

Kyra soon finds she's falling again for the smooth talking hustler she was determined to leave behind. Redd's not impressed by her luxury cars or mansion. He's prepared to conquer and destroy by any means necessary. And soon she finds that her carefully orchestrated reality is unraveling fast.

How far is Kyra willing to go to protect her secrets? And when Redd threatens her "perfect" life she is left with one choice: play him or get played. Which will she choose?

Undisclosed is a sexy romantic read full of suspense and heat. Its too hot for tv and too hot to miss. CAUTION this story is not for the faint of heart, read at your own risk. Buy your copy and learn just how dirty Kyra intends to play this game, even if it means everybody might get played.

PROLOGUE

Yo ass got til Friday to get the hell out of this state!
Get out or find your home in one of these bayous!
I'll feed yo ass to the gators and they will never find you
You been warned!

THE SUDDEN ATTACK of the words jolted my heart and left me in a state of disbelief. This was not at all how I expected my Thursday to go. Every nerve ending within my body exploded with infuriating heat, engulfing me in anger. Now part of me wanted to wait it out and dare a bitch to come at me. That was the real in me talking, but the smart me said there was someone just as real out there; waiting to prove her point. The thud of the door hitting the wall as I entered my home echoed my emotions. I slammed the door shut and threw my bags against the sofa.

"Think Dominique, think girl!" With the speed of a sprinter, my mind raced to create a plan. Staring at the white piece of notebook paper I found on my door I knew it was from a woman and most likely it was from my man's wife. I say my man cause he took care of me, he paid for this house, kept my pockets full and made sure I had nothing but the best. It didn't matter to me that he had a wife at home, his wife wasn't my problem, it was his.

At least that's what I thought. For years I knew this woman existed, but again, she wasn't my problem. Until now, now his pain in the ass wife was making a formal introduction and I heard her loud and clear. Had I met Queen under different circumstances we may have been cool, we shared much of the same taste, especially when it came to men.

I always knew who Queen was, everyone did and I had even met her a couple of times, but she just thought I was on Redd's payroll. She didn't know I was the main side chick dipping into the pockets she thought belonged to her.

My footsteps created a path of dismay as I walked the length of the room. Shit! What was I going to do? My heels clicked against the mahogany colored wood as I marched from one end of the living room to the other. I stood still for a moment, taking in my surroundings. My apartment was everything a girl like me could hope for. From the muted steel colored upholstery to the pops of purple throughout the room, it was all me.

I didn't want to leave it, but if it was Queen who sent me the threat, I knew she had the means and the power to follow through. I mean, she had the whole hood backing her. Queen had been with Redd since high school and I knew when it came down to it she had a team waiting to get a piece of me just cause she had told them to.

Some of these bitches were so thirsty to be in her presence they would kill on command. Redd and Queen were hood royalty and every nothing ass nigga and dusty hood bitch was dying to be in their court.

I've never been a stupid woman and I didn't plan on starting now. I made up my mind at that very moment. No use staying so that I could prove I wasn't scared. I would be lying to myself anyway. I walked to the back of my apartment and moved the picture in front of the large wall safe that Redd used to stash his valuables.

He had it installed right after I moved in. I agreed to stash the cash here and he agreed, I just wasn't allowed to know the combination. Or so his dumb ass thought. Anytime he opened it he made me turn my back or leave the room. What the dummy didn't know is when I turned my back; I faced a mirror and saw his every move.

"2-10-5-7," I said the combination aloud as I turned the dial. My fingers trembled, Redd had a key to this apartment and came and went as he pleased. I didn't expect him, but I never knew what to expect from him. I glanced towards the door and dashed towards it to bolt the top lock. At least that way I would hear him unlocking both locks and give myself a little extra time to hide what I was doing.

Once I made it back to the safe, I eased the door open and saw stacks and stacks of cash. I don't know exactly how much was in this safe. All I saw was racks on racks on racks, it was enough cash to get me the hell out of the state of Louisiana and some place better, some place where I knew I could be safe. I stuffed the money into the biggest purse I could find and closed it. Taking only the clothes on my back, I got in my car and drove straight down I-10 until I arrived in Houston, TX.

This is the place I will start over, this is where Dominique Simoneaux will re-invent herself.

ONE

SITTING at the dinner table next to my husband I admired him, he was truly handsome. The light from the dimly lit reception hall bounced off his smooth ebony skin, landing on his chiseled chin and full lips. After twelve years of marriage, we still had a passion that burned hotter than any fire. I knew how to be the lighter to his fuse, and I would always be here to support anything that would lead him to greatness. We were yet again at another benefit his firm was sponsoring.

I don't know if we were feeding the homeless, clothing the children or donating blood, his company was always trying to save the world and I could barely keep up with which cause they were fighting for.

I smiled and interacted like a good little lawyer's wife. Trent was a partner at one of the largest firms in Houston. He had broken through the barriers and was one of the few African American men employed by Smith, Masters & Jamison. We were the Jamison part. Boredom was creeping in while listening to the many speeches and bad jokes. I leaned into my husband and excused myself.

"Baby, please excuse me," I leaned into my husband and I whispered in his ear.

"Where you off to Kyra?" Trent's mouth spread into the million dollar smile that helped him acquit guilty people every day.

"The ladies room." Smiling, I slowly pushed my seat away from the table to stand. The black evening gown I wore clung snuggly to my hips. With my body swaying to the music that played in the background, I made my way to the restroom. Pushing the heavy door open, I walked in and quickly surveyed the stalls.

"Whew, I'm alone."

I needed the quietness this restroom offered. My back landed against the wall as I deeply inhaled the floral aroma of lavender and jasmine and then exhaled all of the exhaustive tension that resided in the pit of my stomach. My eyes roamed the room, taking in the nice decor. The restroom was decorated like a small sitting room with plush sofas and oversized chairs where one could wait in comfort.

No long lines would form outside of these doors. The marble countertops sparkled as if they had been newly polished, glistening in the warm recessed lighting that made them seem to glow.

The door opening interrupted my contemplation of the countertops. I moved closer to the sink to allow the woman entrance and to limit any unnecessary interaction. The woman's smile seemed to be carved into her creamy skin. It struck a chord of familiarity with me.

Trying not to stare I fumbled through my purse to find my lipstick and compact. I dabbed the sponge against my face to refresh my makeup. Through the reflection in the mirror, I could see her eyes on me. For an unusually long time, her eyes drifted over my features. Without taking my eyes off of her I snapped the small black case closed. What the hell did she want?

"I use MAC too, it's awesome isn't it?" Her voice sang the sweet song of a Louisiana native.

"Yes, it is." I smiled and continued to mind my business. My interest in her conversation was only surface deep, I would prefer not to be bothered and surely she couldn't have stared me down that long just to tell me she likes the makeup I use.

"I believe I know you." She tightened the space between us and was now far too close for my comfort. My deep breaths and exaggerated sighs should have been signs of my budding annoyance. Didn't she come in here to use the restroom? I was curious as to why she hadn't done so.

"I don't think so," I responded with a smile and began to place my cosmetics back into my bag. I watched in the mirror as her eyes burned deep holes into the side of my face.

"Yeah, Yeaaah, I know you, your name is Dominique, Dominique Simoneaux, am I right?" It was more of a statement than a question. I finally turned to face the woman.

I laughed, "I think we have a case of mistaken identity. Let me introduce myself," I extended my right hand to her. "My name is Kyra Jamison, and you are?" She reached to shake my hand. I noticed her immaculate French manicure and diamond rings she wore, pricey diamonds.

"You can call me Queen." I sensed a bit of sarcasm in her voice. She spoke as if I already knew her name. Her eyes were on fire, ignited with anger. She looked at me as if she attempted to look through me.

"Queen, that's very unique. Well, I am pleased to meet you. I have to excuse myself though, my husband will be giving a speech shortly, it was nice talking with you."

Hurriedly, I exited the restroom. Something about this woman made me uneasy and I was more than happy to excuse myself from her presence. I practically ran back to my table and the comfort of the familiar faces. Just as I was about to take my seat I heard that voice behind me.

"Dominique, you forgot your purse." I turned to receive the small Dior bag I was carrying.

"It's Kyra, and thank you very much for bringing this to me. I do appreciate it." With one swift motion, I collected my purse from her and turned to take my seat. This was her cue to walk away from the table. My purse was returned, her presence was no longer needed but instead, I watched as she grabbed the nearest empty chair and invited herself to the table.

"Mr. Jamison," She spoke. "How are you?" Trent looked at her as if she were an alien. I could tell he did not recognize her. Her head flew back as she released a boisterous laugh. "I work as a paralegal in your firm. You know, I'm assigned to most of your cases."

A spark of recognition flickered in my husband's eyes. "Queen, great to see you. I hardly recognized you without your glasses and your hair down. How are you this evening?"

"Well, that's the power of contacts and a flat iron." Again her loud laugh echoed through the room. For reasons unknown to me, I didn't like her. Her shifty eyes and knowing stares made me uneasy but it seemed that I was the only one to notice them. I didn't participate much in the conversation because her mindless chit-chat and country grammar reminded me of times I didn't care to think of.

"Sweetie, Queen relocated to Houston after Hurricane Katrina."

"So, how long ago was that again?" Why would I care when and how she got here? I smiled but honestly didn't care. I could tell my husband was trying to engage me in the conversation. He wanted his forever entertaining wife to emerge.

I knew she wouldn't be making a debut as long as that woman

sat at the table. I nodded and mumbled various things to entertain my husband's pleading eyes, but I was lost in my own thoughts.

The cadence of her voice held me captive as I gazed at her. The only thing that kept me from screaming at the top of my lungs was the hundreds of people in this room. Watching this woman was like watching a train wreck. You want to look away but you can't. Her energy intoxicated the table. She seduced them all with just her presence.

I sank back into the plush cushion of my chair and watched as they clung to her every word. My friends hungrily waited to devour her, greedy for more of her witty conversation. It was obvious that her beauty had captured them all. From the corner of my eye, I watched her every move.

It was easy to see how she had captivated the table, she was beautiful. Her smooth cappuccino colored skin and bright smile could fool anyone. Those almond-shaped amber eyes were incredibly innocent, but I knew different. Those same innocent doe-like eyes threw daggers at me when no one was looking. Between smiles, she would glance at me and wink with perceptive eyes. What was it that she thought she knew?

My stomach did summersaults as I watched her toss her long brown tresses and bat her lengthy Covergirl eyelashes. The night was finally nearing an end and I was ecstatic. I wanted to jump for joy as we walked towards our car.

"Would you and your date like to join us for drinks at our home Queen? A few of us from the firm are going to retire and have a few drinks, a little after party if you will." My husband could be very persuasive with just a smile.

"Now how could I say no to the boss." Queen stepped away from us long enough to call her date over. The one she had abandoned while she sat at my table. They moved towards us for what I assumed would be more introductions.

"This is my husband Lawrence." We all took turns shaking

Lawrence's hand. I shuffled further and further back. I wanted to disappear. Lawrence's eyes locked with mine as he extended his hand towards me. I had to drive myself to touch him. His grasp was frigid and cold, almost as cold as his smile.

"How beautiful" The words slipped secretly from his lips, only audible to me. I noticed the Chinese letters tattooed along the side of his neck. Under the Chinese letters was one simple word in all caps, Redd. I snatched my hand back and retreated into the safety of my husband's shadow. Lawrence towered over me, his tall slender stature intimidating me. I trembled from the strength of his stare.

His piercing eyes wandered over my body slowly as if he was memorizing every inch of my curves. I searched for any and every reason to avoid eye contact with them. Every nerve ending my body possessed tingled with terror. I had to figure out of how to get out this situation.

I began to walk towards the car and opened the door to get in. I would normally wait for my husband but they made me anxious. My retreat to the car placed needed distance between us. I exhaled as my body sank into the plush leather seats. Resting my head on the headrest, my husband's pearl white Maserati became my refuge.

There were no roaming eyes or knowing stares in this car, I was finally alone. I shifted in my seat to see if I could spot how close they were in the rearview mirror. They were approaching. I knew I wasn't going to be able to play hostess tonight and the only way I could get out of it would be to fake a headache.

I know he hated when I seemed uninviting and I tried to keep him happy, but he was so worried about appearances. The car door opening was the finger snap I needed to bring me out of my trance.

"Kyra, why did you leave like that?" His smooth harmonious

voice was concerned. He patiently waited for my answer but his eyes were consumed with worry.

"I have a headache baby." My voice was low, weak, and begging not to be questioned. This answer seemed to be enough because he never said another word. With every minute that passed, we came closer and closer to our home. The closer we got the more nervous I seemed to become. I didn't want these people in my house. I didn't know them and whatever they seem to have against me could only seem to get worse with inviting them into my personal space. I sat motionless as the car pulled into the three car garage. I almost forgot to breathe.

"Kyra, we're home." I heard his unspoken question, why hadn't I moved. I pushed the door open and stepped out. The mindless chatter in the background of the intruding lady, Queen floated through the garage, getting increasingly louder the closer she got.

Her voice carried through the hollow garage and with it traveled a pending disaster. I couldn't say why I felt this way, but it was something about the spark she carried in her eyes. I noticed it from the moment I saw her, her eyes said she was a woman with a vendetta, and vengeance would soon be hers.

Everyone talked while sipping midnight cocktails. Music played as the party started to really pick up. Any other night I would be right next to my husband, having a hell of a good time but tonight was different. Tonight I couldn't seem to pull it together.

All night I've felt both Queen and her husband threw glances with hidden messages, and somehow I was supposed to know what it was they meant. I was done with their cat and mouse game. I placed my hand on Trent's knee and leaned towards Trent. His facial hair brushed against my lips as I planted a kiss on his cheek.

"Baby, I think I'm going to go lay down. This headache is

getting worse and worse, I'm going to take something and go to sleep." I was in no mood for a party. I finished my theatrics hoping he fell for this fake ache.

"Can't you stay a little while?" I looked regretfully as Trent gave me the sad puppy dog look.

"Baby, I-" He interrupted my sentence with a motion of his hand.

"I understand, I hope you feel better." He gently kissed my hand as he led me to the long hallway that ended in the master bedroom. I couldn't close the door fast enough as I entered the room to finally find the peace I had been searching for all night.

I slid the straps of my sequined gown off of my shoulders and stepped out of it as it slipped off of my body and onto the floor. There was a low knock at the door. I wondered what Trent wanted. It was unlike him to leave a room full of guests. He was always the ever entertaining, always hospitable host. It must be important.

I walked to the double wooden bedroom doors, turned the lock and walked back to my dressing area without even turning around to greet him. Just as I reached for my robe, he spoke.

"Still just as beautiful as you have always been." The unfamiliar voice echoed throughout the large room. I turned to face the stranger.

"What are you doing in my room? You need to leave. Now!" How dare he just stroll into my room and watch me as I undress. That was beyond rude, it was repulsive.

"It's nothing I ain't never seen before."

"Leave, damn it." I felt like a small child in the company of a scary stranger. He cautiously moved towards me as his eyes began to dance over my body.

"Ohhh going back to our roots are we, I don't hear little miss proper no more, I hear Dominique from New Orleans, the one that grew up in the hood." His lips curled into a sinister smile.

"Where you been hiding all night girl? Now that's the person I remember."

An uncomfortable silence stood between us. My heart pounded, pumping five times faster than normal as I stood motionless, scared to even allow my self to swallow.

"You really have cleaned up nice. I see how you live, fancy cars, million dollar homes, diamonds for every day of the week; tell me Dominique, did my money help you get here? You know the money you stole from me. I never forget a debt. No matter how long it's been, and thirteen years still ain't long enough for me to forget 500,000 dollars. Baby, that's half a mil and right about now I'm needing that plus some interest." He stopped talking only long enough to take a breath, then he moved closer to me.

I held my robe in front of my body attempting to cover myself. I was naked and I didn't want to be bare in front of this man. The silky threads slipped from my hands as he snatched my robe away from me exposing my body. I could feel the cold air caress my nipples as they began to become alert from the chill. He mistook this as an invitation. Lawrence's hand gently stroked my breast. I slapped his hand away.

"Get the hell out of my room, I'm not going to tell you or your crazy ass wife again, I'm not who you think I am, my name is Kyra, not Dominique!"

His eyes were full of determination and that determination seemed to be fueled by anger. With the quickness of a cheetah, he grabbed my neck and pushed me against the wall. His nails dug into my skin as he rendered me immobile by placing all his body weight on me. He was so close I could feel his erection press against me. The more pain he seemed to inflict the more excited he seemed to become. His hot breath burned against my skin as he moved close enough to whisper in my ear.

"Bitch, stop playing with me, I know you, from the curve of

your hips to the scent of your pussy. Your hiding days are over, it's payback time." With the end of his speech, he released me. My body tumbled to the floor as I struggled to catch my breath. A minute longer and I'm sure I would have passed out. My heart was racing. Gazing up at this man he appeared larger than life. I shrank back into the corner, I wanted away from him. He glared at me and then just as quickly as he came, he was gone.

***

Within the next six hours, I was in Houston, Texas. The big city left me in awe. I didn't have any relatives here so I was all alone. The first night I spent sleeping in my car and that became old fast, besides I didn't need to. I knew any motel I landed at wouldn't ask questions. I had been here for a week, ducking and dodging like the law was after me. Hell Redd was worse than the law and if he ever caught me I would be dead.

I needed to come up with a plan. I had way too much cash on me and had to find a place to stash it and a place to stay. I ended up someplace off I-45 S. I didn't know what type of neighborhood this was, but I also didn't care. As long as I was around people that didn't know who the hell I was.

I grabbed the boxed hair dye I purchased from the first beauty supply store I could find. Not wanting my curly locks to fall out, I read the directions repeatedly. Once I felt confident I wouldn't mess it up I applied the kit and allowed it to work its magic.

I squeezed the towel to remove the excess water from my head and stared at my reflection. My hair had been transformed from its natural sandy brown color to jet black. It was different but I needed more. I grabbed the gray handled scissors I purchased and began to snip away at my hair.

I cut it in bold layers the best I could and used the bottle of Hawaiian Tropic to make my skin three shades darker than my normal caramel colored complexion. Granted it wasn't a total transformation but I did look different.

After days of listening and taking in my surroundings, I learned next door neighbor had the hookup. He sounded like someone I definitely needed to see. I needed a way to get myself established in a new city as a new person. I walked to his apartment.

"Hey Berto, what's up." His name was Humberto but everyone called him Berto for short.

"What's up, Mami?" He looked at me with raised eyebrows, waiting for me to state my case.

"Yeah, I heard you the guy to come to if I need things," I stressed the word things. He knew what was up so no sense in saying what I really came for. Basically, Berto and his brother Andres are the people you see when you need to get legal. I was legal, but my legal name would get me killed so I needed a new one. I started to open my mouth to explain, but before I could get a sentence out, Berto interrupted me. It was like he was reading my mind.

"Mami, I don't need your explanation. Keep it to ya self, as long as you payin' we can do bizness." He said. That was cool with me, the less people knew about Dominique Simoneaux the better.

"Cool, I will also need a degree in something like business or finance in that package. It needs to look good on my resume and if you know someone who could verify the info that would be even better."

"Yeah, I got you, you just have the money, a fifteen thousand for the first package, five thousand for the degree. I have it for you in two weeks." With that said, he snapped a picture of me and then I was dismissed and on to the next person.

True to his word, my package was ready for me two weeks later. I happily paid him from my stash of money careful not to let him see just how much I had. Once he left I went through the contents of the package. Damn, he was good cause this shit looked legal.

I had a new Texas issued driver's license, a social security card, credit cards in my new name, a Master's Degree in Finance, and a bomb ass resume with references and everything. Dominque has officially disappeared, it's time to do things a little different and Kyra Williams definitely knows how to live.

TWO

SLEEP EVADED me the entire night. I begged for its comfort, even solicited help from Ambian but my nerves were too bad. Fear had battled fatigue and won. I had a delusional couple insisting I was this Dominique and I didn't know what to do. I laid in the bed staring silently at the ceiling until the promising signs of daylight crept through my window.

If I couldn't get rest perhaps I could relax by taking a warm shower. I delicately shifted the comfy covers from my body and planted my feet into the plush carpet. The bed moved as got up, I looked over my shoulder to make sure I hadn't awakened my husband. Trent was sleeping peacefully, ignorant to all the turmoil I was facing.

As soapy suds slid down my body I weighed my options. I was so consumed with my own thoughts that I didn't hear Trent when he walked through the door. He moved groggily through the bathroom as I eyed him through the frosted glass shower door. I couldn't help but think to my self how well I had done. His physique was like a work of art; each muscle chiseled to perfection. Thanks to an hour at the gym every day before work, his stomach was firm, with a well defined six pack. For my husband, appearance was everything.

My eyes roamed the length of his body stopping only when my gaze met his, we were both watching each other. A feeling I hadn't felt in years washed over me. It was like fire. It was the heated, searing passion that burned hot in the beginning of our marriage, but the years had made us complacent. I was praying he would surprise me by being spontaneous and divert my attention from its unwavering hold on my situation.

He stepped into the shower with me and pressed his lips against mine. Our tongues moved in unison as he pulled my body close to him. This was out of the ordinary for him. Trent had a routine he followed religiously, and his day couldn't start if anything was out of order.

Our kiss was deep and passionate. He hungrily explored every inch of my lips, neck and then body. His hands eagerly probed my body, excitedly trying to take in every inch of me. He held me tightly, so tight you would have thought he believed I would disappear. We kissed the way we did when we first met, before all the fancy cars and diamond rings. When he was fresh out of law school and I was a branch manager for Wells Fargo. This reminded me of the young passion that he once showed me.

Trent held my hands above my head and kissed me lightly on my breast. The suds still rolled down my legs as I began to get weak from the intensity of his kisses. The water danced erotically on our skin as he pressed himself against me. I could tell he wanted more. Unexpectedly, he grabbed me by my hips and turned me around so that now my back was to him.

He clasped my hands and held them behind my back as I became his prisoner, his hands my cuffs. Slowly he entered me. Each thrust was long, deep. Our bodies were close, touching as he moved inside of me. The water splashed against my hair and back, the warm fluid flowing over us, mixing with our perspiration of lust. He became more intense, moving faster, thrusting harder. I couldn't help calling out his name.

"Trent, baby, you feel so good" I needed more of him.

"You like it rough don't you? Take it, can you take all of me baby?" He began to thrust harder, whispering to me how good I felt, how deep he was, and how he was determined to make me cum. He pulled my hair, causing my head to tilt back against his chest. As if on cue, we both reached our orgasm.

"It's going to be hard to say goodbye to you." I thought I heard Trent whisper in my ear. I quickly dismissed it, too exhausted to decipher his jumbled jargon. I had no words to speak. My body was weak with ecstasy, and for a moment in time, I forgot my problems. I stood frozen, staring at the man who had changed my life. Just as quickly as he had come into the bedroom, he was gone.

Once I heard the click of the door shutting, I turned to the mirror and inhaled deeply. As soon as my moment with Trent was done, all of my problems came rushing back. Surveying my reflection in the mirror, I dried my jet black hair and parted it so that the long layers framed my face. It rested delicately on my shoulders as I used my flat iron to gently bend the ends.

The corners of my eyes curved upward as I smiled at myself, content with the woman that stared back at me. The light above the mirror danced across my eyes and reflected a vibrant chestnut brown color with a tiny hint of hazel. My eyebrows were arched to perfection and my luscious lips would give any of the Kardashians injected lips a run for their money. Once I finished styling my hair I began to dress for my date with the Galleria, if nothing else I needed to get out of the house and keep busy.

I parked my car and walked towards the mall. I still hadn't figured out what to do. The garage looked empty for a Friday afternoon. My steps echoed as I walked to the entrance. I heard movement behind me. I turned around expecting to see someone but there was nothing there. I continued to my destination attempting to shake the feeling of being stalked.

From store to store, I purchased any and everything I felt I wanted. Shopping seemed to always take my mind off whatever was bothering me and the fact that I was surrounded by thousands of people also gave me comfort.

I could get lost in the crowd. I left the mall with bags in hand. Hours and hours of endless spending had taken its toll on me; hopefully, I could go home and sleep. I walked into the dimly lit garage. Even though it was daylight, the air was hazy and it appeared to be much later than it actually was.

The massive structure surrounded me making me feel small and completely alone. I had made a poor choice parking so far away and in a corner. I should have just valeted. Uneasiness fueled my steps as I raced to the safety of my car. I unlocked the door and breathed a sigh of relief, then strapped myself in behind the wheel. The sound of the engine starting brought calm to my racing heart. I checked my rearview mirror before shifting the car into reverse.

"What the fuck?" I squinted to get a better look at the black figure that eyed me through the tiny mirror. I didn't know who or what the hell that was staring back at me, but I knew one thing I would fight like hell. I searched for something, anything to defend myself but before I could turn around I felt a slender arm seize my neck. I was rendered immobile as I felt the deathly embrace squeeze tighter.

The arm slinked around my neck like a serpent to its prey. The more I struggled, the firmer the grip. I pulled forward attempting to break free, but the more I pulled the stronger the grip became. I couldn't see my abductor but I could feel the warmth of angry frenzied breaths on the back of my neck.

"Remember the note, bitch? I meant it then and I mean it now. There are plenty of bayous in Texas you can find yourself in." Queen. Without releasing her grip the slightest bit, I felt her reach to my left and unlock the door. The passenger door flew opened and he slipped into the seat beside me.

"Hey there little lady, whatcha lookin' scared for?" I cut my eyes towards the man sitting next to me. His lips curled into a hateful scowl, and his eyes reflected the sentiment.

"Because I've told you I'm not who you think I am." My voice was muffled and distorted because of the lack of sufficient air.

"Bullshit." She spat as she squeezed my neck. Every time she spoke her hold on me became tighter. I struggled to breathe.

At this point, I began to weigh my options and it was evident I didn't have many. I would continue to be terrorized by this couple. I thought if I stuck to my guns, maybe they would believe they actually had a case of mistaken identity. I don't exactly look the same as I did then. I've lost weight, tanned my skin, changed my hair, and had worked hard to get rid of my native New Orleans accent.

The way I speak and interact with people is different, but somehow they had found me. They saw through my disguise and even though I made certain to cover my tracks, I obviously didn't dig a deep enough hole to bury my secret. From the corner of my eye, I could see Redd's menacing stare.

"Damn it, Redd, why can't you just leave me alone? The money I took was owed to me, yeah you paid my bills and put change in my pocket but that's all you did. Then this wife of yours threatened to kill me, what choice did I have?" I was shedding my mask. Dominique had surfaced.

"Finally she admits it." His cold hard stare made the tiny hairs on the nape of my neck stand at attention. Tiny prickles of panic coursed the length of my spine as I waited for him to finish. "I should kill you now, but dead men don't pay." My eyes widened as the sound of his laughter floated through the air. None of this shit was funny, he was talking about my life.

"I don't have anything to pay you." Queen still held me by my neck and I was unable to move.

"Come on now girl, don't insult me. I know you holdin' somethin'. I've been to your house. I know how you livin'."

"I don't make the money my husband does. I can move about 250,000 without it being noticed. I have to move it gradually, so he doesn't know, but that's all I got. It's been twelve years and I had to use that money to get on my feet."

Trent and I had a joint account, most of our money went into one account and there was no way in hell I could move that type of money without Trent or the bank realizing it. Trent would flip if a few hundred dollars were out of place, I could only imagine he would lose his shit over $500,000. This was the only way I could keep my life from falling apart. They would just have to take payments.

"That's all you got? What you mean that's all you got? You take all the money I stashed in that apartment and then the police raid me and put me out of business and before I could get back on my feet and get my business running again, that bitch hurricane Katrina came through and ran my ass out of the only place I called home. Now you want to sit in your expensive ass car and tell me that's all you got. Hell naw, I need everything you took from me plus some interest. Listen you get me my money or I go tell your new sugar daddy just who you really are." He scowled.

"No! You can't do that!"

"Yes, I can, and I will unless you get me my money. You got one week." He leaned in and kissed me on my cheek. As he kissed me I felt Queen tighten her arms around my neck. Tiny stars circled around my head and then I saw only black.

I was awakened by a security guard tapping on my window. I don't know how long I had been passed out but my head was throbbing. I wondered for a moment if it had all been a bad dream.

"You can't sleep here." A security guard's pudgy finger tapped at the window. I quickly waved off the guard and started my car. I noticed a letter on my windshield. I hit the button to roll the window down and reached for the note. My heartbeat quickened as I read the note.

Yo ass got a week to get me my money!

Get it or find your home in one of these bayous!

You been warned!

This was like déjà vu. My past had caught up with the present and the evidence of it was staring me in the face.

***

With my new found identity I was on the hunt for my new life. I took a long look at my surroundings. Kyra Williams was much too classy to live like this so I made plans to upgrade myself. I decided as soon as Berto dropped off my stuff that I needed to find a safe place for my money. I wasn't gonna be like Redd and have that much cash on me, and I would not be getting my shit from no chop shop.

I needed to figure out a way get what I wanted without all the unnecessary questions that went along with dropping that much cash. And if I walked in with that much cash there would be questions. I glanced over at the package I had gotten from Berto, This was the key to my new life. If I wanted to be legit, all of my shit had to appear that way.

The next day I decided to test out my fake driver's license at the courthouse to get a DBA. I've done enough research to know what I needed to open a business account. After finishing up with the nice clerk I immediately went to a bank to open an account.

I would be able to make larger cash deposits without anyone suspecting anything. Not that the bank should question where the hell I get my money but I thought better of walking into a bank with 500k trying to make a deposit, so over the weeks I funneled money into my business account. I would make weekly deposits sometimes several times a day for thousands of dollars. I hadn't quite gotten it all in yet but I would.

I had enough to start Kyra on her way. Kyra had her shit together, good education, even better work experience, and exceptional credit. Good, cause you couldn't do a damn thing in today's society without credit. Unless I went back to my old ways and I planned to do a complete 180 with my new found freedom.

Kyra needed a new home, a home to reflect her successful status and a car to go with it. I jumped into my old Nissan. It was time I roll in something a little classier. I remember when Redd gave me the car. I thought I was rolling in style with my leather seats and sunroof, but Redd had me fooled.

The funds he gave me were limited. It was just enough not to fall. I never had anything so everything that he gave me seemed like a lot. While he and his wife were pushing Benz and Bentleys all through the city, I was behind the wheel of a Nissan Altima.

Don't get me wrong, the car was reliable but when it came down to it I deserved the best too. Until I saw how much money he actually kept at my place I had no idea he was bringing in as much as he was. Back home he was at the top of the food chain when it came to his operation and I knew he was pushing drugs back and forth across state lines, not to mention how he dabbled in providing female companionship for the lonely.

I knew if he had that much money stashed at my place there was a lot more where that came from. I knew he kept a stash at his home and his mama house. I didn't know quite how much money he was bringing in but I knew it was a lot. No wonder Queen was ready to kill my ass.

I pushed Redd and his money from my thoughts as I arrived at the car dealership. I drove down Interstate 45 until I spotted a place with luxury cars. I looked around assuming I was in north Houston since I was heading north and had been for close to forty-five minutes.

The last cross street I saw was FM 1960. I was lost but maybe I was exactly where I needed to be, on one side sat a Mercedes Benz dealership and the other Jaguar.

Hmmm. What's a girl to do?

I made a quick u-turn and headed towards the Jaguar dealership. A smile crossed my face when I saw all the new toys for me to choose from. Instantly I knew I would be leaving with a new car to match my new attitude.

THREE

I WAS WALKING proof that people are capable of extended periods without sleep. Queen and Redd had caused a rush of adrenaline that kept me in permanent overdrive. This part of my life was supposed to be over with. With each passing year, I gave less thought to the possibility of being found, it had never crossed my mind that my past could catch up with me. I haven't been Dominique Simoneaux in years. I didn't use that name or communicate with anybody from home and no one knew where I was.

My husband knew nothing of my past and that's the way I wanted to keep it. But I wasn't sure how long I could keep my secrets buried if I couldn't get my hands on the money they wanted.

My heart seemed to be constantly in a quickened state. It pounded so hard I was sure I would have a heart attack before this was over. Trent was ignorant to the many misfortunes holding me captive. I wanted so badly to just make them go away, to make them disappear, but I knew without the money they would be a constant part of my life. All those years ago I vowed to change my life and who I am and until now I had done a very good job of being Kyra. I had come too far to turn around. I needed a plan or I was going to lose everything.

I nearly burned a hole into my carpet pacing back and forth. Anxiety flooded my body as I searched for a way out of this abyss but came up with nothing. I couldn't withdraw that much money without it being noticed. I had a little more than 200,000 of the money that I took from Redd. That was my fall back money in case anything ever happened but I kept it in a CD.

I used the money to restart my life. I purchased a car and home and gradually paid them off. I briefly thought of selling the house that we now rent but that would take too long and I would have to answer too many of Trent's questions. If it were one thing Trent was good at was asking questions, it was his job. My only choice would be to break my CD with the bank and pay a hefty penalty. Maybe they would accept a down payment of some sort and allow me to make payments.

The two hundred thousand plus the two hundred fifty-thousand I thought I could slowly take from our joint account would at least be most of the money I had taken. Damn, this was extortion. I thought of going to the police but swiftly dismissed that idea. The thought of me, Kyra Jamison, living under a false identity, and on the run from my former pimp and drug dealer looking to the police for help. I almost wanted to laugh at my damn self. My misdeeds would surely have me sitting behind bars if I tried that.

The sound of the front door opening interrupted my thoughts.

"Hey baby, how was your day?" Maybe asking my husband about his day would take my mind off of the horrible days I've been having.

"Another good day in court! My client was completely exonerated of all charges, didn't even have to do probation." He gloated. He was arrogant, and he loved to win. I imagined those were the things that made him so good in court. He thought that the world was his to own, there was only one way to see it and that was his way.

"Do you think he was guilty?" I was intrigued. I knew what kind of clients he represented. His firm was the one to go to when you need to be acquitted, guilty or not.

"Kyra, why would you ask a thing like that?" A sly smile spread across his lips. "A man is innocent until proven guilty, and prosecution couldn't do that, so my client walks." He still hadn't answered my question. I guessed that was the lawyer in him.

I watched him as he began to remove his clothes. He walked passed me without so much as a kiss. Sometimes I longed for the attention that he used to show me. I know that we have been married for a while but for once I want to feel as special as one of his clients, I wanted the undivided attention he gave his clients, instead of feeling disconnected.

He neatly laid his clothes on the chaise sitting in the corner of our room. My mind wondered as I stared towards that corner. That was the very spot that Redd cornered me in. I could feel the icy touch of his hands on my body. My heart skipped a beat. I had to figure out a way to get rid of them. They were the past and I had no intentions of going backward.

I decided to gather Trent's clothes to take a trip to the cleaners. Every one of my nerve endings was on fire. I couldn't be still and somehow driving always seemed to help me think.

"Our accountant called today." The sound carried through the room, followed by long uncomfortable silence. "There were several purchases made on Saturday and because of the amounts and back to back charges he wanted to make sure that your card hadn't been lost or stolen." He finished. Trent hated when I spent money like that. My back was turned towards him but I could feel his eyes burning into the back of my head.

"Yes, sweetie I went shopping Saturday remember." I know he didn't remember because I don't believe I told him but that was my defense.

"Well, that must have been some large purchases if he thought the card had been lost or stolen. Just what did you buy?" He stood silently waiting for my answer, but one wasn't coming. Instead, I changed the subject.

"A little of this and that you know, it was a me day. I'm going to run your clothes to the dry cleaners. I'll be back soon." With that said I kissed him on the cheek, grabbed his clothes and moved towards the door.

While driving, the wheels of my mind spun out of control. I attempted to devise a plan to get rid of Redd and his evil wife. My new life had taken me far away from thinking like Dominique. My day today survival used to depend on the hustle, my ability to get over and get out of sticky situations. I needed to find that again, I knew it was somewhere deep inside of me.

My plan of taking the money from our account was out. If the accountant noticed a few purchases he would definitely notice money leaving our account on a regular basis. Driving in circles, I rode the freeways with no destination in mind. Cars sped by me as I traveled along the Sam Houston Tollway. To be honest I wasn't quite sure how I had ended up on the tollway. I exited and turned my car around.

How in the hell had my life turned into this shit show?

I had no desire to return to my old ways. I loved my husband and I believed he loved me. No marriage is perfect but this life is better than the way I was living before. Granted Trent and I had had our problems. There were times I felt devalued and unap-preciated.

Even though there was no spontaneous passion constantly

erupting between us, I had grown to love him over the years. Most of all he was my safety net. Because of Trent and his profession, I no longer needed or wanted a sugar daddy. I didn't have to prostitute myself for dollars or deal with any of the things I've had to do in my past. Before I was a mistress, now I'm a wife. I supported Trent in his career path, even played a part in catapulting him to success.

I'm married and as the law goes in Texas half of everything he owns was mine. Redd could ruin everything for me and reduce me to nothing. He could expose me, my illegal fake identity, and cause me to lose the only stability I have ever known.

My eyes welled with tears. My emotions seemed to constantly teeter between anger and desperation. I was over this weepy ass bullshit. I realized Kyra needed to take a backseat. It was time to think like Dominique.

"Think girl, think!" I willed myself to become the woman I once was. The by any means necessary chick that showed up and could get out of any fucking situation you pushed her into. It had to be done. Here I was again attempting to get away from Redd and Queen.

I knew I couldn't get them all the money but if I could devise a plan for him to make money I might be able to get rid of him. I snatched my cell phone off of my nightstand and scrolled through my contacts looking for the saved number. I tapped the screen to make the call. I wanted to meet with him.

"You got my money?"

"Maybe I got something better."

"Yeah, well your pussy's good but that shit ain't better than money!" Everything was either sex or money with him.

"I'm not talking about pussy, well I ain't talking about my pussy. Just meet me so we can talk, and leave your wife at home." I hit end after I told him where to meet me.

We decided to meet at a nearby Starbucks. This was the first place I could think of that could manage to be public and private all at the same time. Most of the people were glued to their laptops and tablets. No one would notice us.

I ordered my usual white chocolate mocha and waited. Sitting in the corner I hid behind a magazine while peering over the rim of my shades searching for Redd. I didn't want to be recognized by anyone.

My eyes were glued to Redd as he walked through the door. His toasted sienna colored skin looked as if it had been just kissed by the sun. Redd's dreads were tightly twisted coils that were now much longer than I remembered and his facial hair was neatly lined up. But the thing I found most stunning about this man were his eyes.

The deep green pools could be shockingly hypnotic. Back then he was just my type. He walked with a swagger that said he knew he was the shit and then that's exactly what I wanted. He was a street savvy hustler who turned sex and drugs into a business.

His height commanded the attention of many as he moved through the building. His slender but muscular body wore his clothes well and his row of perfect white teeth peered from under his smile as he noticed me in the corner. Those piercing eyes watched me as he sank into his seat.

"So do you have my money?" The words rolled from his lips, jolting me back into the present. He wasted no time getting to business.

"I have some of your money."

"Some is not all baby, don't you think your time will be better spent by getting me the rest of my money!" Redd's smile was almost a snarl.

"I already told you I can't move that type of money from our account. It would be noticed." Trent's observation was a gentle reminder me that he's always watching the finances. It would be a stupid move on my part to go anywhere near that account to repay my debt.

"So what you want, to try in talk me out of getting my money, well forget it. You stole from me and I want what's mine. I need it." The tone of his voice told me he did need it. He was desperate for it, and desperate men did desperate things.

"Look Redd, I didn't have a choice, your wife threatened to kill me." I felt a need to explain. I never had a chance to give my version of events. I'm sure Queen's story was unfairly skewed in her favor.

"You had a choice, you made it and never looked back. Now you have another choice to make. Either get me my money or deal with the consequences. I think you have a lot more to lose than I do when hubby finds you're not exactly who you claim to be. Once he knows who you really are and leaves your ass, I'll come again to collect, but the next time payment will be your life."

I decided I'd had enough of this conversation and tried to steer it in another direction. I needed to run my plan by him and get him to agree. This was a way to get us what we both wanted. I wanted silence and he wanted money, I knew my plan could bring him that and then some.

"Hey, you remember back in the day when sex was your big business?" I didn't want to say pimp even though I guess that's what it was. He wasn't what you thought of when you thought of a pimp, he wasn't smackin' hoes or taking all of their money, he was good at providing horny men with sexual pleasure and I had a plan to take his know how and my expertise to build a business that would make money fast and quickly remove him from my life.

"What does that have to do with anything?" I could hear the

annoyance in his voice. Once he got in the drug game he pretty much abandoned prostitution.

"It has to do with everything." I smiled. "Let me build you the best little whorehouse in Texas."

***

I cruised the streets in my brand new Jaguar feeling like a new woman, a reinvented woman. I shed my old skin and the new person I was wasn't going to be a gutter girl any longer. These degrees Berto got me were the real deal, stamped signed and sealed by the school. I don't know who his connect was, but they were damn good.

It wasn't hard to get an interview with Wells Fargo, I was hired on the spot after feeding them everything that was typed on the resume that was prepared for me. With all my credentials, they would have been foolish not to hire me.

After my interview, I found a gorgeous apartment and put a deposit. I was informed that a decision would be made after a credit check. I smiled when they said that knowing there would be no problem with Kyra Williams credit. Within hours my phone was ringing telling me I had the apartment. Things were finally looking up for me. I loved being Kyra.

I admit I was a bit concerned about Redd, if he found me I'm sure he would kill me. So I devised a plan that would keep him busy for a while. I reached for my new cell phone and made a call.

My fingers trembled as I touched the keypad. I dialed the number on a card I received when Redd was being investigated.

It had been at the bottom of my purse for ages. I didn't know then it would come in handy and I actually never planned on using it. Whenever they tried to approach me about Redd I denied even knowing him. When it came to Redd I was loyal. I would have never turned on him, but now I saw things differently.

"May I speak with Detective Bradford?"

"Speaking." The voice that hissed back was less than patient.

"Hello, I received your card a few months ago concerning Lawrence Richardson, I have some information that may be of value to you." His long pause told me I had gotten his attention. I even think he put down his doughnut for a moment.

"Who is this?"

"Just know that I'm someone who can help you." I didn't care to leave my name. I went on to tell him information that only I was privy to. Not enough to get Redd locked up, just enough to give the police a reason to look and him a reason to hide. If the plan went my way, Redd would so busy with keeping them law off his back he wouldn't worry about me. In time, I hoped he would forget all about me and the money I took.

FOUR

REDD READILY AGREED with my plan of creating Houston's very on Bunny Ranch. Any plan that made him money made him smile. My little plan was now in motion. I cashed in my CD and agreed to meet with Redd today to find a suitable space for our joint venture.

I maneuvered my car into a nearby parking spot across from the apartments Redd and Queen shared. My eyes roamed the area taking in all that I saw. This area reminded me of one the first areas I lived in. The rent was cheap and the area was rough.

Redd moved slowly across the street as if he wore a bumper. Blowing horns and shouting drivers cursed Redd as he made his way to the car. Once he spotted my car he opened the door and got in.

"What's up D?" His lips curled into a seductive smile and I instantly knew what that look meant.

I rolled my eyes ignoring his adolescent attempts to lure me into his arms. We wouldn't be talking about anything unless it was about business. I knew better than to open that door. There was too much history between us. Whenever I got around Redd I became incredibly nervous. There was no doubt in my mind that I loved Trent. Being with him had changed my entire world, but when Redd was near my body involuntarily reacted.

Heat rushed to my face as I inhaled his sultry scented cologne. I didn't want him to know he had that affect on me. I was doing my damnedest to hide it. Curiosity got the better of me as I shifted my eyes to look at Redd. The straight leg jeans he wore were dark in some areas and faded in others and his shoes were as white as the winter snow.

The aviator style Gucci sunglasses reflected my profile. He was watching me watch him. I quickly turned my attention to the traffic in front of me, pissed that he caught me watching him. Damn he looked good.

I zipped my car in and out of traffic trying to get to our destination and get out of this car. I needed him out of my personal space. His presence was suffocating me, surrounding me so much I could not catch my breath. I exhaled, trying to slow my quickened pulse when I felt the tender touch of his slender fingers inch up the length of my leg. He acted as if I wouldn't notice. He cautiously rubbed my thigh, almost as if asking permission by the hesitation in his touch. My thighs tightened as I felt the stir of arousal between my legs. His touch, although I hadn't felt it in years, was familiar against my skin.

Everything inside of me signaled that this was a bad idea. I needed to get rid of him and allowing this would make that even harder. The voice in my head screamed again and again to stop this, but the words never escaped my lips.

My body craved the rush that he was giving me. I struggled to keep control of the car as Redd pushed my legs apart and worked his way to my inner thigh. His powerful hand moved seductively until he found my lace panties. I wanted to succumb to the desire, to allow this man to touch me in every way I remembered but that inner voice finally snapped me back to reality.

"Stop!"

"Don't act like you don't like it." He smiled slyly as the words to tumble from his lips.

"It's not about whether I want it or not. It's about what's right and wrong and this ain't right. I'm married and just in case you forgot so are you." My eyes darted at him as I drove, angry at him for trying to cross that line, and even angrier with myself for wanting him to.

"That never stop you before." He sounded offended.

"Maybe I'm not the same person as before." We drove the rest of the way to meet the realtor in silence. Thankfully, he kept his hands to himself. I stilled tingled between my legs from our close encounter.

Nestled in a wooded area was a gorgeous two-story home. There was a large iron gate that stood open and allowed entrance into the driveway. As I drove the semi-circular path I noticed the manicured lawn. The curved driveway led me to the front of the house where I stopped the car and parked behind the realtor's car.

I knew before even seeing the inside this was perfect. Secluded from all, this would be the perfect place to run his business. Part of me couldn't believe that I was helping him, but the survivor in me would do anything to ensure my well being.

I stepped out the car and walked towards the front door. The sprawling double doors were edged in cherry colored wood with the center being a mixture of bronze and glass uniting to create a breathtaking design. The shady realtor's chatter was merely background noise as I stepped into the house. I pretended to listen as he went through his sales pitch.

I really didn't understand why he was going through the motions of actually trying to sell us the house, he should have known through our connect, that this deal was as good as closed. This realtor's only real job was ensuring our names weren't connected to anything. If things ever got out of control the paper trail would lead to some nameless person that probably didn't exist.

Stepping back into my old world was both familiar and foreign. I watched as Redd and the realtor eagerly probed every inch of this house. I broke away from the group and began to roam the halls alone. I needed time to focus on how the hell I would pull this off. I stumbled across a long hallway which led me to the master bedroom. It's impressive size overwhelmed me and instantly the wheels of my mind started to turn.

We could use this room as the presidential suite or VIP room, and we could charge a ton for it. My heels sank into the plush carpet as I made my way to the bathroom. In the center sat a sunken marble jacuzzi bathtub. The left side of the room was completely mirrored from floor to ceiling and the marble counter-tops matched the tub and shower tiles perfectly. I stood in silence and contemplated the possibilities. I was so lost in my own thoughts I didn't hear when Redd walked in behind me.

I could see his reflection in the mirror, watching me watch him. He closed the space between us, never saying a word, then I felt the strength of his embrace around my waist. It was always Redd's unexpected desire for me that drove me wild. It was something I craved, but Trent was rarely spontaneous.

"Can you still do that thing with your tongue?" Redd whispered into my ear. Memories of our past caused a slow smile to spread across my face. It felt good to be wrapped in his arms. Just like before, my mind told me to stop him, but part of me that refused. Somewhere I still loved this man. At one time I craved him, needed him, and wanted to be his everything. My eyes closed as my body gave in to the kisses he planted along my neck.

Without thinking, I turned towards him and found his supple

lips. Our tongues teasingly united as we kissed. His right hand moved up my spine ending at the nape of my neck before provocatively pulling my head back. He lifted me onto the marble counter and pulled my skirt around my waist. His fingers eagerly probed the fleshy folds between my legs. Years have passed since I felt this man touch me but it was as if he remembered every spot that triggered a response.

"So if you're not the same old Dominique, why are you so wet?" His piercing eyes probed me, waiting for an answer. He waited, but there was no response. I didn't have an answer. I wasn't the same person, at least I hadn't been in all these years but now Dominique was surfacing and I couldn't stop her.

My left leg dangled to the floor while Redd held the other. He dropped down to one knee and pushed his face towards my center. He slid my lace undies to the side while his tongue swirled and pushed from left to right. I shivered with delight as he brought me to the brink of orgasm and then pulled away, which only intensified my desire for him.

Our eyes connected as I ran my tongue across his lips, savoring my own juices. I heard the rip of tearing fabric, but I couldn't care less about the expensive lingerie. I watched as the wispy fabric floated to the floor. I blindly reached for his pants and undid his button and zipper. I reached inside and wrapped my hand around the warm thickness that swelled even more as I touched him. My hands ran the length of his shaft repeatedly before tenderly rubbing the tip of my thumb across the head.

"Damn." He groaned signaling he was ready to feel more than just my hands on him. I pulled his pants further down completely exposing him. He rubbed against my clit, teasing me, denying us both the pleasure we obviously desperately craved.

"You ready for me."

"Yes."

Inch by inch I could feel him fill me completely. My body felt the sting of both pleasure and pain as my body opened up to receive him. Somewhere in the back of my mind, someone was screaming stop, but it was a faint whisper compared to the voice that called for this man's touch.

"I know you missed this good dick!" Redd breathed into my ear. "Say it, tell me you missed Daddy's dick!" He demanded, but I wouldn't speak. I didn't want to give him the satisfaction of knowing no one could touch me the way he could. Redd was always so spontaneous, so fulfilling. He moved faster, thrusting harder with each stroke.

He slowed his pace and pushed deep inside of me. My hands tightened across his back before moving upward to pull his lips towards mine. Our tongues danced as our passion took control of us. With this man, every way he stroked me was the right way. My body allowed all of him, swallowing every inch as he moved in and out of me.

"Say it, I know you love me, and you love the way I fuck you!" He still demanded more of me. I began to move my hips in sync with his thrust. I pushed, he pushed, and my breast bounced to the beat of our lovemaking.

"Damn, you feel good!" Redd whispered into my ear before running his tongue across my lips. I could tell he was about to climax, his strokes became more intense. He even felt harder as he tapped the bottom. I wrapped my legs around his waist, pulling him even closer.

His hand clasped around my neck. My body stilled in obedience with his unspoken command. Short gasps slipped from my lips as I became overwhelmed with pleasure. My skin developed tiny bumps as we became more intense. He took my erect nipples into his mouth, lightly biting them. My entire body tensed and shuddered. I could feel the warm juices flowing from my middle, down my thighs and onto him as I came. I finally opened my eyes as Redd began to cum, he pulled me even closer as he released himself inside of me.

My weakened body tumbled against Redd. I needed to catch my breath. I blinked twice trying to focus. Redd had my mind so gone I completely forgot about the realtor, but he hadn't forgotten about us. In the shadows of the doorway he stood, watching us as he held himself in silence.

***

Making that call to the police was one of the best ideas I had. That would get Redd off of my back, he would be too busy with the police to worry about me or his money.

Today was my first week at my new job. I was bored out of my mind and quickly attempted to learn what my resume said I already knew. I did learn one part of my job quickly and that was delegating. All that I couldn't figure out I designated another employee in my department to complete. Sitting at my desk I reviewed tons and tons of accounts.

I needed to get out of this place. I hadn't had a real job in so long that sitting at this desk was driving me crazy. I grabbed my purse and walked towards the door, just as I was going out a man was coming in. The door swung open so wide I was knocked off balance and fell to the ground. My first response was to jump up and whip his ass. I know that's what Dominique would do, but I had to think about what Kyra would do.

"I'm so sorry." His deep voice captivated me. He extended his hand towards me as a gesture to help me to my feet. His smile was alluring. He gazed at me with chestnut brown eyes, coffee colored skin and an immaculate body that showed through his expertly tailored suit.

"What's the hurry?" I said as I attempted to dust myself off and straighten my clothes. I guess he found my comment funny because he chuckled. He still had not released my hand.

"I apologize, really, let me make it up to you by treating you to lunch." He offered. I didn't know this man from Adam, but that didn't mean I didn't want to get to know him and a girl's gotta eat. I tilted my head to the side watching him out of the corner of my eye.

"Can you start by telling me your name and then maybe I will consider lunch." I stared in silence, not wanting my eyes to give away how I truly felt about lunch with him.

"I'm Trent Jamison." He handed me a business card as he spoke. I agreed to lunch and found myself walking with him and completely swept away by his conversation. We talked, and not the kind of talking that Redd and I did. Not street talk, so to speak, it was real talk.

He told me how he was fresh out of law school and working for one of the biggest law firms as a junior associate. He continued to talk, possibly in an attempt to impress me. What he didn't realize is the more he talked about him. The less I would have to talk about me.

FIVE

AFTER I DROPPED Redd off at his apartment I used my alone time to think. I was embarrassed by my actions and I couldn't understand what had come over me. Perhaps the excitement and nostalgia of it all had caused me to lose every last one of my senses.

With Redd's return into my life, I had to think and act like I did when the streets were my home, but that definitely didn't mean I wanted to rekindle that type of relationship with him. I was done with being Redd's faithful concubine, years away had shown me I was capable of better.

I pulled my car into the garage and breathed a sigh of relief when I saw I was home alone. Piece by piece I began to pull my clothes from my body as I headed towards the shower. Somehow I thought I could wash away my illicit behavior. No matter how much I desired Redd, no matter how much chemistry we had, I could never allow what happened between us to happen again.

I found comfort in my bed. I enveloped myself in my blankets welcoming the quiet comfort. I gazed at the ceiling intently, hoping that somehow the answers to my problems were there. I tapped the home button of my iPhone to check the time. It was after midnight, where was Trent?

Maybe he is just working late.

It wasn't enough room in my brain at the moment to worry where Trent was. Thoughts ran a marathon in my mind as I assessed the day's events. I couldn't believe I had allowed myself to get caught up with Redd. The very thought of going to back to those days repulsed me and I could not understand why I had succumbed to my desires. When I left Louisiana I still loved Redd.

I thought the years and distance would put an end to my fairytale ideas of our love, and until now I thought it had. One thing was accomplished though. We had found a place for his business. I knew I didn't need Redd as apart of my life anymore, but for some reason, I felt confused.When you know better you're supposed to do better, but every time I thought of the way he touched me my body trembled. Being around him allowed all of my old feelings to surface, which I truly didn't want and thinking of what happened today only made it worst.

I found myself so aroused I had to touch myself. I allowed my hands to fall below the covers. Slowly I made my way to my center, thinking of the feeling of ecstasy I was lost in today. I touched myself, feeling all of my moistness. My nipples swelled with the anticipation of my own touch as I moved my hands slowly, teasing myself.

The sound of the bedroom door opening interrupted me. Trent's movements were catlike as he moved through the room. His steps were extra cautious in an attempt not to wake me. I could either pretend to be sleep or get satisfaction for this burning between my legs. I decided to get satisfaction. Maybe if I directed my energy and desire towards my husband, it wouldn't leave room for my lust for Redd.

I moved the comforter away from my body. "Trent?" I called to him, hoping he would move towards the sound of my voice.

"Hey, I didn't know you were awake." He almost sounded disappointed.

"I'm awake. Why don't you come put me to sleep?" I said in the most seductive voice I could find. I remember there was a time this man was insanely excited at the thought of touching my body. Now at times it seemed as if it were a bit of a nuisance.

"Can you wait until I get out of the shower?" He said.

"I would prefer if you would come extinguish this fire now!" I slowly removed my gown and stood in front of him. Our room was chilly and my nipples stood at attention. I moved closer to him to rub against him. The closer I moved to him, the further he stepped away.

I touched his smooth skin and pulled his hand towards the bed. "Make love to me." He pulled back and stood away from the bed.

"I will make love to you, but first I'm taking a shower." He swiftly moved towards the bathroom, closed the door and locked it. I stood in the middle of the floor, naked and baffled. There was a knot forming in the pit of my stomach. I felt rejected and I didn't understand why it was imperative that he take a shower at this very moment. It's not like he works outside, he sits at a desk and in courtrooms.

Feeling defeated, I climbed in my bed, beckoning the comfort of sleep to take away the sting of my rejection. After what seemed like hours I heard the bathroom door open. The freshness of his newly cleansed body invaded the room. I felt Trent climb into the bed. His hands gently rubbed my thighs as he tried to pull me close to him.

My eyes were closed so I didn't have to make eye contact with him, and I didn't respond to his probing hands. Pretending to be sleep,

I never so much as peaked at him. Eventually, he got the message and decided to go to sleep. At least one of us could sleep because I couldn't. Trent didn't usually make me feel rejected, perhaps ignored at times but I know that's because he is consumed with work.

This felt different. I had never had a reason to question Trent's feelings for me, but tonight left me in a totally different place. I turned my back to Trent and looked at the clock. It was three in the morning and I knew I had a long day ahead of me. I closed my eyes tight, praying for sleep.

The next morning I awoke in an empty bed. Saturday mornings Trent usually slept in but he was long gone. I pushed my hand towards the nightstand and shuffled its contents from left to right until I found my phone and dialed Trent. It rang once and quickly went to voicemail. That was odd but I didn't have time to figure it out.

Perhaps he went to the gym. I jumped up and prepared myself for the day. The fact that he wasn't here was a plus. That meant that he couldn't question me. I stumbled to our walk-in closet and found attire for the day. Still struggling against sleep I groggily stumbled into the bathroom and tapped the faucet to turn on the water. I doused my face with the warm refreshing liquid.

I grabbed my runaway locks and pulled them into a ponytail as I applied make up. I wanted to feel sexy today. No, I needed to feel sexy today. Redd insisted I shop with him for home decor. I should have said no but he had me in a bit of a bind. I couldn't believe I had handed that man two hundred thousand dollars without so much as blinking my eye.

Well, yes the hell I could, I think if I wouldn't have I might have really been found in a bayou somewhere. I was trying to buy my way to freedom. Once he started making money he was going to let me go. He better let me go.

On my way to meet Redd I decided I needed to talk to him

about my debt. We needed a mutual understanding. I parked in the same spot I had when we had gone to view the house. I noticed him standing near his apartment, talking with a man. I don't know what they were talking about but whatever it was it looked serious. He moved in almost a jog to the car.

"What it do D?" He said as he opened the door and climbed into the car.

"Hey Redd, what's up?" I was dry as hell. I didn't want him to think we were about to start round two.

"You!"

"No, I'm not, look I think that we need to talk. What happened yesterday can't happen again. Ever. I don't want to go down that road again and have your crazy ass wife looking to kill my ass." I could tell by the expression on his face he wasn't trying to hear what I was saying. Silence fell over the car as he glared at me. I drove in silence for a moment before I spoke again. "You have to agree that this is about business."

"I don't have to agree with shit. I don't know what makes you think you calling the shots, I'm in control of this here, just like I've always been!"

"You need to lower your voice, like I said, I'm just trying to make sure that the things that happened yesterday don't ever happen again. This is business and when you start making your money back, I'm out. Hell, I've given you half the money I owe you. Paid your down payment for your house and handed you the rest of your money. How well you do is up to you."

"You got that wrong baby girl, it's up to you too. If I don't make my money then you'll be working for me forever. I don't know why you don't just relax and enjoy the ride. This was your idea, remember. " He smiled and moved his hands towards my legs. He gently squeezed my thigh as he gazed at me.

"Stop it damn it, I told you that shit was over, this is strictly business." I pushed his hands away from me. Even though I moved fast, he moved faster. Redd grabbed the steering wheel.

"Stop it!"

"Pull this shit over right now!" He was so forceful it scared me. I didn't plan on being in an accident today so I turned down a dead end and pulled over. Even though it was daylight, being in a wooded dead end scared the hell out of me.

"What is wrong with you? Don't do that, you could have killed us both." I inhaled deeply, I was finding it hard to catch my breath.

"Get out the fuckin' car!" His gaze was so intense it paralyzed me. I guess I didn't move fast enough because before I knew it my car door was flying open and I was being yanked out of the car by my hair. My legs struggled to keep up with the fast pace of his tugging. I fell to my knees unable to firmly plant my feet on the ground.

Redd peered down at me before grabbing me and pulling me to my feet as if I were his puppet. I faced him defiantly. I wasn't going to give him the satisfaction of letting him know I was scared as hell. That's what this asshole wanted. He shoved me towards the car and pushed my face against the hood. The heat from the car stung as my bare skin pressed against the metal. I felt probing hands under my skirt as he found my panties and yanked them away from my body.

"Redd, stop." I attempted to stand but he shoved me back down while pushing my skirt around my waist. I struggled to push him off me, but Redd grabbed my hands and restrained them behind my back. I was now his prisoner.

"Pleas stop, don't do this." I pleaded with him to stop. I couldn't see his face, but his forceful motions told me he wasn't listening.

"I'm not stopping, you want me just as much as I want you. We're not over Dominique, not until I say we are." He pushed himself inside of me. I could hear cars speeding by as he moved in and out of me. I knew I should have stopped him. I shouldn't have allowed myself to be bent over the hood of a car in the middle of the day, having sex with someone who was not even my husband.

I wanted to scream rape, but that's only what my mind said. My body was calling for every thrust he gave me. His hands held me tight, inflicting just enough pain to arouse me even more.

"Yeah, you like that dick, say it!" Yesterday I hadn't given him the satisfaction of verbalizing what my body knew. Today was different though. His forceful, take it nature drove me over the edge. As he pushed in and out of me the wetter I felt myself getting. Before long I was meeting his thrust, rolling my hips in eager delight.

He released my hands and allowed me to grip the hood as he dove deeper and deeper in me. The thought of being caught or watched by people driving by only made me want this man more.

Redd pulled himself away from me and turned me around. My bare ass now sat on the warm hood as he found his way inside. I still hadn't allowed myself to speak but I didn't know how much I could take before my mouth gave away what my body was feeling.

"Say it. You love this dick don't you!" His commands were persistent.

"I love that dick!" Moans escaped my lips as I came. My body was motionless as I lie on the hood of my car, a car that my husband gave me and paid for. The funny thing was, even though I knew I should have felt bad for what I just did, sexual ecstasy would not allow me.

***

Meeting Trent had completely changed my outlook on what I wanted in a man. He was different from all of the guys that I met before and that's probably what I liked about him. When I was Dominique, I looked for the guys with the fattest pockets, the biggest dick, and the street rep to match.

But now, I wanted to do things a little different. I mean look at where my choice in man had gotten me. I was away from everyone and everything I loved. At times I longed for home, but between Redd and Queen looking for me, I knew I wouldn't be going anytime soon.

I sat at Starbucks waiting for Trent to show up for our afternoon coffee break. We worked so close to one another that this had become a daily thing for us. I got to know him and I can say I liked what I saw. So what he didn't walk with street swag and his attire was clean and tailored instead of jeans and kicks. I did like the way he made me feel.

While waiting my cell phone rang and broke my peaceful silence. I looked at the caller id and noticed the 504 area code. Shit. Why would anyone be calling me from 504? I trusted no one enough to give them my number, not even my mother. As far as the state of Louisiana was concerned, Dominique Simoneaux had disappeared never to be heard of again. Curiosity won and I answered the phone.

"Hello."

"Who is this?" A husky voice spoke to me. "You know it doesn't even matter, I have a message for you. Mind your fuckin' business! Shit don't stay anonymous in Detective Bradford's precinct. I got your number, and soon Redd will know who you are and where you are so if I were you I would sleep with one eye open bitch!"

The phone line went dead. My hands trembled as I placed the phone down. Trent had walked up during this conversation.

"What's wrong baby?" I couldn't even answer. I didn't know how they had gotten my number but somebody had it. I knew I would cancel this cell phone before I had made it back to my desk.

Trent stood over me still concerned. I couldn't let that call get to me. Houston was a big place, and obviously they didn't know who I was they only had the number. I be damn if I run again. If Redd came after me, he would damn sure get a run for his money. If he found me it would be because I slipped, and I didn't plan on slipping.

SIX

TWO WEEKS HAVE PASSED since my encounter with Redd. I was preparing to see him tonight, which was supposed to be about business but with Redd it always ended up personal. I had not been intimate with my husband since our spontaneous shower session, and that bothered me a little, but Redd made sure to keep me busy so I couldn't worry too much about Trent.

I sat at my vanity table and watched Trent gather his things for a shower. He walked in and immediately moved towards the bathroom. Usually, he would undress in the bedroom and neatly arrange his clothes over the chair for me to gather and take to the cleaners. That didn't happen tonight. Odd, extremely odd. I leaned against the bathroom door and scanned the room for his clothes.

"Hey baby, where are your clothes? I'm getting them ready for the cleaners." I saw where his clothes were sitting but I was more interested in his response than his clothes.

"You know baby, don't worry about it, I will take the clothes to the cleaners." I watched him through the glass as he took his shower. There has been something very strange about his behavior. He never took clothes to the cleaners. Honestly, Trent never did any of the things he deemed trivial. He left that to his dutiful wife to do.

"So you got room for me in that shower?"

"Actually baby I'm about to get out." He stepped out and swiftly kissed me on my cheek then pushed passed me. I stood in the doorway by myself. I didn't really want to take a shower, I just wanted my husband to respond to me in a way that said he wanted me. But nowadays, it just felt as if he were trying to push me away.

He has left me with the feeling of rejection one too many times. He honestly didn't realize who the hell he was messing with. I walked back to my vanity and continued to apply my make-up. I was leaving, if Trent needed space, it would be space he got. Redd and I were doing a bit of business scouting. I started gathering my clothes but it was as if Trent didn't even notice that I was leaving; did he even care?

I finished my makeup and headed to put my clothes on and grabbed a pair of heels. I stepped in front of my full length mirror to inspect my appearance. The woman that stared back at me oozed confidence and sex appeal. The black faux leather skirt I wore was fitting, and hugging every curve of my body. My dark sheer shirt hung loosely at my waist. The deep v-neck exposed my silver bra.

"I'm leaving," I said as I closed the garage door. I didn't give Trent time to answer me let alone question me about where I'm going. In the exact same spot I always waited in, I watched as Redd left his apartment. Queen stood at the door, planting a kiss on his lips before he exited.

The sight of those two in a tender embrace made me nauseous. Kyra shouldn't care one way or another but Dominique didn't like to see them all over each other. Whatever. I discarded the thoughts of them from my mind. I had my own man to worry about.

"Let me drive tonight," Redd said through the open door.

"I can't let you drive my car."

"Yes, you can, get out and let me drive you tonight." I thought about all the things that could go wrong by letting him drive my car. Forget it. I stepped out of the car and climbed into the passenger side. I was tired of playing chauffeur. I let my seat back and enjoyed the ride. Redd looked towards me and as always he touched my thighs.

"So you gone give Daddy a taste of that tonight?" Redd asked.

"You sure you only need a taste?" I flirtatiously laughed as I shifted in the seat, exposing my legs just a bit more. I planned to have a good time tonight. No worries about home or how strange Trent was acting. I reclined in the seat and sank into the smooth plush leather. Slowly my old personality was gradually becoming dominant.

Tonight was supposed to be about business, but I just wanted to have a good time. Redd parked the car and before I could open my door he was at the door helping me out. We walked in side by side. The smoked filled room was warm as nearly nude females walked the floor.

It was Redd's idea to find our talent in a strip club. I guess some girls would be willing to do anything for a quick buck, I used to be one of them and in some way I still am. Coming to a strip club is not something my husband would ever think of doing, and definitely not with me. Redd led me to a VIP room in the back of the club.

I felt all eyes on me as I moved seductively beside Redd. We were a couple to be admired. I tossed my hair as my hips rocked to the beat of the music. Once we reached the room I sat down, crossed my legs and requested a drink. I needed a little something to take the edge off.

Sipping on my drink, I watched as one of the girls entered the room. She bared a striking resemblance to Beyonce. Layered golden tresses fell to her shoulders as she undid her hair clip. Her eyes shifted my way and then to Redd before fully entering the room. She knew she was here for an interview. Redd knew the owner of the club and he had given us a list of girls willing to work, keep their legs open and their mouths closed.

She stood in the middle of the floor watching me. I could feel her eyes roam my body practically pleading with me to look directly at her. Her body glistened with hues of gold. Sipping on my drink I never gave her the eye contact she desired. She moved slowly, seductively; exuding sexiness with each step.

"I'm Obsession." Her voice was sweet yet sultry. She moved towards Redd. The point of these meetings was to get a feel for the girls. To see what they looked like and how they moved. Obviously, Obsession had a plan of her own. With each step she took she removed a piece of clothing. Not that she was wearing all that much. By the time she reached Redd she was completely naked.

This woman's body was the epitome of beauty, it was the kind of body that women envied in the gym. She was a bronze colored goddess that moved as if she was floating across the room. Her brown skin was smooth and rich. She kneeled before Redd and with one quick movement was swallowing him whole.

I didn't even see her pull it out. I watched her technique. She watched me. I would be lying if I said this didn't turn me on. Redd rested comfortably against his chair with his head back. I could tell he was enjoying this.

I squirmed in my seat, my legs crossing and uncrossing my legs. My nipples hardened and pulse quickened.The more I watched, the hotter I became. My hands traced lines along my thighs. She saw me watching her and began to really put on a show. She pulled a Magnum from I don't know where and ripped the package open.

She straddled Redd backward, placed the condom on the tip, unrolling it with her hand as she lowered herself on to him. This chick had tricks and shit. She bounced up and down and her hips rocked back and forth. Redd threw his head back and gripped her hips. He pulled her into him forcefully and if the look on her face was any indication, she was enjoying every bit of it. The more she took it the harder he gave it. I watched as he eyes rolled, his body shook and he grabbed her hips in an attempt to hold on for a wild ride.

Just before he reached his climax, she stood. I could see him glistening with her juices. She stepped back and slowly walked towards me. My pulse quickened with anxiety and anticipation as she closed the space between us. Her moving my way scared the shit out of me. She didn't wait for permission to touch me, she simply took it.

She leaned towards me, touching my chin to slowly lift me towards her, then kissed me. Her kiss was tender and sweet, but full of passion and desire. Her tongue moved with mine. It was so intense it made me weak. She was working her way down my neck and to my breast.

Being with another woman was something completely new to me. She spread my legs as Redd positioned himself behind her. Obsession was now on her knees with her head nestled between my legs. I could feel the swiftness of her tongue as it traced tiny circles along my clit.

Redd locked eyes with me as he slid inside of her. Her body jerked as he pushed further inside of her. She worked her tongue and he worked her. Her fingers now moved in and out of me, causing my muscles to tighten. I could feel myself about to climax. She pushed her hips back to meet each of his strokes. The harder he pushed from the back, the further her fingers thrust inside of me.

I couldn't take it anymore, the stimulation was too strong and

I succumbed to this wonderful feeling. Redd wasn't far behind, I could tell he was about to cum. He swiftly slid himself out of Obsession and released a steady stream of his seed onto her apple shaped ass.

Obsession was a woman who truly knew her profession. She was definitely hired. After she left we saw a few girls but none as impressive as Obsession. We made a list of the ones we wanted to work with and they would meet us tomorrow at the house. Everything seemed to fall into place.

***

I have to admit, when I received the call from back home it scared the crap out of me. I retired that part of my life, but here it was again staring me in my face. Needless to say, I threw that phone in the trash, and immediately went to Trent and persuaded him to add me to his account as a share plan.

Knowing the kind of dude he is, the old me would have taken advantage of him. I would have taken him for everything and left him broke, busted and confused, but Kyra did things a little different. I would allow him to stick around. I wanted him to stay.

I had plans on us being together but before we could I needed his pockets to be a little fatter. As a junior associate he didn't make shit and I didn't have time to be the doting wife in the corner watching him climb the corporate ladder. I couldn't deal with that.

I wanted to do things differently but one thing I couldn't deal with was a broke ass struggling man. I saw potential in us as a couple, with me pushing him we could be a power couple, the couple that all envied.

Today I was meeting Trent for lunch in his office. When I walked in I noticed a salt and peppered haired man eyeing me.

Mmm, I see he likes a little chocolate swirl in his vanilla. I smiled. Trent was walking towards me. As we left to the break room I heard him speak to old, gray haired guy. I soon figured out this dude was in charge . He watched me as he stopped and chatted with Trent. They talked about boring stuff that held no interest to me.

I could feel old guys eyes, roam over my body. While I watched him watching me the wheels in my head began to turn. I know I told myself I was going to become a new person, but perhaps I could employ some of my old techniques to help my new man get ahead. He just needed a chance.

As we moved towards the break room, I looked over my shoulder and winked at the salt and peppered haired man. When I did that he smiled and turned beet red. I licked my lips and blew kisses at him while Trent talked about getting some type of promotion. If I had my way he would get more than a promotion. I am talking corner office and partner status.

"Trent baby, who is he?" I tilted my head towards the man.

"Oh, that's our founding partner, Jacob. Smith. Let me introduce you two."

Trent introduced us, completely oblivious to mister salt and pepper's hidden desire. It didn't matter. I just needed a way in. A signal to him that he could have what he wanted, for the right price.

Our introduction was short. Trent and I turned to leave but Mr. Smith never took his eyes off of me. He continued to watch me, so I put an extra little twist in my hips. He was losing his damn mind. I knew it was a matter of time before I could get him to do anything I wanted him to do.

SEVEN

I WAS HEADED down a dangerous path. Redd did something to me, he did something for me. It was like old times. There was a time when I felt like he was my best friend. He was my man and my everything. It didn't matter to me that he was married. I never saw it that way. I knew he was with her, I even played my position but in my mind, he always belonged to me.

I sat on the edge of my bed consumed by my thoughts and overwhelmed with confusion. Lawrence Richardson was nothing but trouble. He was as unstable as a schizophrenic on crack. Like a ticking bomb he could explode at any moment. I had to keep myself from going there.

I watched Trent as he slept. We hadn't been together sexually in weeks. I hadn't even noticed because I was being fulfilled by Redd. I knew this was ridiculous and I didn't want to be caught in the situation. Trapped between two men, wanting to be with them both.

Dismissing those thoughts from my head I moved towards our closet. There was no need to burden myself with thoughts of things I couldn't change. My past was kicking my ass. I had to get

Redd off of it and keep Trent from knowing. I was more than accustomed to my lifestyle and if Trent ever found out who I really was I would lose everything.

I dressed for our meeting with the girls. There would be six girls to start. That was more than enough. Everyone was supposed to be in attendance, even Queen. I didn't want her anywhere around me but Redd insisted. She knew people from working at the law firm, and she was given the task of spreading the word to those she knew would be more than willing to pay for it.

The plan was to target lawyers and judges, athletes and business owners. People who could lose everything just for knowing about this place. I slipped out the house unnoticed. On my way there I made a mental note to surprise Trent for lunch at his office. There was a time we had lunch together every day, but it has been so long since we have been able to. I guess we have been so consumed with ourselves we haven't taken the time to think about each other.

Getting caught up in this crazy life didn't make matters any better, but I felt that I had to fight for my new life. I was playing the survival game and I wasn't prepared to lose.

I parked my car and briefly admired the home. The home that my money had purchased. I remember eagerly handing over money to Redd, eager to get him out of my life, but now I'mm conflicted.

"Got damn it!" I know this bitch didn't just slap me. I didn't know what the hell her problem was but we weren't about to start this again. My first response was to grab my face but as soon as I realized she slapped me I lunged for her throat.

"What the hell is your problem?" My hands desperately sought to strangle her. Redd jumped between us as many of the girls watched in amusement. My arms stretched around him desperately trying to strangle her

"You are my problem, bitch you have always been my problem!" I had no idea what was going on. I walked through the door and was greeted with a hand. "And you Redd, why you takin' up for the bitch, move out my damn way."

He stood as a wall between her and I. This was the very last time she was going to put her hands on me and get away with it. When she saw that Redd wasn't budging she went around him and walked towards the door.

As soon as she walked by I stuck my foot out causing her to trip and fall into the wall. She wasn't going to keep putting her hands on me and threatening me. I was ready for a fight. At one point Queen did somewhat intimidate me, but things were different now. She was no longer going to intimidate me with her Queen Bee status. She wasn't Queen of the hood anymore. She didn't have dumb young girls eager to prove they were loyal to her anymore.

Redd helped Queen to her feet and pushed her towards the door. She watched me as she walked away. Her eyes were daggers that cut me with every piercing glance. I was frozen ready for a fight if she tried to bring it. As far as things between Queen and I, shit would be changing. I was damn sure tired of her putting her hands on me when she felt like it, and then Redd always jumping in to break it up. Redd walked back in the house laughing.

"What the hell is so funny to you and what's wrong with your damn wife?" I was irritated that he thought this situation was funny. "She shouldn't even be here. What the hell does she have to do with what we are doing?"

"She's here because I say so, don't forget who running shit. You just make sure this shit jump off so you don't have to come up with the rest of my money. As for my wife, finding out that you still got it bad for her husband gets you a guaranteed ass whippin.'" Redd walked away from me as if the conversation was over. I swiftly followed behind.

"What do you mean found out I got it bad for you?" He smiled slyly and walked away. It looks like I wasn't getting an answer from him anytime soon. I walked to the back of the house to quickly regain myself. I checked my appearance in the mirror that hung at the end of the hallway. My face was still red from Queen's slap and now I had to go back into a room full woman and be the boss. I hated that bitch.

Walking back into the front room I could hear idle chit-chat from the girls. As soon as I stepped into the room an eerie silence fell across the room. Their smirking mouths and teasing eyes taunted me. Queen had confronted me in front of all these women and I knew it was just matter of time before one of them would try to test me too.

I decided to make the best of a bad situation and attempt to turn this around. I stepped up to speak. The first thing I did was make a mental note of the females that were now present. I saw Obsession sitting on Redd's lap in the back of the room. She was one to be watched.

"I'm sure all of you know exactly what you are here for. The key to this type of business is discretion. If you don't have it and you run your mouth, you need to walk towards the door now." I paused briefly. No one moved. "Secondly, your stripper names are out."

I could see rolling eyes and smacking lips but I didn't care. "So you need to think of a name to use when you are here, and anything with ending with isha, ika or quisha is out." I knew I was pissing them off, but again I didn't care. "Please choose your name and before I leave to day I will approve it."

I went into my bag and pulled out a list I had made. "As far as money you keep forty percent of what you earn, the other sixty goes to the house." I was interrupted.

"What chu mean we only keep footy pressent?" I didn't even remember her name, Fantasy or something like that. I would have to give her a crash course in diction, cause this hoe couldn't talk. At least she didn't have to use her mouth for talking much. I walked towards her and stood within inches of her. I was so close I could feel the heat from her breath.

"I mean just what I said, you don't like it then move towards the door." I tilted my head, smiling sarcastically. We locked eyes. It was a game to me and I was going to win. I never broke eye contact. I wanted this bitch to try me. Redd needed to see results and fast and that wouldn't happen unless he was getting paid. I knew he would make the rest of what I owed him back, but the quicker he made it the faster he could release me from my debt.

"I can walk and tell everybody about what you are doing." She snapped back.

"Yeah you can, but we have our ways of dealing with snitches." She stared. I stared back. She had no idea that what I was saying was to merely intimidate her. She sucked her teeth and said nothing more.

I continued for the next thirty minutes uninterrupted as I laid down the ground rules of the house. If we were going to charge high dollar then they would want to get their money's worth. I walked the girls through house assigning each of them a bedroom. They could choose to sleep here or elsewhere at night, it didn't matter to me as long as they were here by noon everyday. I wasn't new to this, before I became Redd's other girl I was his highest paid girl and I could teach these girls a thing or two.

"Familiarize yourself with your room, rearrange things to your liking. I will return with Redd soon. Obsession walked with me. She moved very gracefully as if she were a dancer. I decided to give her the master bedroom. I knew she would be the star, and knowing that I would charge more for her meant I was willing to give a little more. In comparison to the other girls she was show stopping. I mean absolutely stunning. I don't know if she had extensions or if that was her real hair. Either way, she wore it well. We reached the master bedroom.

"This is going to be your bedroom." I opened the door revealing the room. There was a king sized bed with a pillow top mattress in the center of the room. She turned to me and smiled. I could tell she was pleased. I lifted my notepad so I could start to write.

"What name will you be using?"

"My middle name, Michelle." I smiled at her pleased. I didn't have to do a lot of explaining to her. She knew the rules of the game and was willing to play her part.

"Can I ask you something?"

"Sure you can." I was a bit apprehensive.

"What's the deal with you and Redd's wife? I thought you were his wife, until she introduced herself." Michelle gazed at me, waiting on a response.

"That's a story for another time and another place." I left the room to find Redd. I didn't care to go into the details of my sordid past. It was better left where it was and that was in the past.

***

I waited outside of the courtroom for Trent. I left work early in hopes of surprising him for dinner. Normally in any relationship, it was all about me, but I wanted to do special things for him. Maybe somehow I felt guilty for the things I hid from him.

My intent wasn't to deceive. Well, that actually was exactly my intent, but in the midst of all of this I actually began to care about him. My plans were to make sure we never wanted for anything. I was just trying to give him a little push. The door to the courtroom swung open and Trent emerged. I stood to greet him, embracing him once he was close enough.

"Hey baby, I thought that I would be done but I'm not. Go ahead and go." He kissed me on my cheek and headed back towards the courtroom doors. Undoubtedly he had to do more work for the lead attorney.

As I was walking back I noticed Mr. Smith behind me. I'm sure he was watching my ass and I felt as if he was following me. I stopped and stood still.

"Why are you following me?"

"I'm not following you." He was beat red. I'm sure I make him uncomfortable, among other things.

"Sure you are and it's a good thing I slowed down old guy. You know you can't keep up with me." I smiled slightly licking my lips to tease him. He watched me as I spoke, staring lustfully at me, unable to conceal his desire.

"Oh, I can keep up with you little girl." This is the first time he has ever tried to flirt back.

"Little girl? If I were a little girl maybe you could, but being a grown woman you--" "Why don't you have dinner with me. Your boyfriend will be working late tonight." He smiled. For an older guy, he was attractive. Not that I would ever consider anything serious with him, but it made what I was about to do a hell of a lot easier. He was being seduced and he didn't even know it.

I agreed to have dinner with him and was surprised. He wasn't boring, a little corny, but not boring. I sipped my wine and mindlessly listened as he talked. I don't know if it was being nervous or if he really talked that much.

My move to Houston was to change, to get away from those things I used to do and those people that wished me harm. But in some ways I hadn't changed. This was for a good cause, I justified. This was to change my life and Trent's, and I wouldn't have to do these type of things again.

EIGHT

I LEFT Redd with his girls. I couldn't be in that house a moment longer. Who knows what freaky things he was dreaming up for them to do, especially Obsession, or Michelle I should say. Queen's slap was a brief dose of reality of the chaos I was dealing with. Redd had a way of getting into both my mind and my heart. I was falling so quickly I hadn't even stopped to remember all the reasons he was less than perfect for me.

He was the man that could make my toes curl. I needed to let go of the wild and crazy world that was Redd's life. Sure it was exciting but I was losing focus. The only reason I was helping him was to get away from him and stop him from destroying my life.

I parked my car in the parking garage across from Trent's firm and headed to the security desk to sign in. I recognized the guard and spoke, making idle chit-chat as he printed out my visitor's badge. I boarded the elevator on my way to Trent's office.

Normally when I would surprise him for lunch he would smile with delight, stop what he was doing and go to lunch with me. His office door was closed as I approached. I paused, tapping faintly to signal my entrance.

"Hey baby." Before I could fully open the door I noticed Queen sitting on the edge of his desk with her legs crossed appearing to take notes. Now when we met her he couldn't even remember her name, now he was having her work with him side by side. I didn't like what I saw.

"Am I interrupting?" I asked, my unhappiness apparent.

"No. I'm surprised to see you here." Trent never moved from his desk. He didn't bother to take his eyes off of Queen.

"Well, I thought I'd surprise you and take you to lunch." My anger was rising. It's as if I wasn't even in the room.

"I can't today, I have two cases I'm working on, I won't be able to get away for lunch, you should have called and checked." Trent finally looked my way. He still never moved from his desk.

"I never had to call before." I stared at him with icy contempt. The fact that this was playing out in front of her was embarrassing and it took every ounce of control within me to keep me from shoving her ass off of that desk. She stared my way, smirking as if she had won some type of silent battle. Trent finally decided to rise from his spot.

"Let me walk you out." Trent walked towards the door and held it open for me. Had I just been dismissed by my husband in front of that bitch? Was this payback for her being put out of the house that day by Redd?

He walked me back the elevator, kissed me on my cheek and left. The woman that reflected in the mirrored elevator doors looked troubled. At this point, I had no control of anything. Redd did whatever he pleased, my marriage, even though everything I felt I was doing was to save it, was spiraling out of control and half the time I didn't recognize my own damn reflection. A familiar voice startled me back to reality.

"Hello, Mrs. Jamison."

"Hi, how are you?" This was a conversation I didn't care to have. I didn't feel like being nice or sociable just because this was Trent's boss. Before a lengthy conversation could get started I was saved by the opening elevator doors. A look of disappointed washed over his face as I left him there to converse with himself.

I made it back to my car and contemplated my next move. I watched as countless people left the building for lunch. Could I really be hurt that my husband didn't want to have lunch with me? I was the one that was cheating on him with Redd every chance I got. I had to stop this affair with him, it's gotta be strictly business. I needed to get my life back. I didn't want to be Dominque. I enjoyed being Kyra. I enjoyed my lifestyle and I loved my husband.

Just as I started my car and was about to pull off. I noticed Trent leaving his office and he was not alone. Queen followed closely as they moved towards his car and got in. He was so busy he couldn't have lunch with me, yet he could take time out to have lunch with her. I knew what this was. Queen was out to destroy my life, literally and I refused to sit by and watch her do so. I picked up my cell phone and dialed a number I hadn't dialed in years.

"Jacob, it's Kyra." I hated having to come to him. I know what he will ask for.

"Kyra, you were just too busy to talk to me, weren't you? It was if I recall, Mr. Smith when you just saw me. You wouldn't even bother to look me in the eye. Now we are on first name basis again." He gloated for a moment but I knew how to quiet that down.

"Jacob, please stop. I need a favor from you." My patience was very short.

"What will I get for it?"

"Confidentiality. I won't run my mouth about things that could leave you with only half of what you've worked for."

"What is it?" He sounded defeated.

"Currently Trent has a paralegal working for him, Queen Richardson. I want her placed with another attorney."

"Queen is no longer a paralegal, she was promoted to an executive assistant job. Trent requested her. My hands are tied on that matter." I could hear him smirking through the phone. He was enjoying this.

"What do you mean your hands or tied? It's your firm." My words were dripping with anger.

"Yes, it's my firm and your husband is a partner in this firm, you do remember that. I'm sure you do as hard as you campaigned for it." His voice had transitioned from defeat to victory in a matter of moments. He knew he now had the upper hand and that his inside information was a blow to my ego.

"Bye, Jacob" I was done for now but this won't be the last. I had no idea Queen was now his executive assistant. I knew that job came with better pay and benefits, I just hoped one of the benefits wasn't my husband.

***

Trent sat silently on my sofa as I prepared dinner for us. I watched him from the kitchen trying to decide if this was something that I wanted. I think I wanted him. I felt that he would change my life and possibly for the better. Together the possibilities were endless. It had been almost six months of us dating.

I knew he didn't have a lot of money but he always seemed to be able to surprise me and shower me with things. My money was diminishing quickly. Working at a bank I did learn the ins and outs of savings and CDs. I had money, but that was my in case I had to run money.

If I had to move and fast I would have something to start over with. Trent and I still hadn't had sex. I was trying to make a new start with him so I told him I was celibate and didn't want to rush things. I wanted to be one of those girls who didn't easily give it away. I felt like Kyra was that type of girl.

We sat down for dinner at the table and talked about things that didn't matter to me. I was tired of working and all I could think about was getting him the salary he needed to support me. I can't say that I was in love with him, but I hoped to love him one day. I placed my fork down and walked toward Trent. With each step I undid a button on my shirt. He watched in silence as I moved towards him.

I let my clothes fall to the floor and began to dance for him. He never moved from his spot. His eyes were glued to my body. I led him to the bedroom and began to undress him. I could tell he thoroughly enjoyed it.

Suddenly I felt Trent's embrace tighten as he took control. This surprised me about him. He turned me over so that he was now on top. His stare was intense. He kissed my neck and ears. My body responded to him. Tiny chills ran up and down my spine as he showed me the real meaning of foreplay. I've had sex before, but this felt different.

"Let me make love to you." I surrendered to his control. He touched me in the emotional places that had been neglected for years. Moving in and out of me he took my body, kissing me as we explored one another. His pace was nice and slow, each stroke deeper than the first.

"I love you Kyra," he whispered in my ear.

Redd never told me he loved me, never took the time to kiss me like this. Redd and I had passion, maybe what we didn't have was love. I had given him all of me. Now it was time to let that go and allow myself to love Trent.

NINE

MY MIND RACED with thoughts of my husband and Queen. I knew she had to be trying to get back at me. My attempt to have her reassigned failed. I could go toe to toe with Jacob but I decided against it. I would save that threat for another day. My first thought was to follow Trent but I decided against it. Instead, I decided to go home and take some time for myself. Anxiety consumed me and I hadn't slept much since that day at the benefit when Queen and Redd walked back into my life.

I walked into my home feeling confused. After seeing the obvious attraction Trent had to Queen I felt conflicted. I know the things I've done are far from right, but it's entirely different when you see the person you love admiring someone else. I had never had to worry about Trent being attracted to anyone else, at least if he was I never knew about it. I walked towards our bedroom and noticed Trent's clothes sitting on the chaise.

I gathered them to take them to the cleaners. As I picked up his clothes I could smell the vague scent of perfume. I sniffed, but I was unable to identify the scent. This just confirmed what I already knew. There was another woman and I was willing to bet it was Queen. I threw the clothes down, disgusted, and decided to take a shower.

I went to the bathroom to turn on the hot water, undressed and stepped in. Showers always seemed to take the pain away. The water to washed over me and took the pain I felt down the drain with it. Somewhere in the back of my mind a voice screamed that I was doing the same thing, so how could I be mad, but I was. My association with Redd was business and it protected my husband as well as myself.

I stepped out of the shower and grabbed a towel. When I walked out of the bathroom Redd was sitting on my bed. It was time to end this nonsense with him. I know I wanted my marriage and I had to stop.

"What the hell are you doing in my house?" He acted as if the bed belonged to him.

"Why the hell did you leave the spot?" His eyes were dead pools that stared at me, empty of any emotion. If he ever felt anything for me I couldn't see it now.

"Because you and your wife are got damn lunatics." My heart rate began to skip. I don't know how much craziness I can take.

"I'm going to excuse you saying that. You get dressed and get your ass back to that house. We starting up tomorrow. We already have clients on the books."

"Just leave Redd and give me time to myself."

"You've had twelve years to yourself on my dime. I told yo ass it was payback time." Redd walked out of the house and slammed the door. I weighed my options and decided to return back to the house.When I got there the girls were all sitting in the dining area.

"What's going on?'

"We're installing cameras." Michelle was the first to speak. I nodded and walked past them to the study which was set up as an office. All of the surveillance screens had been setup in the office. As each of the room cameras became operable I could see the bedrooms. I looked around the house. I had helped Redd build his establishment better than he could ever hope for.

This was ten times better than anything he had going on when he was set up in New Orleans. I watched as the girls went back to their rooms. They all began to do meaningless task, all except for Michelle. She appeared to be studying. A stripper with a book wasn't an everyday sight.

Something about that intrigued me. I wanted to know more. I knocked on her door, this was my best attempt at not being rude I mean this was technically my house. After a few seconds she opened it.

"Hey Dominique, what's up?" I almost corrected her and told her my name was Kyra but remembered I told them to call me that. They would never know who Kyra Jamison was.

"Nothing, I stopped by to make sure you had everything you needed for tomorrow."

"Everything is great. I'm just doing a little studying. Let me ask you something. Even when we are not working is it okay if we stay here."

" I don't mind but you may want to just clear it with Redd." I knew Redd well enough to know if he didn't feel like he was in charge he would go crazy.

"Sure I'll do that. So you ever gonna tell me the story between the two of you. You guys looked like you were together the night I met you." She was nosey. I came to ask the questions not answer them. I didn't even acknowledge that she had asked the question.

"So you are studying, what are you studying?" I looked over her shoulder trying to get a glimpse of what she was reading.

"I'm in school, this whole stripper hoe thing is temporary. Honestly, I am just doing it to get by. It's a lot easier to shake my ass for major tips than to work an every day nine to five for minimum wage. I'm getting a degree in Forensic Accounting, this is the last year so I'm almost done with the self exploitation."

What the fuck was forensic accounting?

"Well, I was just making sure everything was good," I said before walking off. I was done for the day no matter what Redd said. I grabbed my purse and walked out the door. I did need time to myself. I felt that I was so far in that I wouldn't be able to see myself out.

***

Mr. Smith sat at the edge of my bed and stared at me. I assumed this was his sexy face. His pale white skin appeared blue in certain places as the moonlight from the open window danced across his skin. He was in no way prepared for what would happen in his life next. I strained to see the tiny camcorder on my tv stand in the dimly lit room. I slyly reached over to press a button to make sure it started to record.

"Why don't we turn some light on, I want to be able to see you as you make love to me." I couldn't care less about making love to this dude, I just wanted to make sure that the camera could see everything that was happening. He just smiled and moved towards me. He grabbed my toes and began to slowly suck each one.

He then traced kisses up my thigh and began to taste me. I have to say I was surprised that he wasn't horrible at what he was doing. I pushed my hips towards him to allow him to penetrate me deeper. After twenty minutes he was done and his sweaty body fell against mine.

I was relieved when he finally left. I hurried to watch the tape and then made copies of it. I made sure to choose positions where his face would be fully visible. I placed a copy in a brown envelope that I would deliver to him first thing tomorrow morning. I washed my body, called Trent and then fell asleep.

The next day I walked into the office with a huge smile on my face and went straight to Mr. Smith's office. He looked at me with surprise. It was one thing to fuck me, it was another for me to show up and barge into his office as if I knew him.

I placed the envelope in front of him. "It's everything we did last night." I laughed. He wore a look of disbelief on his face. "Yes, I recorded it. It's insurance. I need you to give Trent a helping hand. He's done with law school, now make him a lawyer and pull him out of that pen of junior associates. Give him real work, real pay." Everything became silent.

"And if I don't, you do know that blackmail is against the law. And I'm a lawyer." He answered smugly as if that was supposed to scare me.

"Did you know fucking a black girl could get you divorced? And for a guy like you, divorce can lead to losing a lot of money as well as reputation when I leak this tape to the press. I don't have anything to lose, you on the other hand, have everything to lose."

"What about Trent, you could lose him."

"I won't, cause you ain't gonna tell. I'm not asking for you to make him partner, he will do that on his own. But you will give him a chance and a salary double what he's making now." I stood before him, silent, but my eyes spoke volumes.

"Why would you do this?" His eyes were pleading with me to stop.

"It's to ensure my future. You have forty-eight hours to make your decision." I turned around and walked out of his office and headed to the lower level where Trent's cubicle was. I suspected after today, Trent would be moving out and into an office of his own.

TEN

MONEY FLOWED like the currents of the Mississippi. With the passing months, Redd's spot went from slow and boring to on and popping. I was amazed by the steady stream of patrons that were in and out of the doors of this place and with my help these men definitely got the most. It was top notch and you couldn't walk through those doors spending less than five hundred. A grand would get you a good time, but two stacks would get you nothing less than full service.

Redd had even set up a bar so to speak, you could get any desired drink or drug you wanted, at an extra cost I lifted my notepad so I could start to write. Discretion was the name of the game. A car rotated hourly bringing and taking customers back to their cars or offices. Because of the location, we didn't have to worry about nosey neighbors wondering what was going on. Our shit was together, and I knew with my help, Redd could be on another level.

I sat in the study with the many video monitors surrounding me. Redd was bringing in the money. He could make ten thousand a day now that things had started really moving. Most of the men that came through the doors were white, many of them with high profile jobs and a lot of money to throw around. I was swiftly paying off my debt and couldn't wait to be free of this. I wanted to go back to my safety net. I wanted to go back to the simplicity of my life.

My old life seemed so far away from me now. Trent spent more and more time away from home. He never seemed to be in his office when I called and the strange scent that I smelled on his clothes was now familiar because he often smelled of the floral fragrance when he came home. The scent of that same fragrance hit my nostrils. I turned to see Queen standing behind me.

"What?" I wanted to keep my distance from this nut. I didn't want to have a fight every time I saw her.

"Are you still fucking my husband?" I turned back around to the computer and continued entering appointment logs.

"Are you fucking mine?"

"Hoe, I'm about to fuck your whole life." Queen turned around and left the room. Good. I would much rather be by myself than to have her for company.

I gazed at the monitors. I looked towards the door to make sure Queen had closed it. The monitors were set up to make sure everything went as it should. None of the girls were allowed to touch the money. All money came to the house first and then the girls got their percentage at the end of the night. They did so well here most of them had quit stripping and made this their full time.

I recognized him from the back first. My eyes were glued to the screens. The sensual cockiness of his walk caught my attention. Its familiarity shocked me and when he turned to face the bedroom camera my heart burst. I couldn't understand how this happened. I watched the train wreck as it happened before me. I stared as he touched her, the ways that he had once touched me.

Tears streamed from my eyes. I didn't know what my next

move should be. I know I wanted to run to the room and tell her to get the hell off of my husband. He reached for what appeared to be marijuana, lit it and puffed as she rode him. The man I saw before me was a complete stranger. I thought of the compromising positions I've put myself into all in the name of protecting him from my history.

I became again what I despised in order to keep his resume impeccable and his reputation top notch. My actions not only protected me but him as well. All the guilt and yo-yo feelings I was having about sleeping with Redd and he's probably been doing things like this all along.

I decided not to move. I would confront him later. I didn't want the embarrassment of the girls knowing my husband was a paying customer. I pressed record to create a video of what was taking place. He would have no way of denying it. I decided tonight we would be coming clean. They took what appeared to be a break. I picked up my cell phone and dialed his number, curious as to what he was going to say.

"Hey baby, are you busy?" I was surprised he answered.

"A little, working on a case, I will probably be working late tonight." Before I could say another word the phone went dead and my eyes told me why. Another girl had entered the room and now sat across his lap as the other sat on his face. I was disgusted by these actions and knew I didn't want to be anywhere near him. If I hadn't been so caught up with Redd I probably would have seen all of this coming.

Unable to watch anymore I left. I went directly home where I played the video with half of his sexual interlude on the big screen. I wanted to make sure that it was playing when he walked through the door. Even though I knew it had to be done, I wasn't prepared to have this conversation.

As I took a shower my mind wondered. I journeyed through the whys and hows of my circumstances. No one did this to me, I am a victim of my own actions and decisions. I took Redd's money. I was the one that decided to handle things my way instead of going to my husband with the truth. And I was the one that was blinded by the feeling of euphoria when with Redd, that I failed to see things happening in front of me. My secrets were coming full circle.

I heard him open the front door and then it closed. Footsteps paced the ceramic tile as he walked through the house, then I heard nothing. Finding my strength from somewhere, I moved towards the family room where I knew he would be. I stopped at the doorway as he watched the screen. He turned to face me as if he sensed my presence.

"What the hell is this?"

"Shouldn't I be asking you that?"

"So are you spying on me?" His eyes were pure venom as he watched me.

"No, but you are cheating on me I see." I watched Trent as he dropped his briefcase and smiled. He never said a word as he walked pass me. I can't say that I wasn't confused. Trent had always been so in love with me, enamored, I mean I was his trophy and now I felt more like a burden. My face became heated as I followed him out of the room.

"Trent, you hear me talking to you!"

"We don't want to talk about cheating. Every day you have somewhere to go. Every night you come in smelling of smoke and alcohol. I know you don't think I'm stupid. You've been fucking someone, so don't pretend you are innocent in everything." He stared at me. Removing his clothing unusually slow.

"You don't know what I've been doing cause you're too busy having sex with prostitutes. This is not us Trent." I was so upset with him that I could have slapped him.

"Isn't that all you are?"

I stood shocked, surprised that I had been called a whore by the man that I loved. Completely lost for words, my anger took control and began to steer my actions. My hands swung as I clawed at his face. He grabbed my hands mid-air and threw me towards the floor. Before I knew it he was on top of me. His eyes glowed with hatred, with anger so strong I feared him at this moment.

"You're my whore aren't you? I pay good money to fuck you, whenever I want. You're no different from those girls at that place, just how many men have had you for just the right price?" He finally released me from his hold as he moved off of me. I rolled into a fetal position, rendered immobile from the emotional bruises he had left me with.

"Trent, you can't mean that?" I pleaded for him to take back his words.

"Like hell I don't." He said and moved towards the bathroom door and locked himself inside.

I struggled to stand up. Both my ego and body were bruised by Trent. I didn't know what just happened or how my husband has lost all respect for me, but I had an idea. Just like other issues in my life, I believed Queen had set these wheels in motion.

***

Everything had gone according to plan. Trent and I were planning our wedding. Trent had a great promotion, and was proving himself every day as one of the strongest attorneys in the firm. I had quit my job and moved in with him.

For the first time in my life, I felt things were going the way they should. It seemed that things in my life were finally easier. Being Kyra was the best thing that ever happened to me. As we worked out the guest list I told Trent the last lie I promised myself I would tell. I had to have a reason why I didn't have any family coming.

He wanted to know why my mother couldn't come and even offered to pay for the expenses for my family to come to the wedding. I knew I would have to think fast, so I did what I knew best. I let the lies to roll off my tongue as if they were pure truth.

"I just don't understand. Shouldn't some of your family want to be here? You never talk about them or anything."

My eyes filled with tears. "I don't have any family. I don't talk about them because my mom and sister both died in a house fire and I spent the remainder of my years in foster care." That was a lie, in fact, my mother still was in the hell hole I left her ass in and I hadn't heard from my sister in years. But I knew if I said they were dead he wouldn't question it.

"Baby, you never told me, I'm sorry" He held me in his arms as the fake tears streamed down my face.

"That's okay baby, your family will be here for us."

"The little family I have here yes, they will make it. I guess it will be mostly our closest friends then. Who comes doesn't matter, this is about us, it's about our union." He hugged me.

Life was what it was supposed to be. I finally felt satisfied that I wouldn't have to run from Redd anymore. Honestly, how could he find me? I think I hid well. He couldn't trace me by cell phone, by the car, I had and I definitely did not have the same name. Dominique was gone.

I lay silently against my husband to be as my cell phone vibrated against my leg. I didn't plan on answering it. I had rejected at least ten calls today from an unavailable number.

"Aren't you gonna get your phone."

"No, I'm enjoying my time with you too much." My answer seemed sufficient enough. He didn't bother to push me any further and I was thankful. My phone continued to ring as we sat in a comfortable silence. I discretely pushed the side button on my iPhone to immediately silence my phone.

I didn't know who it was that was calling me, but I knew I didn't want to be found. There was no way after I've done so much that I would risk losing everything. I moved closer to Trent attempting to shake away the negative feelings that the consistently ringing phone gave me. I no longer wanted to deal with being Dominque.

I was Kyra now, I was soon to be a lawyer's wife, I had a career, and I would have a family. I was everything that Dominque could never be. I felt the phone vibrate one last time against my leg.

"Baby, give me a second, I gotta go to the bathroom." Trent looked up from the book he was reading and shook his head okay.

"Kyra, you don't need my permission to use the bathroom." He laughed, I guess finding it absurd that I needed to announce my journey to the toilet.

"I know babe." I headed towards the bathroom and closed the door. I reached into the back pocket of my jeans to retrieve my phone and firmly pressed my fingerprint against the home key to unlock it. I had a total of 20 missed calls and they were all private. I hit the voicemail icon, brought the phone up to my ear and began to listen.

I instantly recognized the deep voice on the other line. Anger dripped from his words and it was a side I had never seen of him before. Sharp breaths escaped between the vicious verbal daggers he threw at me. It seems his proper tone and ivy league vocabulary had escaped him.

The more I think about it Kyra, the more pissed off I become. Do you really think you can blackmail me? Bitch please I invented blackmail. Just know you have fired the first shot! It's about to be a war.

For a brief moment, I looked at my phone in disbelief. Could this man actually be serious? I tapped the trash icon with the tip of my thumb, discarding, message and any memory of Jacob's threat. What could he do to me? He didn't even really know who I was.

ELEVEN

THE LAST WORDS my husband spoke to me played over in my head. I was unsure of how to take what was happening. My life had literally begun to fall apart and I felt powerless to do anything about it. Hurt and anger engulfed me as I waited for Trent to come out of the bathroom. I watched the door, seething with venomous fury. Last night Trent arrogantly walked away from me and refused my pleas for attention.

I honestly just wanted to get to the bottom of what was happening, I am fighting so hard for this marriage, compromising who I am now for who I was before, all to protect him from my past.

"Treeeeeent!" I screamed to the top of my lungs. I refused to be ignored. When it came to Trent I felt guilt and blame for anything that ever went wrong in our marriage. I took on all of the burden and stress of the relationship in order to make him happy. In order to make him into the best possible version of himself, I was willing to sacrifice pieces of me.

I jumped up from the seat I was rooted in all night. Trent was in the bathroom far too long. I moved swiftly towards the door determined to break it down if I had too. My satin robe flowed behind me as I created my own tornado of anger. One after the other my small fist banged against the door, demanding to be heard.

Just as I went to hit the door for the millionth time it swung open. Trent was standing before me fully dressed. His lips curled and twisted with annoyance as he stared at me waiting for me to speak.

"Where are you going Trent? We need to talk."

"I don't have anything to say to you, I thought I made that clear."

"This is our marriage, it deserves a conversation." My eyes pleaded with him. I was silently begging him to find some form of the compassion like he used to feel for me. He lowered his gaze for a brief moment, breaking our intense eye contact. For a moment I saw a flicker of an emotion other than anger from him and then just as quickly as it came, it was gone.

He pushed past me and walked into our bedroom. I followed as fast as my feet could carry me. He reached for a bag sitting on the foot of the bed. I squinted my eyes in complete disbelief; it was my luggage that he was lifting.

"What are you doing with my bag?" Was he leaving?

"I'm helping you with your things so you can get out." The look in his eyes scared me. He spoke evenly, with a cool tone that said that he didn't really care. Tears filled my eyes.

"I'm not going anywhere!"

"Yeah, you're getting the fuck out now, I'm done." His words said he was serious. I was hurting; he was angry, neither one of us were thinking in our right mind. I had to persuade him to talk to me. I planted my feet into the ground as if to say, "I'm not going." The standoff had begun.

I didn't need to speak any words at this point to let him know I wasn't leaving. I believed I had sacrificed all that I am not only for my survival but the survival of this relationship; he wasn't going to just toss me out like trash.

"I'm not leaving."

"Yeah, you are." Trent grabbed the packed bag, dragged it to the front door and then tossed it out. The force with which he moved terrified me. I squinted my eyes attempting to recognize the man that I had once knew. This was a stranger to me. Still refusing to leave my home, our home, I stood firmly, willing him to talk to me so that we could work whatever issue we had out.

I was baffled by all that was happening around me, it seemed that my life was completely turned upside down. One moment this man was completely in love with me the next moment it seems as if he hates me.

The sound of Trent's booming voice snapped me back into reality. Before I could focus on what he was saying I felt the firm grasp of his arms wrapping around my body. He forcefully pulled me from my spot.

"Let me go!" I kicked and pushed attempting to get away from him. My legs desperately and unsuccessfully fought aimlessly against the air. The robe that covered my semi-nude body began to slip away, exposing my bare skin just as my husband's actions were exposing the callousness of his heart.

I felt a surge of pain shoot through my body as my ass met the hard cement driveway. He was throwing me out like garbage, and worst of all hadn't so much as given me an explanation as to why.

"Trent, what is happening, what did I do to you to deserve this? I'm not the one who was caught cheating, I'm not the one that obviously has a thing for my assistant, and I'm not the one that refused to talk about it. "

Last night I walked through the doors of my home fully prepared to come clean, I wanted to put everything on the table and move forward with the life and image I had worked so hard to achieve.

"You know exactly what you've done, and for you to try to sit here and play innocent disgusts me. Did you think I was stupid? Did you think I would never find out who you really are?"

"Trent I'm exactly who you know me to be?" Even though I didn't fully believe the words, I was convinced they had enough truth in them to speak them now.

"I don't know who you are, but I do know this, Kyra Williams did not exist before 2005. There are no school records, no birth records, and no established credit, absolutely nothing. Kyra Williams-Jamison does not exist." Before I could respond, the door abruptly slammed shut.

***

The day that some women dream about was finally here. Dominique was not one of those women, but Kyra was. I turned in the full-size mirror completely enamored with my own reflection. I would have never had this type of life in Louisiana. Back home I was someone different, someone who didn't get diamond rings and wedding gowns. I was the one men used to fulfill their fantasies, but today all that had changed.

I opted for a simple ceremony; something small and intimate is how I explained it to Trent. It would be just us, I would walk down the aisle to meet him, he would take my hand and we would exchange vows. I limited the guest list to just his immediate family and a few friends. I could never let him know it was because I had no contact with my family and friends.

He could never know that I had stolen from my married drug-dealing boyfriend after receiving a death threat from his psychotic wife. No, small and intimate sounded much better.

A light knock at the door interrupted my thoughts. I walked to the door to unlock it. I guessed it was probably someone from the venue to let me know that it was time. I grasped the knob to open the door. I put on my "I'm so excited to be getting married" smile because I was expecting to see the little white lady who had led me to this room, my smile quickly vanished.

"Jacob." He stared at me, his smooth porcelain colored skin slightly tanned from the summer sun.

"Kyra." He pushed his way into my room.

"What do you want?"

"Here," He handed me a pastel pink envelop with the words, on your wedding day printed on them. I ran my finger in the corner to rip it open and pulled out the contents. Reading the front of the card, it seemed like no more than a kind gesture to a bride on her wedding day, but I knew Jacob a little better than that. The messages he has been leaving me say that this is not a friendly meeting.

Inside the card were pieces of paper. I squinted my eyes as I read the paper. I could feel the blood drain from my face, as my past and my present collided.

"What is this?" I questioned.

"It's my insurance plan."

"Jacob I - -".

"I'll talk. You just listen. This is my insurance plan! You can either play the game my way, and I'll stop looking or do it your way and watch me show you how blackmail really works."

"I don't know what this is." My tongue tripped over the words. I was so nervous I was stuttering. I knew exactly what it was. I could read very well. It was a background check on Kyra Williams. It said everything I had paid thousands of dollars for, but the thing that made my heart beat a million beats per minute was the picture he had included inside of the card. It was a mugshot.

"Yeah, you know what it is. You thought you could play with me little girl? I didn't get to where I am today by playing by the rules. You should have done your homework before you decided to blackmail me. I don't know who Dominque Simoneaux is, at the moment I don't care, but try to blackmail me again and everybody will find out. Police included."

He walked over to me and lifted the many layers of my dress. I didn't know what to do, this man how somehow gotten the upper hand in my own game. My mind raced trying to come up with my next move. I felt his hands slide between my thighs and gently brush against me.

"We're not done until I say it's done. You want your husband to keep climbing, then we do things the way I want, when I want. As long as you keep my secret, I'll keep yours." He pulled away from me and without saying another word, left.

TWELVE

HOW THE HELL had he found out? How much did he really know? Questions swirled around in my head as I drove aimlessly. My heart was still racing thinking about the coldness Trent displayed. In this very moment, I wanted to be just as cold and cruel to him as he was being to me. It was obvious that I am not the only one with secrets. It was becoming more and more apparent to me that Trent harbored probably just a many secrets as I did, maybe even more.

The man I just saw was not the man that I married. Trent was the man I thought would never hurt me. When I found him he was so different from what I was used to. He put me first, I felt special, like he had eyes for only me and would protect my heart by any means necessary, and I, in turn, was willing to do any and everything to make our marriage and him successful.

My eyes were dry from shedding so many tears. I had no more; the only emotion I could feel was anger. Anger that I had gone to such lengths to protect a man who in the end only saw me the same way as any other man had. A possession. I felt alone, and the one thing I didn't want to be right now was alone.

I picked up my phone to call Redd. I didn't know what I thought he could do for me but whatever it was had to be better than feeling the way I did. Anything was better than this empty, dark feeling that was starting to take control of me. I would deal with Trent, but I had to clear my mind to do so. I never thought I would be confiding in Redd ever again, but as I drove he was the only one I could think of that I could talk to.

"Hey, where are you?"

"On my way to the house, what's up?"

"I'll meet you there." I disconnected the call. I didn't want to talk on the phone, but I did need to see him. Before all of this, before Queen found out, before I robbed him, when we were back home and just us, he actually did make a good friend. I knew I could expose all of me to him because he knew all of my flaws, and he would give me his honest opinion about what I should do next.

I pulled my car into the private driveway and parked. I grabbed the rearview mirror and looked at myself. My eyes were puffy and red from my endless crying, my hair which was usually always in place was messy and disheveled; I was a hot mess. I grabbed my purse and attempted to somewhat put myself together. I didn't want any of those girls to see me like this. Once I felt satisfied that I was as together as I could be under the circumstances I got out of the car and went in.

It was unusually quiet in the house, but at the moment I didn't care to question it or even mind the silence. I welcomed it. It was early in the day so most of the ladies hadn't come in yet. This was the time Redd and I usually used to go over the books. I walked in and headed towards the master suite. I knocked gently before entering making sure that the room was empty. Once I entered I headed towards the master bath, water always worked wonders to clear my mind.

Piece by piece I began to remove my clothing until I was

completely naked. I moved towards the oversized tub, slid in and started a warm flow of water that washed over me. I felt safe submerged in the warm pool of water. I stared at the walls, at first void of all emotion, and then the dam broke. Everything I had been running from had rushed in from every end. I was engulfed in turmoil, nothing was right in my life. The more I struggled to hold on to control, the more I began to lose control.

"Kyra?" Her sugary sweet tone broke through my thoughts of self-pity. I turned to face Michelle. My vulnerability showed. "What's wrong?"

"Nothing." My voice was nearly gone from all the yelling I had done with Trent.

"I can tell there is something, but you don't have to talk about it."

Good, I thought to myself as I turned away from her, before increasing the intensity of the jets on the tub. I closed my eyes and sank deeper, hoping she would take the hint to go away.

"What are you doing?" The unexpected movement of the water startled me. I sat straight up and stared at Michelle sitting across from me.

"I'm taking your mind off of whatever is bothering you." I'm not sure what made her think that me soaking in this bathtub was an open invitation. I pulled my legs closer to my body, uncomfortable with being in the tub with her. I know things had gotten out of hand with her and Redd at the club, but it wasn't that type of party.

That was a one-time thing that I did not plan on repeating. The further I pulled away the closer she seemed to get to me. I was in the furthest corner of the tub, there was nowhere else for me to move. She didn't say any words, just stared at me, intensely, instead of looking at me she looked through me. Her hands moved up my legs as she pulled me into her. I could feel the warmth of her body against me.

My mind argued with my body, I wanted her to stop, but then I didn't. I wanted to feel something else other than the emotions and pain that had taken permanent residence in my heart. If I felt something physical, I wouldn't think about raging emotions.

I began to let down my guard. My legs relaxed and slightly parted as she found her way between them.

"Uh-hmmm!" The clearing of his throat was an obvious but immediate attention getter. "I thought you wanted to talk about something." He smirked as he watched me uncomfortably lift myself from the tub.

"I do want to talk." My cheeks were red with embarrassment. I didn't want to be caught in such a compromising position by Redd. I would never live it down.

"Why you running? It's nothing I've never seen before."

I pushed pass him and headed into the bedroom. I stumbled as I slipped my clothes on but soon realized I had much bigger problems to worry about than Redd finding me butt naked in the bathtub with her. I finished dressing and turned to face both of them. Michelle hadn't spoken a word. She carelessly stood naked in the room as if nothing was happening. In her world it seemed to just be her. Maybe she was waiting for a repeat of the night we had met her.

"We need to talk." My eyebrows raised slightly to give him the signal that this was an important conversation. He instantly understood. That's the one thing about Redd and I, we never really needed words; we always had so many other ways of communicating.

"Michelle, you gonna have to table your little lesbian love affair, we got business." She exited the room, not bothering to even put her clothes on before. Redd walked behind her and closed the door.

"Now, what is so important?"

"He knows."

"He knoooooows what? And who the hell is he?"

"Trent."

"Oh, your punk ass husband."

"I'm serious." I needed him to take this seriously, depending on what he knows we could go down for all this shit we are doing. Anger began to build within me. I was doing all this so he didn't find out who I was and he knows that I am not who I am.

"So what your husband got to do with me?"

"He knows something Redd, he was in here yesterday. When I went home to confront him about it he flipped the hell out. Grabbed my ass, through me to the floor called me his whore and choked me until I almost passed out, Then..."

"What the fuck you say he did? Choked you? And that nigga still breathing?"

"Wait, then this morning he threw my ass out the door."

As I recounted everything that had happened, I could see it was finally sinking in. Redd was finally catching up.

"How did he find out?"

"I don't know, but if I had to guess I would say he was tipped off by your dumb ass wife. I don't even know how much he knows. I gotta figure that out first. He was pissed Redd." I shook my head as if I could dislodge the thoughts of what had just happened.

"He just said that he knew my name wasn't really Kyra."

"It doesn't seem like he knows shit."

"It sounds like he knows enough."

***

Three months have passed since my wedding day and the day Jacob showed me a completely different side of himself. I couldn't figure out what his angle was and I didn't know how to contain the information that I knew he had on me. Right now even though everything was peaceful I was smart enough to understand that he had the upper hand.

An overwhelming wave of anxiety passed over me. Every piece of my well-designed life had been carefully placed liked the blocks of a Jenga tower. It looked good, but one wrong move and it would topple over into ruins. I had to think of a way to get out of the conundrum I found myself in.

When I met Jacob I thought I had completely read him. He looked like an easy mark that I could control and he had played along well. I wondered just how long Jacob had known I wasn't really who I pretended to be.

I looked around our apartment. I liked my life. It felt nice not to have to worry about the threats that came from leading the street life. With Trent, I had found some sort of normalcy and a place to hide in plain sight. With my "tips" I gave to the NOPD I felt certain I no longer had to fear Redd coming after me, at least for now. My only real threat was coming from the very person I thought I had control over.

I was drowning in nervousness. Every single nerve ending tingled with anticipation. I couldn't live like this. I knew what I had to do. Rushing to get dressed I ran to my bedroom. My first mind told me to get sexy, but I believed I was far beyond that with Jacob. I seriously doubt given everything that has happened that my sex appeal would do anything. I slipped on my shoes and headed towards the car.

Once I arrived at the office I went to the lower level. This is the area we always met in, it was restricted and could only be accessed with a key card, this way we were less likely to be seen together. I used the one Jacob gave me when I thought I was seducing him. I sat in the parking garage trying to figure out the right words to say.

I just needed assurance that we could keep it between us. From what Jacob has been showing me it would be best to appeal to his ego rather than anything else. How in the world had I missed that? My body fell into my plush leather seat as I sat in my car contemplating whether to send a message asking Jacob to meet me downstairs.

Just as I found the courage to send that text, I noticed a black SUV pull into the garage. Normally this wouldn't seem strange, but it's the way it crept through the garage. The car moved slowly through the dim area and rolled to a stop right as it reached the elevator.

I sat forward to get a better look. The man that exited the rear driver's side door was tall and muscular; he looked a lot like Trent from behind but he was taller and darker. I couldn't make out his face, he never moved beyond the shadows of the garage.

Not wanting to be seen, I sank as deep as I could into the driver's seat without obstructing my view. The light from my screen illuminated the inside of the car. I quickly exited the unsent message and opened my camera. I dimmed the screen as much as possible and began to record the scene before me. I eyed the man up and down.

It wasn't Trent, this man was older but just as handsome. His skin was the smooth texture of milk chocolate. His custom tailored suit fit his firmly toned body perfectly. I watched as he walked along the side of the SUV and stood next to the elevator. He eyed his watch impatiently as if he was waiting for someone.

The dim light in the waiting area for the elevator washed across him but I didn't recognize the man. Something about his features seemed familiar. I struggled to attempt to connect the pieces of my memory. Did I know this man or was my mind just playing tricks on me? I could feel the chaotic bumping of my heart as I watched.

The shuffling sound of the elevator doors opening invaded the silence in the parking garage. Jacob exited and greeted the man. I could barely hear but I could tell that these two were very familiar with one another. It didn't make any sense to me. As if on cue the driver got out of the car and opened the back. As the door went up, I saw what I thought was a body flailing around.

My heartbeat quickened. My mind rushed to make sense of what I was seeing. I wasn't new to any of this, and what I saw looked like someone who was about to meet their end. The driver grabbed the man inside and threw him to the ground. He struggled to gain his balance as the driver stood him up. His hands were tied to his sides and his mouth was taped. The driver reached and snatched the tape from his mouth before retreating back to his spot in the car.

The man stood defeated. His slumped composure told me he had no hope of things going his way. Jacob moved towards him and without so much as saying a word, he punches the hell out of him. The sound of flesh hitting flesh echoed through the garage.

"Didn't I fucking tell you if I ever caught you stealing, you would pay with your life?" Jacob's snow white skinned reddened as he spoke through clenched teeth. I don't think I had ever seen him this angry. Until the day of my wedding, I would have never thought that he could so much as get angry. But clearly he could. The man didn't answer only looked at him with I could only guess was pleading eyes.

"Where's my money?" The man moved closer. His body language was menacing. The closer he moved to the man the faster my pulse quickened. I would not want to be this man. He had broken the number one rule. He got caught.

"I have it, I'll give it back, please." The man in the suit tapped on the back a truck and the driver got out of the car again, this time carrying an iPad. He handed it to Jacob. After a moment of pressing and swiping he spoke.

"Give me the passwords," he demanded.

"G-g-e-t-t-h-A-t-$_4-M-e," The man said through frightened gasps. I watched as Jacob swiped and tapped some more before handing it back to the driver who stood silently to the side.

"It's done, all of your money will be back in its rightful place by the close of business today." He turned to look at the man who was now shaking. "Thank you." A sinister smile spread across Jacob's face and then disappeared.

"Don't make a mess in my garage." He said to the driver and then pressed the button to enter the elevator. I wanted to look away but I couldn't. I sat in paralyzed, horrified as the driver turned into a hitman. He grabbed something from the truck, wrapped it around the bound man's neck, and squeezed until his body went limp.

I sat waiting in my car afraid to move as I watched him throw the body in the car and leave. I didn't want to follow them out so I sat and waited for what I thought would be enough time for them to have left.

I hit end on the recorded and quickly scrolled to my unsent message. I erased it; thankful I hadn't sent it. After what I just saw I wanted no trace of me being here and I no longer thought it would be a good idea to mess with Jacob, but I knew this recording would buy me a bit of insurance in case he came for me.

I hoped I never had to use it but if he exposed me it would be mutually assured destruction, I would take his ass down with me. I didn't understand everything that had happened but I understood one thing, Jacob wasn't exactly who he claimed to be. My best bet would be to lay low, be a good little wife and not provoke him to spill my secret.

THIRTEEN

THE WARMTH of Redd's body wrapped around me like a child's favorite blankey. I felt safe in this very moment. The sun peaked through the semi-closed blinds creating an ethereal glow throughout the room. If I had it my way I wouldn't move from this spot. Lying next to him reminded me of the times I had run away from, things at times somehow seemed perfect, but always fleeting. The bed gently moved as Redd began to wake and turn to face me.

"Good morning," He lifted his head, his eyes still half closed.

"Hey."

"What?" His partially opened eyes were twisted in confusion, or maybe it was annoyance.

"Everything Redd, what the hell am I going to do about Trent?"

Redd sat up in the bed now fully awake. His face was twisted in annoyance. His expression told me he didn't understand how my life seemed to be crumbling around me.

"Do nothing about that nothing ass nigga."

"That nothing ass nigga is still my husband, all of my money everything is tied up in joint accounts. I gave you everything I had separately to clear my debt with you. Remember!" I moved to the side of the bed. I was annoyed that he didn't seem to understand what was happening.

"Look Dominque, fuck that nigga. We got the spot, we making money. You don't need him. Besides, it's always gonna be mine anyway." Redd walked over to the side of the bed and pushed me back against the plush mattress. My body immediately reacted as he began to kiss me against my neck. Slowly he moved down, using his tongue to trace sensual lines leading to my nipples.

My back arched as his touch commanded my body. As Redd's hands traveled the length of my body, my thoughts of Trent slipped away.

"Damn." Redd shouted reaching for his phone. I sat up to peek at the screen.

My Queen

I quickly read before he moved to answer. So much for my welcomed distraction. Queen seemed to be in the midst of everything. I watched as Redd left the room to speak to her in private. I assumed she was calling because he didn't come home last night. I began to put my clothes on and sat waiting for Redd. This again reminded me of our old times and our fleeting moments. Things always seemed perfect and then they weren't.

I shrugged my shoulders and proceeded to put on my shoes. It didn't matter figuring out things with Redd was further down on my list. Things would never really be different. As long as Queen is around we would always be in the exact same place.

"Where you going?"

"I gotta figure some stuff out."

"Look I told you, don't worry about that motherfucker. He wasn't ever right for you. You just ran to the first nigga that didn't remind you of me." He laughed.

"I ran because your wife threatened to kill me."

"She wasn't gonna kill you."

"Well, I wasn't gonna stick around and fuckin' find out." I walked over and grabbed my purse and car keys. "I'll be back. I'm going to my house to see what I can find out while he's at work. I know you think it it's not important, but he was here, and if he wanted to, with one phone call he could shut us down."

I left Redd standing there to digest the information I gave him. This shit had to be contained. If Trent so much as blinked in the direction of the police they could have us on prostitution, drug possession with the intent to distribute, not to mention my entire identity was false. I didn't have time to live in Redd's world where everything would be okay. I had to move fast and find out what was really going on.

I jumped into the only possession Trent had left me with and raced to my home. Trent should be at work and it wasn't really like him to come home in the middle of the day. I glanced at the clock on the radio. It was 12:54 pm, that gave me approximately two hours to find some piece of evidence that would fill in the blanks for me. Trent had seemed like everything I desired in a man, but what I desired at the time of arriving in Houston was anything that was different from Redd.

Until twelve years ago, I led my life in the streets. I lived by the streets and always knew I would die in these streets. But when I met Trent all of that changed. I started to believe that I could really be this woman with the perfect life. I believed I could really be Kyra.

After a thirty-minute drive, I pulled up to the house I had until the other day called my home. I sat in the car staring at the massive structure. The French provincial style home was the perfect balance of art and symmetry. I loved this home and being forced out of it was like losing a loved one. I exited the car and headed towards the large wrought iron double doors and entered the keypad entry code. I doubted if Trent changed the code, he always left those things to me and in the past, I had happily obliged if that meant I got to keep playing Kyra.

I could hear the click of my heels hitting the marble floors as I made my way towards his home office. If Trent had any evidence or secrets they would be hidden behind this door. I grasped the cool knob and turned to allow myself entry. An eerie nervousness washed over me. I had every right to be in this home yet I felt as if I was breaking and entering. I was nervous about what Trent would do if he found me in here. He had shown me a side of himself I had never seen before. He was never aggressive or violent with me until now.

I found my way to the plush desk chair and sank into its indulgent comfort. My hand danced around the touch screen to awaken the computer. Blue light illuminated from the screen; the blinking cursor was demanding I put in a code. Code? I had no idea what that could be. I never bothered this computer because I had my own laptop, and until now I completely trusted Trent to be the predictable man I had always known.

Attempting to crack the mystery of how much Trent knew I hurriedly typed in multiple guesses trying to unlock the computer. With each wrong password the screen shook and made a loud noise as if to say "Bitch try again." I stared blankly at the screen. According to the big bold letters above the password box, I had one attempt remaining before I was completely locked out.

My body fell against the back of the leather chair. This was my last try. What could it be? I rummaged through papers and files hoping to find some clue as to what the password was. I grabbed a black leather planner that I had never seen before. I flipped through the pages. Each page held three columns with different numbers in each one. I had no idea what this was, but I only had one try and there was no way I had time to try all three pages of numbers.

I flipped through the back of a book and saw letters scribbled on a blank page. It had no labels, no other words; it only had the eight characters hurriedly scratched on the page in Trent's handwriting. I slowly typed the letters in knowing this would be my last try. I hit enter on the keyboard and watched the screen go blank before the bright screen light was back. It worked. I tossed the book to the side and scanned his open documents. Trent never closed down any of his browsing or window history.

I browsed the first open window I saw. It was opened to a banking page, but I didn't recognize this bank. I hit the password box and to my surprise login and password information automatically populated. Once I logged in the amount almost blew me away. There was twenty-million dollars in this account.

I clicked to scroll through the transaction history. Money had steadily flowed in and out of this account on a regular. The history was never ending which led me to believe the account had been opened for a while. I clicked on the pdf version of the bank statement. It had my name and address but it was something that I had never seen and I didn't set up.

"Son of a bitch!"

I searched his history and found three accounts in my name. And we aren't talking about a little money, these accounts held millions. All this time I thought I had my secrets and turns out he had far more. I didn't really understand what any of this meant at the moment, but I did know something was way off.

In my old life, I would have never been so stupid. A man would never have complete and utter control over my life. I wanted to have a "normal" life so bad with a man I thought I had control over I had completed neglected to see things for what they really were.

My face burned with anger as I searched for any idea of

where this money could be coming from. I looked towards the open closet door and saw a safe. What the hell was in there? I jumped out of the desk chair so forcefully the chair rolled back and collided with the wall. The jarring thud of the chair hitting the wall startled me, but couldn't stop me from getting to that safe. I stared at the black steel box, concentrating on the buttons. What was it with the men and safes?

Redd had a safe but was too stupid to realize he couldn't keep opening it with me there without realizing that I would eventually figure out the code. Now I stood before a safe that I didn't even know Trent had but I would crack it too. I stared at the buttons and noticed that four of the buttons were slightly more worn than the others. The wheels in my head furiously turned. I was going to figure out the code.

I stepped back and eyed the keypad, and then just by chance I decided to try his birthday. It couldn't really be that easy, could it? The most worn keys utilized the same numbers as his birthday. 0-8-1-2, I slowly entered the numbers into the glowing keypad hoping it would accept the code. There were three beeps followed by the sound of something turning, and then it granted me entrance. For such a smart man his ass sure seemed dumb. The password might as well have been password.

I reached in and pulled out the contents of the safe. There was nothing overtly suspicious as a perused the envelopes and papers. I saw his passport, a few credit cards, and some paperwork. My eyes stealthy roamed the contents of the safe, attempting to devour as much information as possible. I wanted to know more about the bank account I had found.

My name was on a lot of the paperwork I found in the safe, there were property deeds, business contracts all listing me as the director. All of these companies I "managed" were all in other countries. I honestly had no idea what I was looking at but whatever it was it wasn't right. How long had this man been using me?

I placed all the papers along the desk, grabbed my phone and quickly started taking pictures of the documents. I would comb through them once I had more time to sit and decipher what all of this really meant.

Peering into the safe it appeared to be empty, but it wasn't exactly eye level so to be sure, I shoved my hand to the back of the black box. I pulled out one last envelope tucked in the back. I undid the clips holding the tanned paper container closed and dumped its contents on the desk as well. A driver's license and passport with my name but Queen's picture spilled out.

"What the hell," I didn't understand what was happening. I scanned the documents; they looked just as authentic as my own. He was planning something, but I had no idea what the hell that was. And what part did Queen actually play in all this? I told Redd countless times that he couldn't trust her. I snapped more pictures before shoving everything back into the safe. I also took down the banking information and password for safekeeping.

I hurriedly placed things back in their original place. Once I was satisfied with the placement of everything I quickly left the house and jumped in my car. I was running out of my own home, but I wanted no chance of running into Trent. After his unusual behavior, I wasn't too sure about his next move. After hearing the clicking sound of my seatbelt being secured, I started the car and hit the gas. I needed to find a place to think, without distraction so I could figure this shit out, fast.

***

I finally settled into life with Trent and I had to admit things were good. Walking away from that bullshit with Jacob had paid off. He had kept his word to keep my secret and I never had to use what I had on him.

I leaned over the pot on the stove and inhaled the rich aroma of the seafood gumbo I was preparing. Even though I had fully become Kyra, there was a little of Dominique that surfaced ever now and again.

"Kyra!"

"I'm here love." Trent walked into the kitchen and kissed me. Here lately he's seemed a little unlike himself. Trent stood in the kitchen staring at the pot but saying nothing.

"Are you okay?"

"Yeah, it smells good baby." Trent turned towards our room and then stopped. His gaze caught mine and he looked as if he wanted to say something.

"What is it?"

"Nothing"

"Talk to me." I had truly come to love Trent and when there was something wrong I could definitely tell.

Trent walked back towards me and pulled me close. His breath was hot against my ear as he whispered. "Let's take a walk." He grabbed my hand and pulled me towards the door. I pulled back to stop him, I needed to turn the pot off.

"Trent, baby we can talk here, I'm cooking." I caressed his face attempting to ease the momentary flickers of panic I saw.

"Let's take that walk. It's been a while since we strolled together." Even though his tone was cool and upbeat, his eyes told a completely different story. He reached for my hand again guided me out of the door. Once we made it towards the entrance of our semi-circular driveway, He finally began to speak.

"There are things about me that I haven't been upfront about. Things that I thought I would never have to say aloud." I looked at Trent, what could he possibly be lying to me about.

"What do you mean?"

"I need to know I can trust you." His words were like a sharp blow. If this man only knew the lengths I went to have his back

"Whatever it is, we'll figure it out." I swallowed trying to clear the lump from my throat. "I know a thing or two about secrets." I faced Trent, maybe it was time for us to both stop keeping secrets.

FOURTEEN

AIMLESSLY I GUIDED my car through the streets of Houston. I didn't want to go back to the house and deal with Redd. He just didn't seem to get it. I felt more alone than I ever had in my life. The support I wanted from Redd was non-existent and what I thought I had found in Trent wasn't there either. I was used to being on my on, but the time I had spent as Kyra had shown me I could have more than what the streets alone could offer.

There was so much information floating around in my head. I found a bank account with my name on it, with millions of dollars in it. I had evidence that Trent was planning something that included Queen, but what?

My first thought was to confront him with proof but I had to figure out what was going on first, figuring out what part Queen played in this was crucial. If I confronted him with no evidence she would know undoubtedly that I knew something and I didn't want to tip off Trent.

I pulled into the Uptown Park shopping center. I loved the Galleria area and I decided that I needed a nice secluded spot where I could think. I parked and headed towards Uptown Sushi, one of my favorite sushi spots. I walked through the door and stood at the hostess counter. The young lady at the desk greeted me with a smile.

"Good afternoon, welcome to Uptown Sushi." I usually had a reservation, but with it being the middle of the day I knew I would be okay. This place got really busy on weekends and evenings, but looking around the beautifully decorated building I knew I would have no trouble with being seated.

"How many?"

"It's just me."

"Okay just a moment, and we will have you seated." She smiled and stepped away. I waited impatiently. I was ready to be seated, have a Lychee martini, seaweed salad, their lickety split roll and devour the information I found in Trent's office.

"Hey!" A sweet and sultry voice invaded my quiet moment. I turned to face the intrusion.

"Hhhhey," The words hesitantly escaped my lips. Michelle smiled; her big brown eyes were deep caverns of innocence. It seemed innocent but I honestly didn't trust it.

The hostess returned, "Will your friend be joining you?"

"Yes, I will," I started to object but decided against making a scene just because we sat at the same table didn't mean I had to talk to her. My plan was to have my lunch and drink in peace. If she chose to tag alone and be ignored, so be it.

She seated us in one of the semi-circular shaped booths along the wall. I slid in towards the middle of the table. Michelle waited for me to be seated comfortably before sliding into the spot right next to me. This booth could honestly fit at least 6 people comfortably, why the hell was she all up on me when there was so much space.

I glanced at Michelle with a raised eyebrow. She didn't seem to notice my unspoken question or maybe she just didn't care. I moved over to give some space between us without making myself uncomfortable and waited for our waitress to take our order.

After ordering I pulled out my phone and started to read over the many documents I had found. Michelle was very silent and I could feel her watching me. Why did she seem to study me so much? Why did she seem to always be around? I placed my iPhone down on the table, now turning all my attention to Michelle. She was openly staring at me, not trying to hide it at all.

"Michelle, how is it do you always seem to be around?"

"What do you mean?"

"I mean you're always around Michelle, lurking in the corner watching, jumping into people's bathtubs, all of that. Why?" I asked the question, never believing that she would honestly answer but it was worth a shot. I am not sure if she wanted Redd, if she thought she was coming for my spot by trying to get close to me or what. It was hard to say. She was never around Redd like this, it was always me she seemed to find those alone moments with.

Maybe they had something going on that I didn't know about and she was trying to make sure that whatever we had was dead. Hell, I don't know what her problem was but I was a little tired of her always seeming to be just coincidently around.

"I'm not lurking." Her head flew back in laughter.

"You're always around or coming around the corner watching me. Now you're here too."

"No, I live there not lurking, and I'm here because I like sushi." She laughed even louder as if I had said something funny. "Maybe I like being around you, you ever consider that?"

"No."

Michelle smiled and closed the gap I had purposely placed between us. "You look like you have a lot on your mind Dominque. You want to talk about something? Tell me what you're really running from."

I decided not to answer. I did have a lot on my mind but I wanted to change the subject from away from me. I picked up my phone and began to read through the documents again.

"What's that?" She asked.

"My business," I placed the phone face down and turned my attention back to Michelle. "So you were in school right, how's that going?" I decided to grill her instead of the other way around. I wanted to see if she could remember what she told me.

She had books and sometimes looked like she was studying but hell I had a lot of things that looked a certain way, so that didn't mean shit. I didn't trust Michelle but since she was always thrusting herself into my space I thought it would be smart to know what and who I'm dealing with.

"It's good, I'm almost done. Was definitely able to pay my tuition off a lot faster than I thought. Thanks to you guys."

"Well, you should thank that one client you have." Michelle just shrugged. My sarcastic tone was lost on her. Most of the girls had regular clients, but Michelle only had one. We didn't argue with it because he paid for her constant availability. He didn't seem like the type but then again I learned a long time ago there wasn't really a type.

He only came once a week, but he paid for her time as if he was seeing her daily. I don't know what she did that was so special to make a man pay for time he wasn't getting. I had even checked the camera to see exactly what his request was, but the only thing I ever caught was him covering the camera.

"I thank him." Michelle tilted her head back and chuckled. My gaze fell on the heart shaped necklace she always wore. I watched as her hands found the gold chain and twirled it around her fingers.

"See something you like?" Her lips curled as her tongue darted around her lips, ending with a slow seductive smile.

"I know things have happened in the past that may have given you the wrong idea, but I like dick."

I needed to make things very clear with her. I wasn't sure what energy I was feeling with her, but I needed her to understand, whatever she thought was happening was not going to happen. Michelle leaned even closer to me as if to challenge my words.

I could smell the sweet scent of her perfume as she inched closer towards me. I felt her hands run the length of my thigh. She pushed my thighs apart and gently pulled my panties to the side. Her touch was delicate and explorative.

"Stop!"

I reached to grab her hand. What the hell did she think she was doing? I pulled away and picked up my phone to go through the information again. I logged into the online account and checked the banking balance again. It's as if I couldn't look at it enough. I had to keep checking to make sure it was still there.

"What are you looking at?"

"You have a problem with minding your business don't you?"

"It looks like banking info, maybe I can help?" I cut my eyes towards her. Damn, she was all in my business. "No, seriously maybe I can help. Business and numbers are my thing, it's what I'm going to school for. You keep looking at your account what are you trying to figure out?"

My instincts told me to shut her down, she seemed like she was always fishing for information. My body fell against the plush backing of the booth as I allowed her words to sink in. Could she really help and what's the risk if I did use her for information? It's not like she knew anything about me.

"I don't need any help." I moved to get up from the table. My finance degree might have been faker than a three dollar bill but I had worked in a bank long enough to know more than a little bit about money. As I reached for my purse Michelle grabbed my hand,

"Maybe you need more help than you know."

I snatched my hand away and headed towards the door, never giving her words another thought.

FIFTEEN

SOMETHING ABOUT MICHELLE BOTHERED ME. I couldn't quite figure her out but I would have to table that for another day. The money was still in the accounts and I hadn't decided what I should do. I knew one thing. I was tired of this victim shit. I felt like I had been abandoned. Abandoned by Trent, a man that I thought genuinely loved me who until Redd showed up I thought I loved back.

Redd and I had our ups and downs but could I trust him. I wonder if we could just disappear in the wind. I pulled into the driveway of the house I used to make money. From the outside it looked like a typical suburban home, no one would ever suspect what really went on behind those walls. I walked through the empty halls searching for Redd.

I needed to feel him out. We hadn't had very much one on one time because I have been so consumed with trying to protect my secrets. But the more I thought about it the more I said to hell with my secrets. Redd was from my past. He knew me and I knew him. It seemed a hell of a lot easier with him than to try to figure shit out with Trent.

It was eerily quiet as I walked into the house. I made my way into the camera room and began to turn all the monitors on. It would be easier to use the cameras to find him rather than walk the whole damn house calling him. I turned my attention to one of the downstairs bedrooms. The camera system had no sound but I could clearly see what was happening.

I watched as Redd lifted Queen unto the bed. His hands greedily caressed her body, touching her the same way he touched me. Their lips met and he hungrily kissed her. She eagerly accepted. My blood boiled as the scene played out. I know that was his wife, but I never had to see it. Back home he kept us pretty separate. I stayed out of her way and for the most part, she stayed out of mine.

"Anything good playing?" Michelle stood in the doorway. Her eyes darted from the screen to my face and back to the screen. "This isn't the first time this happened you know."

"Not the first time for what to happen, Michelle." I breathed through clenched teeth. It was almost as if she was amused. She slinked sexily towards me, never taking her eyes off of me.

"It's not the first time he's fucked his wife here." I watched as a smile spread across her lips. Was she trying to get under my skin? Her words hit me with the force of a tidal wave. Here I was thinking of cutting Redd on my newfound fortune, but cutting him in would mean cutting Queen in too.

"I thought he was yo man? Maybe that's what you thought too?" She leaned back against the monitors, twirling her heart locket between her fingers. The screen began to glitch; it had never done that before. I dismissed the glitch and Michelle's question didn't even deserve an answer. I didn't have time for this bullshit.

The hurried clicks of my five inch heels hitting the wood floors echoed throughout the house as I dashed towards the back of the house where Redd and Queen were. Damn, I really couldn't figure this shit out. Queen seemed to be playing both sides, a position I knew all too well.

"What the fuck is she doing here?" Redd lifted his head from between Queen's legs, obviously surprised by my presence. He stared at me while wiping his face with his hands. In this moment I began to wonder what in the hell did I see in him. I had allowed yesterday's feelings to cloud today's judgment when dealing with him. He tilted his head to the side and smirked before he began to speak.

"If I'm here she can be here, who the fuck are you to question me about my wife?" Queen jumped up from the bed, throwing her clothes back on in one swift motion.

"Bitch, I swear I'm so tired of your ass. I shoulda got rid of you a long time ago."

Queen started to lunge towards me but was soon stopped by Redd. She always seemed to be stopped by Redd.

"I got this," Redd stretched out his arm to silence Queen before continuing. "Dominque we do what we do and that's it. This is a business arrangement. You owe me money, money that you stole from me. You're fun to fuck," he laughed, "and fuck with. But this, this right here," he pointed towards Queen, " is Wifey, you just my hoe."

Redd's words hit me with the force of a Mack truck. Everything we had been through seemed to flash before my eyes. I know this started as a business arrangement but years and years of him laying in my bed said it wasn't. The only reason I left with that money was because of his wife. I deserved that shit. Who did this nigga really think he was talking too?

"Your hoe nigga? That's not what your ass be saying and claiming when you inside of me. Fuck you and your wifey, you know she's fucking my husband right."

Queen moved Redd's hand to the side and moved towards me. Her hair was disheveled from her brief sex session I interrupted. Her eyes were ablaze as she walked. This bitch looked like a woman who was quickly becoming unhinged. Queen stood so close to me I could smell the scent of Redd's dick on her breath. She leaned in and whispered so that only I could hear.

"I'm not only gonna fuck your husband, remember what I said bitch, I'm gonna fuck your life. Nice and slow. I'm gonna tear this shit up."

"I am so done with this shiiiiiiiiiiit!" I shoved Queen's small frame against the wall and away from me. Before she could react I was on Redd. I scanned the room for the nearest object that could do the most damage. My eyes quickly fell on the bedside lamp, not even bothering to unplug it I grabbed it and hurled it towards Redd's head. They have me fucked all the way up if they think I'm just going to sit here and deal with their shit. I grabbed my keys and bag and headed for my car.

"I'm gonna kill that bitch Redd."

"Fuck her, she ain't never been shit but a side bitch with main chick ambitions. Our plan solid, we don't need the bitch no more." I didn't know what plan he was talking about and I didn't slow down to find out.

"Where are you going?" Michelle followed closely behind, jumping in my car as I unlocked the door.

"Michelle, I don't have time for this bullshit, get the hell out of my car." I don't know what games she was playing, or why she thought it was cool to jump in my car like we besties, we ain't shit. Half the time I can't figure out her angle.

"You seem like you need someone on your team, let me be that for you. You held me down, gave me somewhere to stay, help me make money, let me help you now."

I didn't know how she planned on helping me, but right now

it didn't matter. I quickly weighed my options, was Michelle friend or foe. After a moment of pondering, something told me it was better to have her as an ally.

"Fine, close the door," I shouted as I hit the gas pedal and sped off.

SIXTEEN

THE OCEAN BREEZE swept across my skin as I stood on the balcony of our Galveston hotel suite. The morning air felt good against my exposed skin as I scrolled through my phone. We had been here for a week compliments of Michelle's client's credit card. I knew my time was winding up and I would need to come up with something fast.

I checked the accounts daily, I knew I was going to make a play for the money but when I did it I needed to be prepared to disappear. I had no discussions with Trent since he threw me flat out on my ass.

"Coffee?" I reached out to take the warm cup of coffee and resumed my gaze into the ocean.

"Still don't trust me huh."

"I trust no one."

"I told you I just wanna help."

"You don't even know me to wanna help me. So what is it that you want?"

Michelle didn't bother to answer my question. She sat next to me, too close as usual and wrapped her arms around me. My body tensed as she pulled me close to her.

"You look like you need a hug."

"I'm not gay Michelle."

"Neither am I." She whispered, pulling me into her. I released a sigh. I was too tired to fight. It felt nice to lean on someone even if I didn't trust that someone. I realized I've had a long history of using sex and people to escape what I was going through, but at this moment I really didn't give a damn. Escape was the magic word and I might as well use her.

She nibbled my neck, moving upward until her lips found mine. She began to kiss me. It was sweet at first, then with each passing second, it filled me with overwhelming desire. I welcomed the distraction. I needed to feel something other than the panic I felt inside that increased with each passing moment.

Her hands explored my body. I had never been this intimate with a woman in a one on one situation but she had me intrigued. I could hear the sound of the Gulf gently rising and falling against the beach as she planted tiny kisses against my body.

The warmth of her touch was welcomed. Softer than Trent's or Redd's ever was, yet just as strong. She pulled my maxi dress above my head, exposing my naked body on the balcony. I briefly wondered if anyone else could see, but the thought of someone watching me turned me on even more.

Michelle nestled her head between my legs. Her tongue pushed forward and parted my lips. She ran tiny circles around my clitoris. This shit felt amazing. Her head pushed further and further into my wetness. She wasn't scared of getting her face a wet, I think she was trying to drown in it and I didn't mind.

My nipples hardened as her tongue eagerly circled my clitoris. I watched as her fire red nails traveled up my thighs, landing on my breast. My reddish brown peaks stood at full attention as she squeezed, intensifying my pleasure. I could feel her fingers slide inside my wetness, her come-hither motion causing her finger to tap against my g-spot.

"I'm gonna make that pussy cum for me!" Damn, she sounded so sexy. She stood above me and slipped her clothes off all in one motion. I admired her body. From where I was sitting it seemed perfect. She stood motionless, never moving her eyes off of me. She peered so deeply into me I had to look away.

I diverted my gaze and allowed my eyes to fall on her full round breast. I wanted to touch her. I didn't know what her next move would be but my body shivered with anticipation. She pushed me against patio lounge chair. Her body moved cautiously towards me, gently pushing my legs apart as she got closer. Her chestnut colored eyes locked with mine as our bodies grazed against one another. The heat from her body further ignited my passion.

Placing my legs on her shoulders Michelle's soft body collided with mine. I felt her full lips connect to mine. Her tongue parted my lips and I could taste my sweetness on her. I wrapped my arms around her and pulled her even closer to me. I couldn't get enough of the feeling she was giving me. Her thumb moved back and forth against my clit.

"Damn that feels so good."

"I want that pussy to cum for me. Cum for me baby." Michelle's fingers slide inside of me two at a time. She thrust inside of me tapping that damn spot and rubbing my clit over and over again. My moans became louder. This shit had my body on fire with desire.

Her touch was feminine but strong, like the culmination of both masculine and feminine energy. My body craved as much of her as possible. I arched my back and threw my head back. This was so close to ecstasy. The evidence of my excitement rolled down my thighs.

" I bet you no man has ever fucked you this good. Squirt for me baby." Our bodies crashed as I started to raise my hips higher, desperate for more. I ran my hands through her hair cupping the back of her head, pulling her towards me, my actions demanding that she kiss me.

My tongue was eager to meet hers as my hips moved faster, and she pushed her fingers as far as they could go. I tightened my legs around her shoulders. I could literally feel every muscle in my body tighten. The pressure was building inside and I was about to burst.

"Oh my gooooooooooood!" I shouted as a wave of pleasure washed over me. A steady current of wetness flowed before my body went completely limp. I could barely catch my breath.

Michelle's body fell against mine with her head resting against my stomach. We spoke no words, but my mind moved nonstop to make sense of what just happened.

"Tell me one thing about you Dominque." She broke the silence.

"There's nothing to tell."

"I think there is, tell me about your husband. What does he do? How did you guys get here? I know you're not going home anymore at night."

"Sometimes you really don't know who people really are. You know." A solemn feeling washed over me and we were silent again.

"Hey, I'm going to take a shower." I wanted to end this uncomfortable silence and I didn't want Michelle getting the wrong idea about what had happened. I had heard all the jokes about lesbians and uhuals and I didn't need her thinking we were about to be moving in together. Michelle sat up allowing me to get up. I could feel her eyes ravaging my body as I walked towards the bathroom.

SEVENTEEN

I STOOD in front of the mirror trying to get my head in the game. Whatever that was between Michelle and me was nothing more than a distraction. I slipped into a pair of skinny jeans and a tank top not even bothering to put on a bra.

I reached for the complimentary lotion and began to rub it onto my exposed areas. I glanced down and noticed Michelle's necklace lying on the counter. I picked it up. I don't know why I cared but it must have meant something to her because I never saw her with it off.

"Hey Michelle, you left your necklace in here." I exited the steamy bathroom and walked toward the sitting area. Michelle was still outside. She stood with her back turned to the large wall length balcony door.

I moved closer so she could hear me. She turned around holding my phone.

"What are you doing with my phone?" I left it on the balcony. I was so distracted by what happened between Michelle and me, I had forgotten all about it.

"Nothing. I was about to bring it in." I eyed her suspiciously. I reached and grabbed my phone before turning to go back in the room. I didn't want her eyes on any of the documents had found in the house. I sat at the foot of the bed and looked towards Michelle. Her eyes probed, I assumed to gauge my reaction.

"You're so beautiful. I can't believe your husband and Redd let you get away." Her statement seemed more like a question. She had hinted so many times she wanted to know more about me. But until I could figure out her angle I wasn't going to tell her shit.

"Here, you left this in the bathroom." I held my hand out, handing her the gold trinket she always wore. Her hand grazed against mine as she reached for it. A jolt of electricity surged through me. What was happening? Her presence was making me uncomfortable.

"Maybe I can give you my heart." Michelle leaned over and clamped her necklace around my neck.

"Michelle...I..."

"Don't worry about it, I don't expect yours. Yet. " She leaned in and kissed me. Her lips were like plush pillows. I closed my eyes and exhaled. It felt good to be desired. Was I that desperate for affection that I was willing to go against everything in me that screamed stop?

"I have to go."

"Don't forget the keycard. I'll be here waiting for you for round two."

I swiftly swiped my keys off of the dresser they sat on and rushed away from the room. I do not have time for this shit. I needed to think and get my ass out of the hole it was in. Trent flipped on me, Redd flipped on me and now Michelle, who I didn't even know was trying to give me her heart.

Sliding into the plush leather seat of the only possession I had been left with, I started the ignition and peeled off. I needed this moment of solitude to think. The same thought had been playing over and over in my head. *Take the money, Dominque* and that's just what I planned to do. I think my time as Kyra had run its course, it's time to leave my past and my present behind and create a future. To do that I would need to go back to where I started.

After an hour in this ridiculous Houston traffic, I landed right back where I started. Not much had changed in this neighborhood, and I was hoping that Berto could still be found.

I pulled in front the familiar small two-bedroom house. Everything still looked the same. The yard was not manicured. There were bars on the window and there was always people on the porch. To an untrained eye there were hanging out, but to someone like me, someone who had seen these streets before, I knew those dudes were not to be fucked with. They were your way in and your way out.

I pushed the driver's side visor down to check my appearance. I pushed my hair away from my face and put on my shades. I eyed the necklace Michelle had given me.

"No," I said as I released the pendant from my neck. I dropped it into the cup holder between the two front seats and exited the car.

"Hey, Berto here?"

"Who's askin'?"

"Dominique" The guys on the steps eyed me suspiciously. One of the men step to the side and began to mumble inaudibly into his cell phone.

"Alright, c'mon." I followed the man inside but was stopped immediately after the door closed. My heart raced. It hadn't been this hard to see Berto the first time around, but something told me that just maybe this was a whole different operation. The man waived one of those wand style metal detectors over me and then patted me down.

"Open your shirt."

"What? Open my shirt? I'm not taking my fucking clothes off." I was confused by his request.

"You will if you want to see him." I undid the buttons of my shirt. Obviously now satisfied, the man stepped to the side. "She's clean. Follow me."

I followed him through the house. It was extremely cold inside. This might have been the same house on the outside, but it was totally different on the inside. There were large screens and computers everywhere. Some of them simply flashing random things I didn't understand, others with people working diligently as if they were in an office.

We finally reached the back room I had initially met Berto in. My eyes swept the room. This room looked closer to what I remember. There were cameras backgrounds and printers set up. But this equipment seemed a lot more expensive than the ones I had seen before.

"Thanks, Juan. That will be it for now." Damn, he had stepped his shit up. He had a crew, a for real crew.

"Hi."

"What's up mami, what brings you in?"

"I need some work done for me."

"Kyra not working out for you?" How in the hell had he remembered that, it's been years? "Sit down." He pointed towards the empty chair in front of his desk.

"It's time to get out of Houston. And I need a little help with moving some money. Maybe you know someone?"

"I got you Ma, what kinda money you want moved."

"It's a lot, and I want it hidden, completely unable to be traced." I felt like I was asking for a lot. I didn't know anything about this side of things. I worked at a bank and faked my way through a lot of that shit. It was only a way to make my fake identity seem more legit.

Apart of me was a little scared to hand access to twenty-million dollars, but I had a plan and this was apart of it. We had done business before and he had given me exactly what I paid for. I pulled my phone out of my purse and typed in the username and password I had stolen from Trent's office.

"This is what we are talking about." I placed the phone in front of him, not even wanting to say the amount out loud.

"Damn, " Berto said while sitting back in his chair.

"Can you do it, can you move it into another account? But so that it can't easily be traced. Is that possible?" I thought that it was, I had seen shit like this on television, but when it came to real life who knows.

"I got you, but it's gonna cost you. For the new identity and to bounce that much money around it's gonna run you thirty percent of what's in that account. You having the passwords will make it a bit easier but there is still a shit load of risk, so I gotta make it worth my while. And that's me being generous because you know, you're a repeat customer."

He laughed and winked at me. My mind quickly did the math. The last time I checked there was about twenty-five million in that account. That meant that this would cost more than seven million dollars. I knew it wouldn't be cheap but after this, I didn't want to be found. This was way more money than I had stolen from Redd, and I knew with this I could be set. What was seven million compared to seventeen million, nothing? I shrugged my shoulders and extended my hand.

"It's a deal. When will it be ready?"

"Come back in a few days."

"One more thing Berto, I need another car."

"Yea, see my cousin." He typed an address into my phone.

Before leaving I left Berto the information he would need for the account. Then he walked me to the door and called the guy who had let me in to see me out. I glanced again at the computers and the people working on them. A smile spread across my face. For the first time in months, I felt excited about something. I was so close to being away from this bullshit I could almost feel the Miami breeze against my skin.

EIGHTEEN

I COULD HEAR the screeching of my tires against the cement as I swung into the driveway of the house I had gotten for Redd. This was supposed to be my way out, but my debt seemed like a distant memory. I was so eager to keep my life together and had somehow destroyed.

I hurriedly exited the car and headed into the house. I was out of money, had no access to my accounts with Trent so I decided to do what I do best, take that shit. Redd obviously had played me. He used me to make his money like he always had. For him, I had always been good business. So I considered this getting back what was mine. I needed just enough to hold me until Berto got my stuff together.

I eased the door open slowly. I didn't believe that Redd was here but you could never know. I moved as fast as my legs could take me. I wanted to avoid running into him. After I had come in and watched him with that bitch he called a wife, I knew it wouldn't be pleasant between the two of us.

A disgusting smell hit me as I moved through the house.

None of the bitches had bothered to clean. This shit had gone from high class to trash in a matter of days. It was filthy and disgusting. I walked pass the mess and moved towards the back area with the security monitors and money. As soon as I entered the room I grabbed the metal box he kept the money in. Every night he was supposed to dump the mini safe so there was never much money here. This was one time I hoped that Redd didn't listen to me.

I grabbed the cold plastic handled and opened it. The black metal box was practically empty. I grabbed the cash that was inside. Sometimes we charged the customers through a fake company but the PayPal card wasn't here. I counted the cash that was here, less than a thousand dollars. What the hell had he been doing? I stuffed the bills into my purse, returned the box to its original position and left the room.

The house was dead silent. I walked towards the front room and took in my surroundings one more time. Redd had played me, and I had allowed it.I was never supposed to be caught up in this bullshit. I was only supposed to be here long enough to pay him his money back and I had done that and more.

My skin became heated and anger washed over me. Standing in this room made me feel nothing but uneasiness and chaos. I had given this man more than his money back, I had given him a resource to constantly make money and his dumb ass couldn't even see the potential. Redd could kiss my ass. I be damned if he would prosper off of me after I was gone.

I thought he was that person I could always keep it one hundred with, but it was the same shit different day. When it came down to it, when he looked at me he saw dollar signs. Nothing more. I heard him tell Queen their plan was solid, and if their plan was to prosper off of what I had built then they were gonna need to think again.

I ran to the garage looking for whatever I could find to do the most damage. I could tear up this whole place, take out the monitors, destroy the beds, but I knew that wouldn't bother Redd, he didn't give a shit about those monitors, that was my idea, and he didn't give a damn about those beds, he'd just tell them to fuck on the floor.

There wasn't really anything in the garage. I turned to leave but not before slamming my foot into a can. I looked down and noticed a small gas can. I don't even know when this got here because Redd didn't take care of the place, maybe the lawn man left it, but who really cares.

I picked up the small container and began to shake. I practically wanted to do a happy dance when I discovered there was something inside. Instantly I knew what I was about to do. I was going to burn this motherfucker down. If they wanted a plan they can plan to do this shit all over by themselves.

I removed the tiny red cap from the nozzle and began to pour it all over the house. I shook the can to cover the plush carpeting through the lower levels and on the staircase. I rattled the hell out of it until there was nothing left. The scent of gasoline wafted through the air, making me sick to my stomach. It was time to get this over with. I went to the kitchen to grab a lighter. It felt good to purge my pass. I can't believe I wasted so much time on Redd.

My hand slightly shook as I clicked the lighter normally reserved for candles. I knew I needed to move fast because with the way I tossed around the fuel it was going to catch fast. I steadied my hand and slowly moved it towards the seat nearest the door. My left hand gripped the handles of my purse. Damn, I should have opened the door.

The flamed made contact with the chair. Tiny flames began to dance across the doused fabric, growing larger as they began to connect. The heat from the mounting fire jolted me into action. I needed to get out of here.

Still clutching the lighter, I ran out of the door and jumped in my car, backed out and was gone. My lips spread into a satisfied smirk, I was finally taking back control.

NINETEEN

MY LEFT HAND clutched the steering wheel as I dug to find my cell phone at the bottom of my purse. It was time to get rid of this car. And it's about time I started acting like myself. Dominque was too smart for the bullshit. Finally finding my cell phone, I dialed the number Berto had given me earlier. The phone rang forever before someone finally answered.

"What."

"Hey, I wanna know if I can come by. I need something new."

"Who gave you this number?"

"Berto."

"Come in an hour. I'll be here." The rude man said, then abruptly disconnected the call. I didn't care if he hung up the phone or not. I needed another car, to get out of this got damn city.

I glanced at the clock on my dash. It was 7:37 pm. I could be there by nine and get this over with. Then head back to the hotel and fight Michelle off until I was outta here.

My cell phone began to ring. I needed to make a mental note

to get a new one of those too. I couldn't have people being able to find me once I was gone.

"What the fuck did you do?"

"What the fuck does it look like asshole?" This dumb ass didn't deserve my time. My thumb found the small red circle and I disconnected the call. I was done with that bullshit. As soon as I tossed it into the seat it began to ring again. I clicked the button on the side placing it in vibrate mode and continued to steer my car towards my next destination.

The lights from the car behind me were glaringly bright. The driver began to flash his high beams on and off. What the hell was he doing? I maneuvered the car into the next lane to allow the car to pass. As soon as I moved over he moved over. It was starting to get dark and I didn't know what kind of game this person was playing. You never know with this city, road rage could come out of nowhere.

I hit the gas and started to haul ass. Because I was unfamiliar with the neighborhood, I wanted to get out of this area as fast as I could. The faster I moved the faster they followed. I jumped on the freeway. I felt like I had better chances of getting away from this pyscho if I could disappear down the highway. My GPS kept telling me to make the next legal U-turn, but right now I wanted to get away from the person following me.

I tried to calm down. It could have been some random guy that liked what they saw. It's happened to me before. But the vehicle behind me continued to follow me a little too long, maybe he was just eager. I checked the rearview again. I didn't see the car. I exhaled a sigh of relief maybe they were gone.

I hit my signal to exit the freeway and turn around. I needed to get this car situation done. I looked over my shoulder to check my blindside moments before the vehicles collided. The screeching sound of metal hitting metal jarred me. My entire body tensed as my car began to spiral down the exit ramp. From wall to wall the car bounced before coming to a complete stop.

Before I could check and see if anything was broken. The black SUV that had been following me pulled up behind me. A man jumped out the passenger side and headed towards my car.

"Noooo, Noooo!" I screamed. I could only see his eyes peering into my window. His face was completely covered but he looked menacing. The man yanked the door open and grabbed me by my hair.

"Get the fuck out bitch!" His commanded. I was completely frozen. What in the hell was happening? I couldn't understand why this was happening. He dragged me by my hair until he had successfully removed me out of the car. Everything moved so fast. My eyes darted from left to right attempting to make eye contact with anyone that would help me. There was no one.

"Move." The man shoved some hard object into my back. He pushed me until I reached the black Escalade.

"No, I'm not getting in there." I didn't know what waited for me inside of the SUV. I pushed back against the man as hard as I could. "Let me go!" The man fell against the safety rail. This was my chance. I began to run, if I could just make it back to my car, dented or not I could maybe make it out of here. I ran around the back of the truck, trying desperately to get back to mine. Thinking I had outsmarted the man, I dashed towards my car which only seemed feet away. I could taste my freedom.

"Where the hell you think you're going?" It was a different voice.

"Agggghhhhhh!" A sharp shooting pain erupted in the back of my head. My hand flew to the spot of the injury as if cradling it would make the pain any less. I blinked my eyes everything was becoming blurry. I shuffled forward, still trying to get away. The more I moved the dizzier I felt. I thought I was moving forward, but I seemed to only moving in circles. I looked up at the street-light above me.

The bright light glowed, then with each passing second, I saw less and less of the bright light. I could feel the force of gravity pull me to the ground, then everything faded from blurry to black.

TWENTY

MY EYES FLEW OPEN. I jolted straight up and attempted to take in my surroundings. I don't know how long I had been in the back of this car or even where I was. My hands were tied behind me and my legs were bound together. I struggled to gain my balance and sit up. I was still disoriented from whatever had knocked me out earlier. The stale air inside the car made it difficult for me to breathe.

There was only one man in the front seat of the car. I scanned my surroundings. I had no idea where I was but this area was dark. There was a massive industrial building in front of me. It looked like it hadn't been used in years. It was secluded, and there didn't appear to be any other buildings or business within miles. It was the perfect place to make someone disappear.

We were parked in front. I glanced to my left and I saw my car had been driven here as well. Guess whoever these assholes worked for wanted to leave no evidence. My heart raced because I had no idea what to expect. All I knew is that I wanted out.

"Let me out of this fucking car."

"Shut up."

The man driving turned around and extended his arm. I could see straight down the barrel of the gun. Tiny beads of sweat began to form in every crevice of my body. I fell back against the seat. Who could be doing this to me? Had Berto already moved the money? He told me a few days and it had only been one. Had somebody found out about the money already? Redd didn't have the fucking organizational skills to pull this off and Trent and I hadn't spoken since he threw my ass out. So who would and could kidnap my ass.

"Get out." I didn't argue this time. The gun in his hand was all the incentive I needed to comply. My feet were tied, which made movement extremely difficult. I shuffled behind the man who led me inside the abandoned building.

"Sit down and shut up."

The man in black shoved me towards the ground. More pain shot through my body as I hit the ground. The room was dim, the only light that entered the room escaped from the open door of another room. I pushed myself back against the wall and allowed my head to hit the wall. I winced from the pain. The room was so quiet I could hear the thump of my heart race inside of my chest. I didn't know how I was going to get out of this shit. Light slipped into the room as the door creaked open.

"Get the fuck off of me!"

I watched as they hurled his body in first then hers. They crashed into the ground, landing one on top of the other before being able to gain their balance and sit up. I eyed them. Her hair was disheveled. If they had handled her the same as me, I'm quite certain my appearance was probably very close to hers.

I averted my gaze towards him. He sat on the ground, bound and tied just like us. I watched his chest rise and fall with each angry breath he took. He finally made eye contact.

"What did you do you crazy bitch?"

"I didn't do shit."

"No, you always do something, scheming ass bitch! I'm only in this fuckin city because you stole from me. Then you burn down my means of making money, now I'm being fucking abducted. Yo, bitch you are a fuckin' curse and whatever this shit is, I'm certain you got something to do with it."

Queen was silent as Redd and I went back and forth. She was slumped over, crying while she leaned against Redd. My lips curled into a disgusted snarl. All the shit this bitch did and she's crying.

"Bitch, stop crying. You bad enough to step to me, to try to have me killed now you crying. Bitch please. We don't have time for this shit. We need to figure out why someone would kidnap us."

"I don't know." His voice was full of annoyance.

"You never know shit Redd."

The door flew open; making a loud thud that demanded our attention. We abandoned our conversation. The quiet left an eerie feel in the room. Try abductors entered the room. I pushed myself as far as I could against the wall, trying to disappear. The guard saw me move back and lunged towards me, grabbing me again by my hair.

He began to drag me by my curly locks into the middle of the floor. My kicks were useless against this man's strength. He tossed my body to the ground like I was a hopeless doll he was done playing with.

"Sit here and shut up." I watched as he did the same for Queen and Redd. We were in a straight line in the center of the room. Red was to the left of me and to the left of him was Queen. I couldn't control my heartbeat. I was more than certain now maybe Trent had found out about me taking that money. I planned to be in the wind before anyone knew anything about that, now I was almost certain I wouldn't make it out of this room.

Two more men walked through the door. The light illuminated behind the first man's head. He appeared to be a tall menacing shadow. The second guy followed with the same shadowy mystery as the first. I squinted to make out their faces. As they moved closer the men slowly came into focus. The kidnappers parted to allow them to pass.

They stood shoulder to shoulder, one of them holding an iPad in hand. Looking at them both you could clearly see who was in charge.

"Now," his eyes shifted from left to right. "Which one of y'all took my motherfuckin' money?" Trent's intimidating voice boomed throughout the room. Every ounce of air was sucked out of me when he spoke. I struggled to breathe. Jacob was with him. I knew what it meant, the last time I saw Jacob with somebody they didn't make it out alive.

"Let me, Trent let me, I can..." Queen shook uncontrollably. She was scared. She was only a shell of the person that I remembered. She always had somebody in her corner to fight for her. Now there was no one. Redd couldn't do shit for her right now.

"You can what?" He stepped towards her with his hand cupped around his ear as if he was trying to hear her. "Pick her ass up."

One of the guys in black grabbed her and in one quick move she was standing on her bound feet in front of Trent and Jacob. Her body shook as tears streamed down her cheeks. I couldn't even lie, I was terrified too, but I refuse to give them the satisfaction of knowing how scared I was.

"So what is it that you want to explain?"

Queen didn't speak. Not one word, she was dead ass quiet. She stood there shaking, attempting to make sounds come out of her open mouth. Her words were incoherent. They sounded like the ramblings of a crazy person.

She turned to look at me. I know this bitch wasn't trying to put her shit off on me. Whatever happened she knew something about, but she was looking at me like I knew what it was. Did this have something to do with their solid plan?

"Why you looking at me?"

"Oh, she working with you? Kyra? But that's not your real name is it?" He directed the last part to me.

"Bullshit, I don't know shit about shit." I made eye contact with the man I've shared a bed with for twelve years. Until now this man had treated me like his queen, now I felt like nothing more than a stranger. My eyes pleaded with him to recognize how sorry I was for bringing all of this into our lives because I thought it would save me, I thought it would save us. He held our locked gaze for a moment and then shook his head like he was trying to dislodge something from his mind.

"Jacob, says that somebody has been dipping into my money. Slowly taking shit that don't belong to them. And I know y'all have something to do with it. And I'm sure this nigga right here" he pointed towards Redd, "put y'all both up to this shit." Trent was pissed. His face was contorted with anger, his eyes ablaze with loathing. I was slowly realizing this is not about the money I was trying to take.

This was about whatever Redd and Queen had been up to. I'm sure Redd was behind this somehow. He thought we were rich and he wanted his share of it. Even if I did give him a way to make his money back, he still wanted more.

Jacob stood silently to the side. He didn't react to any of what was going on and I wasn't surprised. I knew he wasn't what he said he was. He was an attorney but I knew a long time ago he was much more than that. This attorney shit just made it easier to hide, move and protect his money.

"Man, cool it with this bullshit. Don't nobody know shit about what you talking about. You lucky these fake ass niggas got me tied down, otherwise, I would be kicking your ass."

"Then get up and kick my ass then!" Trent walked over and

kicked the shit out of Redd. "Motherfucker, you think you can whip my ass? Do you know who the fuck I am?" Trent balled up his fist and hit Redd so hard he fell backward. I had never seen Trent act like this. He had always been so quiet, but the man that stood before me was assertive. He was bossin' up on Redd, and I wasn't sure Redd had what it would take to handle Trent.

"Bitch made motherfucka, it ain't shit to hit a man that's tied up."

"Let him loose," Trent demanded and the men went to work. Redd ran towards Trent, but before Redd could land a punch, Trent was hitting him. Striking him, blow after blow. Blood spewed from his open wounds. He stumbled falling back. He wasn't shit without a gun strapped to him. Without that steel courage of his, he was nothing.

"Stop it! It was me! I transferred the money, I didn't think you would find out. It was so much money in that account. How could you notice a few thousands?" Queen was speaking up to save Redd. She swung her head towards me. "This is all your wife's fault. It's because of her, she ruined our lives. She took our money and built a life with you, and we had nothing. I just wanted her to feel the same."

Trent walked towards Queen. "So you thought you could play me? All that pushing up on me and fluttering your eyelashes my way was so you could steal from me? " Trent bent down eye level with her and spoke through clenched teeth "You're going to put my money back. You took from me, now I'm gonna take from you." He nodded towards Jacob and he proceeded to work the same magic I had seen him work in that underground garage. Queen rattled off answers to Jacobs questions. Within moments it was done.

"It's done." Jacob had watched all of this without so much as blinking. This was just another day to him.

"Give me your gun." Trent stretched his hand out to one of

the men. I watched in horror as he gripped the handle of the gun. The loud echo of Trent loading the chamber filled the abandoned warehouse. My body was numb as I watched Trent take slow deliberate steps towards Redd, who was struggling to regain his composure. He stumbled to his feet and tried to hit Trent. Trent raised his hand with lightning speed and then the pop of the bullets flying through the air stopped Redd in his tracks.

"Noooooooo!" Queen screamed as Redd's lifeless body fell to the ground. Blood oozed from the open wound in the middle of his forehead. His eyes were void, staring into nothingness. There was no coming back from that. Queen wailed, her bound hands clawing on the ground, as she struggled to move towards Redd's corpse.

I wanted to say something but no words would come out. My body shook uncontrollably. What the fuck was happening? Trent nodded towards the men then made his exit from the room. He stopped mid-step, just before walking out the door and turned towards me. Our eyes locked only for a moment, then he was gone.

As if that was their cue, the henchmen approached us and slammed the butt of the gun into our skulls. I watched Queen go out like a light. My head throbbed with pain, but I knew on the inside I was a survivor and I was going to make it out of this alive. If I could hold on to my consciousness then maybe I could make it out of this room alive. With everything in me, I fought against the dizzy feeling.

"Why?" I looked up at the man. I struggled to form my sentences, "Please just let us go. Jacob, help me, help –," The crashing sound of the doors tumbling open stunned me. I turned towards the sound of the noise.

"FBI!" Swarms of armed officers rushed into the room, guns drawn. Everyone in the room scattered. I struggled to stand to get out of the way of the men rushing the room.

"Dominique! Dominique! You alright?" Michelle rushed towards me. Her arms wrapped around me and pulled me to my feet. Her hands were all over me touching me checking me, confusing the hell out of me. I stared at her but she seemed different from the woman I had spent the past few months around. Her hair was pulled back into a neat ponytail, she actually had on clothes and vest and badge that read FBI.

"Michelle? What the fuck?"

TWENTY-ONE

"I DON'T THINK she knows much."

"Agent Viera, she has a rap sheet longer than my nine inch cock. She's into everything from prostitution to fraud. What about this woman makes you think she's innocent of anything."

Their hushed voices floated through the cracked door. This was not apart of my plan. I was supposed to be gone not here. I sat in the sterile gray interrogation room listening to them discuss me. My hands and feet were released from the makeshift shackles that Trent had me bound in and had been replaced with the cold steel of handcuffs. A buzzing sound floated through the room and then she was standing in front of me. None of this made any sense.

"Michelle, what the fuck is going on?"

"I'm S.A. Amina Viera." I stared at her in shock. My mind raced to connect the dots. That's why she was always around. That's why she always wanted to know things. She's been playing me all along, trying to get information out of me.

She sat down in front of me and began to layout pictures in front of me. "Tell me what you know about the TCC?"

"The what?"

"Third Coast Cartel, don't play dumb, we know you know." The man spoke up.

"Let me handle this Jones," She waved him off and then moved towards me. Whenever she was around she eyed me like I was her prey and now I know why, I was. I held my head down, not wanting to make eye contact with her. She lowered her head, forcing me to look at her. Her eyes begged me to answer her. "Dominique, this is not looking good for you. Tell us what you know."

"I don't know what you're talking about Michelle, or whoever the fuck you are."

"Tell us what this means." Michelle hit a playback on a tablet device and I heard my voice. I was on a phone call, trying setup things to get the hell out of Houston but I wasn't going to tell her that.

"How did you get that?" My mind was moving at lightning speed trying to put things together. I understood but I didn't understand. How did I end up in a damn interrogation room being accused of anything?

"The locket I gave you." She looked at me almost apologetically.

"So you're telling me, you fucked me, gave me some bullshit ass speech about giving me your heart, and then put a listening device on me? And how did you know where to find me?"

"I put a tracking app on your phone. Listen Dominique, you were our way in. We already know your husband is the head of the TCC organization. We also know that the paper trail leads back to you. What was Redd and Queen's role in the organization? What was yours? Talk to us and make it easier on yourself."

Her sneaky ass was out there messing with my phone that day. I had to admit this chick was slick. When she went under-cover I guess she went deep. Michelle moved in closer to me, her eyes continually pleading to make contact. Did she really think that shit was going to work?

"I'm not telling you shit. You tell them about all the times you sucked my pussy bitch. You were undercover alright. How did any of that shit help further your case because I never had shit to tell you?" How dare this bitch tell me she bugged me and followed me and she wants me to give her information?

The agent in the corner laughed as he watched our exchange. Every instinct in me told me not to trust her. All that running into her everywhere. Every bit it was an orchestrated dance to try to get me to spill whatever it was she thought I knew. Anger swelled within me, there was no way I was going down like this. I knew nothing about the Third Coast Cartel.

"Give us a minute Jones." Jones questioned the command but quickly exited the room. Michelle got up and moved towards the camera in the room, hit a button on the remote. She pulled a chair close to me, too close as usual and reached and touched my hand-cuffed hand.

"It wasn't all just me undercover. I felt something."

"Bullshit. You were trying to use me, but I can't help you. I don't know what you're talking about."

"You know more than you're saying. Every questionable account is in your name, property, and everything."

I glanced at the pictures she laid out on the table. A lot of them were lawyers in Trent's firm. I shook my head and sat there in silence. I had no idea how I was going to get out of this. Michelle said she had felt something, could I use that. Probably not, she was obviously an undercover agent. She faked feelings for a living.

Michelle stood and walked back to her file. Her demeanor had changed, and she was all business. She flipped through the pages. I could see one of my mug shots on top. She read in silence for what seemed like forever before she began to speak again.

"I've been on this case for two years. Your husband runs a tight ship. You were my way in. Now help me and I'll help you Dominique. You're facing a lot of charges, prostitution, drug distribution, embezzlement. The list goes on and on so you better start remembering something fast. Or make no mistake I will lock your ass up faster than you spread your legs. I've been working too long on this case and somebody is going down for this shit."

Her words swirled around in my head. I could tell by her tone that she wasn't playing. She felt something but not enough to save my ass from going to jail. I couldn't go to jail, not when I had over 17 million dollars waiting for me in an account somewhere. This wasn't apart of the plan at all.

"Hellooooo, are you listening? Your husband Trent Jamison, is believed to be the leader of the largest drug distribution rings from here to Miami. No one gets close to him. No one new gets in, but somehow you did."

More and more words spilled out of her mouth but I couldn't stop thinking about how I could get out of this. Think Dominique. Damn, I prided myself on knowing how to get out of a situation but how in the hell could I make that happen being handcuffed to this table. These people thought I knew something. I didn't know shit.

"Queen Richardson is in a coma. Lawrence "Redd" Richardson, went in that building and didn't make it back out. Now, why were you there? How were all of you involved?"

She was hitting me with repeated verbal blows. Redd was dead and Queen was in a coma. I sank back into my seat and let the information sink in. I was the only witness, besides Jacob and the men and since they were the ones holding the guns I doubt they would say anything. This means my version of the story was the only version of the story.

"Get me my phone. I'll talk but I need a deal. I want immunity."

"For immunity your info gotta be good Dominique."

"Just do it." I could finally see the light at the end of the tunnel.

TWENTY-TWO

THE LIGHT PEEKED into the dim room as I eyed the blue sedan parked outside. For the past three days there was always a car parked outside. I turned to face Michelle.

"How long will I have to stay in this damn house?"

"For however long you have to be here. Now sit down."

"Bossy bitch." I took a seat and eyed her. As she leaned forward to pull something out of her bag her hair fell across her face. I could see how she had become a distraction. She was beautiful. I had watched her for months thinking she was nothing more than a stripper turned escort. And she had played her part well, she knew how to use her sexuality and had used it well to break down my defenses. But it was nothing more than acting. The woman I saw before me wasn't Michelle, even though I thought I could somehow see pieces of her.

"Here's your immunity agreement." She placed papers in front of me and grabbed the clear plastic bag that held my phone. "This better be good. I've pulled a hell of a lot of strings to get this done." She shoved her hand inside of the evidence bag and handed me my phone.

I took it from her and powered it on. While it powered on I started to read the agreement. She had come through. It granted me full immunity. I grabbed the pen she set out and signed it quickly. If she wanted a good story she was going to get a damn good story.

"You have it all wrong." She held her hand up to stop me from speaking.

"I need to record your statement." She pulled out a small camera and stand from her bag and set it up. "Continue."

"I don't know anything about Trent's involvement. You say he runs this organization or whatever but I honestly don't know what his role is, but the man that is calling the shots is Jacob, him and some other guy."

"How do you know this?"

"When I met Trent, Jacob blackmailed me and told me he would expose me if I didn't sleep with him." I lied. Well, it wasn't a complete lie. "He found out my history with Redd and basically sent for them."

"Sent for them for what?" Michelle looked like she was getting annoyed.

"I refuse to continue sleeping with him and that's when Redd and Queen showed up. Instead of outing me to Trent he used them. They found me because of him and when I went to confront him I saw this." I grabbed my phone and accessed my iCloud drive. I found the video I had managed to keep for years and hit play.

The phone screen lit up with video of Jacob in the garage torturing and then ordering the killing of a man. I watched her as she watched in confusion.

"Why are the accounts in your name?"

"They set me up. Jacob knew my alias was fake and hoped they could never be traced to me. He convinced Trent it would be best to make someone not affiliated with the firm as a manager on the account."

I grabbed my phone and showed her the documents that Trent had. I had decided to keep him out of this. I would deal with him. I flipped through my phone and showed her the documents I had photographed, including the identification with Queen's face.

"When Redd showed up demanding his money back I did the one thing I knew how to do to make money, and that's sex. I thought I could help him make his money and go on with my life, but they had other plans." I am really hoping she believed this shit.

"Who's the other man in the video?"

"I don't know. I only know Jacob. He's threatened me, you have him ordering a killing and he was there the night you arrested all of us. He's the head I know it."

"We know he's involved." Michelle paused the recording before continuing. "You will have to testify and until you do you will be in WITSEC."

"Witsec?"

"Witness Protection."

"And how long will that take."

"As long as it takes. Within a few weeks you will be moved and given a different identity. Nothing new to you though." She rolled her eyes and began to pack her things. As she did, I scrolled through my phone and found Berto's number and hit erase.

"I'll take that." Michelle reached and grabbed my phone from my hands. "It's evidence."

I knew that was coming. I recited Berto's number over and over again, he should have been done with my stuff.

"So what happens to my accounts, my house, why can't I go home?"

"Because if you do nine times out of ten you'll be killed. I don't think you realized you've been dancing with the devil all these years. We can't find Trent, and we know he's involved somehow no matter what you say. All assets will be frozen. I want you to understand. You won't be Kyra, you won't be Dominique, you can't go back."

Michelle stopped packing up her things and walked towards me. "It wasn't all fake Dominique." She leaned in and planted her lips against mine and kissed me. What kind of head game was this girl playing? "I worked hard to protect you. This will be your second chance, don't fuck it up.... Goodbye."

Michelle left and I was alone. Well, not completely alone there were those guys outside. I paced the floor back and forth. Things were just not going according to plan but I was going to get out of this. I be damn if I someone else decided what type of life I lived. I looked out the window. I was getting dark outside.

The men did hourly checks. I glanced at the clock on the wall. I had forty-five minutes before the next time. I grabbed my shoes and headed towards the back door, peaking out before leaving to make sure no officers were in the back.

I opened the door and then and dashed across the yard faster than Usain Bolt. I reached the fence and threw my shoes over into the next yard before pulling myself over. I repeated it over and over before I made it to a street. I never planned on testifying shit but I had to give them something that could keep me out of prison. There was no way I was escaping from behind bars.

I moved through the dark streets until I found a convenience store. I didn't know what area I was in but I was about to get the fuck out of here. I strolled in looking as normal as I possibly could, given the circumstances. I walked to the counter.

"You got a phone I can use?"

The clerk looked at me as if I was foreign. "Yeah." He breathed and handed me the cordless device. I quickly keyed in the number I had committed to memory. He answered on the first ring.

"I need a favor, there is another grand in it for you." This would be the most expensive ride I ever took. "Yeah, send someone to pick me up at this address. And hurry." I gave him the address and disconnected the call. I looked at the clerk.

"If someone comes looking for me I'm not here." I walked towards the restroom. I didn't know if the clerk would cover for me or not so I needed them to hurry. I ducked my head out the restroom to see there was anyone out there. A black Escalade slowly turned into the parking lot. The car window rolled down and I recognized the guy driving as one of the guys from Berto's spot.

I ran towards the car and jumped in, thankful that he had come through and not just forgot about me and stole my money. I rested my head against the headrest as we drove away. I couldn't wait to get my shit and get the hell out of Texas.

TWENTY-THREE

I STOOD on the balcony of my new beachfront condo. The Miami breeze washed across my skin. Three months later and I still couldn't believe that I had gotten away with that shit. As soon as I reached Berto's, I boarded a plan with my new identity and my millions.

"Hey Baby." That voice could always get my attention. His steamy baritone lulled me back into the present.

"It's about time you get here." I turned to face him and wrapped my arms around him. "I missed being in your arms." Trent kissed me deeply. It had been months since I felt this man. I pushed back to look at him.

"I missed you too Kyra. I just had to make sure my dad got out of the country before coming here. Are you sure there is no way he could be identified on the video you gave the Feds?"

"It's Amani now." I laughed before continuing. "His face was never visible in the video. But the bigger question is what happened? Why you go off script? We had a plan babe."

I had been dying to ask him this question. "We were only

supposed to frame them and Jacob. No one was supposed to die that night."

The night Trent walked in the house and told me I didn't know who he truly was I knew this man was down for me. Our house had been under surveillance for months and Jacob had become more and more disrespectful.

For years he had been skimming off the top, thinking he was calling the shots, so we had to dead that shit. And when Redd showed up I saw it as a perfect opportunity to be done with both of our threats. Being honest Redd had me going just a bit, a little caught up in those old feelings but nothing could ever come between Trent and I. We were one and the same. He was me and I was him.

"Yeah and there also wasn't supposed to be any Feds until I called in the tip. But desperate times babe, that nigga had been fucking my wife and stealing my money, he didn't deserve to live and Jacob bitch ass should have been laying next to him but someone needed to take the fall for that shit."

"Redd didn't know what he was walking into when he came back but none of that matters baby we good."

"Are we? What about the cop?"

"What about her? She was a wildcard, I had no idea I was even on her radar. I don't know how she made me, but it's been dealt with. I think I gave her enough on Jacob to keep her busy."

Trent kissed me again. Every time our lips touched he gave me that feeling. Somehow all the things we had been through rekindled the fire. Every time he touched me I felt butterflies. I knew this man loved me unconditionally. He had accepted my flaws and I had accepted his. He had proven that he was gonna be my rider for life.

"You talk to your connect here?"

"Yeah, we gone be back on top in no time." He wrapped his arms around me as we watched the waves crash against the beach. As soon as I got to Miami I found us our own little piece of paradise and I knew he would find his way back to me. No matter what happened we always agreed to meet in Miami. Our escape plan didn't go as we planned but we always knew we would find each other again.

"We will run these streets baby, but this time no secrets okay." My head fell back against his shoulders and I exhaled. "This time around, full disclosure."

Ready for Undisclosed 2? Get your copy today!
Undisclosed 2: A Tale Obsession and Revenge

UNDISCLOSED 2: A TALE OF OBSESSION AND REVENGE

BOOK TWO SYNOPSIS

How far is too far in the name of love?

When Khari makes the ultimate sacrifice for her mother and sister, she finds herself in the clutches of a savage. Dro, a merciless king of the streets, first sees her as a possession but soon finds the only thing he wants to possess is her heart.

Together they build an empire of desire and seduction, trading and selling men their ultimate fantasies. But what happens when those sweet dreams turn into vicious nightmares?

An unlikely enemy emerges determined to take what he wants, setting his sights on their territory. But when Dro disappears Khari is caught in the crosshairs, she is left with one choice:

Find the threat and seek revenge.

Khari was taught by the best, handle your enemies by any means necessary and they'll soon learn beside every savage is a boss b*tch.

PROLOGUE

THE ELEVATOR CHAOTICALLY JERKED, throwing the passengers against the walls as it descended to the lower level. All five of the unsuspecting passengers stood in dead silence as the elevator hurled to a jolting stop. The frenzied ride caused them to shiver with fear.

The night was beginning to take a drastic turn for all of them. Plummeting elevators more often than not evoked a fear of death. No one planned to die today, and it was their hopes that they would arrive on the lower level safely.

Then get this business over with. The elevator stopped on the bottom floor with a booming thud, they all waited anxiously for the doors to open, but nothing happened.

"What kinda raggedy ass bullshit is this?" A voice called from the back of the elevator. The nervousness was apparent in her voice. All the passengers turned to look her direction before the small space went completely dark. Five sets of eyes struggled to see even though nothing was visible but the eerie, empty darkness.

"I have my cell phone." Buttons were pressed and the phone

momentarily illuminated the area. There were five people on the elevator with a multitude of thoughts surging through their minds.

I need to get the fuck off this elevator.

I can't believe this motherfucker tried to play me.

I only brought two syringes. Is that gonna be enough?

"Somebody press the damn button so we can get some help." Five hands went towards the red button partially made visible by the small bit of screen light from the cell phone but nothing sounded. The power was completely out and the elevator didn't appear to have any type of backup battery system.

The light on the screen bounced around all their faces before the room went completely black again.

"It's dead."

"Damn."

Everyone wanted off the elevator. And for a while, the only thing audible in the small space was the rise and fall of people breathing.

Can I still pull this off?

"Everybody calm down, I know y'all ain't scared of a little dark." He nervously laughed.

I have to do this.

The cap to the first needle was twisted softly off and dropped casually to the floor. Even if anyone had been paying attention it still wouldn't have been heard. The silence was thick with their own anxieties, causing any sound to be absorbed by the boisterous silence.

Damn, I can't see. . . I can't let that stop me.

The needle plunged into the first person, feeling like a tiny mosquito bite; then the plunger ejected the clear substance.

"What the hell was that?" On to the next one, plunge stick plunge stick, until three of the five people were hit. This caused a commotion but the cover of darkness hid their attacker. Moving swiftly, the second syringe emerged, this time the top being swiftly removed and tossed.

The others were starting to pass out. It didn't take long at all but it wouldn't last. There wasn't enough injected to keep them all out for long.

The needle plunged deep into his neck, releasing enough of the substance to keep him out. He struggled against the woozy feeling but it was useless.

Now, how do I get out of this elevator?

The elevator jolted again before the doors opened. Looking around four of the five now were completely knocked out against the floor. There was no time to take in the scene. Lifeless bodies are heavy, and no one really knows how heavy until one has to drag one from the scene of a crime.

The adrenaline was the only thing that propelled this plan into action. His body was pushed into the trunk of a car.

First part complete.

Frantic steps led the way back to the elevator. Thankfully everyone was still out.

You can do this.

With one smooth motion the syringe was deployed into the last passengers neck, seeping out the very last drops of the liquid. Everyone laid slumped in the elevator completely unconscious. Nothing had gone according to plan, yet everything had gone completely as planned.

OCTOBER 2, 2000

"Keisha! Open up this fucking door!" The beating on the door echoed throughout the quiet house. I had no idea what was happening. I rolled over to get a peek at my baby sister. She was sound asleep, oblivious to the turmoil I could feel about to happen.

I squinted my eyes trying to get a better look at the clock on the nightstand. It was three in the morning. My mother knew we had school the next day. Annoyed, I pushed myself out of the bed and shuffled my way towards the sound of the commotion.

"Ma, you don't hear the door." I screamed towards her bedroom. I wasn't sure if she was here or not but since whoever was on the other side of the door was screaming her name, it was her problem to deal with.

"Khari, shut the hell up!"

"Why you yelling at me?"

My mother's tone annoyed me. I wasn't the one who had some man screaming my name outside of the house.

"What you did this time Ma?" It was always something with her. I just wished she would get her shit together. My mother turned to look at me. Her eyes glossed over with panic.

"Shut.the.hell.up!" She hissed as she walked towards me, pushing me into the back of the house. "Get your sister and lock yourselves in. Do not come out." Her nails scratched my arm as she shoved me into my bedroom.

"What's going on Khari?"

"Nothing Punkin, lay back down." I lied to my fourteen-year-old sister, there was obviously something going on, I just didn't know what. The sound of something crashing against the wall sent a chill up my spine. Who in the hell was this man and what did he want with my mother. I pulled the door open enough to see what was going on in the front room. Our house wasn't very big and from where I stood I could see through the doorway that led to the front room. Punkin came and stood beside me, hugging me. I knew she was scared and I was too.

"Who is that?" She whispered. I shrugged my shoulders. I didn't know who it was.

"Don't Dro. Please don't" My mother's screams filled the house. I could hear the uncontrollable sobs escaping her lips and I wanted to do something. I just didn't know what.

"Where is my shit, bitch?"

"I didn't, I, Please." She sobbed, pleading through sorrowful cries. My chest tightened in terror.

"Ahhhhhhh" Ma let out a blood-curdling scream as her small frame flew into the wall. He was tossing her around as if she was some damaged raggedy Anne doll. My mother's head slumped to the right as her arms and legs dangled lifelessly in the air. Her body doubled over as she gripped the site of her pain. Her face was twisted in agony as she struggled to speak.

"Let me explain. I can get you your money back Dro. What I gotta do? Please I got kids, think of my kids." My eyes darted from her to him and back to her. His tall toned frame towered over her small five foot two stature.

"Your kids? The fuck I look like, CPS hoe? Yo kids would probably be better off with out your trifling ass."

My heart pounded so hard I thought it was about to burst out of my chest. He walked over to my mother, wrapped his large hand around her neck and slowly pulled her to her feet. He was smiling as he gently brushed the strands of her curly hairs from her face. Tiny chills coursed my body as I struggled to keep myself as calm as possible. I didn't want to let what I was feeling on the inside manifest on the outside. If my sister saw me panic that would only make her upset. And this seemed like the type of situation we needed to keep calm about.

"Open your mouth." She began to shake her head no, obviously knowing that nothing good would follow.

"Keisha it wasn't a fucking request!" His hands moved so fast I didn't even see it happen. I just knew that it did. He shoved the end of a gun into her partly opened mouth. Blood dripped down her lips from his forceful entrance into her mouth. "Yo old ass ain't got shit I want. I only have one way of dealing with thieves."

I wanted to do something but I didn't know what. I know my mother had told my sister and I to stay in the back, but just maybe if I came out he would know someone was watching and wouldn't do what I thought he was going to do.

I turned to face my sister. Her terror filled eyes stared back at me. I pulled her close to me and hugged her tightly, then pulled away to get a look at her, brushing the tiny curly coils from her face, searching for the right words to say to give her comfort. I wanted nothing more than to stay in this room, but I couldn't. My mother's life was at stake and I had to do something. Anything.

"You trust me right?" She smiled weakly and nodded her head yes. " I want you to stay in here Punkin. Everything will be okay." I gave her one last hug before I dashed down the dark hall towards the living room.

"Don't!" He averted his gaze from my mom to me. I could tell he was startled by my sudden presence in the room. My mother cut her eyes towards me, unable to speak with the metal barrel lodged between her lips. A stream of tears rolled from the corners of her eyes. Her normally rosy skin was completely void of any color.

My vision blurred from the tears that gathered in the corner of my eyes. My mother wasn't the best in the world but she was what we had and all we knew. There had to be someway to save her from this. I just wanted him to stop, for this to stop. My mother's small frame shook as she let out somber sobs.

"Please don't. What if I do it? What if I work for you? Just please don't kill her! I will work off all of it. Please mister don't," The rushed words tumbled from my lips. I shook my head from side to side. The man tilted his head to the right, exposing the large roaring lion tattoo on his neck. He eyed me up and down, weighing his options, me or my mother's death.

He was a formidable sight. His bulging arms and towering height paralyzed me. Everything about his presence scared the hell out of me. Tiny beads of sweat dripped down my spine. I didn't want to go, but if that meant my sister didn't have to watch our mother get murdered in our living room, then I would do whatever.

"How old are you?"

"Eighteen."

He licked his lips before shoving my mother to the floor and putting the gun back into his pants.

"Alright." He moved towards me and grabbed my arm and led me to the front door. The cool night air washed over me as he opened the door and pushed me out. I half expected my mother to scream stop or to plead for him not to take me as I looked back at her on the floor. She watched silently as he led me out the door. The expression on her face wasn't horror that I had traded my fate for hers; it was relief.

ONE

CLOUDS OF SMOKE surrounded me as I made my rounds
through the upper level of the club. Summer nights like this kept
the place packed. There was no shortage of eager men and
women to get into our doors. Lines wrapped around the building,
patrons eager to enter. We had the sexiest, most exotic women in
all of Miami. I made my way to the bar.

"Let me get a shot of tequila." By tequila the bartender
knew I meant Patron. Tami, slid the cold clear liquid towards
me and smiled. Even our bartenders and wait staff were sexy. I
swallowed my shot and leaned against the mahogany colored bar
top. I gazed towards the woman on stage. It was her, and women
like her that kept our clients addicted to this place. My eyes
were glued to her as she clung to that pole as if her life
depended on it, and in truth it just may. Her bare legs slipped
snuggly around the pole as her body slithered around it like a
serpent to its prey.

Greedy hands reached and grasped for her body as she
moved through the crowd, taking slow deliberate steps. Piece by
piece her clothing fell to the floor. With her magnificent body she

commanded the audience. Her hips held them prisoner as she swayed to the beat of the music.

"You see something you like?"

"No Andre, making sure my club runs like it's supposed to."

"Your club? Don't let Dro hear you say that." I rolled my eyes at Andre.

"Hey bae." Andre leaned over and gave Tami a kiss before she ran off to fill her next drink order.

"What I tell you about fucking the help, Andre?"

"Well, you've made it clear that I can't have you." He leaned in towards me, too close if you ask me. He was entirely too comfortable with invading my personal space and if Dro saw it he would become unhinged. I stepped over a few steps to put some distance between us.

"Where's my husband?"

"In the office, talking to a dude about some business arrangement. This his second time here, Dro done already told him he ain't fucking with him like that. I was on my way down there now."

Andre started to walk to the elevator in the back of the club. Wanting to know what was going on, I followed closely behind. I hopped on the elevator with him and took the short ride to the lower level where the offices were. I could hear an unfamiliar voice carry through the walls.

"Have you considered my offer?" This man spoke with confidence. His sultry baritone voice dripped with evidence of an Ivy League education, but there was something undeniably street about him too.

I stopped at the doorway but didn't enter the room as Andre had. Dro's face was twisted in annoyance at this stranger's presence. I could see the vein in his neck pulsing.

"I told you when you showed up the first time I wasn't interested."

"Well, get interested." His tone was even, almost as if he was unfazed by Dro's visible anger.

"Look nigga, don't come up in my shit poppin' off. You don't want smoke with me, trust me."

"No, what I want is a deal with you. Do you realize I have one of the largest organizations in the south? Do you know what that can do for you? I'm not talking thousands; I'm talking millions. All I need is your port access. Let us bring them in with your girls." The man paused. He seemed to know a lot about Dro's organization.

"Do for me? I'm self made nigga, I don't give a fuck bout your organization. I ain't getting mixed up in your shit. What I got going is one hundred my nigga, I don't need your ass trying to take over my shit."

"Partnership, agree and I don't have to take over." This man's voice never rose. He never flinched. He sat in that chair threatening my husband as if he were casually offering him a drink

Dro paused before speaking. His head swayed to the right and I immediately knew he was contemplating putting a bullet in this dude.

"Get the fuck out, Trent."

"Think about it." The man smiled and walked towards me. He paused for a moment, his gaze sweeping across my body as he took in my features inch by inch and then left. I walked over towards Dro and placed my hand on the back of his neck. Something I had learned would calm Dro a long time ago.

"What does he want?" Andre spoke.

"That dude from Houston, he wants to bring his drug shipments in with the containers."

"Oh." Andre paused undoubtedly choosing his words carefully. "You know if you ever wanted to expand into that my cousins got Miami on lock. Remember we talked about it before."

"Yeah and I remember saying, hell fuck no. What we got is good. Ain't no need adding to it."

Andre didn't say another word. He knew by Dro's tone not to push it. Even though they were tight, everyone knew who the alpha of that bro-lationship was. Dro stood and wrapped his arms around me, his muscular embrace enveloping my tiny waist. I pushed my body as far into him as I could and exhaled. I wanted to tell him that working with this dude might not be a bad idea.

Millions for just allowing him access to our containers could change our lives completely. But just like Andre, I knew with Dro, there was a time to speak and a time to just shut the hell up.

The cold windy night air whipped the raindrops chaotically through the gloomy sky. Tears streamed down my face in the silent car ride.

"What are you crying for?"

I looked at the man and shrugged my shoulders. The answer to his question should be obvious. Uneasiness sank in as I felt his eyes constantly roam my body. My mind raced with thoughts of what he could make me do to pay off my mother's debt. I didn't even know how much money she had taken from him. Things happened so fast I didn't have any time to ask, and honestly it wouldn't have mattered.

"What's your name?" His voice sounded less intimidating than it had with my mother, but it still scared me.

"Khari." My voice was barely above a whisper.

"I'm Dro."

He wasn't telling me anything I didn't know. My mother's pleading voice played over and over in my head. She had said his name so many times it was stuck on replay in my mind. Dro didn't try to make any more small talk while we rode. He hit the button on the radio, filling the car with bass hitting so hard it coursed through my entire body.

Grateful that he had broken the ominous silence with the cadence of Lil Wayne's rhythmic voice, I leaned back into the seat and tried to calm down. My thoughts drifted back to my mother. She looked relieved that I had traded my fate for hers. I couldn't believe it and I didn't understand how after Dro had violently beat her and shoved a gun into her mouth, she could willing let me leave with him. What if he did the same thing to me? Did she even care if he did?

She obviously didn't, my mother allowed me to walk out of the door with him to save her ass.

"Get out." Dro hissed at me. I hadn't noticed that we had stopped let alone that Dro had stepped outside of the car. I unbuckled my seatbelt, opened the door and slid off the leather seat. I followed behind him, careful not to allow my bare feet to step on anything. It had all happened so fast I didn't even have time to grab shoes. I had left the only home I knew with only the clothes on my back.

I trailed closely behind Dro as we climbed the steps to the top floor. My body shivered in the night air waiting for him to open the door. I entered behind him and closed the door. I stood at the entry way taking in my surroundings. It clearly was a man's apartment. The sofa was black leather with recliners at each end. It faced a wall mounted seventy-two inch flat screen television.

"Why you just standing there? Sit your ass down."

I found the nearest seat and planted myself in it. I shook my legs up and down, struggling to shake the nervousness that had settled in the pit of my stomach. I had so many questions to ask him but I was too afraid to say anything. Dro disappeared to the back of the apartment, reemerging with a blanket.

"Here, sleep on the couch for now." He turned to leave the room. I looked out the window. The sun had begun to rise in the early morning sky and slipped through the closed blinds. For any normal girl my age, this would signal the beginning of a great day. But for me, these rays of happiness were only a trick of light; today wasn't the start of a great day, this was the beginning of my worst nightmare.

TWO

I MANEUVERED my pearl white Jaguar into the lower level parking area for the club. My heels clicked as I exited the car and walked towards the elevator to take me to the office floor. I checked my reflection in the mirrored doors as the elevator lifted me to my destination. The black lingerie I wore under my coat peeked through the top exposing my lace-covered cleavage.

I tousled my voluminous raven curls as I got off the elevator, leaving the scent of my vanilla bean body scrub and Chanel Mademoiselle perfume floating through the air. Dro had been so upset since the meeting with Trent. Talking to Dro about his proposition had been on my mind. I wanted to bring up that fact that it could possibly be a good idea but I needed to soften him up first.

The door to Dro's office was open. Andre's voice carried through the quiet hallway.

"Ummm hmmm." Both men turned towards me. My hand rested against the doorframe as my hour glass figured curved into an S. Andre stared at me before breaking his gaze. A moment longer and Dro might have knocked his ass out.

"Can you give us the room, Andre?"

"Yeah nigga, get out." Dro never bit his tongue. Andre's eyes connected with mine before leaving the room. I knew what he wanted. I also knew that shit would never happen. After he left I closed the door and locked it.

I made my way across the room, my hips swaying seductively with each step. I connected my phone to his office sound system and waited for music to fill the room. Tank's melodious voice filled the room. Dro sat at his desk leaning back in the chair; one hand laying against his leg while the other stroked his chin. His eyes burned with desire as he looked me over from head to toe. The intense emotions in his eyes betrayed his calm cool exterior. His eyes were low and full of desire as I climbed on top of his desk and stood over him.

My hands traced the curves of my body as I rolled my hips in a circle while slowly undoing the belt to my coat. My hips rocked and swayed to the beat as I allowed the melody of the music to control my actions. I dipped and rolled seductively teasing him with every move. I closed my eyes as I lifted my hands above my head while slinking my hips from side to side.

My hands slipped down, pass my lips landing on my supple breast. My nipples peaked from the folds of the delicate lace fabric. His excitement excited me. Dro shifted in his chair, his erection becoming visible. The more I moved, the more it inched down his leg. I tingled with anticipation as I unbuttoned and removed my first layer, exposing the lace corset and fishnet stockings.

Dro moved the chair closer to the desk and began kissing my legs. His hands ran up the side of my thighs before he stood and lifted me down to the floor. Our eyes connected and did a dance of desire all their own. He leaned in to kiss me, softly biting my bottom lip before pulling away. I pulled his shirt over his head exposing his bare chest. My tongue traced circles around the curved lines of the lion tattoo that started on his neck and ended across his chest.

"¿Me quieres? He loved when I spoke Spanish to him.

"I'll always love you." Dro answered back.

I slid off the desk unto my knees and unzipped his pants. He sat down in the chair and faced me. The man that stared back at me was a man in love. His eyes were ablaze with passion and yearning. Heat pulsed from our bodies as our connection heightened.

"You are mine." He whispered before the fullness of his lips connected with mine. My legs wrapped around his waist as he picked me up and sat me back on the desk. I yearned to feel him inside of me. My legs tightened around his waist, silently signaling my need for fulfillment.

His lips never left mine as his fingers slipped between the tiny holes in the fish net stockings I wore. He spread his fingers causing the fabric to rip. Dro dropped to his knees and nestled his head between my legs. I could feel his tongue gently tease my throbbing bud. He kissed my lower lips as I arched my back. I wanted more.

My hips rolled as the intensity of his tongue kisses increased. He circled my clit, licking and then sucking until pools of wetness flowed from me. He pushed my legs above my head, locking me down with one hand while using the other to softly tease my folds. He slipped his fingers inside of me, stroking my inner walls. This was both pleasure and torture. My body yearned to feel him inside of me. I was on fire with desire.

"Baby." I gasped for the words. "I need to feel you."

"You need?" Dro rose and pulled me into him. I wrapped my arms around him pulling him as close into me as possible. His tongue slipped between my lips leaving traces of my sweetness as we kissed. Tasting me on him excited me even more.

He pulled me to the edge of his desk and slowly slipped

inside of me. My body gave way, molding to him inch by inch. Perspiration dripped from our bodies as we slowly moved to our own rhythm.

Dro slipped in and out of me. Pushing deep inside of me until he reached my bottom.

"Mmmm, right there baby!" Moans escaped my lips as I rolled my hips meeting him stroke for stroke. I wrapped my arms around his neck and kissed his chest before pulling myself off the desk. Our bodies collided as Dro gripped my ass. I locked my legs around his waist and bounced. I gripped his dick with my walls, squeezing the tip every time he pushed inside of me.

"Damn" He growled.

"You like it when I'm in control don't you?"

My back curved from pleasure as I threw my head back.

"Control huh? I control this pussy baby!" He grabbed my hands from around his neck and pushed me back. My body was completely suspended in the air with only Dro to hold me up. He pushed harder, deeper, faster; showing me who was in control. My nipples hardened as his speed intensified.

"Whose is it?"

"I'm yours baby." I screamed as I released my juices all over him. In that moment, just like every moment before, I completely belonged to him.

The blaring sound of a honking horn woke me. I sat up and glanced to my left, expecting to see my sister before my reality hit me. I hoped everything I remembered from the night before was just a dream. But I didn't have that kind of luck. I slid my feet to the floor and sat up on the sofa.

I looked out the window, watching the cars come and go. The streams of light that floated into the room as I fell asleep were long gone. The sun dipped low in the sky as tears dripped down my cheeks. I looked around the dimly lit room. There was no sign of Dro. I cautiously walked through the house. I didn't know if he had left or if was maybe in another part of the apartment.

I tipped around the room to confirm that he had gone. My shoulders dropped as my body exhaled. I didn't know how to take or what too expect from Dro. He hadn't told me how I would be working off my mother's debt. He hadn't even told me what her debt was. I supposed those were all things I should have considered before I readily agreed but it was the only way I could think of to save my mother's life.

I walked back to the living room and sank back into the lush leather sectional.

"Fuuuuuuck!" The ball of anguish in the pit of my stomach found an outlet through my screams. I needed to release some tension. My stomach consistently churned since last night. I felt helpless in a hopeless situation. Was my mother even worried about me? I spotted a cordless phone in the corner and dashed towards it. I could call and let my mom and sister know I was okay. I needed to check in on Punkin, make sure she was okay.

I hit the on button and dialed the number in as fast as I could. My hand was shaking as I lifted the phone to my ear.

"What the fuck you doing?" His voice was deep and menacing. Within seconds he was on me snatching the phone from my grasp and ending the call.

"I just wanted to use the phone." My gaze fell to the floor. My heart sank as my chance of calling to check on my family left just as soon as it came. I just needed to know they were okay, and that I wasn't here for nothing.

"No calls and no leaving. Put this on and then sit your ass down." The stranger threw clothes my direction before plopping himself down into one of the recliners.

"Where's Dro?" I didn't know who this man was. Why was he here?

"Dro will be back in a minute."

I headed towards the bathroom with the clothes he had just given me, happy to be able to put something on. I slipped out of the t-shirt I had been sleeping in and stood in front of the bathroom mirror naked. I grabbed the black tights and held them up. They looked close enough to my size but at this point I didn't really care.

Just as I started to slip my feet inside I felt a breeze from the door opening. I turned, startled and instantly attempted to cover my bare breast with my arms.

"I..I..I'm almost done." I stammered. I didn't know what he wanted. I couldn't possibly know what to expect from this man that was watching me through the partially opened bathroom door as I changed my clothes.

THREE

I BIT the corner of my lip as I gazed at Dro. He swiftly pulled his shirt back over his head and grabbed his cell phone.

"You ready?" Sounded more like a statement than a question.

"Yes." I paused briefly, choosing my words carefully. "Have you thought any about the deal that guy offered you?"

I spoke cautiously not wanting to ruin the sexual high we were both riding, but this time was a better time than any to ask. He didn't like it when I started asking questions or making suggestions. Our past had taught me when it came to business, Dro was guarded.

I couldn't just start making suggestions without getting him to let his guard down. When Dro got things into his head they kinda stuck there and more often than not I would have to try to gently persuade him to make the smallest changes.

"That bullshit with the ports. Hell no I ain't thought shit about it. Why you asking?" He eyed me suspiciously.

"Just curious baby."

I leaned on the edge of the desk to slip my shoes back on. I glanced at the time on my cell phone. It was almost 10:30 pm.

We needed to make it to the port by 11:30 tonight. I decided to let this conversation go for now. It would only cause more harm than good at this point and we had more pressing business to tend to.

"I'll go get the truck and meet you downstairs."

Dro shook his head as he buttoned his pants. I unlocked the door and pulled it open. I jumped back not expecting to see anyone standing on the other side. How long had she been standing on the outside of the door?

"Tami, what are you doing down here?" Her smooth honey colored skin glistened under the lights in the hallway.

"Um, I'm sorry, I didn't want to interrupt you guys." A slow smile spread across her face as her eyes darted from me to Dro and back to me again.

"Tami!" I called her name attempting to bring her out of whatever thought bubble was preventing her from answering my question.

"Oh yeah, " she stammered, obviously remembering there was a reason for her awkward intrusion into our moment.

"Andre sent me to ask if you needed him at the port tonight?" The last few words were slightly a few octaves higher than her initial tone, placing more emphasis on port than anything else. I turned and looked at Dro. It was careless of Andre to send his newest piece of ass to ask about the ports.

"And why couldn't Andre come ask me that shit himself."

"Umm, he was busy with someone at the door." Tami took a few steps back, she seemed a little shaken by Dro's tone. Tami's face twisted with confusion. I watched her as she struggled to decide with her next step should be.

"Just walk away," I whispered and shut the door before he could say another word.

"That nigga reckless." The words slithered from his lips. I watched as his chest began to rise and fall. The smallest things could set him off and once he was off it was hard to get him back on. I walked over to him and wrapped my arms around him, cradling his head in my hands before kissing him.

"It's cool baby. Let's just leave." We walked out the door together to the garage. We had business to handle and it wasn't going to handle itself.

We rode in silence. I drove, giving Dro time to calm down before we got to the port. I maneuvered the obsidian colored Escalade onto a side street near the container yard.

"Do you want me to drive it in since Andre's not here?"

"I got it." I could tell by the expression on his face he was annoyed at Andre's absence. I slipped the SUV in front of the parked Peterbilt. Dro jumped out and headed towards the truck and climbed in.

Once he was safe inside I sat back against the plush leather seat and watched him pull off. This was the part that Andre normally handled but Dro always wanted to make sure that things ran smoothly. Tonight was one of those nights things were not running smoothly at all.

Nervous energy enveloped me as I waited for him to drive out of the yard. For this to go right everything would have to be timed perfectly, from the shift change to our inside guy being paid and the container waiting for us, everything was dependent on a certain schedule so no one got caught. As a team we moved fast and left no evidence. Everyone had their part to play.

The hum of the large truck signaled its arrival before I could see it. The lights shined brightly as he turned down the dark street with the container on back. He had made it in and out with no incident. Dro parked the truck behind the Escalade and turned off the engine.

I raised the rear seat to allow more room as Dro opened the container. The metal latched creaked as he lifted and pulled the doors open. The lump in my throat wouldn't allow me to swallow while I impatiently waited for the doors to open.

Once they were finally opened, I could see inside. Dro reached for each woman and hurriedly helped them off the truck. The first one off handed me a package and climbed in without speaking a word. Then each one followed until they were all inside the car.

Dro slammed the door shut and hopped in the driver's seat. He grabbed his phone and tapped the screen before putting it to his ear.

"It's done, now get your ass over here, clean up and get the truck out of here."

He disconnected the phone and we pulled off into the night. The real work was about to start.

Adrenaline surged through my body as I watched his reflection in the mirror. Why would Dro leave me with this man? Is this how he planned for me to pay my debt back to him, being a toy for his boys?

"You can let me see it. Dro said you here to work. You Keisha daughter right?"

"Yes." An anxious ball of nervousness built up inside of me. I could feel the fine little goose pimples taking shape on my skin as he slowly moved into the small space.

"Can you suck a dick like your mama?" He rubbed his hands together and licked his lips. The man stepped towards me and started to unzip his pants. I was frozen in pure fear as he slowly closed the space between us.

"Stop. I don't do that." I stepped back but the more I moved away from him the more he moved towards me.

His hands groped and prodded my body, as I desperately tried to squirm out of his grasp. I twisted from left to right, slithering from his clutches, only to be captured moments later. No matter what I did, I couldn't get away from him.

"I bet that pussy tight."

My heart skipped a beat. I was young, not naïve and I knew what he wanted. I slipped to the side of him and ran out of the bathroom. I needed to get away from him. He dashed after me, grabbing me around my waist and tackling me to the floor. A jolt of pain ran up my spine as he landed on top of me. He clawed his way between my legs and forced them open. My frame was small and I knew I was no match for him but I couldn't just let this happened.

I begin to kick and push as hard as I could, but he didn't budge. I could feel his cold calloused fingers trying to probe their way inside of me. I shoved my legs together, closing them as tight as I possibly could. Anything to keep him from having his way with my body.

"Drooooo! Help! Stop! Please stop!" My screams were like silent whispers falling on deaf ears. Dro wasn't back yet. My vision blurred as tears puddled in the corners of my eyes. This could not be happening. I shut my eyes tight praying that he stopped, but knowing that he wouldn't.

"What the fuck is going on?" The front door slammed against the wall as Dro entered the apartment. My eyes darted to the sound of the noise. The man broke his firm grasp on my thighs and started to pull himself off of me. As soon as I could free myself I jumped up and hid behind Dro.

"Man what the hell are you doing, I said watch her not rape her." Dro's voice boomed. I could tell by the look on his face he was not happy about what he saw.

"Ain't nobody raping this hoe."

"That ain't what it looked like to me. Looks like you were trying to take what wasn't yours nigga!"

"What it looks like was you interrupting me about to get some pussy."

Whaaaaap!

The sound of Dro's fist connecting with the man's face echoed throughout the apartment.

"Who the fuck you think you talking to?" Dro spoke, his head tilted to the side. His face was twisted in fury. His chested heaved with rage. Dro's eyes dared the man to make a move.

"Dro man you tripping, I ain't doing shit that I ain't never done before." He winced in pain as he grabbed his chin.

"This ain't before, nigga if I tell you to watch that's all you fucking do. If you touching and ain't paying that's stealing. And you know I don't fuck with thieves, I fuck them up."

They stood in silence for what seemed like forever. Finally, the other man interrupted the still.

" I ain't got time for this shit. I'm out." He left without uttering another word to Dro, slamming the door behind him.

Dro reached down and grabbed the clothes I had lost in the struggle.

"Put these on."

"Thank you for stopping him." I tried to make eye contact with Dro. He had saved me from that man. I wanted him to know I appreciated him not letting that man have his way with my body because he could.

"Don't thank me, you can't pay your mother's debt giving away free pussy." Dro's face curled in disgust and then he left the room.

FOUR

I PULLED the blanket over my head hoping to keep the day ahead of me away. Dro stirred in the room, getting ready as I laid motionless on the bed. Maybe if I didn't move or make a sound I would just disappear and my responsibilities would too.

"Baby."

"Yes."

"Get up." He whispered into my ear and then slowly pulled the cover from my face. We had a long night and I was in no way looking forward to any of the things I had to do today.

Dro tugged at my arms, pulling me to my feet. His arms instinctively wrapped around my waist and pulled me close. I nestled my head against his shoulders and exhaled. You would think after years of handling this I wouldn't be phased by it, but every time a new shipment came in, it put me into emotional turmoil and if I were being completely honest, I really didn't understand why. I headed to the bathroom to get ready for the day. After taking a shower and putting on clothes I grabbed my envelope and laptop then left.

I maneuvered the car in and out of traffic as I headed to my destination. This was always a long drive but as the term goes, we don't shit where we eat. Our location for the girls was nowhere near the club, our home or the port they came in through.

After forty-five minutes I finally reached the house. I parked the car and sat for a moment. I needed to get my head in the game.

Khari, time to boss up!

I stared at my reflection in the mirror. It was no time for weakness and I've never been weak so let's do this. I grasped the handle on the door and got out of the car. I walked swiftly towards the small three bedroom home. To anybody just passing by it looked like a normal house. Nothing out of the ordinary ever seemed to take place here, but if walls could talk there would be many secrets to tell.

I punched in the unlock code on the keypad and disarmed the alarm system. I walked in the unusually quiet house. Normally when new girls came in there would be chatter and talking but today it was none of that.

I walked into the living room and saw all the women gathered around the center of the floor. My eyes darted from left to right searching for the source of their undivided attention.

"Oh my God!" I rushed to the side of the young girl that was lying in the middle of the floor. I fell to my knees next to her.

"¿Mírame, puedes hablar?" She turned in my direction, as I requested but she didn't speak. She appeared to be struggling to speak.

"¿Alguien hablan inglés?"

"Most of us speak English señora."

"What's her name? How long has she been like this?"

"Rosita. She's been sick most of the ride over, today she just passed out on the floor. We don't know who to call for help." The dark-haired beauty explained.

I jumped up and dashed towards my phone. I scrolled

through my contacts looking for her number. The phone rang an incredibly long time before someone finally answered.

"Doc we need you a little earlier than we expected."

"It'll take me about thirty minutes before I can get there."

"Get here as soon as you can."

I disconnected the call and turned my attention back to the girl on the floor. I looked at her, she couldn't have been any older than twenty years old. I'm pretty sure she got on that shipping container thinking her entire life was ahead of her and it could be possibly ending before it ever got a chance to start. What thoughts ran through her mind now? She was helpless, struggling to breathe on the floor of in a house she didn't know, in a country she didn't understand and with dreams that may never be fulfilled.

Guilt washed over me. Last night I was more concerned with what I didn't want to do, maybe if I had done more than just let them in the house I would have noticed Rosita was sick. But I hadn't even taken a second glance. I just opened the door and said I would be back. That talk that I needed to have with my husband was long overdue.

My mind wandered to the conversation that he had with Trent. Maybe I needed to look a little more into who he was. What he was offering just may be our way out. I knew Dro didn't think we needed an out, but the more I looked at the young girl struggling to breathe on the floor the more I was convinced we could be done with this shit.

Three weeks passed since that man tried to rape me. I could learn a lot by just staying quiet and paying attention. I now knew that his name was Ace and he worked with Dro. Had worked with him for years. Dro handled the women and Ace handled the drugs. They were partners in mostly everything but Dro seemed to be the one calling the shots.

Ever since that day I had tried to talk to Dro about what I was gonna have to do but this man still scared me. Even though he had stopped Ace from having his way his last statement stuck with me. He was so callouss as he effortlessly tossed out his idea of selling my body. I didn't plan on being a prostitute. I had never even had sex and if my first time had to be under some sweaty old ass man, then no thank you. I had to think of a way to get out of this.

I eyed Dro moving back and forth. He seemed busy but I didn't know what the hell he was doing. It kinda looked like a bunch of nothing.

"Dro," he kept walking.

"Dro!" I found the courage to speak a little louder.

"What?"

"Can I talk to you? Do you think you can tell me what I'm going to be doing and how long I'm gonna have to do it? I don't even know what my mother did to you."

"She stole from me. She took my shit and you're done when I get that back plus interest."

My back stiffened. "And how much did she take?"

"Enough, anything taken from me is too much, but your mama been doing this shit for too long." He answered and then stood to go back to what he was doing.

"Wait, so what will I have to do?"

"I told you, sell that pussy!"

"I don't wanna do that, can I do something else, anything else? I ain't never done that before!"

"Even better, that means I can auction your ass off to the highest bidder."

Dro left the room before I could speak another word. I was tempted to follow behind him to try convincing him that there must be something I could do other than sell my body. I knew he owned a strip club in the hood, I was even willing to work there. I just didn't want to sell my body.

My mother was a hoe, and her mother was a hoe, it wasn't a cycle I wanted to continue. That's why I held on so long to my virginity. In my family sex didn't seem to mean anything. I had always been taught that my vagina was just a tool to get what I wanted and needed.

I looked at it a little different. When the time came to give my body to someone, I wanted it to be special. It would sound foolish to my mother, probably even sound a little crazy to my baby sister and definitely my grandmother, but to me it was right.

I fell back into the sofa and let the tears I had been holding back stream down my cheeks. Dro walked back into the room fully dressed. I hurriedly wiped the tears from my face, not wanting to show him my weakness.

"I'll be back."

"Ok."

Twenty minutes passed before I moved from my spot. I was scared Dro would walk back through the door. Once I was sure he was gone I grabbed the phone and tried to call my mother.

"The number you have dialed has been disconnected or is no longer in service. If you feel you have reached this recording in error, please check the number and try again."

Disconnected? What the hell was going on? Why would the number be changed or disconnected? I bit my nails as I tried to figure out my next move. Maybe if I could get home to my mother we could all run.

Before I could reconsider I was out the door. The evening air was warm as it washed over me. I walked for blocks before I started to recognize the area I was in. My feet ached with pain from walking for miles in the cheap dollar store flip flops I wore.

By car, the drive from my home hadn't been far but by foot this hike was brutal. I wanted to stop but I kept moving. I needed to get as far away from Dro's apartment as possible.

FIVE

I RACED down the highway trying to make it back to the club. My heart did sprints as I steered the car through traffic. I couldn't seem to get the thoughts of Rosita out of my head, laying on that floor, gasping for air. When this all started I told myself it was harmless. I convinced myself that these girls were ready and willing participants. They knew what they were getting into and that had been enough to ease my conscious.

But after years of this, I knew better than that. I knew that some of the girls came willingly, and others did not. The older ones usually came willingly. They were the ones that got in those containers in search of a better life and a sugar daddy. They were the ones willing to trade their freedom and bodies for a little while if it meant they got to live a halfway decent and comfortable life.

But I also knew that girls like Rosita, they young ones most likely didn't come willingly. They were probably more like me. They were the ones that were the only way out for their families. They got in that container because it's what their mother or father told them they had to do. They were the ones willing to sacrifice themselves for the sake of their families, not realizing that if family gave a shit about them they wouldn't have to do this in the first place.

My car slid into the parking lot in the front of the club. I rarely parked up front but today I didn't have time to circle the block and enter through the garage entrance. I jumped out of the car and headed towards the front door.

I was moving so fast I didn't have time to stop our collision. I crashed right into that guy, Trent. His hard body pressed into mine before I stepped back to pull myself together.

"Excuse me." He said.

"No problem I didn't see you." And that was the truth I had been so consumed with getting inside to talk to Dro, I hadn't noticed the doors opening or him exiting.

"Why are you here?" I couldn't understand why he would be here. Every time he showed up Dro shut him down. I think I secretly hoped Dro had a change of heart but I knew better than that.

"I was hoping to talk to your husband, but it seems as if he's avoiding me."

"When Dro says no, he means it." I thought I would give Trent a little heads up. It would take a lot more than him just showing up to try to convince him. Dro wasn't like that, he said what he meant and meant what he said.

"And when I say I want something I mean it."

I blinked twice not bothering to speak. Something about the way his dark brown eyes shined with determination let me know I didn't have to say anything.

"This is my last time being nice about this. Make sure he understands the next time I show up, it will be to take it. We can do this the easy way, or we can have war."

Trent smiled showing a row of perfectly white straight teeth.

Did this dude seriously just try to low key threaten my husband through me?

"There's my car." Trent strolled away ending our conversation. He never even bothered to look back my direction.

I rubbed my forehead before pushing my hair from my face. I really didn't have time to think about this bullshit. I needed to get inside and talk to Dro. I wouldn't be passing on his message either. If Dro knew I would never be able to persuade him to work with Trent. He didn't take threats lightly, and for him to say it to me was even worse. I continued inside and made my way to Dro's office.

"We seriously need to talk!" I burst through the door and hurriedly got to business.

"About?"

Dro's chair swiveled in my direction. He leaned back and smiled. This was one of those moments I wanted to smack that dumb ass look off his face.

"Dro, it happened again." I threw my bag in the small chair before I sat on the edge of the desk. I crossed and uncrossed my legs trying to unsee what I had seen.

The entire ride back to the club I thought of the best way to approach the subject with Dro. I had pretty much tiptoed around it instead of telling him how I really felt, but now there was no way I could just sit idly by waiting for this to happen over and over again.

"What happened again?" Dro scrolled through his phone not even bothering to look my direction.

"Another girl died. We can't keep playing Russian roulette with these women's lives."

"What happened?" Dro finally put his phone down and looked at me.

"Apparently something was already wrong, Dr. Monroe thinks the girl had some type of embolism, I don't know the specifics Dro damn, does that shit matter. This is the seventh girl that hasn't made the trip."

"Khari," his tone was low as he called my name. Whenever he called my name like this that meant tread lightly. I adjusted my tone and continued.

"Baby, what I'm saying is we can't keep doing this, maybe you need to think about doing business with that guy."

"I would say losing only seven ain't bad for the number of girls we have brought into this country. And as far as working with anybody, you know I ain't doing that shit Khari. Been there done that, and I ain't going back to the bullshit involved with it. This we got going on we got this shit down to a science, we are in charge, and we control it all. If I add someone else you already know that shit can get out of hand. No."

"But Dro..." He held his hands up as he stood. I immediately stopped talking, instantly feeling defeated.

"We pay the doc enough money to make these things go away, so it's done and dealt with. And we move forward.

Almost two hours passed after I left Dro's apartment. I walked down the street I grew up on. It was dark but my surroundings were familiar. I just needed to get to my house and talk to my mother.

On the long walk over, I worked out a plan. I didn't have any money, but hopefully Ma had enough for gas. We could leave, all of us and go somewhere else. Anywhere else.

I finally made it to my house. There was a black car parked outside that I'd never seen before. I cautiously walked towards the car to peer inside.

"Punkin!" I snatched the door open, thankful it was unlocked and pulled my baby sister out of the car. The old pervert in the front looked at me as if I was crazy.

"Get your nasty perverted ass out of here, you fucking pedophile!" I shouted at him. His face turned beet red and then sped off.

I held my sister by her shoulder wanting to shake some damn sense into her. What the hell happened in the last month since I had been gone? My sister could be sweet and innocent, but the girl I saw before me was far from it. Her face was painted with so much makeup I hardly recognized the girl underneath. Without me here to stop her from buying into my mother's warped sense of reality, she was transforming into a miniature version of the woman who raised us.

She snatched away from me and crossed her arms. "What you want!"

"I want to know what the hell is going on? Were you in that car doing what I think you were about to do? You are fourteen years old! You have no business..."

"No business what? I wasn't doing anything anyway. I'm almost fifteen and why in the hell would you care? You left!"

"I left because I had no choice!"

"You lying trifling bitch!" My sister swung at me, her fist landing on the left side of my face. What was really going on? I had always tried to protect my sister from all the things that would undoubtedly invade her world. We had always been sisters and best friends. I could not wrap my mind around what was happening.

"Stop it." She was still trying to hit me. I grabbed her hands and held them behind her. She was gonna have to calm down so we could talk. I had no idea why I had become all those things. Why she was so angry? And why in the world did she want to put her hands on me?

"Mama told me you left with that man because you didn't want to be here anymore. She told me that he came here for you that night. He beat her so bad she can't even go to work."

"Those were all lies Punkin." Work? How did she call what she was doing work?

"Naw, I saw you leave with him. You were going to have mama killed."

What the hell was this girl talking about? I know she didn't see everything that happened but she had to know that I would never put either one of them in danger. That was all my mother. Her version of the truth was laced with lies and misdirected perspective. None of this was what really happened. She was right there with me. How could she remember anything differently than what I had?

I grabbed my sister and dragged her into the house. Her legs kicked and punched as she fought against it every step of the way. I managed to pull her through the door, even though her flailing limbs were hard to control.

"Ma! Ma!" My mother was sitting in the living room like nothing was happening.

"What are you doing here Khari?"

"I came back so we can get the hell out of here. Let's just leave so that we don't have to worry about him trying to kill nobody." I worked my words out a million times over in my head on the walk over. In my mind, I imagined my mother leaping at the opportunity to have her family back together.

No matter what we had to do to achieve it, we could have all been together. We didn't know anything other than being together and even after everything that has transpired, being with my mother and sister was what I was used to.

"The day you left out the door you died to me Khari. You belong to Dro now." The weight of my mother's words landed on me like a ton of bricks. She spat verbal venom at me as if I was the one that had put us in this situation, acting like I'm the one that stole from a deranged man.

"No Ma, I left out the door so you wouldn't have to die. So what are you talking about?" I rolled my eyes at her, trying to make sense of the dumb shit she was saying. " Do you know what Punkin was about to do outside?"

"She was about to get some money but you fucked that up. Now you owe me fifty for the money you just lost us."

"Mama she's fourteen!" I couldn't say that enough. Was I the only one who thought a fourteen-year-old shouldn't be on the street turning tricks?

"I know how old she is I gave birth to her. It was just a blowjob. It's the first time she ever even tried to make some money on her own. I ain't got her having sex. Since I can't work no more right now somebody gotta bring in the money." My mother got up and limped towards the kitchen. It was then I noticed the cast on her leg and arm.

Her once beautiful features looked haggard and damaged. My mother was one of those rare beauties, the kind of woman that had the ability to stop men in her tracks with her amber green eyes and sultry smile. As a child, I beamed with pride whenever anyone told me I looked like her, but the woman here now was only a broken shell of her former self. Dro's beating had really taken its toll on her.

"Punkin you know I would never just leave you guys, and you know I did this so mama wouldn't die right. You don't have to sell yourself. I don't care what she tells you, you ain't gotta do that." My eyes filled with tears.

"All I know is that you left, and mama is hurt so somebody gotta step up. And when I finally hook up with the dude across the street I can make even more money for us. I'm gonna do what you couldn't Khari. So don't fuckin worry about me or mama. We gone be good."

I had no words. I sat down on the sofa and waited for my mom to come back out of the kitchen. This was crazy. We needed to get in that car and get the hell out of New Orleans. Ideas tumbled back and forth in my head. I had to find a way to convince her that this was the best and only option we had. Leaving could somehow protect us all. Just get in the car and drive somewhere this street thug had no reach. North, east or west didn't matter to me, we just had to go. My head snapped towards the noisy door flew open pulling me from the thoughts.

"I told you no leaving." Dro rushed in and grabbed me by my shirt. He yanked me to my feet bringing me face to face with his anger.

"I didn't tell her to come here Dro, and I called you as soon as she got here." My mother called him. Again she willingly planned to hand me over to him. My safety and what I had to go through didn't seem to matter at all. What I would endure, was nothing as long as she got to keep breathing. She didn't care what happened to me. My mother hadn't even given my idea a chance. At that moment my heart broke. I just wanted my family, no matter how fucked up it may have been it was mine. I turned my head towards my sister. She didn't say anything, just turned and left the room.

Dro pushed me out of the door. This time I didn't bother to look back. There was nothing left for me here.

SIX

EVEN THOUGH I couldn't shake off the guilt of losing another girl, I did what needed to be done. No part of our well-oiled machine could function properly if everything wasn't in place. I pulled out the envelope the woman handed me when they first came in and began to go through the contents while Dr. Monroe checked all the ladies.

The doctor had been with us a while. We didn't run just any type of operation, we catered to the rich, the elite businessmen of Miami and beyond. We wanted to make sure they got what they paid for. For those men, buying these women were fulfilling a fantasy. They wanted to have the perfect women and that meant checking her from the inside out.

"How much longer?" Dro walked up behind me, peering over my shoulder why I looked through the package to make sure everything else was in order. I had a list of all the women that were in that container. This list let me know everything about them from their names, ages, remaining debt and I also had their identification.

"Doc's almost done. We just have to make sure that everything is together for the party, we want top dollar don't we?"

"Yep, that's right, make me my money! I'm about to go get security straight and then we can leave." Dro laughed, playfully slapping my ass before walking away. My body tingled a little each and every time he touched me. I turned my attention back to my original task.

"Can we talk?" I rolled my eyes before turning to face the doctor. I knew by the tone of her voice she was about to ask for something.

"Sure we can, just let me get Dro."

"No, I can talk to you." I suspected she believed I was the easier of the two to deal with.

I waved my hand, signaling for the doctor to follow me into the other room. I would prefer not to talk business where anyone could overhear.

"So what can I help you with?"

"I need more money."

She didn't waste any time getting to the point.

"I believe we pay you well, Dr. Monroe." She was nervous. She glided her fingers back and forth over the gold necklace she wore. Moving it left to right as if she was considering carefully what her next words would be.

"Yeah you do, but not well enough to have to deal with the bullshit that comes along with the job." She paused I'm assuming for effect. "I was only supposed to make sure they were healthy when they got here, short and sweet, be in and out."

"Well, I th..." She cut me off.

"But now you have me getting rid of bodies. Do you think any of this is easy. My connections can only go so far. Every time I have to call in a favor that means I have to make it worth their while. Which means more money, which means it cuts into my bottom line. It ain't worth the risk for what I'm getting"

I never considered what and how the doc did the disposal and honestly I didn't care. As long as it was done who the hell cared. I briefly considered what she had said. I decided to see how much she was talking about. If the amount was reasonable then maybe I could handle it. Dro wasn't going to like her asking for more. He always considered himself fair when it came to paying the people working for him. When they start asking for more he thought they were just being greedy.

"So how much are you asking for?"

"I want an extra fifty k for every time I have to put myself on the line like that. If you can't do it then get rid of your dead bodies yourself. And consider this when you guys are evaluating my request, I know where the bodies are buried."

Dr. Monroe left out of the room, not giving me a chance to speak. Did that bitch just try to threaten us? I watched her walking away. She didn't have to throw in any threats, I was willing to hear her out. Her disloyalty left a bad taste in my mouth and I also knew Dro wasn't going to like any of her demands. If I told him this, her dead body may be the one she needs to worry about.

Riding back with Dro I expected him to yell at me for leaving, maybe even hit me, but none of that happened. It was extremely quiet in the car. Every few seconds his eyes darted to me and then back to the road.

Maybe he was waiting for me to say something but I didn't have anything to say. What could I possibly say? Nothing meant more to me than my family and it seemed to me that all of that was gone within a matter of seconds.

"I would have killed her if she wouldn't have called me."

I was fighting to hold back the tears as I eyed Dro, angry that he was trying to take up for my mother.

"You could have only killed her if you could find her." I crossed my arms and stared out the window, closing myself off to any more conversation with him.

"And you don't think I would have?"

"I would have made sure of it. By the time you came looking for us we would have been long gone." My tone was defiant. If my mother had given my plan a chance we could have been far enough away that he would have never seen any of us again.

Dro didn't say anything else. A slow smile spread across his lips as if he had a secret that only he knew. I looked out the passenger window into the night sky. I was silently toying with the idea of just walking away from it all. I could wait for my next opportunity and just leave but as much as I wanted to hate my mother, I knew if I left she would pay with her life. Even though she had torn my heart into a million pieces, I still didn't want her to die.

I squinted my eyes trying to shield them from the blinding light that bounced off the side mirror. I watched as the car darted in and out of traffic. The car followed close behind. I wasn't sure if it was a coincidence, so I glued my eyes to the mirror, observing both Dro's and the other car's actions. Dro changed lanes, seconds later they change. Second lane change, they changed again. Every move Dro made, the car made. I counted at least four times this car made a move to stay close but just far enough behind.

"Dro."

"What's up?"

"There's somebody behind us."

He maneuvered the car from lane to lane, checking the mirror to see if the car followed his motions.

"Damn," Dro looked at me as if he couldn't believe I had caught something he didn't.

"I catch a lot of things." I briefly wondered why someone was following him. But I didn't care enough to ponder it more than a second. I had my own issues I had to figure out.

The car sped up behind us before pulling around and speeding off. Dro glanced at the rearview mirror, before seeming to dismiss the entire ordeal.

"We need to make a stop. And since I can't trust your ass back at the apartment you're coming with me."

I shifted in the seat and continued to look out the window. I didn't ask where we had to go or what he had to do. It didn't matter to me. I was starting to understand I was his prisoner and there was probably nothing I could do about it.

The car rolled to a stop as we pulled up to a small building. I read the lit sign above it. **Club Addict**

I scanned my surroundings attempting to take in every bit of it, committing it to memory. The small two-level building set right off the highway, allowing easy access and the parking lot was moderately full.

"Come on."

I got out the car and shut the door. I have never been in a place like this, but this last month had been filled with I have never moments. Walking through the door I expected to see women and dancing and poles but there was none of that.

"Man, Ace been here, I don't know what the fuck going on with y'all, but he took all the girls and he hit your office up too."

"What?" Dro replied as he moved towards the back. I moved as fast as I could struggling to keep up with him. Once we made it to the office he stopped dead in his tracks. He rushed to his desk and pulled out a lock box. The lock was broken off and it was completely empty.

"Yeah, that's what I'm saying, this nigga came in here wildin', screaming he made you! How you ain't shit without him. Man, we got a house full of people and we ain't got shit."

I watched the exchange between Dro and this man. It was tense. Dro's face was twisted in anger as the man frantically talked. Ace was the dude that tried to rape me and Dro had stopped him. Had all of this been because he stood up for me?

My I don't give a fuck attitude dissipated at the realization of this moment Dro stood up for me. No one ever did that before. Not even my mother. She always chose herself over me. I quietly slipped away from them as they talked and began to walk through the club. I stepped through the door to the right and found what appeared to be the women's dressing room. I walked towards the mirror and let down my hair. I wasn't sure what all of sudden made me want to help him. Maybe it was because deep inside I knew helping him would be helping me.

SEVEN

THE WARM WATER from the shower beat softly against my skin. There was so much on my mind since the last girls came in. Talking to Dro about working with Trent had been useless and as far as the rest of the girls I still had a job to do.

I pushed the thoughts as far out of my mind as I could. Until I can figure out how to change it I guess I shouldn't dwell on it. The shower filled with steam as the preset temperature increased. I placed my hand behind my neck and rubbed to release some of the tension.

"What's wrong baby?"

I turned and wrapped my arms around him. I was upset with Dro for not understanding where I was coming from, but at the same time, this man had been my refuge for so long. I knew what type of man he was. He was the type of man to commit and see things through. He was the *if it ain't broke don't fix it* type and to him, nothing was broken.

He cupped my face in his hands and locked eyes with me. Slowly he pulled me towards him and kissed me.

"It's gonna be alright baby. Think about it this way this is how we make our money, and this is how so many other families eat. Because of us. We take all the risk, but it's worth the reward baby."

I wanted to believe the things he said. Wanted to look at myself as some type of hero but who was I kidding. This was human trafficking. This was enslavement, whether voluntary or not it was wrong. I thought about how I volunteered myself for my family. In a way, I felt like that was both a blessing and a curse. Honestly, Dro was the best thing to come out of that bad situation. And even though our relationship wasn't always perfect I knew one thing he always had me and I was always gonna have him.

I pushed up towards his lips and kissed him. His fingers ran through my wet coils as he pulled my head back and kissed me on my ear and then down my neck. The further he moved down my body the more intense his kisses became. My body quivered with anticipation as his tongue roamed my body.

"We have to go," I whispered into his ear even though I didn't want this to end. My lips lingered on his ear for a few moments longer then I stepped out of the shower. I grabbed my towel off of the rack and walked towards our bedroom.

"Where do you think you're going?"

Dro walked up behind me and wrapped his hands around my waist, kissing my neck as he turned me to face him. Dro cupped my face and gently pulled me towards him, pressing his lips firmly against mine. He tossed me against the bed and was on top of me in one quick motion. His aggressive nature always caught me off guard but it always turned me on.

Dro's sepia colored skin pressed against mine, still wet from the shower. I hungrily searched for his lips, desperate to feel his tongue dance against mine. Our lips connected causing a surge of electricity to course through me. He knew how to touch me, kiss me, taste me, and completely please me in just the right way. He kept me yearning for more.

My legs gripped Dro's waist as he guided himself inside of me. Feeling him slide inside sent chills through my body. He slowly pushed deep inside of me while looking me in my eyes. Any time we connected it was as if our souls touched.

"Mmmmm" I exhaled a sigh of desire. Our bodies rocked back in forth connecting deeper and deeper each time he stroked. Dro flipped me over and I was on top now. I rocked my hips back and forth and then up and down, throwing my head back in pleasure. He was allowing me to control the speed. His hands grasped my hips and then slinked their way up, landing on against my breast. He squeezed softly, igniting my desire even more.

I leaned down and kissed his lips. I knew we needed to go. Tonight was a big night, but every moment with Dro was worth it. Things would just have to wait.

I grabbed a tube of mascara and went to work on my appearance. I wanted to do something to help the situation. Dro had stopped that man from putting his grimy hands all over me and I felt like this little problem he was having was because Dro whipped his ass that night.

I scanned the room for something a little sexier than the black tights I wore. I pulled my pants off. My black lace panties would work fine, I just needed a top. I tossed around the abandoned contents of the room and found a black strappy, lace bralette. I put it on and turned to face the mirror. I wasn't the sexiest stripper that you have ever seen but it wasn't bad. I grabbed a pair of shoes out of the corner. The heel had to be at least six inches high and the entire shoe was pretty much straps that laced up my legs. They were a little too small but I forced them on to complete my look.

I walked out of the room to peep the scene of the room. Some of the men had already left, others were yelling about the cover to get in but ain't shit happened yet. I told myself over and over again I could do this. I wanted to help him but I also wanted to find a way out of him making me sell myself. I had other strengths but I just needed him to see that.

I spent several years dancing in school, granted being on this pole might be a little different but I could figure it out. I walked out and stopped by the DJ.

"Can you play something for me to dance to?" I asked barely above a whisper.

"Who are you?" His eyebrows and nose scrunched into a ball of confusion.

"I'm just helping." He shrugged his shoulders.

"What you want me to play?" I had no idea what I could

dance to. If I were being honest at this very moment I didn't care what he played.

My eyes swept over the crowd. This was a rowdy group and although I wanted something slow and sexy something told me that wouldn't be a hit with these men. "Play Wobble Wobble, 504 Boyz."

"Alright," He said before speaking into his mic. "Y'all mother-fuckas settle down, we got something special definitely worth the wait. Get ready to throw that money!"

The beat dropped and all eyes were on me. Butterflies tumbled around my stomach as I walked onto the stage. I was nervous as hell but I was determined to do this. I began to move my hips from left to right. I knew this crowd was going to need to see more than me tossing my ass from side to side. I gripped the cold metal pole and worked my way around it. I didn't know any pole tricks but I definitely knew how to move my ass.

I started off slow slipping around the pole. I held onto the pole and dropped low. I decided at that moment to get over that scared shit. I began to follow the lyrics of the song, wobble, shake it and dropping.

I bounced my ass up and down, isolating my muscles. Left, right left right, drop into a split, then twerk some more, dip low shake it, on all fours bounce it. Any move that I could think of I did. The more I moved the more money they threw. Men gathered around me, throwing dollars against my body. I felt both exhila-rated and demeaned at the same time.

I tossed my hair from left to right, looking back at the men throwing their money at me. In the corner I noticed Dro standing, watching. I locked eyes with him, glad that I had caught his atten-tion. He stroked his chin, never breaking our connection. A sly smile spread across his face, and then he was gone.

EIGHT

I WALKED around the club making sure everything was in order. The room was dimly lit with only candlelight to see your way. Even though this set a sexy mood, it was all about anonymity. The train of my full-length gown trailed behind me as I walked through the doors to enter the main level of the club. This party was for the elite, and by invitation only.

I glanced at my phone to check the time. Guest would arrive soon. I checked the bar areas. There would only be select servers working for us tonight, and they would be rewarded nicely for both their service and secrecy.

"Ladies can you step over here for a moment." All the women rushed towards me. Once everyone stood in front I proceeded.

"Here, put these on. You are to wear them at all times. Only speak when spoken to. Your jobs tonight will be to serve only. You do not see anyone, you do not hear anything and you speak nothing of this night after today."

The girls knew the rules but I always went over it with them before any event. They all put on their masks and walked away. I moved on to the front of the building.

"You got the list?" He nodded. "Make sure everyone is wearing a mask before they come in."

"Sí," Sergio responded. He had been the head of security for years. He would guard this door with his life. Only those with invitations would get through these doors.

Dro walked up and kissed me on my cheek. I was good at hiding what I really felt inside and getting to the job at hand. This was one of those moments. I knew what had to be done, and I knew it was necessary so everything else was irrelevant.

"Ready baby?" He asked.

"Yeah, people should start to come in soon."

I scanned the room and saw Andre walking towards us, with Tami on his arm. What the hell was he thinking? I could feel the frown lines forming on my face. He knew this shit was out of line.

"What she doing here?" Dro spoke first. I grabbed his hand and squeezed gently. I didn't want him to go off with guest slowly entering the lounge.

"I thought she could work tonight."

"Then you thought motherfuckin' wrong nigga!"

Dro was always abrasive, always said exactly what he meant and never gave a crap about how you received it.

"Andre let me talk to you." I pulled him away from her and walked out of hearing distance. I thought it would be better if I talked to him. I didn't want my husband to lose his temper on such an important night. Dro stood there watching, as he always did, ready to step in and take care of it his way if need be.

I turned to face Andre. "You understand she can't work tonight, right?"

"I don't see why not, you and Dro always work together, she my girl now."

"But weeee don't know your girl. She's only been here a minute, not long enough to trust her with this and you know that." This wasn't the first time Andre tried to push Tami on us, but this was definitely a time we could not allow this shit.

"This is some bullshit Khari, you know we all supposed to be making the decisions but all you and that nigga seem to do is tell me what the fuck to do." His chest heaved up and down as he spoke. The conversation was becoming more heated than I intended.

"We don't know her Andre!"

"I know her!"

Dro rejoined the conversation. "You don't know shit about shit, Andre. Especially that bitch over there. She leaves now! Before all of our guests arrive. You know what the fuck is up!" I watched defeat spread across his face. Andre didn't say another word just walked back towards her and escorted her away.

Good. Mad or not we didn't have time to deal with shit. I stroked Dro's chin to calm him down. I continued to do my scan of the room. There were seven upper level VIP sections, all facing the stage. Each section was completely closed off from the other. With an exceptional view out but no view in. Anonymity.

The room lights went even dimmer and a single spotlight shined towards the stage. It was almost time. I slid my masquerade mask over my face as I had done many times before. Guests were entering and being led to their private areas. My nerves were on a rollercoaster ride.

Actually, every night that I've had to do this I've been somewhere between panic and paranoia. Dro walked to the back taking his position. He felt it was his job to watch over his wife and his club. His eyes stayed glued to everything the entire time and if anything was out of line security would step in immediately.

The tip tap of my heels against the stage echoed through the quiet club. The music lowered to a silent hum. You could almost hear a pin drop.

The sequined gown I wore plunged deeply in the front exposing my perfect cleavage while hugging my curves. My hourglass figure demanded their attention. And I needed everyone's attention. I closed my eyes and exhaled, then proceeded in my sexiest voice. My tone dripped with the promise of sex and seduction.

"Welcome, to Club Fuego. Where the atmosphere is hot and our women are fire!" I slinked sexily across the stage before continuing, "We have nine exotic beauties for you tonight. Please place your cell phones in the box to the right. They will be checked until bidding is complete. Please use the tablet inside of your room to sign into your bidding account."

I paused giving all the guests time to complete the requested tasks. We didn't want anyone to have access to their phones for any reason. Each room contained a lockbox, requiring a four digit access code that only the server could provide at the end of the night.

All of the tablets we used for bidding would forbid access to any outside links or sites. You had to have an account to participate. Once signed in, bids would silently show on the screen. The winning bid was then processed and transferred from the account immediately. Every piece of everything we did had to flow together perfectly.

All guest were given this information. Most understood it was to protect us all. I glanced at Dro. He nodded giving me the signal that everyone was signed in.

"Winning bids are processed immediately, there are no refunds or exchanges. All sales are final."

I motioned for the first woman to walk towards the stage. Her long legs played peekaboo with the gown as she walked towards me.

"We have Marlia. Marlia is from Guyana. This ebony beauty is twenty-two years old, speaks four languages and is eager to please. The bidding starts at one hundred thousand." I walked away leaving her standing in the middle of the stage alone, so the guest could put all eyes on her.

Bidding continued throughout the night until seven of the nine girls were as we like to call it, *placed*. It sounded a lot better than *sold* to me.

"What was that?" Dro asked as we were leaving the club. I watched his muscles flex and stretch beneath the t-shirt he wore as he locked the doors. I had been with him all this time but never really noticed how attractive he was. His skin was the color of brown sugar and cinnamon, swirled together and slightly toasted. His six foot five height commanded attention, and his posture exuded authority.

"What was what?"

"Stop playing, you know what the hell I am talking about."

"I was trying to help." I stopped and turned towards him. The light from the moonlight reflected in his deep brown eyes, drawing me in even more. How had I not seen him, I mean truly seen him before?

"Who said I needed your help."

"You didn't have to say, just like I didn't have to say I needed yours the day Ace brought me the clothes." There was a long awkward pause between us. Dro's eyes began to roam my body again. He stroked the neatly trimmed facial hair as if he was considering something.

His hand softly caressed my hair, twirling my long strands around his fingers as he looked at me. He didn't say a word, but then again he didn't have to. His body language said it all. He moved in close to me. He had a way of looking at me that felt like he was looking through me, into me. I had felt it before but honestly thought he was simply trying to see how much he could sale me for. I had seen him be hard, callous even, but on more than one occasion he had shown me a softer side. Until now he had been a menacing terror that shook me to my core every time he came into the room, but I was beginning to see a tenderness in him and I hoped it wasn't just what I wanted to see.

"So are you trying to say you didn't appreciate what I did up there tonight?" The words slipped softly from my lips. I wasn't necessarily flirting, or was I? "I know I made you some money."

"You probably would make me more if you worked it off in other ways." Even though he said this, it didn't sound as threatening as it had in the past. I think he almost made a joke.

"But I don't think that's what a nigga really wanna do is it?" I mimicked his way of speaking, laughing as I moved closer to him. I could feel something stir below, not a feeling I was familiar with but I definitely wanted to explore it more.

Dro turned his head abruptly towards the sound of an oncoming car. My hands flew up to block the blinding light. I squinted, blinded as a car flew into the parking lot. The driver slammed on the brakes causing the car to come to a screeching halt. The window rolled down slowly. Something wasn't right.

It looked like the same car that had followed us earlier. Dro turned around just in time to see the barrels of the gun creep out of the cracked window.

"Get down!" Dro jumped on top of me, pushing me out of the way. A storm of bullets rained down. I hid behind a column as close to the ground as I possibly could. Dro pulled out his gun and started to return fire before the car sped off.

"You alright?" Dro reached out towards me, pulling me to my feet. I shook my head. The adrenaline coursing through my body stunned me into silence. The only thing I could think of doing was running. Dro grabbed me and dragged me towards the car.

"Let's get the fuck out of here." That was a great idea. I followed the man who had saved me. Again.

NINE

STANDING AT THE BAR, I watched the guest leave with their women. Once all of them left, I breathed a sigh of relief. It was over. Well, almost over. Dro walked over looking very pleased with himself. He handed me the tablet and I looked over the account. Tonight wasn't bad at all, we brought in nine hundred and twenty-five thousand dollars, in one night. This money wouldn't stay in the account. We would slowly filter the money into the club and then into a different account.

I handed the tablet back to Dro and smiled. "I'm going to pay the servers." I walked behind the bar and grabbed my bag. The seven servers walked towards me. I handed them their envelops with payments as they returned the masks to me. They all started to leave. I glanced towards the door and saw one of them had forgotten to give me the mask back.

"Hey, wait! I need the mask!" I said as she walked out the door. How had I missed collecting hers? I dismissed the thought and went about blowing all those damn candles out. I gathered the mask that were on the bar and put them in the bag I pulled them from. I had a total of seven. What the hell. I know I saw one of the girls walk wearing one so how did I have all seven of them?

"Where's Andre?" Dro looked around. He was nowhere to be found. Just then we heard his voice from the front of the club.

"I'm over here, we got company." His raspy voice echoed through the building. Two masked people walked into the club, one male one female. I watched as the two entered the room. How had they gotten past Sergio?

Dro walked towards me and pulled me closer to him. The couple made it to the center of the room. They walked in as if they owned our club. Sauntering in wearing masquerade masks as if they had been invited to our event.

"Are we too late for the party." That voice. I remembered that voice. Trent was back. Just as he said that four more men entered behind them. My eyes roamed the room, three of us, six of them. If he got in I'm sure Sergio was long gone by now. I usually told security once the guests were gone they could lock up and leave.

"You look stunning in your mask" His gaze fell on me as he spoke. I hadn't realized I was still wearing it.

"What the fuck you doing here? I told your ass repeatedly we ain't got no business together."

"And I told you, either take my offer or I take it by force! I have a shipment that needs to come in within the next two weeks. Like I said, either you take the offer or I take your operation by force."

"Yeah, and just how the fuck you plan on doing that." I watched the woman standing at his side. I couldn't see her face because of the masquerade mask, but her eyes were visible. There was something oddly familiar about her, something about her eyes. She was silent, hadn't yet said a word. Who was she? She eyed me up and down, undoubtedly a little twisted the man she was with was complimenting me. Who gave a shit about any of that?

"It's late," I said. I didn't have time for this shit. Tonight had been exhausting and now it seemed that a clusterfuck of problems just kept rolling my way.

"Did you give your husband my message?"

I stared blankly at Trent. What in the hell was he doing? Trying to make it seem like I've been having secret conversations with him? The last thing I wanted was Dro thinking I was communicating with this dude behind his back.

"What fucking message?" Dro's eyes burned with anger as he turned to face me.

"Like I said," eyeing both the man and the woman, "it's too late for this shit. Leave, please." Dro's hands crept to his waist as the four of us stood frozen in a standoff. Andre still hadn't walked into the room and the fact that this man brought hired goons with him didn't make me comfortable. I thought I was far beyond bullets flying over my head, but I knew if Dro felt the slightest bit threatened he would handle it.

"I don't think you understand what's happening here." She eyed me through the holes in her mask. "Negotiation time is up." Who the hell did she think she was. She sounded like some gutter trash trying to keep up with her husband, but she was lacking both the etiquette and obviously the education. The front door of the club opened again. We all turned towards the commotion.

"Is this the motherfucker I keep hearing about? The nigga from Houston that thinks he can just stroll into Miami and set up shop? This is my territory." Her Haitian laced words carried through the large room. Andre finally entered behind her. Along with, from the looks of it, her entire crew. She stood in the center of the group slightly ahead of them, letting all of us know she was their leader.

Margeaux. I knew who she was, who in Miami's seedy underworld didn't know? She walked in dressed in all black, thigh high boots, and center-parted bone straight hair that hung past her waist.

"What is he doing here?" Her eyes cut towards Trent. I briefly wondered how she even knew who *he* was. Andre. Had he told his cousin Trent was here?

"Who the fuck are you to question me?" Dro poked himself in the chest placing emphasis on the word me. His eyes bulged slightly as he stared her down. His head swayed to the side as he watched her. "I don't know what make y'all niggas think you coming into my spot running anything. Andre, what's going on. First of all, why the fuck you over there?" His arms flailed about pointing in the direction Andre was standing. Andre moved to Dro's other side.

All of us stood facing one another. Dro's hand hadn't left his waist. I knew exactly what that meant. I didn't know if I was going to be able to keep him calm and I was a little nervous that we seemed completely outnumbered. These assholes were messing up my night. Everything was spinning out of control.

Andre shrugged his shoulders as if he didn't know what was happening. I watched how he stood quietly not interacting, its as if he was retreating to the background far enough not to be directly involved but close enough to look as if he was.

"You know who the fuck I am!" She spoke again. "You willing to do deals with dis motherfucka but not me? Where I'm from that's disrespect nigga, you don't help somebody walk in on my territory. Try to take over my shit, when I helped you build your shit " Damn, what was she so pissed about. Dro never offered her a seat at the table so how could she even part her lips to say she's being disrespected.

"Bitch fuck you and your territory! You ain't help me build shit."

I grabbed my phone and shot a quick text to Sergio. I saw things getting out of hand.

"Baby, calm down. Let's talk to them long enough for Sergio to show up with our people and then put them the hell out." I leaned into Dro and whispered into his ear so the others couldn't hear. I was trying to buy us some time, and also remove us from being completely outnumbered.

Dro nodded his head in agreement after a few moments of silence. "You," he pointed at Trent, "and you," now pointing at Margeaux, "come on, the rest of you stay here while we talk." We began to walk towards the elevator to lead us to the lower level.

The woman he was with took a seat at the bar while the others stood around. Andre followed on the heels of his cousin. We squeezed into the elevator, and I silently prayed for Sergio to hurry up and get here. I didn't trust any of these people and the faster I could get this over with the better it would be.

The elevator jerked several times before stalling. We all looked around a little shaken by the bobbing lift. It stopped momentarily jerking again before the power went out and we were in complete and total darkness.

After a long ride to the middle of nowhere, Dro parked the car in front of a small one-story home. Soft light escaped through the sheer curtains as I struggled to get a peek inside. Dro hadn't said much of anything the entire ride here. I could tell he was deep in thought.

My heart rate had finally settled and I was beginning to calm down. The entire ride over I watched the mirrors to make sure that car wasn't behind us. Once we crossed over the long ass bridge on Lake Pontchartrain, he continued driving for another 20 minutes or so. I had never been this far out, honestly had no reason too, but right now anywhere seemed safer than New Orleans since people were shooting at us.

"Where are we going?" I asked Dro, feeling a little more comfortable with him since our earlier exchange. He didn't respond. I didn't like that he was ignoring me but I decided to leave it alone. Dro only gave me information when he was ready to. I didn't expect that to change overnight.

We got out the car and I followed him to the door. I watched as he fumbled with keys. Once he found the right key we entered. The house was modestly furnished but it felt like a home. Where in the world were we? The small home sat in the quiet swamp. There was nothing out here but murky waters and alligators.

I stood behind Dro as he fumbled with his keys before finally finding what he was looking for. The door slowly opened making visible the softly lit room. A woman slept soundly on the sofa as we entered. So many questions ran through my mind, who was this woman.

Even lying down I could see she was beautiful. Her skin was the color of coffee with a touch of cream. Her hair was a mess of soft auburn curls falling over her face.

"What are we doing here?" I whispered to Dro.

"Sit down."

I found the nearest seat and planted myself in it. My heart raced not knowing what was coming next. He walked over to the sleeping woman and knelt beside her. He softly brushed the hair from her face before he spoke.

"Mamá, despierta, wake up." Dro spoke Spanish? The woman started to stir. Sitting up on the couch, she blinked several times before her eyes widened in surprise.

"M'ijo!" Her arms wrapped around Dro. I watched him with her. His hard exterior shed in her presence. This was his mother. The love in her embrace was evident. I couldn't recall my mother ever hugging me like that.

The talked, most of it I didn't understand because I didn't speak Spanish. She finally looked my way.

"Alejandro, who is this?" She motioned her hand towards me. I stared at her. I sat motionlessly, I didn't know what to expect from her, or why we were here. The woman stood and walked to me.

"Qué hermosa," she touched my face and looked back at her son, awaiting his answer.

TEN

I RUBBED my neck while struggling to open my eyes. I felt as if a ton of bricks had hit me. My eyesight was blurry and I blinked desperately trying to get a better look at my surroundings.

"What the hell!" I heard Margeaux's thick accent from outside the elevator. I struggled to stand on my feet.

"Dro!" I shuffled out of the elevator. I spotted Trent, then Margeaux, and Andre, but no Dro.

"Where is he?" Tears rolled from the corners of my eyes.

"That's a great fucking question!" Margeaux was visibly agitated. She charged towards me, grabbing me by my disheveled gown. "Your husband is the only one that was not in that elevator when I woke up. What the fuck did he drug us with!"

I didn't have any words for her. I grabbed her hands and pushed them away from me. I wasn't about to fight with this woman. We were all trying to wrap our minds around what happened.

Andre grabbed his cousin and pulled her away from me. The look in her eyes told me she was pissed. She watched me out of the corner of her eye while Andre tried to calm her down.

"She doesn't know what happened any more than we do. We were all knocked out in that elevator."

Andre walked towards me and pulled me close to him. I would normally tell him to back up, but I fell into his arms. I needed the comfort he was offering now.

"Where is your husband?" Trent spoke through clenched teeth.

"I should be asking you that! Maybe you did something to my husband?" I turned to face him staring him straight in the eyes. If it was a fight he wanted I'd give it to him. I scanned the room, I remember before it all happened that I had sent a message to Sergio. I spotted him coming through the door along with five other members of his team.

"Sergio," He sprinted towards me.

"I need you to get everyone off the premises. I want them gone."

The pounding in my head made it hard for me to concentrate. I walked towards the elevator. I needed to get to Dro's office.

"Where the hell do you think you're going?" I could hear so many people shouting at me but I didn't have the time. I stood in front of the elevator but stopped frozen. I wasn't getting back on that thing. I headed towards the back and raced down the stairs as fast as my feet could carry me. I rushed down the long hallway and threw the door open expecting to see Dro sitting behind his desk. The office was eerily empty as I slowly walked into the room. I felt sick to my stomach as I stood in the office alone.

For all these years Dro has been by my side. Together. We did this together and now I felt completely alone.

"So what's going on? Does Dro have some type of plan you guys forgot to clue me in on, again?" Andre had crept into the room. He moved so silently I hadn't noticed he had even come in.

"There is no plan Andre."

"So where is he?"

I breathed an exasperated sigh. "Why in the hell do you guys keep asking me that? Like you said wasn't I laid out just like the rest of y'all in that damn elevator?"

I shook my head trying to shake away the thoughts of tonight. Everything seemed completely out of hand and I had no idea of what my next step should be.

"What are we going to do Andre?"

Andre shook his head. I can tell he didn't know what the next step should be any more than I did.

"I don't know Khari, but whatever it is, I got you."

The soft mattress shifted as I stirred. It felt so good to actually sleep in a bed. I sat up and took a look around the room. It was sparsely decorated, but comfortable.

I could hear Dro and his mother talking. I followed the sound of their voices until I found the kitchen. I listened to them talk, most of which I couldn't understand. There were bits and pieces of English, but they spoke mostly in Spanish. I had never thought much beyond the Dro that I saw every day. Who he was and where he was from was all a mystery to me.

I watched her. I hadn't had many conversations with her but she had welcomed me into her home, gave me her spare room. The smell of eggs and bacon wafted from the kitchen through the doorway where I stood.

"Come on in here and get you something to eat." Her voice was heavily laced with an accent from a country I couldn't identify. I walked in and took a seat on the table next to Dro. I fixed my plate from the food that sat on the table. The concept of eating as a family was a bit foreign to me. My sister and I would eat together all the time but rarely was my mother ever around to share those moments with us.

His mother locked eyes with me and then darted towards Dro. "Are we robbing the cradle now Dro?" She spoke in English so it was obvious that she wanted me to understand what she was saying. She looked back at me.

"We didn't get a chance to talk much last night, My name is Gabriela."

"I'm Khari."

"Khari, pretty. And how old are you Khari."

"I'm eighteen."

Gabriela pushed her lips together and nodded her head, slowly.

As if she was processing what I said and deciphering whether or not I was giving her the truth. Dro's phone rang, breaking up the sporadic conversation we were having.

"I gotta take this," Dro said to his mother. My eyes followed him as he left the room.

I ate in silence trying to overhear Dro's conversation. I could tell it was heated. I heard Ace's name, then something about a hit.

"So what do you have my son into?"

"Nothing."

"There's something going on, I can tell with the way you look at him. He never brings a girl here, into this house. So I'm wondering what makes you special?"

"Mamá, I need to handle this nigga." Gabriela stood to her feet.

"What I teach you, Alejandro?" Her entire posture changed. Her deep brown eyes went from sweet to hard. This seemed like the kind of woman you never wanted to be on the wrong side of. "Something needs to be handled, handle it. Por calquier medio. And I mean it, by any means!"

ELEVEN

I ROLLED to my life desperately seeking the warmth and comfort of Dro's body. My hands instinctively reached for him but it wasn't there. My eyes flew open and stared at the empty space. I was so used to waking up and feeling his presence that his absence had me shook. I sat up and let my head fall against the headboard. I felt lost and confused. What was my next move?

There was one thing I knew. I couldn't just sit in this bed waiting for things to happen. I needed to figure this out. I pushed the blanket off of me and stood to my feet. The first thing I was going to do is get to that club. Until Dro came back we had to continue business as usual. And business, as usual, means that we would still have to make money.

I jumped in the shower and washed yesterday off of me. My neck still a little sore from being stuck in the elevator. I hurriedly slipped on a pair of jeans and headed out of the house.

I parked in the parking garage and entered through the back entrance. I could tell by the light that dipped into the hallway there was someone in Dro's office. Excitement washed over me and I ran towards the open door. Was he in there? I raced through the door and then was stopped dead in my tracks. What the hell was Andre doing behind his desk?

"What are you doing in my husband's office?" Tami sat on the edge of the desk facing him as he leaned back in the chair. What was happening?

"Chill out Khari, I came in early so I can see if we can figure out what was going on."

"I don't see how we included her and not me." I walked towards the desk and opened the drawer Dro kept his iPad in to grab it. I bumped into Tami as I was opening the drawer. Hopefully, she got the damn picture and moved the hell out of the way.

"Can I talk to Andre a minute?" Tami looked towards Andre with her eyebrows raised.

"Just give us a minute baby." Tami walked out the door looking hurt but who cares. I've told him time and time again to stop pushing that girl on us.

"Why do I keep having to tell you the same damn thing over and over again?"

Andre leaned back in the chair, his eyes closing into tiny tight slits before responding to me.

"I don't think I like the way you are talking to me."

"I don't think I like the way you are acting. Instead of being in here with her all in your face we need to be trying to figure out this Dro situation." I was starting to feel like I was the only one that cared that he was missing. Last night Andre said he had me. I took that to mean that he would help me. This didn't appear to be helping me.

"Khari," Andre stood and walked towards me. "I told you last night I got you. I just figured somebody needed to be here so we could figure out what was happening. I honestly think it was that nigga Trent."

"I don't know Andre." It could be a lot of different people. "What makes you think it's him?"

"Just a feeling I got. Look we gone figure this shit out. I told you I got you." Andre said. "In the meantime, we gone keep it pushing, okay. Don't worry we gone find him."

Just as he finished Tami walked back into the room with Margeaux following close behind. We eyed each other in silence as she walked in.

"Andre, what's she doing here?" My head swiveled his direction. I thought he said he was helping me with Dro, what the hell kind of help could she offer?

"Where's your husband?" A sick smile spread across Margeaux's face.

"You tell me! You the one ran in here last night with the problem." My fist clinched into two tiny balls. I was mad enough to want to hit her.

"Khari," Andre looked at me. "I am going to get to the bottom of this, but we gotta keep the business going. I'm second to Dro, his right hand. I'm gonna make sure this shit stay tight until we get him back. Believe that!"

He sat back down in the chair and Margeaux took a seat in front of him. I am not sure what he thought he was going to get out of her but I was going to make sure that I stayed right here to find out whatever it was he thought she knew.

I didn't know if I could trust what was happening but what choice did I have. Andre had helped us build this club and business into what it was but under the leadership of Dro. Could I really trust him to do the right thing while Dro wasn't around? They talked, mostly about meaningless things. None of which I thought could help.

Margeaux cut her eyes towards me and then proceeded in Haitian Creole. I sat back a little my eyebrows raised. Mmmm, they effortlessly changed the language just as Dro and I did a million times before when we didn't want someone to know what we were talking about.

"¿*Tienes hambre?*" Her voice carried from the kitchen into the small family room Dro and I were in. I stared at him waiting to translate or respond. I had no idea what she was asking.

"Yeah Mamá, we're starving." He replied. I guess she had asked if we wanted to eat. I was definitely on a steep learning curve in this house with the two of them but the more I was around them, the more I wanted to know.

At breakfast, her entire demeanor had changed after Dro's phone call. The tone of her voice went cold, almost scary and then just like the flip of a switch she was back to her. It seemed a little crazy but I would take that kind of crazy over my mother's any day.

Dro hadn't said too much since then. I wanted to know what we were doing. We hadn't talked about the stream of bullets that flew over our heads just a couple of days ago. Dro and I had a moment that night we were shot at. Before that happened I could have sworn he was about to kiss me and I couldn't stop thinking about what if he had.

He watched television in silence as I sat curled on the sofa. I wanted to say something to him, wanted to talk like we had been doing the other day. But I just didn't know if he was open to it. I shifted a little closer to him. I wanted to see if he would respond in any way.

Dro's eyes cut towards me and then back towards the television. I shifted a little bit more closing the space between us again. There were a lot of thoughts tumbling around in my head regarding him. Could he feel the same spark I was feeling?

I reached out and softly rubbed against his hand. He didn't stop me. "Alejandro," I called him the name his mother used. He turned to face me and smiled. Had I ever seen Dro smile?

"Who told you that you could call me that?"

"That is your name isn't it?" I smiled back. Dro was scary, and I was starting to think a bit crazy, but I saw something else in him too. I thought on more than one occasion why didn't he just get rid of me, why was he still letting me hang around. I know he said he was going to get his money back but I had a feeling we were far past that.

"Khari," Her voice interrupted our silent conversation.

"Yes ma'am," I turned to face her, snatching my hand away from Dro.

"Come help me in the kitchen, bonita."

I glanced at Dro before making my way into the kitchen. I turned on the water and washed my hands. I knew my way around a kitchen fairly well and didn't at all mind helping her out.

"What can I help with?" I asked.

"Can you cook?"

"Yes, I do okay." I smiled at her and waited for her directions.

"I will teach you to be better than ok."

"Ok," I didn't really know how to take that. Her expression was kind and loving, but her tone seemed to say something else.

"I can tell you want my son, but right now you are a little girl. If you want my son to love you, you need to be a woman. Not a little girl. My son is strong. He is a lion and if you want to be with him you have to be a lioness. You have to be built for this life."

After that, she went back to giving me directions to complete her recipe. Her words replayed in my mind. I didn't feel that I was a little girl, especially what I had been through in the past month. Who my mother was never really allowed me to be a child. I always had to step up. I knew how to take the lead. I stopped chopping the onions and looked at her.

"I'm built for it. You have no idea just how much I am."

TWELVE

AFTER MARGEAUX and Andre pulled their little language swap on me I decided to get the hell out of there. They obviously wanted to discuss something they didn't want me to hear. I don't know what that was but I was going to get to the bottom of it.

It was like there was a ticking time bomb counting down the minutes. I needed to figure this out, I needed to get my husband back. I sat in my car and flipped through the calendar on his iPad. I was trying to find out when he planned the next shipment of girls to come in. There was no way I wanted Andre having access to Dro's information.

There was a scheduled shipment set to come in the next week. Without Dro, this wasn't doable. I grabbed my phone it was time to start making some moves. I needed to call his cousin in Columbia and put a pause on the next shipment. I hit the saved number and waited for an answer.

"¿Aló?"

"Julian, hey it's Khari."

"¿Qué Mas?"

"Bien, Everything's good" I lied. I didn't have time for pleasantries, but I needed him to go along with what I needed. "I was calling about the next shipment. Did you receive your last payment?"

"Sí."

"Good, we had a good night. Dro told me to give you a call. We are gonna have to reset the date for the next shipment. He will call you as soon as he gets a chance."

I could tell by the silence Julian wanted to ask more questions but decided against it. I was thankful. I wouldn't be able to handle another shipment without Dro. I didn't want to handle another shipment at all but I definitely wouldn't do it if he wasn't by my side.

My next move would be to check on the remaining women from the auction. I leaned back into the driver's seat and made the long drive. My nerves were jumping in every direction, but I knew I had to pull it together.

I had to calm down. I turned the air on high and increased the volume on the radio. I was hoping the cool air and music would calm the panic that was increasingly rising within me.

Kehlani's *Gangsta* blasted through the speakers as I sang along word for word. Listening to these words always reminded me of Dro. He wasn't like any other man that I ever encountered in my life and no one could love me the way he could. Tears trickled from the corners of my eyes. Without him, I was completely lost. And not knowing how long before I was reunited with him caused what had to be separation anxiety. I cried and sang along with the lyrics after putting the song on repeat. I needed my husband back.

As soon as I pulled into the driveway I noticed that there was none of our security parked out front. That was more than odd, it was unheard of. Neither Dro nor I could be here twenty-four seven, and even though most of the girls wouldn't dream of running we always made sure there was somebody here with them.

"Hello," I called out as I walked in the door. There were two girls that should have been brought back here that night. "Hel-loooooo." No one responded. I walked through the entire house looking for the women. Where the hell could they be?

I shoved my hand into my purse to recover my cell phone I had just tossed inside. I hit Sergio's name. I was going to get to the bottom of this.

"Sergio."

"Sí."

"There were two girls that should have come back to the house after the party, Lucia and Carmen. They aren't here."

"We waited but no girls showed up. We thought everyone left the night. Lo siento señora. I don't know where the girls are."

As sorry as he was it didn't matter. This was a disaster. Where the hell would they have gone? So much happened that night at the club I didn't know where to start looking for them or how they had even gotten away.

"Señora, do you think that Dro has them?" The fact that Sergio thought that my husband would disappear with some random women made me livid.

"No Sergio, I do not think that. We don't know what happened to Dro, but I know one thing, we better hurry up and fucking find him, and them."

Curled up on the small porch swing that sat in the front, I allowed the warm Louisiana breeze to lull me into calmness. This is the most peace I've felt in a long time. My home life was so chaotic. There was always so much going on that I would struggle to find moments like this.

I hadn't thought about working for Dro, or about what my mother had Punkin up to. I hadn't thought about any of the things that usually weighed me down and often felt like too much to handle. The squeaking screen door opening pulled me from my daze.

I smiled in her direction as she stepped out onto the front porch with me. I hadn't had much time alone with Gabriela but she seemed nice enough. Her eyes were always watching me and her son.

After our last discussion in the kitchen, I knew she questioned my relationship with Dro. Well, in all honesty there was no relationship with Dro. I thought I felt a spark between the two of us but that has never been explored and could quite possibly be a figment of my imagination.

She walked towards me and sat down next to me. I repositioned to allow her more room on the small porch swing. For a moment we both sat in silence. I didn't know what to say to her so I said nothing.

"So, Khari, tell me how you ended up with my son."

I turned to face her but didn't know how to respond to her. I didn't exactly want to tell anyone the reason I ended up with Dro. It was easier for me to allow people to think I was just another one of his girls. The truth was much harder to face.

When I didn't respond she didn't press it. She sat back in the seat and allowed us to be still. The breeze tossed the leaves from the large magnolia tree that stood in the front yard. I could see her sitting silently from the corner of my eye. Dro treated her differently than I had ever seen him treat anyone since I had been with him. I think I wanted him to treat me like that.

I contemplated telling her my truth, but before I could get the words out Dro walked out onto the porch, disrupting our quiet peace.

"I need to head to the club and check on some things." Dro blurted. I stood to my feet ready to follow him back to his club. "Naw, chill, stay with my moms. I'll be back."

"Oh, okay." I sat back down confused. I guess he thought he had brought me too far out to run.

"We'll be fine Alejandro," She patted my knee while urging him to go. "You should have never allowed this situation to get this far out of hand. Handle it. Then get back here there are somethings we need to discuss with your cousin Julian."

Most of the time I didn't understand half of what they talked about. Mostly because when they talked it was in Spanish but the parts I could understand didn't make much sense to me.

I sat back and watched him walk away. Gabriela stayed on the swing with me, softly pushing us back and forth. The steady fluid motion lulled me into a place of calm. I looked at her.

"I'm with him because it was the only way to save my mother's life."

I spoke no other words. The tears trickled slowly down my cheeks. Gabriela didn't verbally respond, she just wrapped her arms around me and pulled me close to her. It was an unfamiliar yet comforting feeling.

THIRTEEN

REST. I needed rest. It's as if my brain was on rapid fire, one thought after another surged through my mind keeping me constantly in a state of agitation. One disaster after another had left me mentally drained.

I drove back to my house so that I could find a moment. I needed to think. Everything was so upside down. I parked in the driveway of our beachfront home. This mini mansion felt completely empty without Dro.

I walked inside and slipped the high heels off my feet. I moved down the long hallway leading to my bedroom and noticed the light slipping from under the door.

Dro

I pushed the bedroom door open. The light was on but the room was empty. He wasn't here. I sank into the bed not bothering to remove my clothes. I needed a moment and it would be back to figuring this out. I had to be able to think things through. Think about where Dro was, and where had Lucia and Carmen disappeared to.

Sergio thought Dro was with them but I knew better than

that. Dro would never disappear, he wouldn't leave with another woman or anyone for that matter. I closed my eyes wanting to cry but knowing my tears wouldn't solve anything.

"Get up!" My eyes flew open and I sat straight up. I looked towards the direction of the sound. His voice had boomed loudly through the room like rolling thunder, causing my heart to race with fear.

I rolled over to Dro's side of the bed hoping to get a hold of the nine he kept bedside. Before my hands could open the drawer he grabbed me by my ankles and pulled me towards him.

"You looking for this?" He held the gunmetal gray handgun in his hands, dangling it before me, taunting me with it. He hit the button on the side and released the clip from the gun, and tossed them both to the side.

"What the hell are you doing in my house?"

I pulled my feet under me and moved as far away from him as I could. I was hoping to inch my way to the other side of the bed and make a run for it. I scanned the room for evidence that someone else may have been present. No shadows in the bathroom. No one behind me. It looked as if it was just the two of us. My chances of getting out of here were good. I knew the layout of my house well and I knew that there was a strong possibility that I could outrun him.

I jumped off the bed and dashed through the open bedroom door. I sped towards the staircase in the back of our home that spiraled down to the garage. From there I could hop in one of our cars and be gone. My feet thudded against the tiled floor, echoing through the quiet house, the sound giving away to the direction I was running.

Glancing back to see how close he was to me, I noticed he was nowhere to be found. I was almost there. Just a few more steps and then I was gone. I took the spiraled stairs two at a time. Out of nowhere, a dark shadowed figure appeared.

"Oh hell no!" Who was this big ass Rick Ross looking ass nigga? I wasn't going to go running into him. I turned on my heels and tried to move back the direction I came. Before I could even get back up the stairs this man was on me. He grabbed me by my waist and tossed me over his shoulders.

"Put me down damn it!" I kicked and screamed hoping to loosen his grip on me but my attempts were futile.

"Here she is boss." The man had carried me into the front room.

"Good, set her ass in this chair and if she so much as flinches put a bullet in her brain."

My pulse quickened as I breathed, struggling to keep my composure. I didn't want to give him the satisfaction of knowing how terrified I was.

"Trent, why are you in my house?" I spoke calmly.

He began to pace back in forth in front of me. I watched him in silence. His impeccably tailored suit and designer shoes said he was all business, but him giving the order for this man to put a bullet in my head said he was straight gangsta.

"Where is your husband?"

"I was hoping you could tell me, you're the one who keeps coming around threatening us. He tells you no and now he's gone. So you tell me Trent, where the fuck is my husband?"

"I don't have time for these bullshit games. Your husband has seventy-two hours to either show the fuck back up and do business, or turn over both your Columbian and Miami port contacts."

Every time he spoke my flesh crawled. I hated the way he barked out orders, I had to wonder if he would have been better received if he wasn't so damn bossy. I rolled my eyes and looked at him. I hadn't completely figured him out, but I knew he most likely meant what he said. That wild look in his eyes told me he wasn't bluffing.

"And if we don't?"

"Don't and you're both dead."

Trent dropped a card on my lap and then turned on his heels and walked out the door, leaving me shaken, both mentally and physically.

"Have you talked to Dro?" I asked as I walked into the kitchen where Gabriela was. I could often find her in there when I was looking for her. We have been here for over a month, much of which Dro has been in and out of the house.

"Sí," Gabriela had taken to teaching me Spanish. Between the telenovelas she watched and her always speaking to me in Spanish I was becoming pretty fluent.

"Where is he? Is he coming back?" She stopped mixing her batter and looked up at me.

"Yes he is coming back, doesn't he always?" She smiled. Gabriela had been kind to me. I think she liked me.

Dro had been in and out, looking for Ace, and still trying to do business and make money at his club. He never took me back there or asked me to work. I knew he had replaced the women Ace disappeared with.

Over the time I've been here, it has become more than apparent to me that his mother was very involved in his day to day. She was sweet most of the time but could flip like a switch.

"Gabriela, " She stopped mixing and looked towards me. "Tengo una pregunta." I spoke in Spanish hoping my use of her native language would set her at ease and not take offense to my question.

"Ask your question M'ija." I smiled. I like when she referred to me as her daughter.

"You know what Dro does, how are you okay with it?"

I had wondered for a long time how she could know her son sold both women and drugs and be okay with it. She didn't seem like the type of woman to be involved with those types of things. It seemed like something my mother would do, but not Gabriela.

She continued mixing the batter. The sweet smell of her unfinished concoction wafted through the air. I was beginning to wonder if she was going to answer me.

"Okay with it, I teach him everything he knows. Columbia is beautiful but my country is hard. Nothing is given, everything is taken. I give him the tools to be a king."

She paused for a moment before continuing. Her voice was just as sugary sweet as always, but underneath was a cold hardness that quietly crept through.

"Now I have a question. You know our last name, si?"

"Yes, Leon," I answered. I had seen it on her mail and around the house.

"Tell me what that means in Español."

"Lion," I was happy to know the answer but had no idea where she was going with this. She continued mixing as she spoke.

"Yes, we are lions, you ask if I'm okay with it. I say yes, because I am a lioness, and it is always the lioness that goes in for the hunt and the kill." Her voice sent chills up and down my spine.

"That's what you meant when you said he needs a lioness?"

"Yes, someone who knows how to do whatever needs to be done. Someone who could go in for both the hunt and the kill. Is that you?"

Gabriela always had a way of ending our conversations with a question. Usually, one that led back to Dro and I.

FOURTEEN

THE BANGING on the front door jarred me. I looked at the panel and saw Andre standing outside. After Trent had left I was uneasy about being in this house alone.

I hit the button on the panel to unlock the door and allow him in. Andre sauntered up the steps into the same room I had been sitting in since Trent left.

"Khari, I've been calling you like crazy, what's going on?" My gaze fell on Andre. I wanted to talk but I was still a bit shaken.

"Hellooooooo, Khari! Khari Leon. You hear me talking to you?"

"Yeah I hear you. Trent was here."

"What do you mean Trent was here?"

"Just what I said Andre, he was here in my house, threatening us. He says Dro has seventy-two hours to show back up and do business or we are dead."

"Well you know I ain't gonna let that shit happen. How long ago was he here?"

"A few hours ago. What am I gonna do?" The last part was meant more for me than for him. I had to figure out what to do.

"Have you tried calling Dro's phone?" What did he think I was an idiot. Wouldn't that be the first thing I did?

"His phone is here. So we can call it all day it's not gonna ring to him. He left it that day."

Andre sat on the sofa across from me. I know he was just as lost as I was. Andre was smart, but that didn't have anything on Dro's street sense, he didn't know what the hell to do any more than I did.

"So check this out, I'm staying here tonight in case that nigga wanna try to come back. We might have to just face the fact that Dro may or may not be coming back. Real talk Khari, you know that nigga unstable maybe he just finally snapped."

"Don't stand in my husband's home and talk shit about him like that. That unstable nigga is the one that gave you your shot. That unstable nigga took you in, gave you a seat at the table!"

I didn't like the things he was saying. I hadn't been able to pinpoint what was going on with Andre lately. He seemed to be all over the place. Maybe his emotions got the best of him and his thoughts.

"Chill Khari, I told you I got you. We will find him." His mouth said the words but there was no conviction behind them.

"I'm going to take a bath." I needed to find a moment to exhale. At least if he was here I would be a little more at ease. I set the alarm on the panel and walked towards my bedroom.

After slipping in the tub and allowing the warm soapy suds to calm me. I slipped into my bed. I had three days, well less than that now to get us out of the shit that we were in. I sometimes wonder how in the hell did Trent even know as much as he did about what we had going on. The thought lingered on my mind as I drifted off to sleep.

"DRO,"

Soft moans escaped my lips. The soft caress of lips brushing against my thigh sent chills up my spine. With my eyes closed I rolled my head back in ecstasy. My legs fell open as I allowed his head to fall between them.

"Baby, you're back!" I whispered as his tongue brushed against my inner thigh. My hands instinctively cradled his head. His hair. I expected to feel the familiar low cut strands, instead,I felt the brush of thick lush curls.

My eyes opened as my lips curled in disgust. I through the blanket back and looked down at Andre.

"Andre, get the fuck off me!" He didn't stop. He wrapped his arms around my legs and held me hostage. I squealed in revulsion. I wanted this nigga the fuck off of me. I saw the gun and clip that Trent had played with earlier on the nightstand. I grabbed it and pushed the clip inside.

Click clock

The sound of the loading chamber caused Andre to freeze. I pressed the gun to his temple. I was not about to be defiled by this man, in my husband's bed. I would kill this motherfucker dead before I let that happen.

"Get...the...fuck...off...of...me!" My words were slow and deliberate. I wanted him to understand that this was not at all happening.

"Khari, really? You pulling a piece on me? The fuck is your problem?"

"You are my problem. What the fuck do you think this is?"

"Get the gun out my face."

"Shut up and stop trying to give me fucking orders. Here is how this is going to go. Put your clothes on and get the fuck out of my house. Our house." I spat the words at him. He had mistaken my kindness for something else. He should know me well enough to know that I could be sweet at first but then as cold as ice.

"Khari, you might as well give up on that nigga. He gone. He done abandoned your ass, and I'm right here. Fixing what that motherfucker broke."

"Get out my house. It's already one in the chamber, don't make me use it!"

Andre put his clothes back on. He had never gone this far. Always flirted but he knew how far to take it. Now that Dro wasn't here he had the audacity to climb in his bed.

I walked towards Andre with the barrel still extended towards him. He grabbed his things and began to make his way out of my house. The look on his face was somewhere between anger and hatred. He threw the door open and walked out never taking his eyes off of me.

Once he was gone I walked to the alarm panel and watched him walk down the stairs. He pulled his phone out to make a call. Who in the hell was he calling? I hit the speaker on the panel to engage the two-way communication. I wanted to hear what was being said.

"Yeah, it's me." There was a pause I assume the person on the other end was speaking. I was just happy that he was speaking in English so I could understand. I'm sure he didn't expect me to be listening.

"Let's do it, time to set the motherfuckin' plan in motion."

Sitting on the front steps with Dro, we both found peace, enjoying one another's company. I was now more than certain that I had a thing for this man. I didn't care that he was almost ten years older than me. Most girls my age had high school crushes. Girls my age thought twenty-two years old was an older man.

But Dro, age twenty-seven and all was the most handsome man I had ever seen. He was dangerous but could be sweet. Getting to know him with his mother had completely shown me a different side to him. Not to mention he had saved my life.

I moved closer to Dro, something I always seemed to instinctively do when he was near me. I paid enough attention to what his mother said to know that real women make moves. I smiled at that thought. Actually, she taught me real women make moves and let their men think it's their idea.

I laid my head against Dro's shoulder. His breaths seemed to quicken as I got closer to him.

"Alejandro." I whispered.

"You're getting too used to calling me that." He smiled. Dro often teased me when I called him that but I knew he didn't have a problem with it.

"Besame!" With each passing day, my Spanish was getting better and better. Dro looked slightly startled and then did as I requested. His hands wrapped around my waist and scooped me up. He pulled me across his lap. I loved the way he took charge. My denim shorts inched up as I wrapped my legs around him.

He pulled me in close, staring deep into my eyes. The connection was pure fire and electricity between us. Dro slowly pulled me closer, pressing his full lips against mine. Our tongues passionately danced. I savored every second of it.

I waited for this moment a long time and this kiss was every-

thing I hoped it would be. I wanted to give my heart to this man. His kiss told me he was giving his to me.

"Now you're mine." He smiled while pulling away from our kiss but never letting go of me.

The creaky screen door opened. "Excuse me," She coyly looked our direction. I dropped my head and giggled. "Alejandro, Julian is on the phone, he needs to talk to you about putting things in motion."

I stood up to allow Dro to stand. I didn't know much about their plans but I knew it was something they had been working on for a while. Dro still didn't tell me much about what was going on, but I felt he would open up to me in time.

"So, what was I interrupting?" Her smooth cocoa skin glistened in the sun. I didn't need to say any words. She knew how I felt about her son before I even did. She joined me on the steps. I was so wrapped up in Dro's family and my relationship with Gabriela, that I had started to rarely think about my own mother.

"Thank you, Gabriela."

"For what?"

"For showing me what a real mother is like," I said. It was true. She might not win mother of the year in some people's eyes but to me, she had become so many things. A mother, a friend, a teacher, the list was endless.

She nodded her head and smiled. Her arm wrapped around me pulling me into a side hug that said, I love you. I rested against her and looked towards the quiet road. I noticed a car in the distance.

"That's odd," I pointed towards the car. No one ever really came this far back here. Knowing Gabriela, I'm pretty sure that's the very reason she chose this place.

"Yes, it is." We watched to see the cars next move. We were both alert, eyes glued to the car. It did a U-turn and we both relaxed. It looked as if they were turning around to leave.

Just when we thought the car was about to pull forward, it peeled into reverse and a hail of bullets shot our way. Not again.

"Get down! Get down." We scrambled to get as low as we could and slip through the door. The bullets were moving far faster than we could. The zipping sound of a bullet passing right next to my head zoomed passed my ears and right into Gabriela. Blood splattered from both her back and her front as the bullet entered and exited her body. Her frame collapsed in the doorway.

"Noooooo! Dro! Dro!" I screamed. Dro came running forward, gun already drawn, shooting towards the car that was now speeding away from the scene.

"Gabriela, stay with me. Stay. No te vayas," I cradled her petite frame in my arms and stared down at her. Her breaths were short. "It's going to be okay."

"No M'ija, it's not." She struggled to speak.

"Don't say that."

Dro ran to her side, calling an ambulance while grabbing her hand.

"Alejandro, look at me." We both turned her way. "Remember everything I taught you. And change her last name," She looked at me. "She's a Leon through and through."

Gabriela's head fell backward as she exhaled one last breath, and then she was gone.

FIFTEEN

I HADN'T SLEPT at all last night, but none of that mattered because I was on borrowed time. I hadn't taken Trent's threat lightly.

I grabbed my phone and typed in his name. I was good for doing a Google search. I needed to know my opponent and well. Any information I could find on him would be welcomed. The only thing I really knew about him at the moment was that he was from Houston. That wasn't going to be enough.

I jumped in the car and headed towards the club. It was early but I needed to beat Andre there. Last night was the last straw. I didn't trust him. I didn't know what kind of shit he was pulling but this wasn't the time or the space to play games. The stakes were high and I didn't plan on losing.

Once I reached the club I pulled into the underground garage and hit the code to open the arm. The buzzing sound let me know my code was rejected. What? I hit it again and again but the loud buzzing sound signaled the system rejected my entered information.

Confused, I drove around to the front of the building and

parked my car. I didn't know what was going on with my code, but I would have to figure out that part later. When I got to the door I noticed two people standing there I did not recognize.

"Move!" The had the audacity to block me from getting into my club.

"We can't do that."

"What the hell do you mean you can't do that this is my club!" I was becoming angry. I pushed past the two guards at the door. The guards I did not hire but was stopped by a second larger man.

"Ma'am. Wait here."

"What do you mean wait here, I'm not waiting for anything this is my club and I will come and go as I please."

I pushed even harder to get by him but he blocked the entire way. I watched as he pulled out his cell phone. He listened intently to what was being said on the other end.

"Okay, Leah is gonna take you back."

I didn't know who Leah was. I followed the ebony colored beauty to the back of the club. What was the meaning of this? I got on the elevator and made my way down to the lower level.

"I can take it from here," I said. I didn't need her to show me around my club.

"Naw, boss say I escort you, I escort you all the way." The woman continued to walk in front of me. Who in the hell was her boss? There was only one boss and no one knew where he was.

"Have a seat." I glared at Andre.

"What is going on?"Are you behind this Andre?"

"Sit down!" He said through clenched teeth. Leah grabbed me by the arm and forced me into the seat in front of Andre. I scanned the room. I had seen these faces. The two at the door, the one who escorted me here, they were all apart of Margeaux's crew.

"Andre!" I tilted my head to the side trying to figure out what his angle was.

"Shut up. I'm talking you listen."

"You mad? Cause I turned your lame ass down, again!"

"Why would he want you if he has me?" Tami walked into the room smiling like she had just won the lottery. She walked towards Andre and sat to his side.

"So who are y'all supposed to be, the new Dro and Khari, y'all desperate asses ain't never gone be shit. This is our club, Andre you ain't got your name on shit over here."

"Fuck a Dro and Khari, Andre and Tami is just fine. He's been telling me about y'all little operation. How you and your husband always trying to cut him out of shit. We done with that, bitch this a takeover." Tami kissed Andre while cutting her eyes towards me, undoubtedly waiting for my reaction. I wouldn't give this bitch the satisfaction.

"He's been telling you shit huh, Andre always did talk too much."

"He even showed me your books, how you do it, everything. I can handle it from here" She gloated.

"I'm tired of fucking around with you. Before I put you out *my* establishment let me tell you how this shit gone go," he used the same words I used with him last night before continuing, "The club is mine, the business is mine, and the money all mine. The containers of women you traffic into the country, I don't need that shit either. I been telling you my cousin got Miami on lock. Now I'm about to show you what this club can really do."

"You done? Cause none of that is about to happen." I crossed my arms, my head falling to the side as stared at me. I could feel my lips curling into a disgusting sneer. I hated everything he represented.

"No, you're done, I'm just getting started. Like you said it's all in y'all's name. How many times did Dro remind me of what was his? I know how you do this shit from the top to the bottom. So you really don't have a choice but to do shit my way. What you gonna do? Tell the police? Bring it on, I'll give them my version and I even have another witness to corroborate my story. Doc, come on in."

"You know there is no way in hell you're going to get away with this, right. You know Dro ain't gonna have it."

"I don't think I'm gonna have to worry about Dro. Have you even heard from him. No, that nigga long gone." Andre laughed and motioned for doc to come stand near the desk.

Dr. Monroe walked around the corner. They had coordinated this. Was this the plan he set in motion last night when he left my house.

"I told you I needed more money for my trouble. Andre is willing to pay adequately for my silence." She tossed her hair and folded her arms. She had a lot of nerve. I was even more disgusted with Andre than I was last night. I scowled his direction.

"Andre, you always were a snake."

"You damn straight, and you just got bit."

"Bitch!" Tami yelled before the entire room erupted in laughter.

The past two weeks have been brutal on Dro. I wish I could do something to ease his pain. Staying in this house had been torture for the both of us. Gabriela's scent still lingered throughout the house. Every corner and item in here reminded us of her. I missed the smell of her food floating through the house. I missed everything about having her around and for every pain I felt, I knew Dro's was ten times greater.

"We are gonna leave this city. First, we get my mom's ashes and then I deal with that nigga Ace." Dro turned to face me.

"Where do you want to go?"

"My cousin said either Miami or Houston would be good to start our business. Big port cities." Up until now, he hadn't discussed much of what he and his cousin Julian was up to.

"What kind of business?"

"Transport. There are a lot of women in Columbia and other countries around it that want to come here. We are gonna make that happen."

"So like trafficking? Smuggling them in?" I wasn't that comfortable with that, but at this point, anything Dro needed I was here for.

"Yeah, but they wanna come, there's lots of money to be made. My moms was helping us. I want to see this shit through you know."

I stroked the back of his head as he laid across my lap. It seemed to calm him when I touched him like this. I wanted to ask more questions about what he was up to but I didn't think it was the right time. I just wanted to give him whatever he needed.

"I think Miami would be nice," I spoke softly. He turned to look up at me. "But before we go we definitely need to take care of Ace."

"She told me not to trust him." Dro's voice trailed off. I could tell he was lost deep in thought. "This nigga been hiding from me. I know he was the one responsible for this shit. I should have dealt with his ass from the jump. He got in his feelings about you, tried to take my business and when I deaded his ass in these streets he retaliated."

I allowed Dro to vent. He had been beating himself up about everything that was going on. He felt it was his fault.

"You say he's hiding from you? You think he would hide from me?" Dro's eyebrows raised. I continued. "Hear me out. I think he might come out of hiding if he heard I was looking for him. It's worth a try. No one is going to tell you, but they might be willing to help a helpless homeless eighteen year old." I widen my eyes to look like a lost innocent little girl. I had seen my mother play men for sport, I believed I could handle this. I wanted to help. This beef he had with Dro was dumb and Gabriela had paid the ultimate price for it.

Dro sat up, locking eyes with me. "You would do that?"

"Yes, I loved your mother, she was good to me. And we both know what kind of mother I had."

Dro leaned in and kissed me, softly, sadly. "I think she was right, it might be time to rename you."

SIXTEEN

ANDRE THOUGHT HE WAS SMART, but he would have to think again if he thought he was going to outsmart me. He had the upper hand right now. He was right, I couldn't go to the police. I couldn't really tell anyone, but what I could do was figure out how to get this shit back on track. He had no idea he had just become my prey, and I was gonna hunt his ass down and slaughter him.

It didn't even surprise me that he flipped so quick. I always kept one eye open around Andre, always watched his moves. People could only pretend for so long and he had finally shown his true colors.

I sat unmoved in my car not knowing which way to go. I was going to figure something out. I gotta think this shit through. First of all, Andre has gotten into our systems and taken control of everything. That didn't surprise me, he was the one to develop it.

I looked at this like a game of chess not checkers, every move had to be calculated. Only certain pieces could make certain moves, but I was the Queen, the most powerful piece on the board. I had a number of unlimited moves that he would never see coming.

I started my car and pulled out of the parking lot. I caught a glimpse of the sign in my rearview mirror. I would be back to reclaim my throne. I quickly dialed Sergio's number. He would be showing up for his shift soon, and I didn't want him to walk up to Andre's thugs and have a conflict.

"Sergio, I need you to meet me at my house."

I drove back to my home and parked my car. I was very cautious this time around, I be damn if I was going to get another surprise visitor. I walked in and went straight to the kitchen to pour a glass of wine. I sank into the couch and slowly sipped while I waited for Sergio to show up.

The doorbell sounded signaling his arrival. I checked the screen just to be sure it was him.

"Khari," Sergio said while walking in the door. "I hadn't heard anything from you I'm glad you called."

"Have a seat, Sergio, we have a problem."

Sergio sat down, his eyes glued to me as I followed behind and sat across from him.

"Have you heard from Dro?" He asked.

"No, not yet."

"This is not like him, he's been gone already for three days and..."

I waved my hand his direction. The last thing I needed was him telling me how long my husband had been gone. I knew better than anyone. It was my bed, my home and my heart that was empty without him.

"We have to find him, and I think I know where to start. I have a couple of things I need you to do for me."

"Sí, whatever you need."

I ran down the entire chain of events for Sergio. Disbelief

washed over his face as I told him Andre's plan to take over. All this time Andre wanted everything that Dro had. With him gone that put Andre in the perfect position to take it.

"So most likely it was Andre that did it." I shrugged my shoulders. Andre had really messed with the wrong one and I wasn't willing to walk away quietly from what was ours.

"He chose to strike when he thought we were most vulnerable, we have to show him he made the biggest mistake of his life." Sergio nodded and listened closely. "The first thing I need you to do is gather your entire team. Keep them on standby. I want you to follow Andre. It's not going to be easy because he has the protection of Margeaux's crew. But once you see your chance take it, take him and stash him at the beach house."

"Won't he be able to leave?"

"Not if you keep his ass tied down. Once you have him in place, wait for further instructions." I knew this had to be played just right.

"Sí, I will get it done. I also wanted to show you this." Sergio pulled his phone from his pocket and flipped through it. I move forward trying to get a better glance at the screen.

"What is it?" I didn't want or need another problem.

"I've been looking into where the women disappeared to. I went to our neighboring businesses and convinced them to let me get a look at their surveillance footage. It seems that our power was the only ones on the block that went out that night.

"Okay," I eagerly waited for him to finish.

He hit replay on the phone and the dark video began to play. He handed it over to me and I watched the soundless video showing the two women getting into a dark van, just not our van. I squinted trying to get a better look at the person they were with. My mouth flew open.

"That looks a lot like ..."

"I know that's exactly what I thought." He interjected before I could complete my sentence. None of it completely made sense.

"The plate is visible. Find out who this van belongs to."

It didn't take long to set the plan in motion. Dro began to tell people he was leaving town. We knew if Ace was still here he would get comfortable if he thought that he was in the free and clear from retaliation.

Dro stayed hidden and I showed up anywhere we believed Ace would show up. I knew that eventually, I would either catch his attention or the attention of someone who knew where he was.

It was my third day back in this shit hole bar. After Dro severed business ties with Ace, he heard that he was working out of here. He couldn't have been moving much, these people barely looked like they had enough money to buy off the dollar menu.

I scanned the room seeing the usual faces I had come to recognize these past few days. I squinted my eyes to block out the sun that seeped through the cracked door as someone was entering.

My entire body lit up. It was him. I was starting to wonder if he was ever going to show up. I knew I couldn't be the one to make the first move. He had to notice me. He had to be the one to start the conversation.

Ace took a seat at the bar with a guy that looked a lot like him, just taller and better looking. I would prefer it if he was alone but I had to take my chance. I sat up and quickly sipped my drink before standing. This place didn't bother to check for any id, they just gave me whatever I asked for.

I walked to the bar and leaned next to where Ace was sitting. I waved to get the bartenders attention.

"Whatcha want?"

"Can I just get some water this time?" She shrugged and handed me a glass of murky looking tap water. I would have much rather had a real drink but I needed to appear to have nothing.

"Water?" I glanced the direction of the voice. "Redd did you hear that shit, baby girl ordering water. Why don't you let me get you a real drink."

I shrugged, rolled my eyes and grabbed the glass to take back to my table. The short skirt I wore clung to my body. I knew if he got a glimpse he would want to follow my ass. At least I hoped he would.

"Don't I know you?" He stared at me as I sat back down at the table.

"Yeah, you tried to know me real good." The saltiness in my voice was real. That was definitely something I didn't have to fake.

"You that bitch that caused all those problems. Where your man Dro at? Last time you had that nigga fighting turning his back on his niggas and shit. That pussy must be fire."

I ignored his question. Ace sat down in the seat next to me and continued talking. "So that nigga left your ass high and dry huh? I thought y'all was playing house and shit."

"I guess not. Cause after shit popped off at his mom's he left. Now I ain't got shit. I can't go home, he's nowhere to be found."

"See you fuck with the wrong one." Again I didn't acknowledge his statement, but I knew it didn't matter to a dude like Ace. This nigga spoke for the pleasure of hearing his own voice.

"I can get you some work." He said. His lips curled into a sinister smile. "Same type of work you were supposed to be doing anyway. But I have to sample it first." Hearing him talk about touching me made my flesh crawl. Por calquier medio, by any means necessary. I could hear Gabriela's words in my mind.

"Okay, I'll do it. But I'll need a place to stay. I'm tired of sleeping on the streets. If you can handle that we can do it."

It's like he couldn't get me out of there fast enough. I followed Ace to his car I got in while he stood outside talking to the man he was with. My heart was racing. I would be lying if I said I wasn't scared but I was in way too far to try to pull out now.

Ace said goodbye to the guy and turned to get in the car. It disgusted me as I sat and listened to how he has taken every-thing from in his words, that nigga Dro, even his bitch. I slipped the prepaid phone out that Dro had given me and shot him a text.

Leaving the bar now. Stay close
Cool

I stuffed the phone back inside of my bag, hitting the button on the side to silence it. I didn't want him to figure out anything before Dro could get to me. I knew he would be staying close behind, but I was going to be alone with him for a moment.

Ace dropped into the driver's seat and we were gone. It took us no time to reach his small apartment. I stepped out looking at my surroundings. This wasn't too far from my old neighborhood, but old life seemed a million miles away from me now.

I followed him inside and threw my bag on the sofa next to where I sat.

"I'll be right back." He disappeared into a back room. I texted Dro again.

1112 Magnolia Way apt 340B
Got it

I walked over to the front door and unlocked it just before Ace walked back in the room. I turned around to face him, slowly starting to pull off the shirt I had on, exposing my bare chest. He walked over and grabbed my breast. His calloused hands rubbing against my delicate skin irritating me.

"I'm about to show you I'm that nigga you shoulda been fucking with all along." He pushed me down on the sofa and began to kiss me. Nothing like the way Dro kissed me. This was sloppy, wet, and nasty. I tilted my head back as if I wanted him to kiss my neck, but I really just wanted him to stop kissing me period.

The door slowly pushed open. Ace was so focused on trying to shove his grimy fingers between my thighs that he didn't even notice.

"Get the fuck off her nigga."

"Dro," Ace looked at me, anger setting in as he was realized he was being played.

"Did you think I was gonna let you get away with that shit."

"That bullet wasn't meant for your mom man I swear." All that shit Ace had talked now he sounded like a little boy.

"I don't give a fuck how much you swear or how sorry you are." Dro looked at me. I grabbed my shirt and put it on and stood next to him. This bitch ass piece of shit had tried to rape me, shot at me and killed Gabriela, he deserved to die.

"You set me up bitch."

"Watch your mouth." Dro barked.

"Dro man come on don't do this."

"Did I fuckin get to beg you not to do this before you put a bullet in my mother? You out here telling niggas that you took everything from me. You ain't got shit but your life nigga, so you gone pay with that motherfucker!"

A hail of bullets rained down on Ace. I'm pretty sure he was long gone after the first few shots hit him, but Dro emptied his clip. Tiny beads of blood splattered everywhere as his lifeless body hit the ground. Dro turned to face me.

"You're mine. I love you. No man will ever touch you like that, ever again." He said as he grabbed my hand and pulled me out of the apartment. I smiled as I swiftly ran behind him and jumped in his car. We sped down the road in silence. I glanced his direction.

"I love you too." Dro continued to drive. He pulled up in front of my house. I looked towards the small home, this is where I grew up, but instead of having good memories this house just mostly held pain.

"What are we doing here?"

"If I plan on marrying you, won't you need your things. Go get your identification and shit, and then we are leaving."

I nodded my head in agreement before I got out of the car. I twisted the doorknob and just as expected it was unlocked.

"What are you doing here?"

"Shouldn't you be at school?"

"Shouldn't you?" She rolled her eyes and continued flipping the channels on the tv.

"I'm getting my id and stuff. I'm leaving." I glanced at her. My sister was fourteen years old with her entire life ahead of her, but if she continued to follow my mother's lead she would be going no where. I believed I wanted so much more for her than she wanted for herself. "Maybe you can come with us." I hadn't talked to Dro but she was my sister and if it's one thing he understood it was family.

"With you? With that nigga that tried to kill mama for you? No thank you."

"Punkin, that's not how that shit went down."

"Whatever just get the fuck on. We don't need you."

I shrugged my shoulders and went to my room to get my identification, and then to my mother's room to get my birth certificate. As I walked back to the front of the house I paused. I was leaving this life behind and I was okay with that. I would never see my sister and mother again, that relieved me and broke my heart at the same time.

"Got it," I said to Dro as I got back in the car.

"Good, now let's get the hell outta here." We drove off leaving everything behind. There was nothing left for us here anymore.

SEVENTEEN

THE TIME on my clock was running out. I was down to thirty-six of the seventy-two hours that Trent gave me. Things were coming from all angles and I just needed this to be over with. I grabbed Dro's iPad and pulled up the browser. I needed to do a little bit of reconnaissance.

I typed Trent's name in the search box. I didn't know his last name or much about him. I made a mental list of the things I did know. He was from Houston. He somehow lost his port access through the port of Houston and whatever he did had to do with drugs. I typed in Trent Houston Drugs. This was a long shot but I hoped it worked. There had to be a reason that he was no longer in Houston and I bet if I dug deep enough I could find it.

The screen loaded and I was amazed how Google pulled up just what I was looking for with so little information. The first link was to the Houston Chronicle. There was an archived story. Evidently, Trent had been a high powered attorney at a firm in Houston. He was believed to be the leader of a drug cartel, but without anything more than substantial evidence he had gotten away free. His wife, Kyra Jamison, aka Dominique Simoneaux, was wanted for questioning. I googled Kyra Jamison.

The screen loaded picture after picture once I clicked on images. There were pictures of them together, separately, at formal events. This list was endless. It looks like Kyra Jamison slash Dominique Simoneaux had done well for herself. My heartbeat quickened as I became lost in the brown pools that stared back at me. She reminded me of my past.

My phone rang. I tossed the iPad to the side and reached for the vibrating phone. I quickly hit the answer button.

"Hey, Sergio."

"It's done."

Sergio had moved fast. Obviously, Andre hadn't really learned anything from Dro. If he was able to snatch him that quick he wasn't paying any attention to his surroundings.

"Keep him under lock and key. Get some of your men over there and make sure he goes nowhere. Did you find out anything on the van."

"No, not yet but I'm working on it."

"Good, I want you and about five of the other guys to meet me at Fuego. We have business."

I disconnected the call, threw my clothes back on and headed back to my car. Since Dro disappeared, my days seemed to be spent going back and forth. I needed Sergio with me just in case something got out of hand. When I was at the club earlier I counted the guys, two at the front, one near the office and Leah, the woman that had escorted me to Andre.

Racing down the highway I sped back to our club. The club that Andre thought he would so easily take. I had a lot of questions to ask him but first to handle this. When I drove away earlier I said I would be back. And I meant it.

I pulled into the entrance of the lower parking level. Sergio was waiting in front of the arm. The car door opened and he ran back to my car.

"It's not letting me in, Señora."

"I know, drive through it."

"You want me to break it."

"Yes."

Sergio nodded his head and ran back to the truck. Within seconds the large SUV was barreling through the lowered arm, ripping it from its base and tossing it yards away. I pulled in behind Sergio and parked in my usual space.

"I need all of you alert. Hands on your weapons cause we may have a problem."

I walked to the door and entered my code. As I expected it buzzed denying me access. I reached in my jacket pocket and pulled out my keys. I rarely used them because it was much easier to use the code and Andre knew that. I inserted the key and unlocked the door. He thought of changing the codes but not the lock. I shook my head and laughed. Amateur.

Leading the way, I walked down the hallway to Dro's office. No one was guarding the door. I guess they thought that changing the codes were going to be enough to keep me out. I rounded the corner with Sergio to my right. His postured read ex-military. He was a giant of a man with thick hard muscles that threatened to release themselves from the tight fabric that trapped them. The other members of his team were just as intimidating. They all followed as I stepped into the room.

"Get the fuck out of my husband's chair." She swiveled around to face me. The two men from earlier stood up obviously ready to defend her if needed.

"And who gone make me?" Tami stared at me. It angered me that she sat behind his desk like she had some place in this. She was no body and whatever hopes and dreams that Andre fed her made her believe that she was now able to call the shots.

I glanced at the papers scattered over the desk. She was going through countless amounts of our information. Our accounting ledgers, our checking accounts, savings, all of the statements were on the desk. Why was she so damn interested in our business.

I didn't even give her an answer. I just stepped to the side and allowed Sergio to enter the room. Margeaux sat to my left. She hadn't said a word to me as I came in the room. She barely made eye contact with me.

The men next to her pulled their guns out. As soon as Sergio saw the motion him and then my guys had all of their weapons drawn. I stood in the middle of a standoff. Sergio's team had brought double the weapons. With both hands raised, they stood statue still with their finger on the trigger, ready to shoot at any moment.

"You're outnumbered. Like I said, get the fuck out of my husband's chair." No one moved, which was really starting to piss me off. I kept my eyes on Tami while speaking to Margeaux.

"Call them off Margeaux. If you don't you already know how this is going to play out. There will be a bullet in you and her before they can even get a shot off."

Margeaux hurriedly spoke to them, I didn't understand exactly what she said because it wasn't in English but they both dropped their weapons. I threw Tami another glance and she finally started to stand up.

"You should have stayed behind the bar, you don't know what you've gotten yourself into."

"No, more like you have no idea who you are messing with." She responded. I called Sergio over and whispered my orders to him. I would deal with her later.

"Margeaux, I want your men out of my club. I don't know what the hell you were thinking, or why you even decided to try this shit with Andre."

"I —"

"No, I talk you listen." I cut my eyes toward Margeaux. "Give us the room, please. I need to catch up with my old friend. Remind her of a few things."

Dro and I drove almost nonstop to reach Miami. We had been here for almost a month and we were just trying to get things setup. His cousin Julian kept pushing us to get things together, but Dro kept explaining to him that we had to take our time and make sure that it's right.

I rested my head on Dro's chest. I twisted the ring on my left hand from right to left. I couldn't believe we had done it. After leaving with Dro that day everything had moved so fast. And now we were married. The way I felt about this man should be illegal, I had never known I could love so deep. To think that of how we started and where we were now floored me.

"Good morning, it's almost time for my class." I kissed Dro and sat up on the bed.

As soon as we got here the first thing we did was make it official, the next thing was to enroll me in school. I took the test to get my GED and I was now picking up some college courses.

Dro and I agreed that if we were going to work with his cousin and build a business, the number of people we brought into it had to be the bare minimum. He had learned from working with Ace that some people can't be trusted. The less people involved the better.

I wanted to know every aspect of the business. The numbers, the logistics and that's why I was taking classes. I was going to learn everything I could about business and accounting. I would make our books look as clean as possible. So when we moved money it looked legit.

I didn't want to live like we did before, with violence all around us and greedy understudies like Ace trying to take his place. We didn't want another situation like with Gabriela, what *we would require was loyalty before everything and if you couldn't meet that, then you couldn't be here.*

"Can you drop me off today. I want you to talk to this guy Andre."

"Andre? You sure he just some nigga from school, you ain't creeping around on me are you?" I laughed but the look on Dro's face told me he was dead serious.

"Alejandro!"

"Well,"

"No, you know you got every part of me."

He seemed satisfied with my answer. I would never even think about another man. Dro was mine and I was his. I would never even dream of telling him that Andre had made more than a few advances towards me.

"So what you think this nigga can bring to the table."

"Well, I've noticed he is crazy smart. This dude can legit create and hack anything. I was thinking he can handle the back-end. We can't just auction women off. We need to do it in a way that's untraceable. The way I see it, we could hire him, just to build a system for us. He doesn't even have to know what he's really doing it for."

Dro shook his head in agreement. We had to get established. Neither one of us knew much about Miami what we didn't know we would learn. I jumped up from the bed to get ready for class.Once we got to my school. Dro parked and I got out. I leaned into the open window.

"I'm going to go find him."

I headed towards the building hoping I didn't have to walk this entire campus to find him. I finally spotted him heading towards the science wing.

"Andre, wait up."

"What's up Khari, finally come to your senses and gone leave that old ass nigga you with for me?"

"What I tell you, he ain't old and that nigga is my husband now cut that shit out." I stepped back. He was always in my personal space. I didn't completely trust him because only a shady nigga tried to come at another man's woman, but I knew it was nothing Dro couldn't handle.

"I can't talk to him now. My cousin just texted me said she needed me over here. I gotta find her."

"No, I'll go help her out, you go talk to Dro. This could be good for you, I know you're having a hard time paying your tuition and running for your cousin ain't gonna get you paid like this can. Go. He's parked in the front, you know what our car looks like right."

"Yeah I remember, my cousin is downstairs in room 506."

"Got it."

I headed towards the hall and found the room she was in. I pulled at the door but it was locked. I knocked.

"Margeaux, it's Khari, open the door. Andre sent me."

"No, tell my cousin to get his ass down here."

"He can't now Margeaux, that's why I'm here." She opened the door, but stood in the entrance not wanting to let me through.

"Margeaux, let me in. What's going on?" The lights in the room were off. I pushed my way pass her and entered the room. I took two steps back. There was a lifeless body sprawled across the ground.

"Is he breathing."

"No."

"What happened?"

"He was trying to push up on me, dat fat motherfucka was trying to rape me." Her eyes were filled with fire. "I pushed him back and he fell against the counter."

"What are you even doing back here with him?"

"He's a customer, he shovels so much coke up his nose I'm surprised it still works."

I analyzed the scene. I could tell she was nervous and this

looked bad. I turned around to get a look at the hallway. There were no cameras on this hall. No one down here, no one saw me come in.

"Did anyone see you down here?"

"No, you know I know better than that."

"Good. Listen we don't have a lot of time. And there is no way we can move this body or hide it."

"Khari what?"

"Margeaux, stop and listen." Because I saw this I could very well look like an accomplice I didn't have time to answer her questions. "Did you touch anything?"

"No. Not that I can remember." I hoped she was right for her sake.

"Did he take a bump?"

"Several."

"We just gonna make it look like he was getting high and slipped that's it end of story."

Margeaux looked at me confused. I understood her mind wasn't moving as fast as mine at this moment but we needed to get out of here.

"Wipe that bag down as good as you can, then spill it." She tossed the white powdered substance around his body. I scanned the room to make sure nothing was out of place. Nothing seemed too out of place. I motioned for her to come on and we ran out of the room letting the door close and lock behind us.

The hallway was empty as she followed me up the stairs in the back of the hall. We slipped out of the door and into the crowd of people as if we had been there all along. My heartbeat was starting to slow down.

"Thank you." I nodded and then looked her way. My mind was still working double time.

"Don't your girl work security at the port?" I knew the answer to my own question. We needed a connection at the Port of Miami to get the containers Dro's cousin was sending from Barranquilla, Columbia. Everything was a go on Julian's end, but we needed a way to get them into Miami and I believe I've stumbled across my access.

"Yeah, why?" She said puzzled. I smiled to myself. Everything was falling into place. All we had needed was a way in.

EIGHTEEN

I WALKED around the desk and sat in the chair. Margeaux watched me without speaking while I gathered the papers and placed them back in the desk drawer. Tami had no business going through our things and it bothered me that Andre had given her open access to all of that information we normally kept under lock and key.

"Margeaux, what's this all about."

"It's just business."

"You know me better than that. It's never just business, you cross the line, it makes it personal."

"Andre is family, I've been trying to do business with Dro for years, do you know how much business we can do in this club alone."

"But you knew we didn't do the drug thing. He told you that time and time again."

"Yeah, but as we can see, he ain't here now which makes Andre in charge."

"Wrong, he's not here right now so that makes me in charge. Andre always did have it twisted."

"You played with my cousin's head, all that damn flirting and shit you did with him, he would have done anything you wanted him to. I'm glad he finally stood up to that nigga Dro and you."

"You sure that's how you want to play this?"

She sat back in her seat and didn't say anything else. Good, because I was going to be the one to have the last word.

"Unless you want to end up like your cousin, I suggest you fall back."

"What does that mean?"

"What I just said. I didn't stutter. Besides, we both know you're only loyal to your cousin when you want to be. You just saw him as a way in, you seem to have forgotten that you at one time wanted his spot."

"That's only because you promised to bring me in."

"I never promised you anything. I've always held the upper hand."

"That was a long time ago, I paid my debt with you when I hooked up at the port. Then you dropped my ass and put Andre on."

"Our business was done. I should have you killed, or worse, report your ass, there's no statute of limitations on murder. How would it look, big bad Margeaux couldn't even handle her shit. I could have left you in that room alone holding a murder charge but I helped you."

"And I helped you. And never made a dime off of it."

"A jail free life should have been payment enough." Margeaux was salty. I could tell by the look on her face she harbored a hidden hatred for us. I was tired of going back and forth with her. I wanted to get straight to the point. Working with a man like Trent could be a trap and if I I had to team up with him, I wasn't going to be forced into blindly handing over the keys to the kingdom. He would have to work with me and pay me a percentage. The more people I could connect with him the better our percentage.

"I have a proposition for you. Until Dro is found I have to make some hard decisions and a lot a shit is on the line. I can't run my business and bring the money in like we have been doing if Trent wants complete control of our shipments. I'm not giving him that." Margeaux leaned in, listening intently. I continued. "But if I can build a big enough team I can have protection against him." Trent showing up in my home, and threatening to kill me taught me he was not a man to be trusted. "I don't know him so I can't trust him, I don't trust you but you know I will have you placed six feet under if you even think about double crossing me again."

"So what do you need from me?" She asked.

"Your crew."

"My crew?"

"Yes, your people will answer to my security team. If they so much as make one wrong move you know what that means for you." I hated having to expand like this and I definitely hated having to return again to violence but desperate times called for desperate actions. If I wanted to gain control over everything I would have to proactively act. And get things done by any means.

"Why would I agree to that?"

"First of all, you still owe me. Secondly, this can be good for you too. In exchange, I'm about to connect you with someone who can help you step the quality of your product up. This can change everything for you.

I leaned back in my chair. I planned on staying five moves ahead at all times. Trent is vulnerable now. But as soon as he is able to reconnect and open those distribution channels again, he would be damn near unstoppable. A man like Trent didn't stop at just getting back on track. I could tell he was a man used to running things and I knew he would have to be watched and we would have to be prepared if he ever decided he wanted war.

NINETEEN

THE LOUD MUSIC thumped through the speakers throughout the club. Business had to continue as usual. I stood in the hallway watching my surroundings. The same spot that Dro normally stood in as I walked through the club. My heart skipped several beats at the mere thought of him.

Sergio crossed the room in my direction. He must have news. I hoped so because time was winding up. I had to make sure everything was going to fall in place. Dro wouldn't be happy about the move I was about to make when I finally got him back, but I hoped that he would understand that nothing I did was ever done without him in mind. Anything I've ever done since the moment I fell for him has been for him, for us.

"I did like you asked." Sergio said.

"And?" I leaned in struggling to hear him over the loud music.

"My contact got back to me. We found out some crazy info." Sergio handed me the phone showing me the information. I read over all of it.

"Where is she?" I asked passing the phone back to him.

"In the back."

I headed downstairs with Sergio following closely behind. Ever since Dro hired him, I knew I could trust him. He was never like Andre or any of the others we could only let so far in. I trusted him with my life and believed he would gladly lay down his for mine. Otherwise, there is no way I would trust him with half of the stuff he did for us. His ex-military background and Dominican upbringing made him one tough ass dude.

"She's in here, Señora." Sergio reached and opened the door for me. I walked in the dark room. Boxes of liquor, supplies, and water lined the walls. This back office was mostly used for storage. I hit the light switch and watched her face contort from the bright light flooding the dark room. I pulled a chair from the corner and sat down in front of her.

Her eyes stared back at me. She was a beautiful woman. I could see how Andre was completely fooled by her. Knowing what I now knew, Dro and I were completely within reason not to trust her.

"Why are you here Special Agent Amina Viera?" She didn't respond. The defiance in her eyes told me I'd have to work to get the answers I needed from her.

"That's okay. You don't have to say a word cause I got your ass. Let me tell you what I do know. You transferred from Houston, Texas. You're only supposed to be working a drug case that has nothing to do with my club. What are you now? Something like a rogue agent?"

She didn't so much as blink. She gave no physical indicators of whether the information I had been given was true or false. But I knew that Sergio's contacts were solid. Once those plates came back as government it wasn't hard to trace the who and where. Besides for a federal agent she had to be stupid. She was seen on camera that night with the girls. And she was here without any type of backup.

"So I'm going to ask you one more time, Amina Viera, why are you here and where the hell are my girls? And what have you done with my husband?"

Tami thrust her chin in the air and stared at me vehemently. Strapped to the chair she was completely immobilized. I told her earlier she had no idea what she has gotten herself into. I believed in her mind she thought there was a way out. I was going to get an answer to my question, and I didn't plan on waiting all day for it to happen.

I nodded in Sergio's direction. He stepped forward and flipped the chair she was sitting in backward. The metal chair crashed to the ground, shooting her legs straight into the air and her head back against the hard floor.

Sergio was silent as he went to work. I stared down at her on the floor. She twitched and turned trying to force herself free. He swiftly stood over her grabbing a bottle of water before straddling her and cradling her head between his feet. He had become some type of human vice. She couldn't move left or right.

Fear flashed in her eyes but she still said nothing. Sergio glanced at me for approval. I nodded and he kicked in to gear, putting his special ops military training to use. The water streamed from the bottle and splashed in her face none stop. Her mouth flew open, struggling and gasping for air as if she was drowning.I raised my hand and he stopped.

"You ready to talk now?" She again said nothing. "Tami, I'm sorry Agent Viera, I do not have all day."

Her eyes cut towards me and then she tightly pressed her lips together. I nodded at Sergio and he went to work. This time he poured down even more water. She wailed and coughed trying to expel the water from her airways but it was no use. Her legs moved back and forth as she began to shake.

"Okay, okay." She tried to speak through gurgled breaths. Sergio looked at me and I nodded. He stepped from over her and flipped the chair to the right, causing the water that had just evaded her nostrils to spill onto the floor.

"Breathe," Sergio said while still tilting the chair to the side. After she started to regain her breath, he sat the chair back up and she was again facing me. I looked down at her, trying to control the sly smile that threatened to spread across my face.

"You ready to talk? Or do you want more water?" She started to shake her head yes. Like I told her, she had no idea what she stepped into. I dropped back into the chair in front of her and waited for her to start."Talk."

"I was assigned to infiltrate Margeaux's crew. She's responsible for a lot of movement in Miami."

"That still doesn't explain why you are in my club."

"My way to get close to her was Andre. The job here was just part of my cover so that I could get close to him. But when I saw Trent Jamison here, I followed that lead. He's wanted back in Texas and you obviously have some type of connection to him. Then I saw what you guys were into, trafficking. I couldn't have hit a bigger jackpot."

The inflection in her voice told me she wanted to be some type of super cop. It sounded like she actually got off on trying to take all of us down.

"What is your connection to Trent?" She got quiet again. Sergio stepped forward and she quickly started to speak again.

"I was over the task force in charge of infiltrating and investigating his organization, but he got away. They both did." Her voice trailed off as she tilted her head down. There was defeat in her voice and a few holes in her story. She was over the task force the person in charge takes the fall. Had she taken the fall for Trent's escape?

It sounded like there was some major fuck up somewhere in this story on her part. Seemed like was trying to redeem herself. That's why she was trying so hard to bring us all down. She bit off a little bit more than she could chew.

"And what about my husband? Do you know where he is?"

"I had nothing to do with that. Best I can tell he has voluntarily disappeared."

"Where are my girls?"

"They are safe."

"Where are they?" This was all happening because I have somehow let them get out of my sight. So much was going on that the night Dro disappeared. I was responsible for their safety and I failed them. I wanted them to be free but not like this. Being stuck with the feds wouldn't be freedom, as soon as they got what they needed I'm sure they would be deported.

"Back at my apartment. ICE will get them once you guys are arrested, and they will be deported."

"You somehow think that you still have a way to win this?" I laughed at her arrogance. She had no backup. If she did they would have been here by now. She wasn't even supposed to be working this case, we weren't a case at all and if she disappears then any evidence of what we have done also disappears with her. I turned to Sergio.

"I want you to get the girls. Get the passports out of my office and give them their freedom. Put them in a hotel for now, and if they want jobs here tell them they have it but we don't own them. If they don't want to work here I will give them money to start there lives. But they are free." I was finally happy to put that part of our lives in the past.

TWENTY

I STARED at my phone sitting on the desk as I swiveled back and forth. It was time to make the call. I grabbed my cell phone and dialed the number on the card Trent gave me when he came at me in my home. Now I felt like everything I knew gave me the upper hand to deal with him.

"This is Trent." His voice was as calm and cool as always.

"Trent, it is time to talk."

"Good choice," he laughed. He was one arrogant asshole but we would see who had the last laugh.

"Can you meet me at my club in an hour? There are some things I want to discuss. And bring your wife, she seems to be apart of your organization. I would like to meet her."

Trent didn't question the how are the whys of my request. He assured me that he would be here within the next hour. That's was just enough time to make sure everything was in place. I didn't trust Trent to show up by himself. He hadn't shown up last time by himself. This time I would be more than ready.

I called Sergio giving him instructions to put security

throughout the club, now that Margeaux's guys were with us that more than doubled the size of our security team. I wasn't trying to start a war, but I definitely wanted him to feel our power.

I sat in the office waiting for Trent to be escorted back to Dro's office. When he first approached us I was felt this may not be such a bad idea, now I felt like I was about to make a deal with the devil.

My phone buzzed with a text from Sergio.

He's here

It was show time. I waited the short time for Sergio to walk them in. There was a soft knock at the door. I stood behind the desk, nervous. I smoothed my clothes down. If anyone could pull this off I could.

"Come in."

Sergio walked in and took his place behind me. I dropped my head to conceal the smile that was trying to emerge. I quickly got it together and looked up at the couple as they entered the room.

She walked a few steps behind him, to his right. Her eyes did a complete three-sixty before landing on me. Nothing about her expression told me she expected or knew anything.

"Have a seat please," they both took a seat in the chairs in front of my desk. Trent settled into the seat as she leaned in close to him, softly touching his knee while never taking her eyes off of me. It appeared she was just as down for her husband as I was for mine. She seemed just as cocky as him. He spoke first.

"I see you finally decided to take my offer."

"I haven't decided anything yet."

"You don't have much of a choice"

"I have all the choices in the world. Make me your best offer."

I walked from around the desk and took a seat on the edge. I needed them both to know just how serious I was. I wasn't going to take some lowball deal and I had enough of everybody trying to fuck me over just because Dro wasn't here.

"Your life should be enough." Trent sat forward in his seat. Finally, I got his attention.

"I don't see it like that, you kill me you have to start all over. Not to mention when Dro finds out you won't have to worry about making any deals from six feet under. That got his attention.

Trent stared at me. His eyes as cold as ice. It shook me a little bit but I wasn't at all going to back down. I knew who he was. I know he was something like a big deal but so was I. And what I had realized over these past few days is that he can't be shit if can't get his drugs in.

"Let's try it again, make me an offer."

Trent whispered something to her and I watched as she typed something across the screen of her phone and held it up. I stared at the screen and almost laughed aloud. He needs me. Needs us.

I stood up. Adrenaline filled nerves bounced around my body. It was the moment that a hunter went in for the kill. When you knew you were about to take that one shot, and attacking your unsuspecting prey leaving it helpless.

"That's an insult. Five hundred thousand is not enough, I clear a million on my own. Even though I had no intentions of continuing I didn't want to let him know that.

"That's my offer."

"Your offer isn't good enough."

I looked at the both of them. He looked a little surprised that he wasn't getting sweet demure Khari. His wife squinted her eyes as if she was trying to read me. I glanced back at Sergio giving him the signal. He left the room. I turned my attention back to them.

"Look, I'm not going back and forth with you. If you want access this is what I want. Firstly, I want thirty percent of the street value of whatever you are bringing in. If you want access to what we have worked hard to establish you're going to pay for it."

I could tell by the look on his face, he wasn't happy with my offer. I didn't care that wasn't going to stop me.

I continued.

"Secondly, I can help you increase your territory. Yeah, I know you have your own but this is Miami not Texas. Right now Margeaux has all of Little Haiti and much of Miami on lock. They won't do shit without her approval." I had embellished her reputation just a bit but I needed him to buy what I was selling. I wanted him off of my ass and the best way was to make a deal. Best way to know what my enemy was up to was to keep them close. If I can make this deal then I could accomplish that with both Margeaux and Trent.

"And besides we are family." I glanced at her sitting in that chair. All grown up but she still was the spitting image of our mama.

"What the hell are you talking about," She looked at me disgusted that I would even insinuate that we could be related. The moment I started to research Trent and her name and picture popped up I knew it was her.

"Punkin."

"Don't call me that." She stood to her feet, looking much like that fourteen-year-old I had left behind. Defiant. Angry. Misguided. I honestly never thought I would see her again. I was hoping this added bonus would be a little more insurance for myself and Dro. I really didn't know how I felt about reconnecting with her. I had done everything in my past to protect her and she never cared.

"What's going on?" Trent asked.

"She never told you she had a sister? I'm guessing if I remember correctly my sister isn't exactly the most forthcoming with things. She's a little sneaky." I laughed. She was.

"Bitch I don't have a sister." She yelled. "You died that day when you left with that nigga."

"Watch it, that nigga is now my husband."

"Let's get out of here. I don't have anything to say to this bitch." Trent didn't move.

"Dominique sit your ass down. You still act like the same little girl from years ago. Besides, I'm not done." I walked over and opened the door. Sergio was standing outside as instructed with Tami. He pushed her into the room her hands and mouth still bound.

"My last surprise." I couldn't stop my smile from spreading this time. "Look what I found." They both looked at her in disbelief. Trent turned to face Dominique.

"I thought you took care of this. What the hell is she doing here?"

"I haven't talked to her, I swear. I don't...I don't...don't know." There was definitely a bigger story than I knew there. I cleared my throat to interrupt their back and forth. That was something they could sort out on their own time.

"I know this is the Fed that almost brought you down before. Let's deal or I turn her ass loose on you."

"That's just as bad for you if you let her loose."

"She would have to find me first. Just make the deal Trent. We can work together, get money and no one will ever have to know this agent even existed."

Trent stepped back looking at Tami and then at Dominique. He was visibly angry. I understood I knew what it was like to be pushed in a corner. I myself had been pushed in the corner, but I had learned to claw my way out of any situation.

"Fine," He extended his hand for me to shake to close the deal. "What are you doing with her?"

"I'll hang on to her for safe keeping. Thank you, we will be in touch with instructions for your shipments. And it looks as if you guys have a lot to talk about. We'll catch up later sister." I smiled as I walked to the door and opened it. It was time for them to go. This meeting was done.

TWENTY-ONE

TONIGHT HAD BEEN EXHAUSTING. I walked into my house and set the alarm. I kicked my heels off and stood in the center of the floor staring at the large ceiling to floor painting that hung on the wall.

My body shook as I walked towards the painting. With everything that I had to do to get to this point, none of it seemed as big as this moment. I slid the painting along the hidden track exposing the small wall fingerprint scanner.

My hand trembled as it connected with the tiny screen. I held as still as I could, waiting for it to flash the green light. Once the print was accepted I could hear the locks clicking. I stepped back and allowed the reinforced door to slide open.

I peered into the small room we had built with the house. The room was stocked with a small bed, bathroom, microwave, fridge, and food. It was a room built for our protection in case we ever experienced any of the same threats we had encountered back home.

I was silent, waiting for him to realize I was there. He turned around as the door fully opened.

"Khari." He stared at me in disbelief.

"Alejandro," I said softly as my eyes pooled. None of this had been easy I just hoped he could forgive me.

"Why? Why am I in here?" He walked towards me his chest heaving with anger. "I've been trying to use my fingerprint and code to get out of here for I don't know how long. What the hell is going on?"

In the beginning, Dro scared me. Now the only thing that scared me was the fact that after this he wouldn't be by my side. I believed he would stand with me that our love would be strong enough to withstand this.

I stepped back as he started to step out of the room. I hadn't yet found the right words to speak so I said nothing. The conversation had played over and over in my head yet it was the only thing I wasn't prepared for.

"Khari! Talk to me. What's going on?"

I flinched with the rise and fall of his voice. "I told you I didn't want to traffic women anymore."

"What the hell does that have to do with you locking me in the safe room? I've been sitting in the fucking room, worried about you. Wondering why I'm here and what happened to you. I was going crazy. ¿Que mierda?"

I knew when he started cursing in Spanish he was pissed. I needed to explain this. I needed to make this right.

"I changed the codes and deactivated your fingerprint. It wasn't supposed to be that long, things got out of hand."

"What things? You still haven't explained to me what the fuck was I doing in there and why you would do that shit to me."

He stood in front of me, his eyes widened in disbelief. He wanted answers.

"Talk Khari!"

"Por cualquier medio. Like Gabriela always said. By any means necessary." He stood staring at me in silence. I knew he was trying to process what was happening. I continued to speak. "Lo siento mi amor. I am sorry I truly am. I never wanted any of this to get out of hand. I only saw it beneficial to do a deal with Trent."

"With Trent? You doing deals with that nigga behind my back. What the fuck?" He threw his hands up in the air.

"Wait let me explain." I touched his arm and he jerked away. I was caught off guard by his action. My touch always seemed to soothe him but it appeared to do nothing in this moment.

"How can you explain this?"

"Dro you could only see the money. You couldn't see our body count steadily rising. You didn't know about doc trying to blackmail us. You weren't even seeing Andre trying to push his way into your position. This was all happening. I was only trying to protect us."

Tears rolled down my cheeks, I was a mess and he was the one thing that could make it right. I continued talking. "Alejandro, look at me. I did this for us. It was never supposed to be this long. Never supposed to get as out of hand but it did. You were always safe here with me."

"Who helped you do this to me?" He clenched his teeth and pounded his hand against the wall. "Who is he?"

"There is no he. No one helped me. I wouldn't do that. I drugged you with the tranquilizers Dr. Monroe kept at the house. I actually drugged everyone so there would be no witnesses to what I was doing. And I was the one that got you in the house. It was hard and I didn't know how long the sedative would last. I pulled the car in the garage, put you in an office chair and rolled you into the room. No one knows about this and no one ever has to know about this." He turned his head to the side and eyed me up and down.

"So what did you do?" His tone slightly calmer than before.

"Trent accepted my terms. He threatened to kill us if we

didn't go along with his plan, so I persuaded Margeaux to work for us under Sergio's direction to build our security up, and I told him we wouldn't bring his shit in for anything less than thirty percent of the street value." I lifted my chin. I was proud of what I had accomplished. I just didn't want it to be at the expense of our marriage. "And we had another problem. That little pushy bitch that kept showing up with Andre was a fed. I shut that shit down too." I gave him the short version of what had happened. I would completely fill him in later but right now I just wanted his forgiveness.

"Sometimes you're so much like her it's scary." By her, I knew he meant Gabriela.

"I'll take that as a compliment." A weak smile spread across my face. I moved towards him. I hadn't felt my husband's arms around me in a week, even though it felt more like months. I pressed my body into him as I always did. I could hear the beat of his heart as I lay my head on his chest. He pushed me back and stared down at me.

"It's not going to be that easy Khari. I'll forgive you but you're gonna have to give me time." He tried to push me away but I wasn't going anywhere. I thrust my body into his. Pulling him into me, finding his lips. I kissed him with a desperate intensity, I needed him to know just how sorry I was.

He didn't react at first, but then he pulled me in and kissed me back. Biting my lower lip and then kissing away the pain. My ass smashed into the back of the sofa as Dro pushed me back, ripping my skirt from around my body and exposing my lace panties. He flipped me around and shoved my body down against the sofa. His forceful aggressive nature told me he needed to take control of this situation. He entered me and my body trembled with anticipation. I molded to him as always, he was the only man I had ever been with. The only man I ever wanted to be with. With each stroke he pushed me close to ecstasy and then pulled me back. His strokes were long and deep.

Feeling him inside me excited me causing me to drip with desire. I knew Dro was an alpha man, he needed to feel in charge and I had taken that away. I had hunted without his permission and he was going to show me who was in charge. I pushed back to meet his stroke, taking him in deeper and deeper.

"Don't ...ever...do...that...shit...again!" He yelled through angry strokes. "Say it! Tell me."

"I won't ever baby, ever again," I said. I knew this was angry I'm so mad I want to hit you sex, but I also knew I hadn't lost my husband, and I would take my punishment, stroke by stroke.

TWENTY-TWO

"BABY," I said to Dro. We were lying on the floor out of breath and overwhelmed. One thing we couldn't deny was our love and attraction for one another. I wanted to be forever lost in our moment but there were some things that needed to be completed. Dro turned to face me waiting for me to continue.

What Andre had done I knew would be unforgivable in Dro's eyes. I felt somewhat responsible for all of it. I had been the one to introduce the two, I had not said anything to Dro about the way that Andre was always trying to flirt with me. I was the one that had put us in this position to almost be overtaken by the opposition. I realized after that day at the club, these were feelings that Andre harbored for us for a long time.

"I have something for you. Let's shower and get dressed and I'll show you."

Dro looked at me apprehensively. I know it's going to be hard for him to trust me as he did but I would never act without us in mind. I was willing to work to show him that I was sorry. I would start by letting him know everything that had been going on and giving him back the ability to handle those things like the king he was.

We got showered and dressed and headed to the car. I started it up and pulled out of our garage while Dro sat silently, undoubtedly trying to figure out where we were going. I broke the silence.

"Baby, I think its better no one knows it was me." I never wanted anyone to know about this. We would always be just as united as we ever were, but our opposition wouldn't see it like that. They would see this as a crack in our foundation, they would never understand.

"No shit."

"While you were gone..."

"Oh is that what the fuck we calling it now? Gone?" He was definitely still mad.

"I am sorry."

"I know." He softened. "Go on."

"Andre tried a lot of shit, he tried to come on to me. After I pulled your gun on him for doing that disrespectful shit, he tried to take over the club." It was imperative that I give him all the details. I know Dro would come to understand that this was protection, not vengeance. I loved him, I hadn't lied to him before, and I wasn't going to start now. "No, he didn't try, he did. Actually kicked me out of our club."

"He did what? I knew that nigga always wanted you." He shook his head. "He always wanted everything we had."

"He did and for a minute he thought he was gonna take it. But you know I would never let that happen." We were getting close. I stopped talking and continued driving.

"What are we doing here?" He said as I pulled into the driveway. "Is there a problem with the girls too?" I hadn't told him about the losing the girls. Instead of trying to ease him into it I decided to just rip the band-aid off and just get straight to it.

"No, I let the girls go."

"You what?" His eyes got bigger. He couldn't believe what I was saying.

"Well, actually the fed got a hold of them I got them back and then let them go. Baby, I will have to tell you the rest of the story, right now let's handle this. Look in the glove compartment." Dro reached in and pulled out the gun, and dropped it into his pants. I knew how he liked to be prepared. I didn't know how he planned to handle tonight but if it was through violence so be it, then hopefully we could move past all of this, get back to us and leave the violent shit for someone else.

We exited the car and walked into the house. It was completely quiet. That was one of the reasons it was chosen. The room was dimly lit. Two of Sergio's men sat on the sofa guarding our two hostages.

"Dro, you're back." They both stood when he walked into the room. I whispered to Dro and he gave them the order.

"Yeah, I'm back. Tell Sergio to get the other one from the club and bring her back here. You guys can go."

They left out and I looked up at Dro. He stared down at the two bound bodies. They were completely bound, gagged and blindfolded. Dro walked over to Andre first and snatched the blindfold from around his eyes. Andre jumped back in surprise. He had been so sure that Dro had left me.

"I hear you got a little rogue." Dro ripped the gag from his mouth.

"Hey man, you're back." Andre pretended to be happy to see Dro. "Man y'all got it wrong let me out of these things man."

"I ain't letting you out of shit. Is it true you climbed into my bed? Onto my wife?"

"Naw man, I ain't done no shit like that. I would never. I know how crazy you are for her."

"So you saying she's a liar?"

"No, I'm saying shit didn't happen like that. That's all."

"I believe it did. I also believe her when she told me that you tried to take my money and my club. Let me get this straight. You tried to steal my wife, my money and my club."Andre eyed me angrily and then back at Dro.

"Y'all on some crazy obsession type bullshit. I don't want that bitch or your club. Fuck your club." Andre was trying to grow a pair. "Besides my cousin will find you and take care of both y'all asses. Do what you have to." Andre rolled his eyes and looked away. Did he really think his cousin was going to come in and save the day?

"Your cousin works for me now. So now what the fuck you gone do?"

"Man, Dro you don't have to do this. This crazy man. I've worked for you for years."

"Right and then you betrayed me. You should know me well enough to know that I don't like thieves. There is only one way I handle thieves." Dro raised the gun to Andre's head. He began to cry and drool all over himself. Maybe he was right, maybe Dro and I did obsess over one another and I was completely okay with that.

"Don't do it! Don't!" Andre shook his head from left to right. I glanced at Dr. Monroe. She shook in fear. Her body trembling as she released muffled sounds through her gag.

Dro lifted the gun and released the trigger. The bullet flew through the chamber and right into Andre. I didn't even look away. I had seen this before. Maybe too many times. Andre had crossed us and the only way to deal with a snake was to chop it off at the head. If you don't, it might slither in and bite your ass. Dro turned his attention to the doctor. He had no questions for her at all.

"I can't stand a greedy motherfucker." He said as he released another bullet into her chest. She hadn't even gotten a chance to plead her case. I stared down at their lifeless bodies. Now two of our three threats were gone.

I looked at my phone to get the time. I checked my text messages to see if I had any missed messages and then calls. There was nothing. I was starting to get a little worried. Sergio should have been here by now. Just as I started to call him he came racing into the house.

"Dro, I'm glad you're back." He said. He seemed frantically rushed. "What happened?"

"He happened," Dro motioned towards Andre's dead body. "But I took care of it."

Sergio's eyes scanned the scene for a moment and then turned his attention back to us. He dismissed what he saw as if it was nothing. His eyes were a little crazed and tiny beads of sweat had started to form along his temples. Something wasn't right.

"I'm sorry." Sergio paused for a moment. "I went back like you told me to bring the fed lady. When I got back to the club she was gone."

"Gone, what do you mean gone?"

"She wasn't there Señora, I had her tied up. There is no way she could have gotten out without help."

"Then let's find her," Dro said. "Find her ass and put her at the bottom of the ocean right next to these two."

EPILOGUE

THEY SAT in the quiet car, both of them scared to break the deafening silence. The anger that swelled in him was like a rising tide, threatening to overtake him at any moment. She was at a lost for words, being confronted by her past with both her sister and the woman that had somehow infiltrated her tough hard exterior.

The moments of her past replayed over and over in her mind. Her husband never knew how many times her thoughts would revert to Michelle or Amina or whoever she was this time around. She didn't want it to be true, but that woman had gotten under her skin.

The minutes on the clock ticked on as they continued to sit in silence. They would never admit it but the turn of events had scared the hell out of them both. What was supposed to be an easy takeover turned into an all out fight. It was a head to head competition and they both hated the fact that they were losing.

His eyes shifted towards his wife. The woman that he spent countless years with but questioned if he knew her at all. He finally dared to break the silence.

"I thought you said she was taken care of. Have you been in

contact with her?" This federal agent had been a thorn in their side and had completely turned their lives upside down. They barely escaped her once and the fact that she was back infuriated him. Not to mention he hated knowing that somehow this woman occupied a small space in her heart that should have only been reserved for him. If it was just sex he could get over that. He knew his wife, but with knowing his wife he understood that somehow this woman had gotten much more out of her.

"Of course I haven't. I didn't know about any of this."

He paused for a moment wanting to choose his next words carefully. They made a promise to one another to be truthful, full disclosure as she had put it, but now it seemed that she harbored even more secrets than she did before.

He tried to dismiss the thoughts. Could he really be surprised? Their entire relationship was built on a shaky mound of mystery, manufactured by the both of them.

"Since when do you have a sister?"

"I stop having a sister the day she left. The day she told me everything would be okay and it wasn't."

"Did you know she was here?"

"No, she was dead to me. I seriously haven't talked to her in years."

He stared at her as she faced him with her eyebrows connecting. He tried to figure out why he didn't believe her. He wanted to trust her but past events had taught him to tread cautiously when it came to his wife and the truth.

Every word that tumbled from her lips was true. Her sister had left her that night and built a life with that man. The man that attempted to kill their mother.

Memories from that night flooded her mind. She believed her sister when she said everything would be okay. She watched with amazed eyes as her sister rushed away to save her mother and her heart broke when she walked out the door.

"Can we trust your sister?" Trent interrupted her thoughts asking the question that was at the back of both of their minds.

"Have you been listening? Hell no we can't trust her. You don't know my sister like I do. She is cunning, manipulative. The day she left she was supposed to be saving my mother, but I honestly believed she did it to escape our home."

Sure her sister had pretended she was doing something great, for all of them but it was for her. Because her sister had to leave she was forced to step up. Her mother made her turn tricks to support them at the age of fourteen. She was angry with her sister and blamed her for the vile and disgusting things she was forced to do in her absence.

"We need to find out just what Michelle knows. Or whatever her name is." She watched him stare out into the moonlit sky. She knew the answers weren't up there. Dominique was ready to act. True to her nature, she was not going to be beaten at her own game.

"Seriously, are you listening?" She turned to Trent.

"Yes, and how do you suppose we do that. It's not like your sister is just going to let us question her."

"My sister doesn't have to *let* us do anything. I need you to remember who the fuck you are. You wouldn't ask permission, you would take that shit. So let's take it."

Trent looked at his wife, marveling in the way her mind worked. He knew the wheels were spinning at this very moment. She had just called her sister manipulative but wondered if they may have been more of the same than she knew. His lips spread into an ominous smirk. He pulled his wife in close and kissed her lips, in love with everything about her cunning mind.

"What's your plan?"

"I think we need to get inside and get her out of there. Once we do that we can question her away from here. I don't trust my sister to take care of it. I believe she would keep this woman locked away to use against us the moment she feels she is not getting her way. She's already asking for thirty percent just for facilitating transport. What do you think she's going to do when she wants more, or when her husband wants more?"

Trent sat back and considered her words. She was right. The only way to know what was going on with the fed was to take care of it themselves.

"So how do we get in." I spotted security all the way around the building."

"All around the building except in the offices. I didn't spot anyone else downstairs. We know Khari left because we saw her leave and we saw the one guy she seems to cling to for security leave too. Let me go in and find Michelle, you stay in back and be ready to go once I get her out."

He questioned if this was something she could do. He thought about the last time they worked together on the same page. They were an unstoppable team. Realizing that, he had no doubt his wife could pull this off.

"Okay, be quick and be careful. If you're not out in fifteen minutes I'm coming in." She leaned in and kissed his cheek without saying another word.

Trent watched as she stepped out the car and headed to the front of the club. She looked calm, like a woman in complete control. What he didn't know was on the inside her nerves did flips.

Once she was completely out of view, Trent pulled the car around to the back, cautiously eyeing his surroundings to be sure there was still no security in the back. He entered in the parking garage having no trouble getting through. The arm that would normally allow him entrance was broken and thrown to the side. He parked the car and turned all the lights off sitting in complete darkness. He planned to pull up as soon as that door opened and the women emerged. He didn't want any chance of his wife getting caught inside.

Dominique sauntered into the club's entrance. She walked in surprised that no one paid attention to her at the door. She concluded that the security didn't know much about the operation, it had been too easy for her to get back in the club, which meant that those guys at the door didn't know who the hell she was.

She walked in and sat at the bar, taking in her surroundings. It was easy to spot who was security and who was just here to party. Her eyes glued to the back of the club. This was the area she needed to get to, unnoticed. She sat for a minute, trying to figure out how she was going to pull this off.

She knew one thing she was good on her feet. She could think herself out of any situation and this would be no different. She had outsmarted Michelle, Redd and Queen all at the same time. Her sister's name was only one more to add to that list.

She began to walk through the club towards the back. She mixed in with a group of women heading to the bathroom, laughing and talking with them to blend in with the crowd. As soon as she passed the open stairway to the offices she dipped into the dark area and kicked her shoes off. If there was anyone down here they wouldn't hear her coming.

Her bare feet softly hit the cold tile as she ran through trying to find her. Dominique knew that she was being held somewhere down here. They had brought her into the room way to fast for them to have been keeping her anywhere else.

Dominique's heart beat furiously in her chest. It was so quiet she just knew if someone else was down here they could hear the chaotic thuds of her heart. She opened the doors to the countless rooms that were down here. Most of them seemed to be empty. She was starting to feel like maybe she had been wrong about Michelle being held captive here.

Finally, she came to a room that at first glance looked like a storage room. Dominique twisted the cold handle and the door opened allowing her entrance. She quickly scanned the room before her eyes landed on her in the corner. Bound. Gagged. This woman looked like she had been through hell.

Dominique walked towards her. Seeing her began to stir a lot of emotions that she thought she had shoved away. This woman had gone out on a limb to try to save her life and get her an immunity deal that Dominique was never going to take. Part of her felt guilty for using her, and Dominique never felt guilty about anything she had to do.

The bound woman looked up at Dominique, realizing it was the woman she had set a grenade to her career for. This woman was the whole reason she had been ridiculed, demoted and transferred from the city she loved. The pair locked eyes, one of them didn't speak, the other unable to, but both of them having millions of things they wanted to say.

"Michelle or is it Tami now?" Dominique interrupted the quiet. She knew this woman by the name Michelle, but knew that wasn't her real name. Dominique knew her name was Amina, an undercover agent who became whoever she needed to be.

Dominique never thought she would see her again. When she left that day, she left knowing there was no reason for them to ever talk again, whether they wanted to or not.

Amina jolted back in the chair as Dominique moved closer, but could go nowhere. She was bound but that didn't stop her from trying. She didn't want to be anywhere near Dominique. To Amina, that woman was nothing but trouble. The kinda trouble that she seemed to fall for each and every time.

"I don't have all day, either you stay here and know Khari is going to kill you or come with me and take your chances."

Neither of those options seemed like good choices to Special

Agent Amina Viera, to her there was only one outcome either way. She would end up dead.

"I'm going to get you out of this chair. Don't give me no shit either." Dominique went to work on releasing her from the chair. Not knowing how Amina would react, Dominique kept her hands bound and her mouth gagged.

Amina continued to weigh her options and decided that going with her had to be better than being tortured by Khari. She stood, stumbling a bit from being bound. Her legs felt nonexistent and each forward movement was excruciatingly difficult.

Dominique turned towards her and grabbed her hands dragging her the rest of the way. Amina was moving far too slow and they needed to get out of here. Dominique had so many questions she wanted to ask, but knew it would have to wait.

Almost there

Dominique sent Trent a text. She needed him to be in place and ready. The corridor seemed extraordinarily long. Finally, they hit the door and exited out. Trent pulled the car around as soon as he saw the door fly open.

Dominique shoved her in the backseat and made a dash to the front and jumped in on the side of Trent. They did it. She couldn't believe they pulled it off but at the same time, had no doubt that they would.

They drove off into the night. Her sister thought she had the upper hand on them. She was still the same. Every move she made was well thought out, Dominique would have to give her that, but she should have never discounted Dominque's resourcefulness. Dominique began to laugh out loud, Trent looked at her. Even she had to admit her behavior was a bit strange. She could see the hidden question forming in his mind.

"I'm not losing my mind I promise." She laughed.

"You sure?" He smiled.

"Yeah, we beat her at her own game. Checkmate, she's all out of moves!" Dominique erupted into hysterical laughter. An hour ago she couldn't see her way out of this now things seemed clearer than ever. She sat back in her seat and enjoyed the quiet ride back to their home. Khari had fired first, but Dominique was confident that she was going to win the war.

Find out what happens next! Sign up for my mailing list to get the next release date, contest give-aways and freebies!

Join the Lit Gang Today!

UNDISCLOSED 3: A TALE OF PASSION AND BETRAYAL

BOOK THREE SYNOPSIS

For there to be betrayal there must first be trust.

Amina Viera is a woman trapped between two worlds. Rocked by the loss of her father, her one and only mission is to bring down those responsible. In the name of justice, Amina weaves together a maze of sex, lies and deceit, getting her closer to her goal but deeper in the game.

And the only thing she has to lose is herself.

Lost in the world of money, drugs and murder, Amina's deep cover lands her in the middle of the largest drug cartel in the South. Between being tortured to kidnapped, Amina's double life is catching up to her fast.

Amina's on the run and out of options. It's either kill or be killed. But when past lovers become enemies, and former adversaries become allies, there's only one problem, who can she trust?

PROLOGUE

"ARE you sure your information is good?" Hushed words slipped from my partner's lips as I eagerly watched our two marks enter the abandoned warehouse. I was a bit annoyed that he kept questioning my intel. I'd gone to hell and back to get this information. I side eyed him, just once I wanted him to trust me.

"Don't be my Dad right now, be my partner."

"You mean your boss. Let's not forget that part, Amina" He took every opportunity to remind me that he was in charge.

"I know that —" His hand thrust towards me, immediately causing me to swallow the words that were about to come out of my mouth.

"Well show me that you know, remember what I always say, if you want to lead you have

— "

"To know how to follow." My father had been saying that for years and I hated it. I was a born leader.

I closed my eyes and rubbed my forehead. My father was everything I wanted to be and he knew it. He pushed me beyond measure, sometimes to the brink of insanity, but there was a lesson in everything he said. I joined the bureau because of him, then begged him to pull strings and put me on his team. I wanted to scream to him back off, but I knew I couldn't do that so I changed the conversation.

"Look, " I pointed towards the two men entering the empty warehouse. We had been watching them for months now, trying to come up with something that would stick.

"You never answered my question. Just how good is your intel?"

"It's good, my confidential informant is sure that he's supposed to be here tonight." He was Cain, a known mid-level boss in the crew we'd been watching. Getting someone to snitch on them hadn't been easy but I finally found an informant that was either brave enough or stupid enough to spill a few secrets.

"We need to come back with a team, a real surveillance team." I could hear the hesitation in his voice. He was by the book, the fact that we were out here without backup made him uneasy.

"But if we don't get something on them now, we may never have this opportunity again."

These guys slipped away every time we got close. They evaded a number of organized crime charges, murder charges, tax evasion, RICO charges, you named it we had tried it, but we could never get close enough to anyone to make anything stick. The low-level wannabes were all too happy to take the wrap, knowing that they and their families would be taken care of.

Dad shrugged his shoulders and closed his eyes. I knew with this look meant, no. Not wanting to give him the chance to speak the words. I grabbed my jacket and jumped out of the car.

The cool New York air hit me as I pulled the coat closed and dashed towards the warehouse. I turned to see my father following me. I knew he wouldn't let me go in there by myself.

"What the hell are you doing?"

"Taking care of things." I cut my eyes towards him, it was time for me to take the lead. I slid behind the side of the warehouse and waited. There were only two men who exited the car and the CI stood at the door.

"Somethings not right." He whispered in my ear. I eyed the scene. There were only two men who exited the car and the informant stood at the door. Nothing looked out of order to me.

"You're just nervous, Viera." I teased. I hated calling him Dad when we were on the job. I turned my attention back to the CI just in time to see three masked men on motorcycles roll through the parking lot. They sped through the empty lot as if on the search for something.My heart pounded in my chest as I watched.The loud hum of the motors bounced off of the abandoned buildings, creating a rumbling sound of impending doom. Tiny beads of sweat rolled down my neck as I tried to contemplate our next move.

"Let's get the hell out of here." My father grabbed me and dragged me towards our parked car. We ran full speed using the cover of darkness to shield us from those men. I dashed to the car and hopped in the driver's seat, starting the car so that we could get away. My stomach buzzed with butterflies, I was worried things could get out of hand.

"Where the hell is he?" I searched my surroundings. The three men circled him on their bikes. I wanted to get out, I wanted to help. I could see my father shaking his head no towards my direction.

My heart pounded ten times its normal rate as I watched them circle him. There was no way out. He reached for his weapon and just when his hand grasped the handle a hail of bullets shot through his body. My father jerked from left to right as the bullets ripped through his body. He shuddered before stumbling forward and then falling backwards. Watching him hit the ground knocked the breath completely out of me. I struggled to breathe.

"Nooooooo!" I screamed as they sped off in the dark night. I jumped from the car and ran towards my father. The parked car we were watching was gone and so were the shooters.

I ran to my father's lifeless body. "No, no, no, no, no." What the hell had just happened? I glanced up and noticed my CI running towards his car.

"Where the hell do you think you're going asshole?" This had all been a setup. I trusted a low-level fuck boy and ended up getting my father killed. I raised my gun towards him, angry that I had gotten played.

I could see he was anxious. There was no way I was letting him leave so he could tell everyone who I was. I pointed my weapon at him and squeezed my trigger. Letting a burst of bullets fly towards his body.

ONE

WHAT THE FUCK had I gotten myself into? This had been one hell of a year for me. 2018 had not been good to me at all. I fought the urge to continue my sobs, I didn't want to give these two the satisfaction of seeing that I was breaking inside. To hell with that bullshit, I was too strong for that.

"What do we do with her?" Trent asked Dominique. My eyes darted from left to right, listening to everything they were and weren't saying.

"Wait until we get back to the house then we will talk. Don't say shit in front of this bitch!"

Dominique turned to look at me, her eyes catching mine and lingering for a moment too long. She pressed her lips together as if to suppress her thoughts and then turned back around. There were many unspoken words between us. Snatching me from Khari was undoubtedly her attempt to protect me, but the thing about Dominique was anything she did to help you would also be to help herself. I hadn't figured out what her motive was, but I knew one thing, she wouldn't have another chance to double cross my ass.

I sat in the backseat of the car as Trent drove recklessly through the Miami streets. His driving was careless, nervous almost. He was a lot different from the man I remembered from Houston.

I made no sounds since my mouth was still gagged and my hands bound. It would be useless to try to reason with crazy anyway, and at this moment I was surrounded by crazy.

They sat in silence. Dominique's eyes shifted, secretly eying me when she thought Trent wasn't looking. I briefly wondered what was planned for me, but I dismissed the thought, I'm sure whatever she has planned I can get out of easier than I could get out of it with her sister. I was more than certain I would be dead by this time tomorrow if I had stayed there.

I shifted in my seat, wincing from the pain that surged through my body with each movement. My body was battered from the torture I had just endured with Khari and her security. If you could call it that.

The car rolled to an abrupt stop in front of a large beach home. I assumed it their home. Trent hit a button and the garage door slowly lifted. He pulled the car in and let the door down. The door flew open as Trent reached in and grabbed me.

"Get out the car." He spoke through clenched teeth, obviously not happy to have me in his presence at all. I struggled to keep my balance as I got out of the car. My aching limbs and bound hands were working against me.

"Hurry up" She screamed at me. I'm not sure just how much faster she thought I could move. "Take her to the back office, it has no windows, only one way in and one way out. Tie her ass down to the bed and meet me in the bedroom."

Trent followed her instructions. It was almost sad that the strong, vibrant ruthless man he was only seemed to be a shell of himself." I darted my eyes towards him.

"Mhhhateer" I tried to speak through the gag.

"What?" I looked up at him, my eyes pleading with him for help. He looked down on me and pulled the gag down to hear me.

"Thank you? Water, can I have something to drink?" I didn't want any water, quite the opposite but I wanted to know if I could get him to lower his defenses. I was good at spotting a window of weakness and I was seeing it in him. I decided to push it a bit more.

"You know kidnapping a federal agent is a crime. You can just let me go now. I know this was her idea, just let me go, Trent, I won't come after you. Just let me go, please."

Trent turned to face me, flashing me an ice-cold stare. His chiseled jaw clenched as he came down to eye level. He was so close I could feel the heat of his breath against my skin. Something in him had shifted.

"Don't think you can play your mind games with me like you did my wife. I consider myself a gentleman, that's why I removed the gag, but you should know, I will put a bullet in your head if you so much as blink at me the wrong way."

He shoved the gag back into my mouth and left the room without saying another word. Damn. Even though I saw a window, it was made of bulletproof glass.

***

The wind whipped the rain chaotically through the sky. The weather teetered between winter and spring, bringing cool air and constant rain. Tears slipped down my cheeks as I watched the six men dressed in military uniforms carry my father's flag-covered casket to his final resting place.

My mother sobbed softly as she took her seat in front of his casket. Five days. That's how many days had passed since this happened and I still hadn't found the courage to really speak to my mother. I knew she had questions, but I really didn't have any answers. At least none that could right what had happened.

The minister closed the service and people started to slowly walk towards their cars. I waited in the shadows, desperate to comfort my mom in some way. Moving slowly, I made my way towards her.

"Mommy," I called, my voice seemed to be trapped in my throat. She shifted her gaze my direction. Her eyes were filled with tears, and the sparkle that usually radiated through her cashew colored skin was barely visible.

"What Amina? What happened?" She questioned as she walked towards me.

"I...I..."

"They say you were there with him. How did this happen?" Her voice cracked as she spoke.

"I can tell you how it happened. Her reckless ass got our father killed." My brother pounced on me like I was his prey.

"You don't know what happened, Kash." I shot back.

"I know you fucked up!" His finger came thrusting towards my face.

My mother lifted my chin. My eyes locked with hers as tears streamed from her eyes. We spoke no words but I sensed her pain.

"Mama, I can make this right. I can make the people that did this pay." I cried out through choked breaths.

My mother let go of my face, a final tear falling from her eye before her stare became icy cold.

"There is no way you can make this up. You fucked up and as usual, someone else paid the price for your impulsive bullshit. Whatever happened can't be undone. The Bureau is covering for your ass but this has your name written all over it."

Her words hit me like a ton of bricks, completely and utterly knocking the wind out of me. My family was all I had, all I knew and I would go to the ends of the earth to protect it.

"Mama, I didn't do this. I wouldn't put Daddy in danger."

"You paid your respects to your father now leave. And don't come back." She turned and walked away leaving me standing alone, which was exactly how I felt in this moment.

TWO

I SAT in the room surrounded in darkness, unable to move, unable to speak, my situation seemed hopeless. Ever since I tried to get Trent to let me go, no one had been back in the room. I couldn't tell how much time had passed. It was hard to know anything when I couldn't see or hear a thing. The room was void of windows and I didn't even hear anything, which told me that I must be in another part of the house separate from them.

I allowed my head to fall back against the bed. I needed to figure a way out of this situation. It's never been like me to give up and I wasn't about to start now. I wiggled my wrist trying to loosen my restraints. I needed to find a way out. My heart beat began to thump uncontrollably as my mind raced to figure out a way out of this shit. Normally when I was undercover I always had a plan to fall back on, but now I had nothing. I had no contacts, absolutely no way out, and it was occurring to me that this time would be different. There wouldn't be anyone rushing in to save the day. There were no agents laying in wait waiting for my signal. If I was getting out of this it was all on me to make it happen.

Yellow light from the hallway slipped through the cracked door. I couldn't see her face but I knew it was her. I didn't move as she slipped in the room. I wasn't sure what she was here for. I watched as her shadowy figure slinked through the room as she made her way to the bed I was tied to.

Our gazes connected as she hovered over me, staring silently. Her eyes danced in the darkness shining brightly while staring at me. Her head tilted to the side as if she was plotting something out in her mind.

"Michelle..." Her voice trailed off into silence as she twirled the faux locs I wore as apart of my cover. I could smell the scent of her Bath and Body Works body wash waft through the air as she moved. It was intoxicating. Her fingers trailed to the side of my face and slipped the gag from my lips.

"What are you doing in Miami, Michelle?"

"It's where my work brought me, what are you doing in Miami, Kyra? Dominique? Whoever you are now."

"You got a lot of damn nerve, Michelle, Tami, Amina or whoever *you* are." She laughed aloud as she called out all of my aliases known to her. The crazier thing was that wasn't even half of the people I've pretended to be my past. I closed my eyes and exhaled. She did have a point, my life was just as much a lie as hers, but at least I was on the right side of my lie. My lies were in the service of good, she only lied to protect herself.

"Let me go and no one has to know about any of this."

"Do you think I'm stupid, you've already tried to arrest my ass once, given the chance I know you will put my ass behind bars in a heartbeat."

"You got it wrong, I didn't try to arrest you, I tried to save you." I turned my head to face the wall. I didn't want her to see any of my vulnerability. I had tried to save her. I obviously saw something in her that perhaps just wasn't there. When it came down to it I put my job on the line to get her an undeserved deal. But in true Dominique fashion, she fed me false information and lies. While I was busting my ass to protect her, she was protecting him.

"Where's your husband?" I probed.

"Why, you want to try to persuade him to let you go, again? I'm the only thing keeping you alive, if it were up to my sister or my husband your ass would be at the bottom of the ocean by now." A sadistic laugh slipped from her lips, but I didn't see shit about any of this funny.

"Will you at least allow me to clean myself, use the bathroom or do you just expect me to lay here and piss myself?" That part was at least true, I hadn't been to the bathroom, hadn't eaten anything and I was dirty from being held captive in a dirty ass storeroom where some crazy ass dude water tortured my ass. A bath seemed like a luxury at the moment.

She tilted her head to the side in deep thought. It wasn't an unreasonable request. I really was dirty. She reached over and began to untie the restraints that Trent used to hold me down.

"Don't try anything."

"I won't."

She pulled me from the bed and led me into the hallway. The light hit my eyes with blaring brightness causing me to squint. I hadn't seen much light in the past few days and my eyes had grown accustomed to the darkness.

Dominque led me through the house to a large bathtub. My eyes scoured every inch of the home as she led me through it. There is no way Trent could be here. The house was eerily quiet as we walked through it. I didn't even hear noise from a television, only the shuffle of our feet as we entered the bathroom.

"Thank you," I said as I leaned against the counter. My eyes roamed her body taking in her beauty, I could understand how she had made so many men look stupid, one smile from her and you were ready to hand her the world. I had even fallen for it myself.

"The toilet is in there. After you're done you can take a bath and then back to your cell!" She pointed towards the separate water closet. "I will give you some clean clothes. " She disappeared to the adjoining bedroom for a moment before returning with a pair of yoga pants and a t-shirt.

After using the restroom I returned to the bathroom. I leaned over the tub and turned the hot water on. I needed it as hot as I could stand it. My bruised and aching body needed the warmth of the water to soothe the pain. Dominique handed me soap and a towel and then took a seat on a vanity stool.

I could feel her watching me as I slipped my clothes from my body. Piece by piece my dirty garments hit the floor. I turned to face her before stepping into the garden tub.

"Wanna join me?" I smiled. "Come on, it won't be the first time we've ever been in a bathtub together." Just the mention of our shared bath made her uncomfortable.

Dominque rolled her eyes and crossed her arms and legs. I slipped into the tub and turned on the jets. The light massage of the water against my body was just what I needed. I put my locs into a bun and sank further into the water. I closed my eyes and allowed the liquid to work its magic on me. For a brief moment, I forgot I was a prisoner and needed to escape.

"This ain't no damn spa and we don't have all day. Bathe and get out!" Her voice jolted me back to reality. I stood to soap my body down, washing every inch of myself, I wanted to get as much of the last few days off of me as I could. Once I was done I stepped out and grabbed the towel she handed me.

I left the bathroom and headed towards the bedroom. I threw my towel against the bed and laid down.

"What the hell are you doing?"

"I like to let the air dry my body, it won't take long. You'll have me tied up again in no time." I answered back sarcastically. I was in no hurry to return back to that windowless room. "Besides, I'm starving." My lips curled into a seductive smile.

"Get your ass up, put these damn clothes on and let's get back to your room. This ain't no damn spa day and brunch bitch. I was being nice to you don't make me have to drag your ass back!" Dominque stood over me, her face contorted in anger. She reached and grabbed for my hand, attempting to yank my naked body off of the bed.

I slipped my hand in hers and pulled her on top of me. She struggled to free herself, but I was quicker. I rolled on top of her and pinned her down.

"Don't act like you don't like it."

"I don't, get the fuck off of me!" She shouted as she twisted and turned to free herself from my grasp. I held her wrist pinned to the bed, slightly squeezing my thighs around her waist to keep her pinned. The more she fought against me, the more excited I became.

I leaned towards her, kissing her neck. With each peck, she softened. A sly smile spread across my face. That didn't take long. I could tell every time she looked at me there was something there. There was something that still held interest for her when it came to me.

"See I know what you like." I softly kissed her lips, parting her lips with my tongue. Her back arched in response to my touch. I released her wrist and pulled the soft fabric of her dress off her body. She wore nothing underneath.

"You wanted it just as bad as I did," I breathed into her ear. She wouldn't give me the satisfaction of verbally confirming that she wanted me, but her body said more than her words ever could.

My head slipped between her legs. I kissed her inner thigh,

before parting her lips with my tongue. My mouth wrapped around her clitoris. She moaned in response to my kisses. I ran my tongue in circles, the more I kissed the wetter she became. I slowly slipped my fingers between her folds and began to tap against her g-spot.

"Damn..."

"I know what your body likes," I whispered.

I moved to the middle of the bed and rested against the headboard. I pulled Dominque between my legs, her back to me. I planted tiny kisses on her neck as I wrapped my arms around her, my hand moving south until I found her wetness.

"Your so wet, you missed me didn't you, tell me. Tell me you missed me."

She said nothing. My fingers made small circles around her clit. Slipping in and out of her and then back around. I grabbed a handful of hair and pulled softly.

"You like that don't you," I could feel her walls tighten. She was close to cumming.

"That's it, cum for me baby, You ain't gotta say shit, your body is doing all the talking." Her hips rolled back and forth, she was eager and greedy for more. I wrapped my hand around her neck.

"Mmmmmm, damn." She moaned. The harder I squeezed the faster she moved. She was enjoying every moment of this. I slipped my hands slightly lower and squeezed firmly. Her body writhed in pleasure before passing out cold.

I threw her limp body off of me. She would only stay out for a few seconds. Less than twenty to be exact. I rushed to the bathroom and grabbed the clothes she had given me.

On our walk to the room, I spotted a rack of keys, I ran towards them and down to the garage. Ten more seconds. I hit the opener and jumped in the car. It seemed like it took forever for the garage door to completely come up.

Putting the car in reverse I rammed through the half-opened door. I didn't give a shit about damaging their door, I had to get the hell out. I shifted into drive and hit the gas and sped off.

***

I sat at my desk seething. After the incident with my father, I was pushed out of the investigation, pushed out my family. I felt like I completely lost everything. I had done everything I was supposed to do. I had been cleared by the Bureau's shrink and it was go time.

I watched as those DEA assholes entered the building. My father was point on this case and I was his second. There was no way I was going to be pushed out of this case. I jumped from my desk and headed towards the room. They were gonna let me in, that piece of shit drug operation was the reason that my father was killed and I would do anything in my power to bring it down. I marched towards the conference room.

"Where do you think you're going?" Director Bryant jumped in front of me.

"This was my dad's case, this was my case. I'm okay. I can do this."

I could tell by his expression he pitied me. "There will be conditions Viera. You go in this room and take a seat. You want on this task force then it's my rules. You got it." I shook my head yes. I understood what he was saying, but I also knew that I would go the distance to catch the people responsible.

I entered the room and took a seat at the front, I planned on listening intently, studying every angle of this case. I knew that day was a setup, I just didn't know who set us up. My eyes searched the board in front of me, there was a pyramid of suspects.

Director Bryant stood next to the lead DEA agent and started the meeting. Some of the names at the lower level of the organization I knew. My informant had given me a lot of information regarding the operation but I had slowly come to realize it was all superficial. None of it would amount to anything and obviously when I thought I was using him, he was the one using me, but he had paid for that with his life.

"We need someone who can go in and infiltrate this organization. We are talking deep cover, you'll have to go in and work your way up the ranks, earn their trust. No one has successfully as of yet." The man's booming voice jolted me back to the present. I shook my head from side to side.

"That shits never going to work." I sighed at the mediocrity I was witnessing. I cut my eyes at Director Bryant, I know I promised him I would keep my mouth closed but there was no way I was going to sit here and let them fuck this up. Again.

"You got a better idea?" The DEA asshole snorted back at me.

I scanned the board following the pictures and names posted above. My way hadn't worked, their way hadn't worked, so that means we needed a new way of doing this. I stood and walked to the board.

"Who are they?" I pointed to the two pictures at the top of the tier. Until now I was only aware of Cain, who was at the bottom of the pyramid. He wasn't a Boss at all, these two sitting at the top, they were the ones we wanted.

"That's Omere and Soraya Francis, hitmen and distro for the entire east coast and expanding as far west as southeast Texas. No matter how we try to get them they always seem to get away. She's currently being held on some bullshit charges, we thought we could crack her, but nothing has worked."

"Put me in with her, make me her cellie, I'll crack her."

"I don't know about that Viera, especially with what happened with your father. Soraya Francis is a big fish. I don't know if your're ready for that." I turned to face Director Bryant. His face was red with anger, his pale flesh giving away his true annoyance with me. I didn't care.

"It's because of what happened to my father that I know I am the perfect one to do this. There is no one that will be more committed to this than me. Trust me, I'm more than ready, I got this. See the thing is Director, if you want to catch a big fish you can't be afraid of deep waters."

THREE

I SPED down the dark Miami highway, not knowing where I was going. I just knew I needed to get away from them. I didn't trust any of these people not to kill me. I left Dominque passed out on the bed. She would be okay, I only squeezed hard enough for her to pass out. I switched from lane to lane looking for anything familiar. Finally, I was approaching the road. I spotted the entrance for I-95 and sped down the highway.

I raced towards my home, not my undercover home but my actual home, but then thought better of it. I'm sure they had some type of LoJack locating system on this car. I decided to head towards the Field Office. If they wanted to pick up their car with a bunch of federal agents around so be it.

The sun rose as I drove the hour long drive to the field office in Miramar. I knew I would have plenty of questions to answer. I spent the entire drive stringing together my story. I had a lot to answer for. I hadn't made contact with my handler and I knew he would be looking for me. As soon as I arrived I parked the car and got out entering the door only to be stopped by security.

"Ma'am," the man extended his arm preventing me from entering pass the lobby.

"Call Agent Trejo." Were the only words I spoke. I didn't have any identification on me of course but we could get this sorted out quickly. I stepped to the side and waited impatiently.

"Where the hell have you been Viera?" I heard his voice echo through the lobby. "You look like shit!" He said as he escorted me to the elevator.

I rolled my eyes I didn't need him to tell me what I looked like, after what I've been through it's surprising I'm still alive.

He handed me a cup of coffee before we entered into one of the briefing rooms. I took the warm liquid and sipped it slowly.

"Again, where the hell have you been?"

"I've been held captive, first by a couple and then by the head of the TCC himself, Trent Jamison."

His eyes almost popped out of his head, leaning forward in his seat. "Jamison is here?"

"Yes, and that's only the beginning. While I was undercover trying to get intel on Margeaux's crew, it led me to an underground human trafficking operation ran out an upscale night club in Miami. This couple is tied to the Jamison couple. I haven't figured it all out, but I can tell something changed. It's like they were building an army. Maybe they were trying to expand their territory. I don't know for sure. I do know those bitches tried to kill me." I said the last sentence under my breath.

The more I talked about it the angrier I became. I barely escaped and that nagging feeling in the pit of my stomach told me this shit was nowhere near over.

I continued to run down everything I learned while undercover. They were watching the wrong people, Margeaux was mid level compared to the likes of Dro, Khari, and Trent. I had combed over both couples operation. It was some next level shit.

Sending me in to watch Margeaux was the wrong move from the very beginning.

Agent Trejo left the room for what seemed like forever. My heart rate finally began to slow. I knew protocol. I was going to have to go to a safe house, but I didn't plan on being out for long.

The door opened and Trejo entered. The look on his face told me whatever he had been out there chatting it up about he wasn't happy about the response.

"Viera all we got is circumstantial. Why didn't you call us in when you first discovered what was going on?"

"Have you ever been undercover Trejo? I was trying to not fucking die!" I stood and shouted at him. He took a few steps back.

"Your burnt and all this is circumstantial. We can't make a case with this." He stepped forward as he continued to talk. " I believe you but you know the federal prosecutor's gonna need a hell of a lot more than this to make the charges stick. So first things first let's get you somewhere safe. Then we can talk about your relocation."

"Relocation? I'm not going anywhere. I plan on being around when we bring these assholes down."

"If that many people are after you there is no way you can stay here. You know the protocol, even though you don't follow it most of the time."

I rolled my eyes at his sarcasm. He had no idea how much I have put into bringing them down. My cover was blown but with all the information I had on them, there was no way I could just walk away.

I followed without protest as he led me to the car. We rode in silence through the busy streets. I glanced out the side mirror watching as the cars whizzed by. There was a black sedan that whipped around the cars. I started to count the number of times it happened. Agent Trejo whipped around a truck. I checked the mirror to see if the car would do the same again. I jumped up and turned towards Trejo.

"There's someone following us." He glanced out the rearview.

"No one is following us." He cut his eyes towards the rearview and then towards me and shook his head.

I looked out the mirror again and the car was gone. Maybe I was just paranoid. Maybe being held captive and tortured will make you think everyone is following you. I rested against the seat as we continued to drive.

The car rolled to a stop as we reached the safe house. It was a small, quaint home with square-shaped bushes and a large tree in the center of the yard. It could honestly be any home in Anytown, USA. No one would easily assume it was an FBI safe house. It was starting to get dark. I hated that I would need to be this far away from anything and anyone. I felt helpless in this situation, but I understood why,, ultimately the Bureau wanted to keep me as safe as possible.

"So how long do I have to be out here?" I turned to face Trejo. He looked at me with raised eyebrows.

"You already know the answer to this question." He walked off and unlocked the door to let me in. I walked into the small house.

"I will be here until the security team arrives, they will watch you and keep you safe until we can move you."

I rolled my eyes at the thought of his fat out of shape ass keeping me safe. I walked through the small house familiarizing myself with my new surroundings. It was much like the house I had left Dominque in. My mind drifted back to that day. The only thing I could think about was bringing that damn organization down, that and protecting her. I gotta stop trying to repair broken things.

I shook the thoughts from my head and proceeded to the back

of the house. I just wanted a bit of peace and quiet. It would take some time to figure out how I was gonna get back to Miami. There was no way the Bureau was going to put me in, I mean how could they, my entire cover was blown.

The headboard banged against the wall as I flopped down on the cement hard mattress. Thank God I didn't have to be here long. I reached for the remote to turn on the television when I heard a loud bang coming from the front of the house.

"Trejo?" I waited for a response. Nothing. I stood and slowly walked through the house, instinctively reaching for my waist. What was I thinking, I didn't have my gun. I tiptoed through the house, making my way towards the direction of the noise.

The night air swept through the open door bringing with it a chill that shook me to my core. I looked down at Trejo's body laying lifelessly on the floor. Moving quickly I rushed to his side, I wedged my fore and middle finger between the fat rolls of his neck to feel for a pulse. Faint but it was still there.

"It looks like I'm going to be the one protecting you," I whispered and then patted his shoulder before reaching for his gun.

Someone was in the house. I stood and scanned the room. Where did they go? I searched, looking for the smallest hint of the direction they had gone. The house wasn't big, and undoubtedly whoever it was, was looking for me. I hit the lights and slipped into the shadows. If they wanted me they were gonna have to find me. Hide and seek bitch.

Moving slowly, I pushed my back against the wall and moved towards the kitchen. I relied heavily on my sense of hearing as I moved trying not to make a sound. Only a tiny sliver of moonlight slipped through the door. Not nearly enough to see anything, so I listened intently for the direction they would be coming from. I knew turning the lights off would cause them to run my way and I would be ready.

I could hear footsteps as I hid behind the small kitchen

island. I squinted attempting to make out a shadow of what appeared to be a man creeping through the room. I rounded the small island and released bullet after bullet in his direction, closing the space between us with each shot.

His body flailed as bullets ripped through him. He fell to the ground before he could even get a shot off. I hit the light switch and stood over his body as he gasped for air. I kicked the gun from his hand and watched. I wanted to know who sent him, but there was no use. I wasn't getting any answers out of him, he was on his way out. Besides, it could be only one of two people.

I went back to Trejo's body and searched for a cellphone. The other two officers that were supposed to be here hadn't arrived yet. Just as I grabbed the phone I heard a ringing come from the dead guy on the ground. I walked over to his body and searched for the ringing sound. I answered but didn't speak.

"Se li fè?"

I didn't understand what the hell that meant but I spent enough time around Margeaux and Andre to know it was Haitian Creole. More than likely this was a hit ordered by Khari. Anger rose in my chest as I thought about all the shit I had gone through within these last few days. I was kidnapped, tortured and now this bitch wanted me dead.

"He's dead." I paused after breathing the words into the phone. " Just remember when I take all of you guys down and you're rotting in your cells, you fired the first shot. If it's war you want, you got it bitch!"

My fingers found the big red button to end the call, not giving her a chance to respond. I grabbed the keys off the counter and headed towards Trejo's vehicle. The moment I reach the car I noticed two officers exiting their car.

"What the hell happen here?"

"Somebody tried to kill me that's what happened. Get Trejo some help, you fucks can't protect me, I'm better off on my own."

I opened the door and jumped in the car. I whipped the car into reverse and sped off, not giving those officers any time to respond. I was breaking all kinds of rules when it came to these situations with the Bureau, but I didn't give a shit. There was no time to think about that. I was desperate to figure out my next move.

***

I stood outside of my parents' house afraid to go in. I walked slowly towards the door, used my key and slipped inside. I know she told me to stay away but I needed to let her know that I wasn't letting this go. I was about to go undercover and I didn't know when I would see her again.

I walked in and saw my brother's jacket thrown over the sofa. The letters on his jacket jumped out at me. I rolled my eyes and continued to walk through the house.

"What the hell are you doing here?" I looked towards the direction of the voice and folded my arms.

"I'm here to see our mother."

"That was some bullshit that you pulled today." His voice was steeped in anger. Kash too in front of me, his eyes on fire with anger. I didn't give a damn.

"You DEA assholes don't get to come take over the case Dad and I worked to break, besides somebody liked my idea cause it's happening. So do your job and keep pushing those papers, while I break this case."

A lot of time I didn't get along with my brother, he honestly had the ability to irritate the hell out of me, I gave him a lot of grief for going DEA instead of FBI but at the end of the day, I knew he wanted the same thing I did, especially now. He wanted to bring down the assholes who were ultimately responsible for our dad's death. Even though he blamed me, he had to know that this was bigger than me.

"Stop it." My mother emerged from the shadows. I turned towards her, making eye contact. "Amina what do you want?"

"I'm going under cover."

"Your brother told me. That doesn't answer my question, what are you doing here?"

"I know you told me to stay away, but I had to come talk to you, just let you know I was going away for a while. I told you, mama, I'm going to catch them." A lump caught in my throat. Nothing meant more to me at this moment than her seeing my sincerity. I needed her to know I would avenge my father's death, no matter the cost.

My mother stared and me. I shifted from left to right, disturbed by the uncomfortable silence between us. Tears pooled in the corners of her eyes. Her stare was full of accusations. She shook her head and walked off. She didn't have any words for me and still blamed me for my father's death. I never meant for that to happen that night. My father died trying to protect me, and I would go to the end of the earth and back to make someone pay for taking him from us. I glanced towards my brother who glared at me.

"What Kash?" My arms flew out from my side.

"Amina I know you think this is a game, but it's not. If we are gonna work this case together you're gonna have to listen. It's a joint task force which means, you can't do this shit by yourself, you —".

I turned and walked away. I didn't have the energy, it's bad enough I have to work with his ass, he was not about to lecture me in my time off. I had enough going on in my head, I didn't need him trying to take up extra room.

FOUR

I WAS paranoid and with good reason. I needed to get the hell out of Miami and fast. They weren't going to stop until I was dead. Khari knew I saw her whole operation, I poured over her books, I knew how and where she was hiding the money, I just didn't get a chance to get proof I needed to shut her down.

"Damn it!" I slammed my hand into the steering wheel. I wanted this to stop but I knew better than that. It never stopped until you made it, my years on the job taught me that lesson. It would only get worse from here on out.

I pulled the car into the driveway of my home and rushed inside. Moving with lightning speed, I headed towards the safe in my bedroom and pulled out my gun, a burner phone and ten thousand in cash I kept stashed there. I was never going to be caught with absolutely nothing, being undercover taught me to prepare for any and everything.

Adrenaline surged through my body as I moved through my own home. I thought it was safe but I couldn't be too sure. I walked into the restroom and stared in the mirror. It was time to let Tami go. I grabbed a pair of scissors and began to cut the faux locs out of my hair. Once I was done I washed my hair and then pulled my hair back into a sleek ponytail. I had been undercover so long and so many times, I could barely recognize the brown-eyed girl that stared back at me.

Grabbing the bag I just packed, I headed towards the door. The world felt so cold now, I had no allies. I slipped into the seat and pulled out the burner phone that I had. I copied a few numbers into it before trashing my cellphone. I didn't want anyone trying to trace me, not even my fellow agents. Even though I knew my job was on the line I had to see this through. It didn't matter what it cost me, I was going to make someone pay for my father's death. I scrolled through the phone trying to figure out my next move. I decided to send a message.

Hey

No Response. I tried again.

Need to tlk, it's Tami, give me a chance to explain things.

I didn't know how much he knew but if I wanted to break somebody, my best bet was going to be Andre. He was the weak link in their organization, and I believed he was in love enough with *Tami* that he would be willing to do anything. He had already shown me he would even double-cross his friend and his family.

I glanced down at the phone but still hadn't gotten a reply. I had almost given up hope he would respond when I felt the phone buzz.

U can't explain this shit
Meet me, it's complicated

It seemed like forever before he finally responded.

When?Where?

In an hour, that restaurant on 5th st you took me to.

Cool

Once I got to the restaurant, I asked for a table in the back and waited. I kept working out what I would say over and over again in my head. Truth be told, I didn't really have an explanation for him. I was just doing my job. Unlike with Dominque, I had no real feelings for him. But right now I need his help, and I felt my life depended on him not knowing that at all.

Customers came and went and still no Andre. I stared at the colorful walls of the restaurant, contemplating how much longer I should wait. Maybe he decided not to show. I stood to leave when I noticed two men eyeing me from another table. I quickened my footsteps, watching them out of the corner of my eye as I tried to make it to the door.

Two more men stood at the door blocking my way out. I backed up towards the direction I came from, looking for a way out, I didn't know who they were with but I definitely knew this wasn't going to be good.

"Have a seat," I turned around and came face to face with Margeaux.

"Where is Andre?"

"Have a seat." She breathed through clenched teeth. The restaurant had become eerily quiet. All of the people eating seemed to have disappeared in a matter of minutes. I backed up towards the table and took a seat.

"Where is Andre?" I asked again. Margeaux looked at me, her eyes briefly showing a spark of pain and then anger. She didn't answer me immediately. She just stared at me, never blinking.

What the hell had I just walked into? Had Andre sent her and her hitmen instead. I sat in silence, my fingers clutching the handle of the gun slipped into the side of my pants. I listened as she ordered a drink. Once the waitress returned with her drink she sipped slowly before finally responding to me.

"Andre is dead."

"Dead? No, I just sent him a text, I just talked to him, how in the hell can he be dead?"

"Li mouri, you dumb bitch. You were talking to me. My cousin is dead because of your ass." I sat back against the chair as defeat washed all over me.

"How did he die?" I wanted to keep her talking long enough to figure my way out of this. I know she was here to finish what she had started the other day. I had killed one of her soldiers, only because he had tried to kill me first, but in her mind, I know to her it didn't matter. Someone always had to pay. I had to die for multiple reasons, that only being one of them.

"I don't know what kind of lies you were filling his head with, but like I said he is dead because of you. It doesn't matter how it happened just know it fucking happened."

"You don't have to do this."

"Do what?"

"Cut the bullshit Margeaux, I know what your orders are. Remember, you've already tried once. But you don't have to do this. We were friends, remember." I reached across the table and touched her hand. As soon as I made contact I heard the click of a gun loading near my head. My entire body tensed. Maybe this was it. I closed my eyes and waited for the inevitable.

"Get the fuck off me." She snatched her hand away and waved at the gun man to put down the gun. "Bitch I'm not stupid."

"I'm simply saying, that maybe shit ain't gotta happen like this. Maybe I can help you and you can help me." Margeaux blew out a long burst of air. This was gonna be much harder than I thought. Leaning back, I started to rethink my approach.

"Margeaux, listen," I paused, choosing my words very carefully. "I'm sorry about your cousin, I never meant for that to happen."

"But it did."

My eyes circled the restaurant, there was seemingly one of her men at every doorway. They didn't plan on me making it out at all. We sat in silence, obviously both contemplating our next moves. There had to be a way into this woman's head. A way to buy me a little more time.

"Margeaux, you don't want to make the people that did this to your family pay?"

"Yes, and you did this to my family." Her hushed controlled tone scared me. She was too calm, which meant she wasn't being controlled by emotion, this had to be logic plain and simple.

I slowly breathed out a sigh. It finally hit me. I had to present her with pure logic, it had to be a win-win situation, otherwise, I was gonna end up dead somewhere in a ditch.

"Technically Margeaux, it wasn't me. I was gonna take care of Andre, whatever happened I had no hand in it. I was being held by Khari. I'm sure you know that. I am more than certain your hit on me has something to do with her."

"I'm done with this conversation." She stood to walk away. Her eyes connected with the man standing next to me. I felt the cold hard steel press against my temple. My heartbeat quickened as I struggled to control my breathing.

"Whatever she has on you I can get you out of. Trent ain't the only player in the game with superior product. Let me help you." Desperation caused careless words to tumble from my lips.

She turned on her heels and held her hand up. The man lowered his arm in response to her silent command. Had something I had said had gotten through to her?

"Fine," Her gaze was ice cold as she looked my direction. "You have less than twenty-four hours to prove you're not full of shit. If you're trying to play me, I'll kill you myself. Put her in the van." Margeaux swung her long bone straight hair over her shoulder as she gave her order and walked out the door.

* * *

The loud metal of the heavy cell door slammed shut. I was finally in. I took in the surroundings of the small cell. All of my nerves were on fire, I was, for all intents and purposes an inmate. My rights and freedom had been stripped from me. It made it feel like the walls were closing in on me.

My eyes locked in on Soraya. She sat silently reading, never looking up to acknowledge my presence. I walked over and sat on the bottom bunk. I sat in silence watching her, wondering how to open up a conversation. No matter the amount of preparation and advice I was given, being here undercover was completely different from any hypothetical situation they could throw at me.

"Get off my bed." Her voice was low but full of authority. She hadn't even glanced my way. I jumped up off the bed, something about her was making me uneasy but I had to find a way to get past it.

"I'm Mina." I stood facing her trying desperately to spark a conversation. She rolled her eyes my direction and then got in her bed.

Each night I went over and over in my head how to get close to her, but she never had much to say to me. When we were out of the cell I noticed she pretty much kept to herself. I could tell the other inmates respect her. There was an underlying secret society here that I was not apart of and I had to figure it out fast.

I sat in the yard watching the different cliques interact. People seemed to group together by the smallest of similarities. A stringy haired white girl in the corner caught my attention. Her disheveled appearance and shaky demeanor let me know that she was suffering withdrawal from something, and for me, that made her the perfect target.

I casually walked towards her and sat down. There wasn't anyone around her and I could smell why, it seemed like she skipped the shower time, all the time. I ignored her bad body odor and proceeded with my plan. Since I couldn't develop a rapport with my cellmate I would just have to create one.

"What?" She yelled as soon as I sat down on the hard stool.

"I thought maybe we could help each other."

"You can't help me wit shit!" She brushed off something imaginary on her arm.

"I assume you can't get whatever you need in here."

"Oh I can get it, I just ain't got nothing to get it with."

"What if I can help you with that?" Her blue eyes lit up with excitement. Her voice raised a few octaves. I turned towards her and my index finger to my lips. I needed her to calm down. "You do something for me, I put two hundred on your books, what you do with it is your business.

"What you want me to do?" She looked fearful but eager. It was that eagerness to feed her addiction that told me she would do anything.

"I need you to start some shit with her." I nodded my head towards Soraya's direction.

"Oh hell nawl bitch, you trying to get me killed"

"No, I got you, just do what I need and it will be alright, I'll get you money on your books and everything will be good. You think you can handle that?"

She hesitantly shook her head. I could tell the addiction was battling her common sense, but with people like her addiction always won.

"When?"

"Tomorrow, around this time. Make it look real. Do your part and I'll do mine."

"Okay, okay, and you gonna give me the two hundred right away right, right away."

"Yeah, I got you."

I smiled at her and walked away. The wheels were set in motion and I was praying that this shit worked in my favor.

FIVE

IT SEEMED like my life lately had been one abduction after another, first Khari, then Dominque, and now Margeaux. At least with her, I wasn't tied up and gagged. I stood and walked towards the small house. I knew we were in Little Haiti. From my time undercover, I knew this was the area that Margeaux ran her entire business out of and I was pretty sure that hadn't changed. She was different from Khari and Dro or even Trent. They lived in the upscale glamorous side of the drug game, but Margeaux she was still trying to get where they were. And that's exactly what I planned on using against her.

"Where is Margeaux?" I said to the man who was sitting in the front room.

He rolled his eyes and continued to play on his phone. I was getting tired of this waiting game. She hadn't been here in two days and I wasn't up for being held hostage anymore.

He continued to ignore me as I walked across the floor. He sat on the sofa half-ass paying attention. His gun was on the coffee table next to his big ass feet that he had propped up. I bent down and grabbed his gun and held it on him.

"I'm not asking again. Where the hell is Margeaux?" He stammered and stuttered, unsuccessfully attempting to find his words.

"Put the gun down." Margeaux's voice rang through the house. She had somehow quietly slipped inside the house. I turned to face her, irritated that she left me this long without so much as a conversation.

"Where the hell have you been?"

"Sit down. You," she pointed at him, "Get out!"

He left the room, damn near knocking her over in the process. I was beginning to relax a little bit but was still holding the gun.

"Put that shit down and have a seat."

I cautiously slipped into the seat nearest me and hit the button on the side to release the clip. I slid the chamber back and released the one inside. If she was gonna kill me I damn sure wasn't gonna hand her the gun to do it with. After I was done I placed the empty gun on the table and sat back. She smirked.

"If I wanted to kill you that wouldn't stop me." I ignored her comment it was time to get down to business.

"I want to help you, but to do that I will need more information."

"You can ask your questions, that doesn't mean you're gonna get an answer."

"I'm going to ignore your sarcasm. I was serious when I said I can help you. I know you don't want to be working for Khari."

"How the hell would you even know about that? For someone who was held hostage you sure do seem to know a lot."

"Cause I was held on the same floor as their office. I overheard quite a bit. It's my job to see and hear stuff, and I'm damn good at it Margeaux. Now why would a boss," I paused for a moment, only using the word boss to stroke her ego, "allow someone who ain't even apart of the drug game to take over her operation?"

I could tell my last statement got under her skin. Good. The angrier she got the more reckless she would become.

"I ain't no snitching ass bitch, so whatever you think you can get out me think again. I ain't got nothing for you or the fucking FBI."

"It's not about that, I just want you to stop trying to kill my ass. I just need to know what she promised you so I can make you a better offer. I've been doing this a minute, I've made enemies, but I've made a hell of a lot more friends and even more favors. So if you really wanna run the streets of Miami, then you let me help."

I sat back in the chair and watched. I could see the wheels spinning in her head. We sat in silence as I let her ponder her next move. I needed her to take this deal. I hadn't even figured out how I was going to pull this shit off, but I would worry about that later. I just needed her to take the bait.

"Trent ain't just gonna walk away from Miami, he got superior product, he got just about every little hood nigga trying to buy from him. I'm caught between his crazy ass and Khari and Dro, and you met that nigga he ain't the one to play with." Margeaux spoke.

"Why did Khari recruit your crew."I was desperate to persuade her to see things my way.

"She said she needed an army."

"Ok, then you build a bigger fucking army and find better fucking product. Let me help you get *unstuck*. Deal?"

"Deal." She spoke firmly by the look on her face, I could tell she was hesitant, but being Miami's top queen pin was too enticing for her not to roll the dice.

* * *

I laid in my bunk all night staring at the ceiling. My nerves were getting the better of me, in a few more hours my plan would be in motion. I didn't know what to expect from a tweaking addict, but at the moment she was all I had at my disposal.

"Counts!" I heard the guard yell right before the door buzzed to release us. I hopped down from my bunk and made my way outside of the door, waiting patiently as the CO made his rounds. As soon as the count was completed we would be free to move about the pod. Soraya always seemed to make her way to a table which very few people were invited to.

Just as I suspected as soon as we were done she was at her favorite spot. She sat silently, occasionally interacting with a few people but mostly keeping to herself. I stared, taking in all of her features. Her jet black hair was wavy, silky smooth and thick. It lay softly against her shoulders as she continued to read a book. I don't know how she managed to make prison orange look good, but she did.

I walked towards her and took a seat. We shared a cell and she hadn't spoken more than ten words to me.

"Hey Soraya, what you reading?"

"A book," I pushed past her sarcasm.

"Can you help me with something, how do we use the phone, they said I needed some kind of code."

Soraya looked up from her book. The expression on her face told me she was annoyed by my presence. I was trying not to come across pushy. In a perfect scenario, this would have been organic, but it wasn't working. Before she could get a chance to speak the white girl from yesterday charged our way.

"Bitch, Nique told me you blocking me from getting my shit!" I glanced up staring at the foul smelling, stringy haired addict. Her eyes were glossed over and her pupils were as big as saucers.

"And who are you? And who the fuck do you think you're talking to?" Her tone never changed but again there was an undeniable authority in her voice. She was used to being in charge, and not use to people going off on her at all.

The commotion caused everybody to stop. Another girl stepped in and tried to pull the tweaker away.

"Bitch what chu doing?" The woman whispered while trying to pull her back.

"Get the fuck off me!" She screamed at the other girl while brandishing a sharpened toothbrush she pulled from her pants.

The other woman threw her hands up and backed away, "Bitch it's your funeral." She returned to her seat and continued to look on like the rest of the pod.

"Why am I cut off?" She ranted and raved. I was starting to wonder if she was a really good actor or if this shit was real. It seemed that there may have been something going on that I wasn't privy too. Soraya didn't answer she just turned to walk away.

"Bitch, don't walk away from me. Answer me!" She lunged towards Soraya with the shank headed straight for her back. I didn't know this was going to get this crazy, I told her to start something not try to kill Soraya.

I jumped up and grabbed her hand. I squeezed forcing her to release the homemade knife. A smile spread across her face.

"Did I do good? You got me right?" I quickly scanned to see if anyone heard what she said. She kept squirming and yelling. If they had not heard her, they would soon. I wrestled with her, shoving her head into the ground attempting to shut her up.

Her eyes widened in confusion. She struggled to regain control of her shank but her frail drug abused body was no match for me.

"Shut up!" I said through clenched teeth. She was seriously going to mess this up. I could see Soraya watching intently as we struggled. The girl continued to try to get my approval, not caring that someone may over hear us and find out this was all planned.

I needed to shut her ass up. Without a second thought, I grabbed the shank from her hand and thrust it in her side.

"The guards! The guards!" Women scrambled about, hurriedly trying to get away as they heard the doors unlocking. Soraya pulled me away and led me back to our cell before they made it in the pod.

"Shit, what if that bitch talks," I spoke frantically. Soraya. took the knife out of my trembling hands. She wrapped it in a cloth and shoved it behind a loose brick near the head of the bed. My eyes widened.

"She won't talk. Trust me."

"I can't trust she won't say anything, she looked out of her damn mind, what was she talking about?"

"On the ground now!" The corrections officer yelled at both of us. We flew to the ground not wanting to give him any reason to get physical. My face laid against the cold hard floor.

"It'll be okay," Soraya mouthed the words to me as the guard tossed our room. I shook my head. At that moment I knew I had just gotten her attention.

SIX

"SHE WANTS me to come in for a meeting." I watched as Margeaux paced back and forth across the floor.

"What the hell are you so scared of?" I quizzed her.

"I ain't scared of shit!" She turned to face me, defiantly staring me down. "You promised to help me get out of this. What if she knows I'm working with you?"

"She doesn't, no one even knows I'm here, so the first thing you need to do is calm down and boss up. Take the meeting, if you don't you will start to look suspicious." She tilted her head to the side and stared at me for a moment. "Trust me."

"The same way Andre trusted your ass, I don't think so."

"Andre wasn't my doing, I would have looked out for him the same way I'm looking out for you. Just go to the meeting, it's business as usual. She's gonna ask about my status. Tell her the truth, your guy tracked me to a safe house and I killed him and got away. Let her do the talking, we need to find out her next move."

Margeaux grabbed her keys and headed towards the door. When she grabbed her phone I spotted a pair of Apple Airpods laying next to it.

"Are these yours?" I picked them up and dangled the small white device between my fingertips.

"Yeah, why?"

"Use them. Here, put them in, your hair will completely cover them. Before you go in call me and I will put the phone on mute. It's a bootleg wire, this way I will be able to hear everything she is saying."

"This really starting to sound like some of your FBI bullshit." She rolled her eyes and continued to walk towards the door.

"It's not. This will allow me to hear everything she is saying. And what you're saying. I don't need you trying to double cross me. I gotta know we can trust each other."

I extended my hand towards her. She reluctantly took them and put one in her right ear.

"This shit better be worth it." She mumbled under her breath as she turned to walk out of the door. I sat down and waited. I was good at playing the long game. Happy that I had thought of it on the fly, I took my seat and waited for that call. I should be able to hear everything. I pulled up the phones app store and scrolled for a call recording app. Not only would I hear the conversation, but I would also record it. If I needed it, I would have it for insurance. Thirty minutes passed before I received that call from Margeaux.

"I almost thought you chickened out."

"I'm about to go in. You sure this is going to work?"

"Yes, I'm putting my phone on mute now," I wanted to make sure there was no unnecessary noise coming from her earbud. I needed the volume as loud as possible so that I could hear everything.

Margeaux must have been walking into the club. I could hear the wind blowing and then the loud bump of music. I opened up the recording app and pressed start.

"Where have you been? I've been trying to get a hold of you."

Sergio. I would never forget his voice. This was the man that had tortured me at Khari's request.

"I still have my own business to run you know. I don't jump just because you or your boss says so." Margeaux accented voice shot back.

"She's your boss too now, recuerda eso!"

"I don't speak Spanish asshole, but I know one thing I'm my own fucking boss."

"We will see about that."

The back and forth between them momentarily stopped. It was quiet again as I imagined they walked to where ever Khari was, I'm assuming in her office. I wish I had a visual to go along with the audio. The dead air as they walked had my nerves in an uproar. There was nothing on the other end for what seemed like forever.

"You can go in now." His voice again. The only thing audible was the click of her heels against the floor. Six steps and then she stopped.

"Dro," She sounded surprised. "I thought I would be meeting with Khari.

"Sit down." His booming voice was intimidating. When I was undercover I spent some time around him. He was one scary dude, the kind of dude who you never knew which direction he was going to go.

"My husband said have a seat." It became silent again. Even though I was listening in on the other end I could tell the vibe in the room was ice cold. A million scenarios went through my head as I listened on.

"We need to talk."

"About what?" Margeaux questioned.

"We need you to take a trip to New York. We need it to be you and not one of your lame as hittas who can't even take out a bullshit ass cop handed to them on a platter!" Dro barked at her.

My heartbeat quickened as I listened intently. Why would they be sending her to New York? The room became quiet before I heard the sound of the door squeak open.

"You've met my brother in law, he needs you to take care of something there, a loose end."

"I don't work for him and as far as I knew you don't either." Margeaux's tone was defiant. It was apparent that she held nothing but contempt for Trent. I would have questioned it too. These two were what seemed like enemies, now they were doing favors for one another. It didn't make sense to me and by the questions Margeaux was asking, it didn't make sense to her either.

"Here, these are the two you will be looking for. They're causing a problem with our shipments. Two containers have been seized, and it's all because of them. I'm not going backward, so we gonna have to find a way to get the supply in, the only way I can see that happening is by making them disappear."

"And if I won't do it? I'm not a hitman or fuckin' assassin, send one of your people or he can go his damn self. All I want is to run my organization and get money. Fuck all this murder shit, I'm done."

"It's not a request, if you don't then you'll be seeing your cousin a lot sooner than you hoped, your life or theirs, it's your decision." Dro's words were haunting.

* * *

I sat waiting for my handler to come in. This room was the only room and safe space we had to talk, so he came in as my lawyer.

"Remind me again of why we gotta talk every week." Every time he showed up it pulled me out of character. Maintaining my cover was all that I could think about and I could do without all the distractions.

"Because it keeps you from forgetting which side you're on. You need it, you need to be able to decompress, that's how you gonna be able to stay undercover."

I rolled my eyes and sat back in the seat. Bryant had no idea what it was like to be this deep undercover. I chose carefully what things I shared and what things I kept to myself, he would never understand the things I had to do just to get remotely close to her.

"So tell me what's going on?"

"I'm fucking in with her, that's what's going on. For weeks she wouldn't even acknowledge my presence now I'm one of the few people that can get close to her." I was proud I had done what none of them had been able to do.

"So you in huh, you got any information yet or y'all just sitting braiding each other's hair?" I rolled my eyes at his misogynistic comment.

"Fuck you." I didn't care that he was my superior officer, he wasn't gonna disrespect me or the work I was putting in.

"I'm kidding, but seriously hasn't she said anything about her organization?"

"The only thing she talks about is getting out, that's it, but I'll get something. How much time is left on her sentence? I just need time. She ain't the easiest nut to crack you know."

"I don't know Viera, it could be months it could be years, it all depends on how her court case goes, we are holding her for as long as we can.

"Okay, can I go now?"

"No, she just had someone added to her visitation. It's a person of interest that we've had our eyes on. After you leave here you will have a visitor. I need you to keep your ears open, you will be at a table nearest her. Can you handle this?" I nodded my head, eager for him to continue. I was born to handle this. "Get as much information as you can and when you get back to that cell you figure out a way to get her talking. We need something more than you guys being besties to bring them down. Don't lose sight of that."

Did he really have to mansplain to me? I knew better than anyone why I was here. This was more important to me than to any of these guys working this case. It was deeper than just getting the bad guy, my father gave his life trying to bring them down, and I would finish the job in honor of his legacy.

"I got this Bryant. I got it." I stood up. I didn't care what else he had to say I was done with this conversation. He signaled the guard and they led me back to my cell. I wasn't sure how much I would be able to overhear but I was going to try.

Even though Soraya was nice to me, she was in no way sharing her secrets. She trusted me enough to keep me close, but not enough to open up. I would have to find some way to change that.

"Inmate!" The guard's loud booming voice startled me. "Visitation. Both of you." Even though I knew it was coming I acted as if I didn't. We were silent on our walk to the visitation room. I took my seat at the table nearest her as instructed. I waited, wondering what undercover agent they were sending in.

"Hey, Mina," My brother's voice carried through the room. I cut my eyes to the left, trying not to let anyone notice I was annoyed. By the time I faced him I had a smile spread across my face.

"What are you doing here?" I hissed.

"Making sure you don't mess this up!" He hissed back. Now wasn't the time or place to hash this out. My job was to look like I was happy to see him and eavesdrop on Soraya. I watched her as Kash made mindless chatter. I pretended to be engaged but kept my eyes and ears hooked on her.

I watched as she quietly waited for whoever was coming. She appeared nervous. I had never seen her fidget so much. Her gazed shifted towards the door and I followed. My heartbeat quickened as I saw the man walking to her table. My eyes widened as I looked towards Kash.

"Hold it together."

"He was there the night Dad was killed." I could barely get the words out. I struggled to whisper to my brother. Everything in my body wanted to scream.

"Pull it together," I shifted in my seat, trying to compose myself. We were close enough to hear them if they spoke at a normal volume. He sat down and stared at her quietly before saying anything. It was something unspoken between them, I knew it wasn't her husband, so who was he?

When they began to talk I struggled to hear what they were saying but I could only hear bits and pieces.

"Why is it always me?"

"Do this for the family."

Fragments of their broken conversation floated my way. This bullshit plan wasn't working. Once my time was up I was led back to my cell. My brother and I hadn't gotten very much from the visit. I had a million questions and didn't anticipate getting any answers anytime soon.

SEVEN

"SO WHAT'S THE PLAN? You heard him, I don't have a choice if I don't do this they do me."

"You got the photos they gave you?" Margeaux grabbed her phone and held it up to her face to unlock it. She wasn't given that much of a choice and I honestly had no idea how I would get her out of this. If she didn't pull this off I knew she was dead, and right now I felt like manipulating her was the only thing keeping them from coming for me and following through.

"Here," she handed me the phone and I scrolled through the photos she had been sent. My heart quickened as I stared at the photographs. I was overcome with one of those nostalgic feelings that stirred both emotions of pleasure and pain.

"Just drive and let me think." My head fell against the headrest as we both sat in total silence. Everything was so upside down and sometimes honestly it was hard to keep my eyes on my true goal. Every day I was just trying to survive.

The car rolled down the highway as we made our way to New York. We were two days into our drive so I knew I better come up with something quick if I wanted to find a way out of this. I could try again to contact the field office but I still didn't have shit, and I didn't want to go back empty handed. I would be looking at some serious disciplinary action and going back with absolutely nothing wouldn't work in my favor.

A hammer in my head pounded away as I closed my eyes, attempting to find peace. It was times like this, times when I didn't know where or who to turned to that I missed my father the most. I had no trouble crossing the line for the right reasons, but this seemed like everything was spiraling out of control.

"So what's the plan?" Her annoyed tone woke me from my slumber.

"What time is it?"

"Time for you to pull one of your tricks out of your ass. This shit better work, don't make me regret not killing your ass. If I do this I'm gonna need immunity or whatever that shit is, I don't want any of this coming back on me."

"Margeaux, I'm not gonna just sit here and let you kill these people."

"What do you care, you heard that shit Dro said, it's either me or them."

"Let me handle it." She parked the car and stared at a building across the street.

"Well, you better figure out how to handle this shit right now cause we here."

I scanned the area. I hadn't realized how close we were. My heart rate increased as I stared at the door. The door that symbolized my past and my future. There was no way I could let her walk into this building and kill them. Margeaux reached past me and unlocked the glove box. She pulled out a nine millimeter and put it in her pocket.

"Just chill, let me handle this. I'm gonna talk to them."

"Why in the hell would they listen to you?"

"Cause I know them."

That was all I said before I got out of the car and made my way to the door. She didn't need all the details, she only needed to know that my past connection could save her current life. Each step got heavier and heavier as I made it towards the door.

I pulled on the door knowing it would be locked but I thought I would give it a try. I looked at the keypad on the door. My fingers trembled as I pressed the numbers that had been ingrained into my head and my heart long ago. The buzzing door caused me to step back. I can't believe that damn code hasn't changed in all these years. I pushed the door open and walked into the quiet space.

"You ain't going in here without me." Margeaux appeared out of nowhere. I was so caught up in my own head I hadn't heard her walk up. I had to get my shit together. There was no way that I could let my emotions take over me now.

As we entered the building much of the surroundings looked the same. It seemed the guard that was usually stationed outside had been replaced by security cameras. The cameras were every-where and which meant we were being watched. Margeaux didn't understand when I told her to let me handled it. But there was no way I would ever be able to stroll inside of this warehouse and sneak up on anyone. They were too smart for that. We needed to be smarter.

"What the fuck is going on? I swear if you are fucking setting me up bitch I'm taking you down with me."

"Margeaux shut up, I told you to let me handle this. Honestly, if they wanted us dead we would have been dead by now. Do you see all these got damn cameras around us? Do you think they are for decoration?"

Her head flew up and swiveled from left to right, looking at each corner that held a camera. We continued down the hallway. I was surprised no one had stopped me as of yet. We came to another door. I reached for the knob and Margeaux pulled out her gun and aimed it straight ahead.

"Put that shit up and let me handle it." What the fuck didn't she understand that she really stood no chance against the people behind this door. Did her dumb ass stop to think why in the hell he didn't come to do this shit himself?

"Humph." She reluctantly slipped her gun back into her pocket and threw her long strands over her shoulder. I twisted the knob and walked through the door first. Before I knew it I was being shoved against the wall and Margeaux was thrown on the floor. My face pressed against the wall as I felt the heavy cold steel at the nape of my neck.

"You must have a death wish walking up in here like you own this shit." The man barked at me. He patted my body down before flipping me around to face him. "What the fuck you want?" His eyes bulged as he yelled. He looked like a rabid dog, drooling and staring, barking and yelping. He held his gun to my head. Margeaux struggled on the floor.

"I need to speak with Omere or Soraya."

"Bitch you ain't gonna be speaking with nobody ever again."

I didn't know who this man was, only that he was young and hungry. I had seen boys like him before. Mindless minions thinking they were something they weren't and ready to prove themselves by any means necessary. I decided to play on just that.

"Go get your boss, trust me this ain't something you wanna do without his approval." The man eyed me in silence. I could only guess he was trying to decide whether or he would kill me or consult with someone.

"I am the fucking boss." He thrust the gun into my face, pressing the metal into my soft skin. My breathing deepened as I tried to maintain my composure. Margeaux's hand inched towards her pocket. I knew what she was about to do. There were five guys in the room all with guns pointed at us, this wasn't a battle she should be trying to fight.

"Mina?"

His deep voice floated through the room. Both men turned to face the direction of the noise.

"You know her O?"

"Get the gun out of her face." Omere calmly spoke as he moved towards me. My stomach did summersaults as he made his way my direction. It felt like every nerve ending was on fire as he stood in front of me. I slowly took him in from head to toe. His jet black wavy hair, his smooth deep dark chocolate skin, the firm muscles that bulged through his shirt, he was everything I remembered. I swallowed the lump that had begun to form in my throat.

"Omere."

"Mina."

"Where's Soraya? I need to talk to you both."

He slowly ran his hand down my face stopping at my chin and then lifted my head up to meet his gaze. I could barely maintain eye contact with him but I couldn't look away. My body was responding as if it had a mind of its own. Heat radiated from me as he stood close.

It was deathly quiet in the room. Then I heard her coming. Her heels clicked against the cement floor as she floated into the room. Her soft black hair was now below her shoulders, much longer than I remembered. The scent of her perfume invaded my nostrils, the two of them standing here, in front of me was almost too much for me to handle. She stood next to him, completing the picture of a perfect couple.

"Everybody out. Take her guest and put her in the back." Soraya commanded.

"You sure boss, I don't think you should trust her, she came in with the unlock code and everything."

"I don't pay you to think, do I? Leave us alone." Soraya answered. Her voice was as I remembered. Calm but strong. She had the kind of presence that made you sit up and take notice.

"Soraya. I, I need your help." I had no idea what I was about to say. What could I say?

"You need our help?" She stepped back, her eyes sweeping my body.

"You still a cop?" Omere looked at me waiting for an answer. Straight to the point. That hadn't changed. I didn't want to answer that question, but I knew I had to.

"I'm still with the FBI, the woman I am with, she was part of a group I was undercover to bust." I chose my words carefully as I gave them pieces of the story.

"Why in the hell would we help you?" Soraya spoke up.

"You told me you would always be here for me, no matter what." I reached for both of their left arms and flipped them over. I yanked my sleeve up and exposed the matching tattoo that once symbolized our union. Three triangles, connecting and intertwined all existing both together and separately equally, on our left arms just like a wedding ring, it was closest to our hearts.

"Don't do that." She snatched her hand away and stepped back. "That doesn't mean anything anymore, you made that decision when you lied."

"I didn't lie. I had a job to do. And as I remember you crossed some lines too."

"That was in response to your — "

"Wait, Soraya. Mina," he turned to face me. "if you need our help we will help you but it ain't gonna come free."

"Boss, this bitch back here got a piece on her." The man from earlier barged in dragging Margeaux along with him. Soraya turned to face me with her eyebrows raised.

"What kind of game you playing Mina?"

"I'm not playing a game. I told you she was sent, but you

know I wasn't gonna let her do nothing to you. I came and honestly asked you for help. I wouldn't let that shit go down like that. I saved your life before, remember? If I stood up to a crazy junkie why would you think I wouldn't try to stop this shit?"

Soraya didn't respond to me. She walked over to Margeaux and stood in front of her. "I would ask Mina but she might lie, so I'm asking you. I hope you are smart enough to know to answer my questions honestly. Who sent you on this suicide mission?"

"Suicide mission?" Margeaux was confused.

"Who sent you to kill us?"

"Khari, Dro, Trent, shit they were all in the room, said something about interfering in their shipments." Margeaux looked nervous and was singing like a canary.

"Well, let's send Khari, Dro and Treeeeeent a message shall we." She pulled a blade from her pocket and in one quick motion sliced Margeaux's neck from ear to ear. Blood gushed from her neck as the life quickly left her body. My hands flew to cover my mouth, struggling to control my surprise from escaping my lips. I hung my head down. I never meant for any of this to happen.

"Clean this shit up." Her minions went to work. She turned to face me before she continued. "Mina, look at me. We not doing that shit from before. No straddling the fence. It's time to decide, are you one of the good guys or are you with us? Cause you can't be both. Think hard but don't think long!" Both Omere and Soraya stared at me, waiting for my answer.

* * *

"You've been really quiet these past few days." I took a seat in front of Soraya. She looked up at me, her eyes glistening with innocence and vulnerability. It wasn't something that I was used to seeing in her. Normally, when I looked at her I saw fire and strength.

A few days had passed since her visit and she had been moody and quiet. These past months taught me that I needed to tread carefully with her, but I had to move this case along. I needed to get something that was gonna keep me moving forward in busting their asses.

"It's nothing." She shook her wavy locks from left to right, like she was trying to shake her thoughts from her mind. From the look on her face it hadn't worked. I decided to try to push a little bit more with her.

"It's obviously something, talk to me. You know you can trust me right?" I eagerly waited for her to respond. I needed her to trust me. Soraya curled her legs up in her bunk and closed her eyes.

She hadn't spoken a word but I heard her loud and clear. This conversation was over. I was starting to feel a little defeated. I had done so much to try to get close to her but nothing seemed to work.

It was bothering me that everything that I did only got me a seat next to her, it didn't allow me insight or access into her personal space.

I stared at the ceiling as I laid in my bunk. It seemed to never calm down in this place. I damn sure wouldn't miss that once I got out of here. Even though the noise floating from the other cells, I could hear soft sobs coming from below. I hung my head over the edge of the bunk and tried to make eye contact with her.

"You okay?" I probed. She still didn't answer. Instead of just letting it be, I jumped down from my bunk and climbed in on the side of her. I didn't know what I was doing or how she would respond I only know that I needed to find a way to break that shell.

"Talk to me." I pushed her to tell me what was going on. I never saw her like this. Granted I hadn't known her that long, but being confined to such a small space with her had a way of making time to move differently.

"You wouldn't understand any of the shit anyway. I mean what you in here for, some white collar shit that got you caught up. You ain't never had to live a life like me. You probably ain't never had to sacrifice shit for nobody."

She spoke, and even with her face turned away from me, I could tell that tears were pushing past her barrier. She was wrong. I may not have known about sacrifice and loss in her world, but I definitely wasn't new to loss. Losing my father to this case had been one of the biggest losses I had ever been through.

"I can tell that you going through some things. But ain't no way in hell you can tell me what I been through. You have no idea about my life." Soraya didn't immediately respond. Then she turned to face me.

We were so close, I could feel her breath against my skin. Her eyes studied me. I remained silent, willing her to talk. I felt like I was close to something, whatever I needed her to do to trust me. Our eyes locked, never breaking contact. There was a sadness in *her that I momentarily felt sorry for. Whoever that man she met with had done a number on her.*

Tears slowly started again. I gently took my hand and rubbed it across her face to wipe away the evidence of her pain.

"You can talk to me." I brushed her hair from her face. Her hard exterior was cracking. If I wanted to push her now would be the time. Every way I had tried had been the wrong way. I had saved her from a fake attack, tried to probe her about her life, everything I've ever done to gain someone's trust I've done to her, and none of it has worked.

I moved closer to her, closing the few inches of space between us. Without a second thought, I kissed her softly on the lips. I have no idea what made me do it. I have never in my life kissed another woman, but if I was reading her correctly this one needed to feel like she could completely trust someone if I ever was going to get her to open up. I didn't know if this would work. It could completely backfire on me.

Her lips were soft, like sweet pieces of marshmallow pressing lightly against my lips. She didn't pull back, she leaned in to the kiss. I broke our connection and then leaned in to kiss her forehead as she released a long sigh.

"It's my father, everything is just all fucked up right now." Soraya slowly began to speak.

EIGHT

"MINA, MINA..." I could hear my name being called but I couldn't answer. I stared at Margeaux's body laying lifelessly on the floor. When it came down to it, I never felt guilty about the shit that happened on my pursuit for justice but this, this had caused some kind of break in me. I promised Margeaux safety and security. I never imagined that this would end with her lying dead on the ground.

"Miiiiiinnnna!" The sound of her voice jolted me back to reality. I watched her as she continued to clean her blade off. "I need your answer." I closed my eyes. What would my father do in this moment? I was tired of always trying to stay one step ahead of everyone. Tired of trying to bring an entire organization down by myself.

Years of my life were spent chasing them, chasing the ghosts of my past, Trying to stand on the side of right had gotten me no further than I was ten years ago. The only thing I really had to show for it was wasted time and a trail of bodies along my path.

"Just let me think," I said to her. Omere looked on never saying a word. My eyes filled with tears as I thought about my options. They were few. I realized I was going to have to let who I was die so that I could make room for my future. I stared at the two of them and thought about all the shit and history we had. It hasn't all been good but they were offering me a choice, I wasn't lying on the floor next to Margeaux so maybe that meant somewhere inside maybe they still loved me. My mind was made up. I knew what I was about to do.

"Fine, I'm in. No straddling the fence, I'm done."

Omere walked over and pulled me close to him. I inhaled his scent. I loved the way he smelled. His strong arms enveloped me as he pulled me as close to him as possible.

"I told you that you would be back." He whispered. I stepped back as a smile spread across my face. Soraya walked our direction and stepped between us.

"It's gonna take a hell of a lot more than her words to prove to me that she's serious. Right about now your words don't really mean shit, it's your actions that will let me know where we stand."

"You'll see, I'll show you."

"Start now, handle this," She pointed towards Margeaux. "Send a message to them. Let them know they just started a war." I knew she was testing me. She knew that as an agent I wasn't supposed to take part in a crime, and in my own way, I tried to obey that rule. The only time I hadn't was when it came to my father and this case. I had teetered on the line of good and bad, it wasn't that much of a leap into this. I looked at her lifeless body and shrugged off my feelings of guilt. If I was doing this I was doing this all the way.

"You want to send a message right?" I glanced from left to right making eye contact with both of them. "Send her as your message," I walked over and grabbed her phone and held it to her face. It quickly unlocked once I had it positioned just right. Omere and Soraya watched on as I opened the camera.

"What are you doing?"

"Sending a message." I created a video of her lifeless body and added it to a message. They would get the picture when they got it.

"You should also probably torch this place. Purge all your video surveillance and let the fire do the rest. The Feds have been watching this place forever," I rolled my eyes. I couldn't believe they hadn't change things in all these years, "and Trent also knows it was you guys interfering with the shipments. Trent is working with a chick named Khari now, her and her husband are fucking nuts and if they sent her, they just gonna keep sending people."

I walked towards them, hoping my starting gesture would be enough for them to start to trust me. I was aiding and abetting them in a crime. More so, I was telling them exactly how to get away with it. Silence filled the room for a while before anyone spoke.

"Javi! Drako!" His voice carried through the building. After a few moments, two guys appeared from the back. "Javi, go gas up the pj, we will be leaving to handle some things in Miami, Drako, y'all erase all of the surveillance and then burn this motherfucker to the ground."

"Cool Boss, what you want me to do with her?" He pointed at the body.

"Let her burn with the building."

Omere turned and sauntered towards the front door. He didn't need to say anything, both myself and Soraya followed. I could see her out of the corner of my eye. She smiled as we walked out. I moved closer to her and reached for her hand, to my surprise she didn't pull away.

Even though I'm sure there was plenty we all wanted to say, there was complete silence on the way back to their place. My gaze drifted to the two of them. Neither one of them made any eye contact with me. I believe we were all a little scared to say what this step meant. What we meant. I wondered what we could honestly be without the boundaries of my job holding me back.

"Javi just texted me, we take off in three hours, the others are gonna meet us there." Omere was always in charge, always moving with purpose and wasn't big on wasting his damn time. I smiled to myself as I waited for what was next. I didn't know what to expect when we got to Miami. As far as I knew we didn't have a plan.

"Don't you think we should talk?" I asked.

"About what?" Soraya turned to face me.

"About everything that's happening. Us, Miami, everything." My eyes widened. What did she mean about what?

Soraya started to slowly walk towards me, kicking her heels off as she made her way to me. Her chestnut brown eyes glistened with a hint of amber, signaling a desire within her. My body tingled as she slowly closed the space between us. As she moved towards me I glanced at Omere. He watched us intently but never moved from the spot he was in.

"I would rather our bodies did the talking." She whispered standing in front of me. Damn, she was so sexy. I could never fight against her sex appeal. She had a way of controlling my desire, harnessing it and then relinquishing the reigns to me and allowing me full and utter control of her body. The closest thing I had ever come to feeling that again was with Dominque. Perhaps that's why I gravitated to her so easily.

I pushed the thoughts of that out of my mind and moved towards Soraya. I slid my hand across her cheek and then behind her head allowing the strands of her hair to flow between my fingers.

"You want me?" I whispered. She slowly shook her head yes, closing her eyes for a brief moment as she leaned into my hand. I pulled her close to me and kissed her lips softly. I pressed slowly, building the intensity between us bit by bit. My tongue slipped between her lips and danced slowly with hers. The more I kissed her the more I wanted her.

Without interrupting our tongue play, I unbuttoned her shirt and let the soft fabric fall to the floor. My hands explored her smooth skin as I found the clasp to her bra and released her plump breast from their restraints. Her nipples hardened as my thumb circled slowly. I pulled away and looked at her before taking her mocha colored nipple into my mouth.

My tongue circled her nipple, alternating between biting and sucking. I used my right hand to slide the skirt from her hips. She stepped forward as it slinked down her legs. She stood in front of me, the dimly lit light bouncing off of her body.

"I missed you." Seductive whispers slipped from her lips as she pulled me close to her. Our bodies pressed together, the heat exciting me more. Strong hands ran the length of my body as we kissed. Omere now stood behind me caressing me with his hands as he slipped my clothes from my body.

I leaned my head against his chest as her lips found their way to my breast. Our eyes locked as his lips connected against my forehead. Heat surged through my body as he continued with a trail of kisses leading to my lips. His tongue slipped inside of my mouth tapping against mine.

My nipples hardened as Soraya bit softly. I turned my attention back to her. I pushed her against the sofa. I kissed her body as her back arched, strategically placing my kisses in every spot I remembered turned her on. I kissed her inner thigh as she softly moaned. From the corner of my eyes, I could see Omere slide out of his clothes.

It's as if every muscle was etched into his finely toned chocolate body. The sight of the both of them here, with me together caused tiny chills to course the length of my spine. Every thought of them, every touch, every glance only heightened my emotions even more, confirming that this was more than just a sexual connection, all of us together felt like love.

My tongue ran tiny circles across her clit. Tasting her sweetness was just as I remembered. I greedily hungered for more. I pushed her legs back and slid my tongue inside of her. I could feel Omere standing next to me, now completely naked. I craved him. Needed him in my mouth and inside of me.

I turned to him and slipped his thickness into my mouth. I wrapped my hand around him and moved up and down his shaft as I pushed him as far inside of my mouth as he could go. He grabbed my hair and pushed me even further as I took in all his inches.

"I want you inside of me." I looked up at him, my eyes pleading for him to extinguish the building fire within me. He didn't respond, just picked me up and laid me on my back. Soraya stood to the side of us watching as Omere slowly slid inside of me. He pressed slowly inside of me, kissing me as my body opened to receive him.

My juices flowed freely as his eyes connected with mine. I looked at her and she immediately understood. Soraya straddled my face as my tongue found her sweet spot. She rolled her hips as I ran my tongue across her as all of our bodies moved in unison, as we rocked each other to ecstasy.

Two months passed since I had gotten Soraya to open up. It was no easy feat to do so. She was so closely guarded that I found myself pushing the envelope with her every single time I wanted to know more. I walked towards the secure room to meet my handler.

Over the months I had been here, things went from weird to normal. It was just another day in jail. Because I was so tight with Soraya no one bothered me. The guard walked me towards the room and removed the handcuffs that held me bound. Bryant sat across from me, staring me down. The last few times he tried to visit I had refused to see him. He sat impatiently waiting for the guard to close the door before he began to speak.

"What the fuck do you think you're doing? You don't miss our appointments, ever. Keep fucking with me Viera and I will pull your ass so fast it will make your head spin."

I rolled my eyes and sat back in my chair my arms crossed, not bothering to even respond to his rant.

"Do you hear me? I'm talking to you!" He slammed his hand against to table and stood to his feet. My eyes swept the length of his body, he was visibly agitated.

"I hear you, sir." I shook off my feelings of defiance. It was definitely a lot harder than it looked in the movies. Being under-cover meant being someone else, and flipping back and forth between those two people was not easy.

"Fill me in." He said as he slipped back in his seat. His cheeks flushed with the color of anger.

"I don't know much, the plan to try to listen in was flawed from the beginning, we couldn't really hear anything, but I did manage to get a bit of intel on her. I know she's protecting some-one. Maybe it's the man that came to see her that day. It seems she is taking the fall because he is telling her to."

"Have you found out anything about her connect, about who she answers to and her actual position in this organization?"My lips curled to the right as he stared waiting for his answer.

"Sir, it's not like she's going to just volunteer that information."

"It's your job to get that information, you don't have anything, what the hell have you been doing all this time?" What did he mean what have I been doing?

"I've been doing what none of the rest of you guys could do and that's getting close enough to know anything about her. I don't have it yet but I know I'll get it." I paused and looked up at the ceiling. All those nights I had spent next to her, holding her, kissing her but never going beyond that point, she still had her wall up. I humbled my tone and continued to speak.

"I believe the guy that came to see her that day is her father." Bryant looked at me, his irritation was starting to subside.

"Now we are getting somewhere. This is it Viera your last chance. Her release date is coming up, we can't hold her anymore. She's got a hell of a lawyer that has shattered any hope of sentencing her. She will get out with time served, so when she is released it will be your job to infiltrate her organization. And please next time we talk come back with more than just who her damn daddy is." Bryant got up and banged against the metal door. On cue, the guard came to retrieve me and return me back to my cell.

Soraya was being released and hadn't said a word to me about it. I felt like I had done everything I could to earn her trust, but it wasn't enough. I had one shot to turn this around. I laid on my bunk thinking about how I would even begin to connect with her on the outside when she walked back into the cell. I sat up and stared at her.

"Soraya." The words were barely audible. She tossed her raven tresses over her shoulder and looked at me. "I just talked to my lawyer."

"And?"

"And I'm just wondering how I'm going to see you again when I'm released. I'm getting out." I wanted this to be the moment she opened up to me. I needed more. I had been fooling myself thinking that my attention to her alone would get her to talk to me, maybe she needed more than just my strength, maybe she needed my vulnerability too.

"There is no us once we get out. I go back to my life and my husband and you go back to whatever white collar shit you were doing before."

"What if I don't want to go back to the same shit I was doing before?"

"Then don't," She hunched her shoulders up and down and continued towards the bottom bunk. I hopped down off my bunk and came face to face with her. I probed her eyes for something, anything that would tell me that she had some sort of soft spot for me.

"I just thought..."

"You just thought what? That things would continue like inside, you ain't ever heard of gay for the stay? It was just a few kisses, it's not that serious."

"Yeah I know," I lied, I thought it was way more than just a few kisses. "But I thought we were friends as well. I looked out for you here, you looked out for me. That can continue, you never told me what you do, but I'm sure you can hook me up with some sort of job." I smiled at her. Soraya's head fell to the right as she took in everything I said. I had to believe I was getting somewhere with her. At least I hoped I was.

"Besides, you already know you can trust me." I lied again.

NINE

THE SUN CREPT through the cracked curtains as I sat up in bed. Soraya lay to the right of me, Omere to the left, our bodies intertwined as they slept soundly. I sat up in the bed replaying the events over and over in my head. When this all started I only wanted to do my job, the only thing I needed was justice. But now that seemed to all be changing.

We landed in Miami a day ago. To my surprise, they already had property here. Even though I thought I knew everything about them, there was still more to learn. They had obviously grown even bigger since I left New York. The old me would be trying to use this time to go through their things, search their phones, dig for info but I was letting that go. And I honestly thought it was going to be harder to shed my old layers than it actually was.

When we arrived Soraya made a call and a full wardrobe in my size arrived here hours later. I was thankful because I was definitely tired of wearing the same thing. I slid out of bed and made my way to the kitchen to scan the fridge for something to eat.

"Good Morning," Omere walked up behind me and grabbed me around my waist, then kissed me on my neck before letting me go.

"Good Morning, love," I swung around to face him, then pushed up on my tiptoes to plant a kiss on his lips. "You want me to make you breakfast?"

"Naw, just coffee is good. Come here." I followed him to the table and sat across from him. His head fell to the side as our eyes locked. The way his eyes focused on me made me feel as if he was looking into my soul.

"So what's the plan?" I asked. We needed a plan.

"I plan to handle shit!"

"I'm sure, but how? How you gonna handle shit?" I asked Omere. Unlike the two of them, I had experience with dealing with all of these people. I got the feeling that he was thinking it would be easier than what it would be. "Omere, seriously how we gonna handle this? These people, they ain't right in the head." I pointed at my temple as I finished my sentence.

"What you mean, Mina? You sounding scared."

"Come on now, you've never known me to be scared, have you? There's no time for scared."

"That's where you come in right?" Her voice carried through the kitchen as she walked into the room.

"Me?" I turned to face her.

"Yes you, see the thing is you are a master at manipulating shit. Right?"

"I'm not manipulating you," I shot back.

"Yeah but we ain't gonna pretend like you haven't before. You stay playing games." She smirked. She was good at pushing my buttons, what happened last night didn't mean a thing, she wasn't letting go of this resentment easily.

I hung my head low, I wasn't going to go back and forth with her, I know better than anyone what I had done in my job to get results.

"Baby that's done." I stood to face her pulling her close to me and embracing her. Her head rested on my shoulder for a moment before she stepped back and continued to speak.

"We still gonna use it. Give us the rundown on them all. We gotta know what we are dealing with."

"This all started in Houston, I got a lead on a case and the rest just kinda fell into place." I ran down the entire story, how I had stumbled on to the TCC in Houston, how I ended up in Miami, me being held captive and how I found my way back to them.

Of course there were things I left out. Like my relationship with Dominique and how I had gotten played when I tried to get her a deal. I felt like that part was better left unsaid.

"So those motherfuckers tortured you?" He barked. Soraya held her hand up towards him, but he continued. "I'm serious, deadass, on everything, that nigga Trent and any of those other bitch niggas are dead on sight!"

"So who put the hit out on us?" Soraya quizzed. I could tell she was trying to get to the facts.

"Trent."

The room became eerily quiet. My eyes shifted from left to right as I waited for their next question, but nobody said a word. An idea tumbled around my head ever since we landed.

"What if," they both stared at me, waiting for me to release the words that had been lodged in my head. My thoughts refused to tumble from my lips. They both sat in silence. Judging from the furrowed brows and upturned lips they were confused as to why I wouldn't speak.

"Never mind." I dismissed the thoughts and went back to my initial question. "Okay, so I'm asking again, what's the —"

Everyone turned to face the sound of the booming knock that

exploded through the house. Who would even know we were here?

"Besides Javi, who knows you're here?" Omere's voice was laced with distrust.

"Nobody."

Damn, they were out there knocking like the police. I wonder if it is the police. Shit! Had they traced me here? I shook my head, dismissing my silent thoughts. There was no way the Bureau would have been able to track me. I didn't have my phone or anything on me that could have remotely given my location.

"Mina, who the fuck is at that door?" She thrust her fingers in the direction of the front door while staring me down.

"Hell if I know," I shrugged my shoulders. How would I know who was at their door, when I didn't even know they had a home here, let alone where it was? I shrugged off her unspoken insult and made my way to the monitor.

"Can't we just use this and see who it is?" The bell rang again before they made their way to where I stood. Omere tapped some buttons and the porch was visible.

"Who is that?" Soraya looked at me as she walked to the kitchen, she yanked out two boxes of cereal, tossing the unopened bags and exposing one .380 and one 9mm. I instantly grabbed the nine. She smiled and went for the .380. Soraya preferred knives, quicker to cut than she was to shoot. But she knew better than to bring a knife to a gun fight, and if she had to shoot, that gun was her gun of preference.

Omere grabbed his weapon from its hiding place and all three of us made our way back to the video display. The man at the door appeared to be by himself. I looked at Soraya and nodded towards the back door.

She shook her head yes and we made our way out of the door and around the side of the house. If he was trying to bring some heat here it was dumb of him to come alone. We silently crept up behind him, not making any sound. He was completely oblivious to his surroundings and too engrossed by his phone.

Soraya moved on the left and I moved to the right. In unison, we both brought the gun to the side of his head as Omere opened the door and pointed it right between his eyes.

"Who the fuck are you?" Omere pressed the gun to his forehead as he waited for an answer.

* * *

"Ugh, what's that smell?" I entered into the small dingy apartment behind Director Bryant. He didn't bother to answer my question. I took in the small one bedroom apartment that would be my home for God knows how long. I was here as long as I was on the case.

"Here," Bryant extended his arm, handing me a cell phone. "This is your phone, and a tracking device. We need to be able to keep tabs on you at all times."

"I, I don't know about that boss, if they find out I have anything that links back to the bureau you know my ass is dead."

"It's for your safety, Viera. Our tech team simply uses the GPS on the phone to pinpoint your location when needed. That's all. Other than that it's just a phone. It doesn't trace back to anyone, or anything for that matter."

I looked down at the phone, pressing the home button to open the screen and the device lit up. I tossed it on the kitchen table and continued into the small furnished apartment. Bryant took a seat on the worn sofa and pulled more things out of his case.

"Come on Viera bring your ass over here so I can brief you and get the hell out of here. After this day I won't be back here, I don't want to be seen with you, but you will still be required to check in with me. Every week just like when you were inside."

"Sir, you know what that does. I explained why — "

"And I explained I don't give a shit, you check in. Every week, if you don't, then I show up and pull you off this case. Take these." I grasped the bulky package from his plump pasty hands.

"What's this?"

"Your identification and some money. The basic stuff. Remember, undercover life out here is going to be different than inside. In jail it's controlled but outside, it's gonna be sink or swim. If you can't gain her trust and infiltrate then it's back to square one. We may not get another chance."

"I understand sir. I'm going to make this happen. Believe me, no one wants to see them locked under a jail as much as I do."

Director Bryant nodded, stood and walked to the door. I was ready for him to leave. I knew this man took a chance on me when he put me undercover, but I was the one for the job.

I needed to figure out how to get next to Soraya. I stared at Director Bryant waiting for him to finish his speech. I shook my head in agreement but not at all paying much attention to what he was saying.

"I got it, Director, I won't let you down, remember I'm doing this for more than just the case, this is for my father."

Our eyes connected and for a moment we were on the same page, and then the doubt returned. It was okay I would prove him wrong. I walked behind him and locked the door. I tore open the package he gave me and began to go through the contents.

There were several stacks of cash inside, an ID with my first name and face but a different last name, and pictures and information of Soraya's whereabouts. I studied the pictures combing over them for every visible detail. I recognized the area but I knew I couldn't just show up. It had to look like we had run into each other.

I changed my clothes and decided to head to the area. I couldn't accidentally run into her if I wasn't hanging out there. I jumped on the subway and within twenty minutes I was there. No matter how much I wanted too, I knew I couldn't just walk up to their warehouse. she worked Doing that, alone, with no back up would be a death wish. Thoughts of my father started to hit me as I thought about the last time I was there.

I blew out a long loud breath and threw my head back. I didn't have time to think about this. I didn't need anything throwing me off of my game. I looked around trying to decide which place will give me the best vantage point to spot her. I decided on a small coffee shop with a large window that overlooked the street. I slipped inside and ordered a latte. It was just enough people to get lost in but not so many that I would lose my mark when I finally spotted her.

I turned to find a table and almost lost my balance. I had memorized every inch of his face. Maybe there was another way in. He moved through the place like he owned it. He was tall, with skin the color of milk chocolate. I walked towards him pretending to be adding more sugar to my coffee. I placed my cup on the small table and proceeded to remove the lid. Just as he started to step away I knocked the cup over.

"Oh damn, my bad." His voice was a low baritone that was so deep and melodious it shook me. I quickly recovered from the unexpected stirring he caused.

"It's fine." I reached to recover the cup from the floor.

"Let me get you another cup. Join me, I mean it's the least I could do." His lips spread into a flirtatious grin. I hesitantly shook my head and walked with him to reorder my coffee. He paid the barista and turned towards me.

"So what's your name?" He said as he walked with me towards an open table.

"Mina," He slipped into the seat across from me.

"It's okay, you don't have to keep me company. Thanks for replacing the coffee. Besides, judging from the band on your finger," I nodded my head towards his left hand, "maybe you shouldn't be having cozy coffee dates with complete strangers." I allowed a girlish giggle to slip from my lips. His non-verbal cues told me he was flirting with me and I was going to completely exploit it.

"Well, Mina, I'm Omere, now we aren't complete strangers." I sipped my coffee as I gazed his direction.

TEN

"YOU GOT five seconds to start talking. Who...the...fuck...are...you?" Omere stared down the man at the door, his lips twisted into a threatening snarl. The man's head jolted up towards Omere and then to the side to get a better look at us.

"Wait, I've seen him before," I spoke up.

"I'm looking for Margeaux, she told me if I didn't hear from her every twenty-four hours to find her. It's been days since she last responded."

"You here alone?"

"Yes!"

Soraya put her gun in her pants and ran her hands up and down his slim frame. While she checked him I kept the gun pointed at his back and Omere to the front. Soraya took two guns off of him.

"You gotta be a stupid motherfucker to show up at my door. Do you know who the fuck I am?" She shoved him into the house.

"Start talking." Omere barked.

"Like I said, I'm looking for Margeaux."

"And why the fuck would you look for her here?" Soraya turned to look my directions. "Mina if this some shit you're pulling, I promise you I don't give a damn about my feelings, this will be the last time you ever get to play me!"

"Soraya, I told you I'm not playing games, I don't have shit to do with this." She was starting to really work my nerves with this. I told her she could trust me.

Our eyes locked and her expression seemed to soften. I turned my attention back to the man. I finally figured out where I knew him from, I remembered him from the restaurant, this was the asshole that held the gun to my head on Margeaux's orders.

"Talk." Soraya grabbed the gun and thrust in his direction. Her voice was steady and controlled. She was a woman in charged and I always loved that about her.

She still wore the oversized cropped shirt she had thrown on when she had gotten out of bed. Each time she raised her hand his direction, her chocolate dipped nipples were slightly exposed. That shit was turning me on. I stepped next to her, not that she needed my help but I wanted her to know that she had it.

"I tracked her iPhone here. Where is she?" He hissed through saliva spurting between his teeth towards the three of us. Even though he asked the question, the haunted look in his eyes told me he knew that Margeaux was gone.

We stood in chilling silence for what seemed like forever. I didn't exactly know what everyone was thinking but I knew they were doing their own calculations just like I was. What was the likelihood he was by himself? Who did he tell he was coming here? And had this just started a war with more than the people they intended to?

"Your friend, she's dead." Soraya spoke bluntly, "It is what it is."

"Dead? What do you mean dead?"

"Is there more than one kind of dead motherfucka? She ain't breathing!" Omere stepped in.

"How the fuck is she dead when you were supposed —" He turned towards me but Omere stepped in front of him.

"Look nigga, kill all that extra shit. I see you got two options, you try to bring some heat our way and end up just like ya girl, or do this shit my way and just go back to where the fuck you came from, forget you were ever here and you get to keep breathing."

"Fuck you, I ain't doing shit no way but my fucking way."

Omere laughed so loud it was almost scary, then with one continuous motion the butt of the gun he was holding connected with the side of the man's head and his body slumped to the ground with a loud thud.

"Go get that rope in the garage." Soraya disappeared. He proceeded to lift the dude into a chair. Soraya returned with the rope and all three of us went to work tying him down.

"I brought the phone." I blurted out. I wanted to be honest with them. I didn't need Soraya questioning if I had done this on purpose or as she likes to say was playing games. "I only brought it because I thought it could be of use, with all her contact and info, I thought it would come in handy. I didn't even think about the fact that once it started to charge it would power back on."

I had made a rookie mistake that could have cost us a lot but if I knew one thing I was quick on my feet. I was going to find a way to flip this around.

"How many of them is it? How big of a fight we got on our hands?" Omere faced me. His voice was calm, non-judgmental, I could tell he just wanted to resolve what he saw as a small setback and move forward.

"Big, honestly until Trent showed up she was the biggest name in the game in Miami, but maybe it doesn't have to be a fight."

"What do you mean no fight? Oh, we most definitely gonna have to handle these niggas." He responded.

"No baby, hear me out." I looked at both of them, wanted to speak quickly before dude came to. "Flip him. Margeaux made an agreement with Trent, well with the couple working with Trent. Technically, if you flip him get him to work for you instead. You put Trent right back where he was when he came to Miami. If you want to stop him, cut out his network, take away all of his allies and connects then leave his ass standing lonely, broke and begging for mercy."

Omere and Soraya smiled at me. She walked towards me and stood next to me, taking my hand in hers while our eyes connected. I was finally gaining her trust. Omere grabbed a bottle of water and walked over to the guy who was still knocked out. He poured the cold water all over him.

"Wake up nigga, I'm about to make you a deal you can't refuse."

* * *

"After two weeks of coffee," I made air quotes when I said the word coffee, "I still don't know much about you." I probed Omere for information, but he didn't even acknowledge my statement. He always seemed to be at this location, at this time, every Friday he was here. I had been waiting to run into Soraya. Of all the surveillance we had of her in this area I had not seen her once. I was here every day, but she never was.

I stared at Omere as he took a seat across from me. This man was just as tight-lipped as his wife. I mean I couldn't get him to say shit. It had taken me months and a little bit of manipulation to get in with Soraya, I didn't have months to do this.

I leaned against the back of the chair, exhausted from trying to do over what I had already done. What was my in with him? I think I overestimated the power of flirtation, honestly, all he ever really did was sit, watch and wait. What was he looking for? I decided I didn't have time to pussy foot. I needed to get things moving.

"Omere," His name dripped from my lips dipped in sweet sexy sultriness. He looked up from his phone, his eyebrows raised waiting for me to finish my sentence. I could tell by his expression that he questions the motives of my tone. He was right to question it.

"Did you come here to stare at your phone or to talk to me?"

"I came to have a cup of coffee, and stare at my phone."

"You could do that at a table by yourself, couldn't you? You don't need my company to do that." He placed his phone down on the table and gazed my direction.

His lips spread across his face into a seductive smile. "I do what I want, when I want and right now that's sitting here." After all these weeks I still had nothing. I was starting to get annoyed. Most men I merely had to flutter my lashes and I owned their asses, but him, he was like a rock. The only thing that held his attention for any amount of time was his phone and this street. I couldn't figure out what he was watching so intently, why was he here, so often?

I watched him as he gazed at his phone and then towards the back of the shop. Without saying a word he jumped up from his chair. I didn't know what he was walking back there for or why he jumped up so abruptly but I was going to find out. I moved slowly towards his direction careful to follow him but not let him know that I was watching. He slipped into a back office I but it was dark on the inside. I tiptoed to the door and softly pushed it open.

My eyes roamed the dimly lit office. I could make out two people at the desk. One person was sitting and the other person standing. The one standing was a woman, it wasn't until I heard her voice that I knew who it was.

"Where is my money?" It was Soraya. Omere stood in front of the desk now, staring down the man who was sitting in the chair.

My heart raced, I've been waiting for this moment but had no idea it would go down like this. I needed to somehow make this work in my favor but from the looks of the gun at the man's head, somebody was about to die.

"What took you so long to get back here?" She asked Omere.

"Never mind that let's just do this and get out." He responded to her.

Soraya had a silencer attached to the end of her gun, by the looks of things it was happening right here, in broad daylight, with all these people around. I didn't have enough information to figure out why there was a gun to dudes head and what part he played in the organization but it really didn't matter. It was time to act. Adrenaline surged through my body.

"Omere, why'd you run away so..." I stopped mid sentence on purpose, acting as if stumbling on the two of them was an accident.

"What the fuck?" Soraya turned towards me, her eyes bulging in disbelief. "What are you doing here? Omere is this what took your ass so long to get back here?" She yelled at him. I turned towards him looking dumbfounded, acting my ass off.

"I ain't seen shit!" I turned on my heels to walk away but before I could get to the door Omere was on me, he pushed it shut and tossed me onto the chair across from the desk. I locked eyes with the man across from me. I could smell the fear pouring from his body. I don't know what he had done to be in this position, but I knew he had to be regretting it.

Was I was going to be able to stop them from killing him? As harsh as it sounded, I wasn't willing to blow my cover to save his life. The case was too important to turn back and blow it all now. He would just have to be collateral damage.

"Soraya, let me go. You know I won't say anything."

"What are you doing here?" She probed.

"Wait, wait. How the hell do you know her?" Omere interrupted us.

"She was my cellmate," Soraya said. "What's the chances that you would be here, now? And you just accidentally chatting up my husband and walk in on this?" The tone in her voice told me that she wasn't really buying this being an accidental meeting.

"Look Soraya, I don't know what you are thinking but I just come here to get coffee, it's close to my new spot. What the fuck else could it be? And besides, after as close as we were inside, you know damn well I ain't with no dumb shit. This shit just happened, but you know you can let me go and I won't say a word."

My eyes darted from left to right. I wanted to convince them that I just wanted to get the hell out of here and go on with my life. But what I really needed was to be in this room right now. For them to trust me and let me in.

My thoughts raced. I had to be quick with my responses and comebacks. I knew Soraya. She questioned everything and trusted nothing and no one. She didn't respond to my pleas, just shrugged her shoulders, as if to say she would handle that in a minute. Her attention went back to the silent man at the desk.

"You've been coming up short while I've been away." She thrust the gun into his temple and twisted just a little. The man closed his eyes, his bottom lip quivering.

"It's been slow, I wouldn't think of stealing from you. You can look at my books, my accounts."

"I don't believe you."

I looked at the two of them and knew this man was about to get it and maybe me next, I really should have thought this plan all the way through.

"Can I make a suggestion?" They turned towards me.

"Do we look like we are taking fucking request, Mina?"

"It's not a request, just an observation, an offer. Remember all that white collar shit that landed me in that cell beside you? Well, let me use it for you. I know numbers, and if this dude is stealing from you and hiding it I can find it."

Soraya and Omere looked towards one another, having a silent conversation that only the two of them could understand. After what seemed like forever he spoke.

"Give her access to your shit, if she finds you been stealing my money we will be back to finish this shit."

The man shook nervously as he reached for a thumb drive and started saving stuff to it. By the look on his face, I knew I was going to find something in those books. For his sake, I hoped he was long gone when I did, because this was my way in and I planned on exploiting the hell out of it.

ELEVEN

"IS THERE anything else you need to tell us before we walk in this building Mina?"

"I've told you everything." I looked at Omere, answering his question. I told him everything he needed to know to confront Khari and Dro. Everything I knew from studying them. The sex trafficking to drug transport and everything in between. Somethings seemed irrelevant, they didn't need to know about my relationship with Andre or Dominque for that matter.

Besides, Andre was work only. I pumped him repeatedly for information and everything I had gotten from Andre I told them. I only knew about Dro and Khari from the small things I witnessed and what Andre shared. I could never get close enough to Khari to get any information out of her. She was worse than Soraya when it came to trust.

"Everything?" Soraya chimed in, distracting me from the thoughts tumbling around in my head.

"Yes."

We sat in the car waiting to get the number of people inside. I knew from being undercover if we wanted to have the upper hand with them we needed to come during the day. At night when the club was open, it was too much security and we were trying to avoid a shoot out.

I turned towards Omere and smiled. "I've told you everything. I know she hooked up with the Haitians to expand her security. I don't really think she trusted working with them, but now that you have them you don't have anything to worry about."

"There is always something to worry about," Soraya added in her opinion. I made eye contact with her as she looked back at me, but I am not going to say anything. Now is not the time to get into another argument with her about whether she could really trust me.

I glanced towards the rearview mirror and watched as three SUVs pulled up behind us. The two men I met in New York stepped out first along with two other men. Then the Haitian guy that showed up looking for Margeaux. I watched the way the men interacted. Neither of them trusted each other, and rightfully so. Omere placed his guys in control but promised this area to the Haitians once they went back to New York. And any promise Omere made he kept. When the man was offered distro for the entire area, he jumped at the offer.

Javi and Drako rushed to the car, interrupting my thoughts. I focused on them and waited as Omere rolled down the window.

"Boss, everything's in place. We have the Haitians set up around the building just in case they with the shits."

Omere nodded and then stepped out of the car. Every move he made was that of a boss. I had no doubt when he walked in this club he would walk out knowing every bit of information he wanted. Soraya and I walked next to him and made our way to the door. My heart raced as we moved towards the building. The last time I was here I had been bound, gagged and tortured. I looked up towards the camera at the front entrance and swallowed. I could feel the tiny hairs on my arm begin to rise. Adrenaline surged through my body, I didn't know what to expect on the other side of the door, but I knew one thing, I ain't never been scared and I wasn't going to start now.

Omere pulled on the door but it was locked. He smirked almost as if he liked the challenge that this was already presenting. He pulled out his gun and pushed us back. His two guys followed suit and aimed their guns at the lock and blasted until it no longer existed.

I stepped through the gun hole riddled door and walked into the familiar surroundings. Soraya and Omere followed close behind. I was the one that knew the layout of the club so they followed my lead.

I scanned the dimly lit club, even in the daylight, it seemed to be a dark secret cave that held numerous secrets. I stopped before heading towards the elevator.

"Why you stopping?" Omere's words tumbled from his lips in a hushed tone.

"Because they will come to us. I've dealt with them enough to know as soon as we hit the lower level they will be waiting for us. I turned towards the dude that came looking for Margeaux.

"Tell your people to enter through the back side door. The more the better and push her, her husband and her pyscho security this way."

He whipped out his phone and gave commands. I couldn't help the sly smile that slipped across my lips. If it's one thing I lived for it was vindication, and right now I felt like I was finally checking off the list of people who had wronged me, but even I had to admit that was a long ass list.

"What the fuck is this bullshit?" Dro appeared as the elevator doors opened, exposing Khari and the asshole who had tortured me. It was three of them to our army. Flipping the Haitians had taken all of their power away.

I raised my gun and aimed it at the bodyguard dude. "Put the fucking gun down." His eyes blazed with defiance. I didn't have time for this shit, this asshole had all but killed me. I squeezed the trigger and let two bullets fly into the shoulder of the hand that held his gun. His hand jerked as the gun tumbled to the floor and he grabbed his arm with his free hand, attempting to stop the blood flow.

I turned my attention to the couple, I could see the wheels in her head turning. Dro's chest heaved up and down as he started to lunge our way, but Khari grabbed his hand and pulled him back towards her. She was smart, obviously the brains. I could tell by the look on her face that she had done the math and knew there was no realistic way for them to make it out. Alive.

"So which one of you motherfuckers wanted me dead?" Soraya's eyes locked on them as she stepped forward.

"What the fuck you want?" Dro barked his head shifting to the side as he eyed us up and down. "I'on know what the fuck you think this is!"

"This, my nigga, is a motherfuckin' hostile take over!"

＊ ＊ ＊

"Do you think you can get him out of there? He's been in with them since the start of his business. It's probably dozens more just like it. They funnel money into these businesses, and then the business washes it clean." I started filling in Director Bryant on what I learned.

"So what's he got on them?"

"I don't know for sure but after looking at all his books, he receives weekly shipments, he marks two weights, the shipping weight and the net weight, the net always has a dollar amount next to it. I think he was washing the money but also using the business as a front to smuggle something in. I don't know what, I do know the money in and out doesn't match up. It does if you don't know what you are looking for, but I know exactly what to look for."

"That's pretty good intel, Viera. Getting him out can be tricky and I don't know if that's gonna be the best move."

I stared at Director Bryant as we had our weekly meetings. I ran through everything I found in the last week. I thought that maybe if we could save the man, offer him some type of protection

in exchange for his testimony, it would help our case. He didn't
have to be anyone's collateral damage, and after what I found, I
was certain he would be headed to an early grave if we didn't do
something.

"What the hell do you mean sir not the best move? You know
they are gonna kill him right?" He was silently staring at me. I
know he has put just as much into this case as me and probably
didn't want to do anything that could jeopardize the case.

"Ok, I will talk with WITSEC see how fast we can move on
this." He answered.

"Move fast, I have to meet with them in two hours and if they
get to him first we lose the first solid lead we have to take these
people down."

I walked towards my car and proceeded to leave. The less I
know about what and how they did things the better. It didn't take
me long to figure out that this man's business was just a front to
launder money for them, and a lot of it. I speculated this is the
reason nothing ever stuck. It's like they were ghost in the game, I
knew they sold drugs, I knew they committed murders, but nobody
ever got close enough to get anything concrete on them. Shit, I'm
about to change that.

1112 W. Fulton Blvd
2:30 PM

A text message buzzed to my phone. I knew it was coming for
Soraya. I had been given only a finite amount of time to figure out
what was happening, and time had just run out. I exited the
highway and headed in the direction of the address. I knew the
location. The warehouse was their base seemingly for everything,
and it was also the place my father took his last breath. As I pulled
up to the location I was hit with a nauseating wave of grief. I
looked into the rearview mirror and wiped the spots of perspiration
from my brow.

"Suck that shit up Amina!"

Now was not the time to fall apart. More of what I needed to know was beyond those doors. I parked, this time in the lot. I exited and walked towards the door.

"Aye, where you think you going?"

"Inside."

"Naw, I don't know you."

"And I don't know your big ass either," I pulled out my phone and showed him the text. "but that ain't stopping me from getting through those doors." I looked the man up and down. It was just like when I was undercover in jail, you did what you had to do and became who you had to become and at the moment I was the bitch that was going through the doors. I had never been so close to completing something as I was now. And I be damn if anyone was going to stop me. I was going to finish this, on everything I loved, on my father I was gonna do what I set out to do.

"Move out my damn way." I pushed past his giant frame and made my way in but stopped dead in my tracks. A tiny gasp escaped my lips but I quickly closed them when I heard Soraya walk into the room. I stared at the man in the middle of the floor. He would never know how close I came to saving his life. I was not at all prepared for what I saw but I quickly fixed my face and walked past him as if it were nothing. The coffee shop owner sat in a chair in the center of the floor. He was free to move, but he might as well have been tied down. He wasn't getting out of this room. Every possible exit way was guarded by some random ass dude who appeared to be doing nothing, but I'm sure they were watching everything.

I stood in the bare open room unsure of what to do, so I did nothing. Better to play it safe than to be sorry. For a brief moment my gaze connected with the man, his eyes pleading for help. I quickly turned my head away. I tried to help him, and if I were to *attempt it now that would mean my life and his. There was too much at stake.*

Voices echoed through the large room as a group entered the room. I recognized Omere and Soraya but the other three men I didn't. Wait, the older one was the man that visited Soraya. My pulse quickened, I knew he was a big part of whatever was going on, and I knew if I could get all of them I would be able to bring this entire organization down. With a mixture of anxiety and glee, I began to move towards the group.

"Did you find anything?" Omere skipped over all bullshit pleasantries and asked the question I'm sure they were all thinking.

"Yeah, the numbers ain't adding up. From what I can tell he is falsifying the information he gives to you and taking a little bit for himself. Small amounts, all under 10,000, so it raises no red flags with the bank, or with you guys for that matter."

I had their undivided attention. I shifted my eyes to the right, watching the man squirm in his chair just a bit as I talked, but he hadn't said a word.

"I can give it back. I still have it all, please." He finally broke the silence. The older man whose name I didn't know yet, walked towards him. I did my best to memorize every inch of their faces.

"Oh there is no doubt you are going to give it back." He waved his hand towards the white man that was with him. "Jacob, get my money back."

Everyone seemed to hang on this man's every command. With each passing moment, I realized that this shit was way deeper than my father or anyone at the bureau could have possibly known. Who the hell is he?

The white man went to work on a small laptop he was carrying with him. He handed it to the man and he typed some things in and handed it back to Jacob. I think that's what he called him.

"It's done sir, it was in an offshore account, total three point five million in separate accounts, it should be available in your Swiss business account shortly sir."

"Thank you, Jacob." The way they spoke to each other you would swear this was a business boardroom they were in and not a stank half lit gray warehouse. I stood next to Soraya and Omere. I was statue still, scared to even breathe.

"Okay then." The other man walked back towards the group.

"So I can go? You got your money back, man I'll leave and y'all can do whatever with the shop, just can I go please?" The man begged for his life.

"Sure. You are free to do what you want."

He looked around for a moment and then raised from his seat and headed towards the door I had just come through. He moved swiftly but cautiously.

"There's just one thing before you go." The younger guy said and then pulled a gun from his back and fired just as the man turned around. His body flew back as blood rushed from his open wound. "You can never trust a thief."

My body shuddered, everything in me screamed do something but what could I realistically do? End up next to him? The man who fired the gun looked like he should be a model on the cover of GQ magazine, the juxtaposition of his looks and his actions floored me. He then pointed the gun towards me.

"Whoa, say don't point that shit at me."

"What do you want me to do with her, Pops?" Pops? Was this his father? So who is he to Soraya? "No loose ends right? We don't know her."

"This call is up to your sister, she brought her in, she's her responsibility."

"I say we deal with it now so we don't have to pay for it later. She's seen too much already." The man continued to push for my execution.

"I say chill the fuck out Trent. Put the gun down, you handle the college shit, let me handle the street shit. You always been a trigger happy motherfucker, calm down." Soraya stepped between me and the gun, and the man lowered his weapon. What the hell had I gotten myself into?

TWELVE

"I DON'T KNOW who the fuck you think you are, this my shit and ain't no nigga walking in my spot talking about a mother-fuckin' take over."

I watched as Dro's chest heaved up and down. His eyes bulged as he stared at Omere. His head shifted to the side as he looked him up and down, his facial expression told me he didn't care about how outnumbered he was, he wasn't going down without a fight.

My time around him was always limited but I knew he had a temper. Khari moved closer to him and placed her hand on the back of his neck.

Omere's laughed was so deep and boisterous it scared the hell out of me. Watching this scene was like watching some twisted movie. Omere started to move closer to Dro.

"And who the fuck is going to stop me?" With slow deliberate steps, he moved towards him. I could see the vein in Dro's neck pulsing. I knew this wasn't going to be a good situation. This dude had to be stupid if he thought for a second he had any out other than the one we were providing him. I looked towards his security Sergio, holding his wounded leg where I had just shot him. Dro had no one.

"The fuck you say to me you bitch ass nigga?" Dro whipped out the gun that rested in his pants and aimed it right at Omere's head. Omere didn't even flinch. Without even thinking I raised the gun I held and pointed it at Khari's head. If he even thought about shooting she was going with him. Khari watched me out of the corner of her eye. Her contempt for me was more than evident given her facial expression. I watched as Khari and Dro made eye contact.

"No te preocupes,"

"Cut that shit out!" I yelled. I knew they spoke Spanish and I knew that they were probably plotting on our ass in another language. I wasn't going to let that happen. Soraya stepped up.

"Shut the fuck up and lower your weapon. If he doesn't get hurt, she won't get hurt." Soraya's mouth curved upward as she stared him down.

"I ain't dropping shit. Get out of my fucking establishment." Dro yelled.

"Get the gun out of my husband's fucking face, or she shoots." Soraya nodded her head towards me. Dro briefly diverted his attention to me and then quickly shifted back to Soraya.

"I don't know who the fuck you are but I hope you know that that bitch is motherfuckin FBI. Y'all rolling in this bitch with a cop?" Dro's chest heaved up in down. I blew out a silent breath, trying to calm my heart rate. The mere mention of me being an agent made me uncomfortable.

"I know who the fuck she is." Soraya chimed in.

"Then you know not to trust the bitch then." Dro spat back.

"All I know right now is that you need to drop your gun."

Khari shifted slightly, like she wanted to say something but she held it back. She turned and faced me head on, making extremely uncomfortable eye contact. She looked at me like she was trying to stare me down. By the looks of it she wasn't intimidated at all by the gun I held to her head.

"All y'all must be dumb as fuck, I'm telling you this bitch is setting us all up." He paused and then turned towards me. "You lucky you got away when you did because I would have gotten rid of your ass a long time ago."

One of the Haitians walked up behind Dro and placed the barrel of the gun to the back of Khari's head. With two guns pointed at her head, I could tell that Dro was quickly reconsidering.

"Drop your pistol, my choppa way bigger!" The Haitian dude spoke again.

"Listen to him, because this is going to be the last time we ask." Dro slowly started to lower his arm and attempted to place the gun back in his pants.

"Naw nigga hand that over, " Omere said and reached to take the gun out of Dro's hands. These were two alpha males going head to head. Once Omere secured the gun, he raised it and swung it across Dro's face. "Don't you ever point another fuckin gun at me."

Dro's hands clenched together just before he was about to hit Omere back but quickly remembered the guns pointed at his wife's head. He stepped back and rubbed the place where the gun had just connected with his face. That was gonna leave a mark.

"What the fuck y'all want man?"

"You would think we could have started there," Soraya said and pushed forward between Omere and me. "You can drop them." She continued. We lowered the guns and Khari stepped closer to Dro. One thing I always noticed anything they did they did together. This woman was ready to take a bullet without so much as a thought if it meant standing by her man. I glanced at Omere and Soraya and wondered if our love ran that deep. I dismissed my thoughts and focused again on Soraya.

"I want to know why you put a hit out on me?" Soraya asked.

"Who are you?" Dro chimed in.

"It's the chick, the chick Trent sent us after. It was just business, we had a deal, we were just holding up our end of the bargain." Khari spoke up.

"So you made a deal with my brother to kill me?" Soraya's eyebrows raised in disbelief.

"Brother?" Khari's eyes crossed in confusion. "We made a deal to take out whoever was fucking with our bottom line. If that was you then yeah, we made a deal to kill you. Like I said it wasn't personal just business. I don't even know you."

"You don't need to know me, all you need to know is that you crossed the wrong people, but I'm going to give you a chance to redeem yourself. Work with us."

"Naw I'm good where I'm at." Dro barked.

"But it's better over here, my brother is desperate, desperate men do desperate things and now because of him you in the middle of this shit. I just need two things from you, your loyalty and his whereabouts. I can pay you twice what he is paying you, come fuck with the winning team." Soraya squared her shoulders standing with Omere to her left and me at her right.

Dro and Khari were both silent, but I could tell that she had Dro from the moment she said double the money.

* * *

I stood in front of Director Bryant, it's been a month and I was in. Even though it was at the sacrifice of someone else's life we had to move forward. Many people had been sacrificed in the pursuit of bringing this organization down. We were wrapping up our meeting.

"I haven't figured out every connection yet Director, but I know this is a family thing. Give me just a little more time and I will find out just how deep this runs." I reached to open the car door. These meetings were always quick, the quicker they were the better I could stay in my role.

"Just one more thing before you go." I turned to face him.

"What went down in that warehouse, you had nothing to do with. Right?"

"No, Director, like I said he was already dead when I got there. I gave them the information they needed and helped them get their money back. We tried Director."

He nodded his head and I turned to leave. It bothered me just a bit that I had to lie to him. I knew I couldn't be involved or a witness to a crime. Knowing the law backward and forward like I did, I knew better, but I wasn't about to blow all of the time I spent working on this case.

I was on my way to meet Soraya. I knew they trusted me but now I wanted more. I needed to know how their organization worked on the inside. I figured out from the first meeting with them that this was a family thing. This organization's hands reached far and wide and sitting at the top of the pyramid was the father. Then I'm guessing her and the brother were second in command.

I couldn't be certain. All my life my father had taught me how to gather intel without asking questions, so I was silent most of the time and kept my questions to myself. I didn't want to seem too eager and Soraya wasn't at all ready to open up about who they were and what they were doing there.

I pulled the car up to a condo that Soraya and Omere shared. I had only been here one time before. Judging from the decor this really didn't seem like anyone actually lived here, it was furnished but not lived in. I suspected they trusted me but only so far and there was no way they were going to lead me to their front door just yet.

I jumped on the elevator and hit the button for the top floor. I stood at the door after pushing the doorbell and waiting for someone to let me in.

"Hey." She spoke as she opened the door. I still noticed how gorgeous and exotic she looked. Her toasted skin and silky hair always caught my attention. "Come in."

"You guys wanted to see me?" I asked.

"Yes, Omere isn't here yet but come on in."

I walked in and sat down on the small chaise and waited for Soraya. She sat beside me and then offered me a glass a wine. I took the glass and slowly swirled it and then sipped watching her as I brought the glass to my lips. I needed to find a way to pull her in again.

"So Omere will be here shortly but I'm gonna get started."

"Okay." I didn't know where this was going. Maybe they wanted me to do another job, I hoped so, that would have given me even more access to their inner workings.

"So first off, you've been doing great work for us. It's been some months and you have proved you can keep your mouth shut and just do the job."

My eyes were glued to her as she paused to take a sip of her wine. I jumped on the inside careful not to expose the way I was really feeling. With each passing day, I could feel myself getting closer and closer to my goal. I exhaled. Soraya and Omere had been cool and if they hadn't been on the opposite side of right we may have really connected. I liked them but I had to keep my focus. Somebody had to pay, this case had been my father's life's work and I was going to finish it.

"So first off we wanna move you out of that crummy ass one room apartment you are in. You can stay here. It's a thank you for the work you've been doing. The better you do the better we pay." She laughed.

"Here? With you guys?"

"No, here by yourself," She turned her head to the side, cutting her eyes to the left to watch me. "We don't live here Amina." She sat her glass on the small table to the right of her and looked at me. There was an awkward silence between us that I couldn't quite read. I was always so careful not to get ahead of myself when it came to her. Just like when we were in jail she was super suspicious of everything. I didn't want to give her any reason on the outside to terminate our arrangement. I needed to do something. I placed my hand on Soraya's exposed thigh. Her skin felt as soft and delicate as I remembered. She had made it more than clear that what happened was only on the inside, out here we were nothing. But I wanted to move things along and this is how I got her to let her defenses down. I wanted her to trust me and I had a feeling if I wasn't family or sharing her bed that trust would never come.

I slid my hand along the open split in her dress and leaned towards her. She turned her head to the side, anticipating the kiss I was trying to place on her lips.

"Look at me baby, focus on me." I breathed. "I know you still feel what I do."

She slowly turned her head towards me, as she did I leaned in to kiss her. She pressed her lips together firmly, preventing me from slipping my tongue inside. I could feel the fire start to stir below as I kissed her.

Dominating a woman like this wasn't easy, getting her to give herself to me was always a challenge, and I think that turned me on. My hand slid further up her thigh, pushing her panties to the side. I could tell she was just as excited as me.

My fingers slipped between her folds, slowly sliding them into her wetness. I moved even closer to her, pushing her body against the chair we were on. I buried my head in her neck. I softly kissed her running my tongue tenderly over her skin before kissing and sucking, then gently biting. My nipples hardened.

"HmmmMmmm." The sound of a deep booming voice vibrated through the room. It seemed to be the finger snap Soraya needed to pull her back to reality. She pulled away and I slid my hand from under her dress. I couldn't make eye contact with Omere, and I couldn't help but scream in my head "Don't fuck this up!" I didn't know what he would feel about what he just saw. My heart raced as I finally looked at the both of them.

"I'm sorry," I said. I had no remorse. I did what I had to do, when I had to do it and I enjoyed it each and every time I was intimate with her. The only thing that could make me regret things would be for that kiss to have messed up how close I was getting.

"We," She moved her hand back and forth to drive her point home, "Can't do that."

I shook my head letting them both know that I understood. Omere was silent and watchful. I wondered if he knew about what happened with us while she was locked up. As if she read my mind, she answered the question that tumbled around in my head.

"He knows about everything that has ever happened between us, I don't hide anything from my husband, and I don't cheat on him."

"I understand, I apologize. It won't happen again."

"Good, because the only way that it ever could, is if it happens with the both of us." Omere looked at me, making direct eye contact as he spoke. I heard his message loud and clear.

THIRTEEN

WE RODE down the highway in silence. After leaving the club I was sure Trent and Dominque would hear something. I found myself trying to constantly prove to them that I was with them.

"I don't know how much we can trust Dro and Khari, so what's your next move?"

"We find out where Trent and this wife of his are hiding and we end this shit once and for all." Omere calmly answered my question.

"I know where they live, at least I believe I can get us back there."

"And how long you been holding on to that shit?" Soraya peered at me out of the corner of her eye.

"I haven't been holding shit Soraya. I playing ball by y'all fucking rules here. How much more do I have to do to prove that to you?" Soraya turned to face me in the backseat, her face aflame with anger. How much more was I going to have to do to prove my loyalty to her?

"I'm telling you this shit as it comes to me, Soraya, I'm not hiding anything." Omere made eye contact with me in the rearview mirror but didn't say anything. When it came to Soraya and I, he tried to let us work out the petty stuff on our own. He only stepped in on the really important things.

I sat back in my seat and crossed my arms, fuming on the inside. If I could let our past go why the hell was she having such a hard time doing so? She was so hot and cold with me, fighting what I know she wanted just as much as I did. Soraya turned around and didn't say another word. Once we made it back to the house we all got out. I had somewhat calmed down.

"Soraya."

I called her as we exited the car. She kept walking and didn't bother to respond to me. I walked into the house and headed straight for the bathroom. I needed to soothe my soul and think about everything that was happening.

I turned the water on, twisting the knob to the left to increase the heat in the water. From the moment I entered into this underworld, it had consumed me. Sometimes it chewed me up and spit me out, but I always managed to salvage something and pull myself together. That is what I was trying to do when it came to them. I saw Omere and Soraya to be one of the only good things that have come out of life ever since the day my father was murdered.

I let my clothes slip from my body, stepping out of them and leaving them in the middle of the floor. I stepped into the shower and let the oversized rainfall shower head pour water over my body. I ain't ever been weak but if I was ever at a point of falling apart it was now.

The water soaked my hair as I stood in the middle of the shower. My eyes were closed as the warm water beat down on my body. I could hear the bathroom door being softly pushed open. I opened my eyes and turned towards the shower door. Omere was standing there staring at me. He had taken all of his clothes off and his chocolate skinned glowed underneath the bathroom lights.

He opened the shower and stepped in. The oversized area was more than enough to accommodate us both. I looked up at him. I didn't have to say any words. He understood me without even having to speak.

"Give her time."

"I am giving her time."

"She took it hard after all that shit went down with us."

"So did I," I whispered as I fell into his chest. Sometimes I wish I could just take an eraser to our past. Remove the things that tore us apart and keep only the good. Omere took his hand and lifted my head up. His strong hands cradled my chin.

"It's going to be okay, she loves you. I love you."

Omere bent down and kissed me. The water beat down erotically on our bodies as we reconnected. His tongue slid inside of my mouth, then worked his way to my ear.

"You don't know how much I missed you."

"I missed you too baby."

Omere lifted my body up, above his head and I wrapped my legs around his shoulders. He took command of my body. He didn't give me a choice of what was happening, all I knew is that it was happening. He nestled his head between my legs and began to taste me. I ran my fingers through his low-cut hair as I threw my head back. My hips moved back and forth as his hands cupped my ass, squeezing tightly as his tongue probed my clit, making circles and figure eights, turning me on even more.

"I want you in my mouth." My need to taste him overwhelmed me. His tongue was kissing all the right spots, I was dripping wet, and wrapping my lips around him would only turn me on even more.

Omere lowered my body. Once my feet were firmly on the floor I dropped to my knees and grabbed his thickness. I looked up at him as I glided him inside of my mouth. He looked down at me, I never broke eye contact with him. He grabbed my head and pushed himself deeper into my mouth. I slowed down just a bit to accommodate his nine inches in my mouth. I could feel the head tapping against the back of my throat. I rocked back and forth letting him tap against my tonsils before pulling back, increasing the suction until the tip of his dick landed on my lips. Using one hand, I moved it back and forth along his shaft, teasing the tip with my tongue as I sucked. I bobbed my head up and down, gagging on it just enough to turn him on even more. Moisture dripped between my legs. I wanted him inside of me.

"Fuuuuck!" He screamed out. I smirked. That's exactly what I wanted to hear.

As if Omere couldn't wait any longer he grabbed me and pulled me up, cradling my body in his arms. I wrapped my legs around his waist and he glided inside of me. He separated my walls as he pushed inside of me, each time he stroked it became more and more intense. I wrapped my legs around him tighter and began to bounce up and down, feeling each and every stroke long and deep.

My tongue greedily searched for his mouth as he dove deep inside of me. Our kisses were greedy and intense, like we couldn't get enough of each other. His hands played between the wet strands of my hair before tightly coiling them in his hands and tugging gently.

My walls tightened around him. He pushed me against the shower wall, pinning my body against the glass. Moans escaped my lips, the pleasure was overwhelming every one of my senses. His strokes were deep, hard, and hungry for every ounce of my wetness. I closed my eyes, letting him make love to every part of me.

I felt the caress of a soft hand across my leg. I opened my eyes and Soraya was standing in the shower. I was so caught up I didn't hear her come in. Her eyes were low, almost sad. They seem to say, *I'm sorry*. She stepped forward, passionately kissing my lips as Omere continued rocking my body.

With both of them here, I was in overload. My body exploded with passion as both of them touched me. I shuddered in ecstasy as my body released a downpour.

* * *

"How the hell did you get yourself into this shit?" I asked my reflection as I stared into the mirror. I peeped into the bedroom. Soraya and Omere lay in the bed, quietly sleeping. It's been more than six months I've been undercover with them, and I could barely tell what was real and what wasn't anymore.

I quietly pushed the door shut. I needed to know what to do. It was times like this that I wished I could talk to my father. He had spent years being undercover, I'm sure he never encountered a situation quite like this but I know he must have had some close calls. I was in deep. My phone buzzed with an incoming text message. It was from my asshole of a brother. His ass was always harassing me.

You got anything yet?
Working on it.

I quickly erased the messages between us. I don't know why he didn't seem to understand not to text me on this number. I never wanted either one of them to walk up on me and my cover gets blown.

I was getting ready for another meeting with Director Bryant.

I needed to give them something, everyone was starting to get a little antsy. The problem was I didn't want to give them Soraya or Omere, and I wasn't all that convinced that they were the ones calling the shots. After dressing I slipped out the door. They were both still sound asleep. At least two nights out of the week they stayed with me at the condo they gave me. I checked the time on my phone. I had less than fifteen minutes to make it to my meeting. I leaned over Soraya and whispered to both of them.

"I'm going to run some errands and then to the store, I'll be back soon." Soraya began to sit up.

"I'll go with you." She groggily stumbled over her words as she squinted her eyes to protect them from the daylight that crept through the windows.

"No baby, just rest. I'll be back soon."

She leaned in and kissed me goodbye. I turned to walk out of the room.

"Where's mine?" I stopped and smiled as I turned around, leaning over her to plant a goodbye kiss on him. I never once thought that this would be my life, but honestly, I liked being with the both of them.

I quickly shuffled out of the house and jumped in my car. Even that had been upgraded. I had gone from pushing a Nissan to pushing the Benz they paid for. My job definitely had its perks.

I pulled up to our designated meeting area. I was late. Director Bryant stood near the banks staring blankly into the Hudson River. I walked up slowly, his back was turned so it was hard to gauge his mood.

"Hey Director Bryant, sorry I'm late."

"Obviously you think I don't have better things to do than to wait on you all day." He turned to face me. His red cheeks and furred brows told me he was more than unhappy with me. There was a long pause between us. I didn't want to speak too fast but the silence was making me uncomfortable.

"I know you have better things to do sir, it's just not that hard to always get away."

Director Bryant pursed his thin lips together, staring down on me with his piercing blue eyes. His expression said he didn't fully trust me. He looked off again. More silence.

"Which one of them are you fucking Viera?" His question caught me off guard.

"Sir, I don't know what you're talking about."

"Cut the bullshit, you're not the first agent to ever go undercover. You think I don't know what's happening?"

"I can assure you, sir, I am fucking no one." I lied. He shook his head in disgust.

"It doesn't matter to me how you get your info just make sure you are getting it and not forgetting which team you play for." He looked towards the car they had given me. "Nice car." Sarcasm dripped from his voice, I couldn't really tell if he was upset or jealous.

"Sir..." He waved his hand in the air to silence me.

"Look Viera, I got the DEA breathing down my neck, you been undercover for close to a year and you haven't given us much of anything we can use. We need results, sooner than later."

"I know sir, but I'm convinced this guy that I think is the father is who we really want. He seems to be the one that is calling all of the shots."

"Have you seen him or interacted with him anymore?"

"No sir, but I can find him I know I can."

"This wouldn't be you just trying to protect your boyfriend." Director Bryant was sure that he had figured it all out.

"Sir, I assure you that's not what's going on," I spoke that one with more confidence. That's not all that was going on. "Sir, I have a plan. I know she meets with him every third Friday of the month. Of course, I'm never invited but I think if I can get a tracker to slip on her car, we can get the meeting spot and pick him up from there. I'm telling you sir, he is the one we want. We get him we bring the whole damn organization to its knees."

"Last chance Viera, last chance." He walked off to his company issued car. I turned around and slipped back into my car. I had found a way to try and protect the people I was falling in love with, even it meant taking down someone they loved.

FOURTEEN

IN THE DEAD of night things could look so different. I drove through the streets attempting to back track. It was dark when I escaped and it was a lot harder to recognize them from pieces of broken memory. Omere and Soraya rode in silence. As I drove in circles trying to remember how to get back to Trent and Dominique's house.

"You sure you know where you're going?"

"No, it was late and dark and I was running for my life, but I'm trying." I popped back. I know they just wanted to know why we were going in circles for the last thirty minutes.

"I know we are close. Just give me a minute." I clutched the driving wheel and made a left instead of a right this time.

"We done gave your ass a lot of minutes." She shot under her breath. I cut my eyes towards her but decided to ignore the comment. It wasn't worth another argument and I knew her personality. She couldn't always help her sarcasm. It was taking some time but I knew that wall was slowly breaking between us.

I pulled up to another stop sign and finally something started to look familiar. I looked from left to right.

"Wait, I've seen this before. I know where I am now." I turned to the right and hit the gas. Anticipation washed over me as I maneuvered the car into the driveway. The garage door was down but clearly damaged. I knew that was from me driving through it when I was trying to get away.

"It doesn't look like anyone is home." Omere looked the house over as he got out of the car. The sound of the ocean waves crashed against the beach was the only thing we could hear. The house was frighteningly dark.

"Move back."

Omere pulled his gun from his waist and headed towards the front door. Soraya and I stepped back and waited for him to clear the way for us. As if on cue we both went for our guns and was ready to back him up at any moment. Omere stepped back and kicked the door so hard it flew open.

We entered the house slowly, unsure of what to expect on the other side of that door. The house was dim but not dark, the little bit of daylight left crept through the windows giving us just enough light.

"Let's split up, Mina you take the back, Omere you go up and I will check the front."

We both nodded, letting Soraya take the lead. We could cover more area by splitting up. Moving swiftly but quietly I started checking all the rooms in the back area. I pushed the door open to the very last room. The room that they held me in, my former cell. I looked at the bed, the restraints they used were still there. There was nothing here.

Even though I was doing my part to search the house, I knew they were long gone. Just being honest with myself, they knew they had kidnapped a federal agent. They probably left as soon as I got away, thinking that I would be back and hot on their trail.

"Hey!" Soraya called from the front of the house. Both Omere and I rushed towards where she was standing.

"Look at this shit." Soraya pointed to the iPad that was propped on the counter it was plugged in a nearby outlet and had full power. There was a pink post-it stuck to it with the word play scribbled across it.

"What the hell is this?"

"Don't look at me, I have no idea. Looks like someone wants to play games." I shrugged my shoulders and relaxed. There was nobody here. "So who's gonna hit play?"

Soraya stepped forward and ripped away the posted. She hit the home button on the device and light illuminated the dim area. Her manicured hand tapped the already open video player and started the video. It was so quiet in the home the only thing that could be heard was our labored breathing. We were all eager with anticipation as we waited for the video to start.

Trent and Dominique's face popped up on the screen. Watching them on the screen was like pouring salt on my open wounds, everything was still fresh on my mind. Trent's eyes were ablaze with a cocky arrogance, it was the same expression he watched me with the night they took me from the club. It was odd to me that he never let on to Dominique that he had encountered me before, he just allowed her to believe that she was the reason that I had stumbled into their lives, when he had been one of my targets all along. Dominique sat to his side, it seemed as if it took them forever to start speaking. Then finally, he spoke. Our eyes were glued to the screen.

"Soraya, sister. You are so fucking predictable. You could have just left shit alone. But you didn't, and I should have stopped this shit years ago. Go back to New York sis. This area is mine now, I got it from here. And if you don't I will mother-fuckin' do what your mother should have done as soon as she found out she was pregnant with you, " He smiled at the camera and made a gesture as if he was cutting his throat. We all knew what that meant. The video ended and all of us just stood there.

"Soraya, why does he want you dead?" I never questioned her about him, I preferred to find out the information on my own, but I didn't understand what was really happening. He tried to have her killed once and now he was attempting to follow through on that threat. I faced her waiting for her to answer me, but instead, she just stared at his face on the finished video.

"This shit is on him, if he wants a fight he can get all the smoke." Soraya pulled her gun back out and shot the iPad off of the counter, then turned and left the room.

* * *

It was time. I needed to put my plan into action. I sat across from Kash as we discussed how to take the father down.

"I put the tracker on her car to find out the meeting location. They meet here every third Friday, here." I pointed to the location on the map in front of us. "To take him down, I suggest that we put agents here, here and here." My finger landed in the spots I felt were crucial.

"Why here?"

"Because of what happened with Dad. This way if they are here there is no way they can sneak up on us." I lowered my head. If only I had listened to my father when he wanted me to come back with back up. This time, Dad, this time around I'm gonna make you proud.

I refocused my attention on the conversation with my brother. We both had fallen quiet. Our father's death was a sore spot for the both of us.

"What I don't understand Mina is why are we only taking down the dad, seems like it would be better to take them all if you could." His brows connected.

"Because he is calling the shots, I think we have a better chance of making it stick if we get him, how many times have you had Soraya in your custody and she's gotten out of it. He even showed up in jail when I was undercover. I'm telling you he is our guy."

It really wasn't any use him debating this with me, Director Bryant had already approved this. We were going after him and that was it.

"Okay," I stood to my feet signaling the end of this meeting. "This is it, we finally finish what Dad started." He nodded at me.

"It's finally finished." I moved towards my brother. I hugged him, we had our differences, but right now he was the closest thing I had to my father, he even looked like him.

Leaving our meeting I felt extremely accomplished. This shit was finally gonna be over. If I had my say in it, Omere and Soraya would never know I had my hand in taking her father down. All the time I have been spending with them I know I wanted a life with them, but I didn't think that was at all possible. But it was something about this relationship that made me finally feel something, and I wanted to protect the people that gave me that.

I looked at the tattoo that they had convinced me to get. Omere told me this was a forever thing. I knew we didn't have forever, all we had was now and that was coming to an end. I drove back to the condo. I needed to work things out for tonight.

"Hey baby." Soraya sat on the sofa painting her nails.

"Hey, where you been?"

"Just checking on the different spots you put me in charge of."

"My books good." She laughed out loud.

"Yes, everything is good." I lied. I walked over and leaned in to kiss her. It was probably the last time.

"Are we still doing dinner tonight?" I knew that we weren't, cause I had been watching her, I knew what tonight was.

"No, we have a meeting."

"Can I come with?"

She leaned and kissed me again. "No."

"Why not?"

"Because you can't, it's business, but it's none of your business." I shook my head up and down and clicked the tv on. I watched the clock. The hours ticked down and I felt anxious. Soraya slipped on her shoes and said her goodbyes. My heart raced as I watched her walk out of the door. This was it, but it was my job and my mission to bring someone to justice for my father's murder. She would lose her father, but at least he would still be breathing. I waited a few minutes to make sure that she was gone then pulled out my phone.

She's gone. They should be arriving in 20. Remember we go on my mark. On my way!.

Got it.

I grabbed my shoes and coat, then left. I parked the car three blocks from the warehouse. I hated that I kept having to come back to the place that had been the source of so much pain for me. I jogged the rest of the way to the surveillance van that was disguised as the telephone company.

My brother sat inside with his eyes glued to the tv monitor connected to the various cameras we had strategically placed around the premises.

"She made it in yet?"

"Yes. Just now. Now, how the hell do we get to him without him knowing?"

"You see that lock?" I pointed to the monitor. "I persuaded them to install them, and I have the code. She normally leaves before him. After that, we only have the men at the door to contend with and that should be easy."

"You ever find out what goes on at these meetings?"

"I was never invited. I tried. But what I do have is the finances and everything that traces back to their accounts. Inside the building, shipments come in and out, mostly from Florida. Don't be fooled, it ain't just drugs they dealing in."

We waited forever. Then they finally made their way out. I saw Omere and Soraya get in their car and drive out. I gave the signal for everyone to move in. Excitement surged through me. We all moved towards the door. My team followed behind me from both ends. I felt exhilarated and in control. My brother was to the side of me as we approached. I hit the security code and unlocked the door. Before they could do anything we were in there.

FIFTEEN

"WHERE HAVE YOU BEEN?" Omere stood in the kitchen as I walked in and sat down the cups I was holding.

"I wanted Starbucks, we were out of coffee."

"Okay, Soraya just got a call from Khari."

"Really?" I questioned as I handed him the cup I got for him and followed him into the other room.

"What did she want with you?" I handed Soraya her cup. I found it kind of strange that she was contacting her, but maybe they had gotten our message loud and clear. I didn't completely know her story but I knew they were deep into shit, trafficking, and drug smuggling. People like that went to the highest bidder and since Soraya and Omere now had the most money, they were the team to link up with.

"We are heading there soon. They say they have some things to discuss with us."

"Okay cool."

My phone buzzed in my pocket but I chose to ignore it. I drank my coffee and waited for them to finish getting dressed so we could make the long ass drive to Khari and Dro's club.

We made it to the club quicker than usual. We all got out of the car, strapped just in case they tried something. We walked to the front and pulled on the door. It was locked. Omere banged against the door.

Sergio came to the door, limping. Good. Now he will think twice about torturing anyone else. Sergio moved to the side to allow us entrance and we walked in. Khari and Dro were seated at the bar waiting for us.

"So what the hell was so urgent I needed to drive way out here?"

Dro glared at Omere as he walked towards him. You could tell there was nothing but contempt in his eyes. He looked him up and down as his veins seemed to post with anger. Khari rose and stood next to Dro, stroking the back of his neck with her hand. I tilted my head to the side, trying to figure that out. She was down for him and whatever she was doing seemed to calm him down.

"We heard from Trent and my sister," Khari spoke.

"Your sister?" Omere and Soraya said in unison.

"You're telling me my brother is married to your fucking sister?" She stared at me as she spoke the words. I hadn't brought up what I heard. I hadn't brought up much about Dominique at all. It wasn't at all relevant, so I didn't say anything.

"Yes, that's what I'm telling you," Khari shrugged her shoulders as she responded.

"If that's your sister how and the hell can I trust you? This can be a fucking setup." Soraya yelled and went for her gun. I raised my hand to touch Soraya's arm.

"I think it's okay baby. From what I've seen, she hates her sister as much as you hate your brother."

"I don't love or hate her. She's irrelevant. I'm not trying to protect her. This is my only family and the only thing that's worth protecting." She pointed at Dro. I briefly wondered what happened in all of their lives to make them turn their back on their blood. We all had our differences, but my family was always my motivation no matter how bad the circumstances were. I protected the people I loved. I shook the thoughts out of my head and tried to redirect the meeting.

"Why are we here?" I asked.

"Trent wants us to bring in a shipment. It's already on its way here. And since you blocked it last time we need to know what's up, if you're really gonna pay us twice as much then we will bring it in, and turn it over to you."

Soraya was nodding her head. I didn't know what idea was spinning in her head but I knew the wheels were turning. All of us waited in silence. Omere stepped forward and whispered something to her. She shook her head.

"When is the shipment supposed to come in?" Soraya asked.

"It's supposed to happen tonight."

"Good. We will pay. Bring it in, but we need you to let Trent think you are bringing it in for them. Get them to show up and we will take it from there. We're gonna end this shit once and for all."

"The shipment comes in at ten. We should have it here no later than eleven."

"Good," Soraya said.

"Yeah, good. Now get the fuck out." Dro boomed and walked towards the elevator in the back of the club. Omere laughed.

"I guess he's still a little salty. But it's not like I give a fuck. Tell that nigga to watch how he talks to me."

"You can show yourself out," Khari said, then turned to follow her husband.

As we left the club I wondered how far was this going to go and could this shit be really coming to an end. My phone buzzed again in my back pocket. I checked the alert.

"What's going on with your phone?"

"It's just some random spam alert I've been getting." I closed the phone and put it back in my pocket.

"Get your fucking hands in the air!" My brother Kash yelled. I went in, gun pointed straight at him. He was here the night my father was killed, for all I knew he gave the order. Shit didn't start to pop off until he arrived.

He turned to look at me. Soraya had his eyes. That part was a bit jarring but I shook it off. One of the officers stepped up and began to cuff him and read him his rights. His eyes were locked on me. We had only met one time but I could swear there was a spark of recognition.

"I know you. Is this my daughter's doing?" He asked.

"Get him out of here." Was my only response. I didn't have any explanation for him. He didn't deserve one.

"DEA is going to hold him until we can get him to Manhattan. He won't ever see the light of day again. Get the rest of them out of here." He swirled his finger in the air and the entire room was handcuffed.

"I don't wanna take my eyes off his ass. I'm going with you."

I jumped in the car with Kash. This was just as much my case as it was his. The ride to Manhattan seemed long as hell. We were *all quiet, happy that everything had worked in our favor. I looked back at him.*

"You're finally going to pay for every fuckin thing you have done. For all the lives you've ruined. You're gonna rot."

"You sure about that?" He laughed. I didn't see anything funny. Kash and I looked at each other and didn't even acknowledge that he had spoken. Anything he had to say didn't matter. My phone buzzed in my lap. I hit ignore. It was Soraya. Again and again, the phone rang and I finally decided to answer.

"Hey, babe," My voice was as sweet as honey.

"Don't hey babe me bitch, where is my father?" Soraya yelled into the phone

"What are you talking about?" I answered nervously.

"I have eyes every fuckin where, you can think I'm playing if you want. Now, this is only gonna work one of two ways. Either you let him fucking go, or you have to let her go." Just as she finished my phone buzzed with a message. I opened up the message and gasped. I hit play, her muffled screams echoed through the silent car. Someone held a gun to her head. I showed it to Kash and his eyes bulged. It was our mother.

"Let my father go. Our you will have to let her go. For good."

The phone hung up and Kash and I just stared at one another. How had this happened so fast? How had they known we had gotten him and how in the hell had they gotten to my mother? I got another message with a location. I gave it to Kash and we headed that way. There was no way we were letting shit go down like this. As we pulled in I couldn't get out the car fast enough. Omere stood outside.

"Where is she?" He looked down at me with both hurt and disgust. His eyes were glossed over with sadness.

"Was it all a lie?"

"Omere where is my mother?"

"Answer me?" He barked.

"No, you don't know how much I did to protect you, now everything is all fucked up. Where is my mother?"

"Inside. You know I'm the only reason she's still breathing. Soraya doesn't take betrayal well."

Entering the building and seeing my mother tied down did something to me. Kash entered in behind me, Soraya's dad still cuffed.

"Bitch!" She lunged towards me. "Get those fucking cuffs off of him now."

"Release my mother first." I cut my eyes to her and mouthed "It's going to be okay." And I hoped it would be.

"How in the hell did you find her?"

"You are not as tricky as you think, in fact, your sloppy ass called her number several times. You didn't think I trusted you so much that I wouldn't go through your phone. Trust is earned not given, and you hadn't earned that shit yet. All I had to do was reverse search and boom. I had her address. You're not as smart as you think."

"Let her go." I nodded towards my mother. Even though she seemed as tough as nails, Soraya looked and sounded like a woman scorned. And scorned women acted with one thing in mind and that's revenge. I needed to get my mother and she could have her father.

Our careers were probably over after this and Kash and I both knew it but it didn't matter if it meant we could get her back. Soraya nodded towards her gunmen and he lifted my mother and walked her over to us. I could see the anger in her eyes. After all of this, she was going to have to go into witness protection. For her own protection. As long as they knew who she was they would never leave her alone.

Kash took the cuffs off of her father and he walked over to her. He stood in front of her and she dropped her head.

"Didn't Trent tell you not to trust her?" He said before

bringing his backhand across the side of her face. The sound of his hand smacking her skin echoed throughout the building. She instantly grabbed her face, attempting to soothe the pain away. She looked up at me. I know she blamed me for all of this. I wanted to protect her but I knew I couldn't. I needed to get my mom to safety. My bother and I began to back out of the door.

"If you ever put your nose back in my business again, I'll kill you." The dad stare was full of venom.

Not if I kill you first. I headed out the door without saying a word. I would find a way to get to him. To make him pay, for everything he had done to me and her.

SIXTEEN

"WHAT THE HELL do you keep doing on this phone?"

Soraya snatched my phone from my hands and turned it towards her. She scrunched her nose up at the screen and then stared at me.

"So all this shit going on and you playing Toy Blast? Really? I need you to focus." She laughed and threw the phone back towards me. I slipped it back into my back pocket giving her my full attention.

"So what's the plan? I mean after all of this is said and done, what are you going to do?"

"You know exactly what I'm going to do. Kill his ass. The same he tried to do to me."

"You really gonna take your brother out?"

"Amina you know the damn story just as well as I do."

"Not as well as you do. You keep a lot of secrets you know."

"I know you ain't talking about secrets after all the things you have hidden from me." She rolled her eyes at me. I wasn't trying to go down that road. We both knew under what circumstances we met, and we also knew that this has grown into something neither one of us ever saw coming.

"Tell me, why? Why y'all hate each other so much?"

"The question is why he hates me so much?"

"So why?"

"It wasn't always like that. I don't want to talk about this shit now. Omere!" She called him into the room. Once he entered she turned her attention to him.

"Is everything ready?"

"Yeah, we got the Haitian crew on standby."

"I only want them there as a precaution in case these assholes try some sneak shit. They need to be close enough to be on the look out but far enough away not to scare away Trent."

"Yeah, that's what I told them. They headed that way right now."

Omere grabbed the keys and headed towards the door. We followed. I'm not sure what anyone else was feeling but my nerves were all over the place. I hopped in the backseat. I mean, could she really kill her brother. He had tried to kill her so maybe so. I had killed in the name of my father before, so who knows what someone was really going to do when emotions got involved. We arrived at the club and walked towards the door.

There were velvet ropes blocking it off and a sign that said, Closed for Private Event. They had thought of everything. Just like when I was undercover and they used the club to auction people off. I reminded myself to tell Soraya and Omere, don't trust these people. I damn sure didn't. I walked closer to Omere as we moved towards the door.

"Are the Haitians in place? I don't have a good feeling about Khari and Dro. We sure this what we doing?"

"This ends tonight." Soraya overheard me and answered for him. We walked inside to an empty room. We sat down at the bar and waited for them.

We heard the elevator ding and just like that it was on. The doors slid open and four people stepped out, Dro, Khari, Trent, and Dominique.

"What the fuck are they doing here?" Trent sauntered towards us, his lips curled in a slanted smile. He seemed amused. Dominque on the other hand, didn't seem amused at all. She looked my way and made eye contact with me. She was pissed.

"I have an even better question. What the fuck is a got damn cop doing here?" Dominique spoke. Her lips tightened as she spoke. Yeah, she was pissed.

"Oh, they know who she is. See that's what she does, she gets in your head, she fucks you and then fucks you over. Do I have that about right?" Trent spoke up.

"So this a fucking game to you?" Dominique screamed. "What you trying to have us arrested. Again?" Everyone in the room turned to look at me.

"Calm down, it was never a fucking game. It was what it was. I needed you to get to them. I offered you a way out, you didn't take it. You can't save nobody that don't want to be saved." I shrugged.

"Cut this shit out!" Soraya screamed. "She's not FBI any more she's with us. And I don't give a damn who or how she fucked to do her job, she's with us now. Enough of the soap opera bullshit."

Soraya moved so fast we didn't even see it coming. Her knife was out and she was on Trent before anyone could stop her. When the knife came out that meant that it was personal. We pulled out our guns and pointed them towards Trent and Dominique.

"You should have stayed in your place little brother."

"My place, you're the one that has no place in this family."

"Everything I've done for you and this fucking family and you're going to tell me my place? I'm the reason you stayed squeaky clean. I'm the reason we are as big as we are. I'm the one that did all the hard work while you were getting your ivy league education. Dad gave me my territory, and he gave you yours. You're the one that fucked yours up."

"You're not the reason for anything but having this FBI hoe stalk us. You're the reason Dad had to leave the country and definitely not the reason we are successful. Get that fucking knife out my face."

"Fuck you, Trent."

"Fuck you, Soraya!" She raised the knife and pressed it towards his neck. He didn't so much as blink.

SEVENTEEN

SORAYA STARTED to slowly press the tip of the knife into his throat. Tiny drops of blood started to drip down his neck. Trent grabbed the knife and pushed her back, bending her wrist back so far she fell under the pain of trying to fight back.

"I told you get this fucking knife out of my face." He twisted her hand so now the knife was pointed at her. I raised the gun to Dominique's head.

"Stop," I yelled. He looked at me.

"You're not going to shoot her. Your weapon of choice is your pussy bitch, and it ain't got no power here."

"But I will shoot you." Omere raised the gun to Trent's head. We were in a standoff, but no one was budging. "Let my wife go."

The front doors of the club opened. Khari and Dro were standing near the doors. Who in the hell had they let in?

"What the fuck is going on?" I had heard this voice only a few times but it had stayed with me. It was their father.

"Dad," Trent and Soraya said in unison. Five other men entered behind him. I watched as they walked into the club, massive men dressed in black with guns that could empty full clips before our pistols were able to get off a few rounds. I didn't see this coming. I looked at Khari and Dro, they were the only ones without guns pointed at them. I knew they couldn't be trusted. I watched the door. Where the hell was the backup?

I was fixated on the door. The last person to enter was a woman. A woman I had never seen before. She walked in like all of the ground was a runway. Her hair long and sleek, her skin was toasted like it had been kissed by the sun on the daily.

"Get that gun out of my son's face."

Omere knew he was outnumbered, clearly, that was a given. He dropped his gun and stepped back and I did the same.

"Give me the got damn knife." She held her hand out and waited for Soraya to hand her the blade. She took it from her and continued talking. "So you were going to kill my son, your brother." Her accent was thick.

"Marisol, he tried to kill me first."

"Do, I look like I give a fuck about the details?"

"You never have,"

"What did you say to me?" This woman did all the talking. Their dad stood next to her but he was silent. Was I wrong all this time about who was in charge?

"I said you never have. Y'all let him get away with murder. Literally. This motherfucker was going to try to kill me. I'm the oldest, I'm the one that does all the hard shit for this family. He don't do shit and everything has always been handed to him."

"That's because he is my son, the real heir. You were lucky I let you stay around. Get on your fucking knees."

"What?" She said.

"Get on your knees. All of you!" She pointed at the three of us and then their gunmen came up behind us. All of us slowly fell to the ground.

"I'm not going to beg you for my life." Soraya shot back at her defiantly.

"Marisol, wait. She's my daughter." Trent's dad finally spoke up. Trent stood behind his parents smiling. He was already claiming victory.

"Tre she's your daughter, not mine." She turned her attention back to Soraya. "You're just like your mother. She didn't know how to stay in her place either and you know what I did to her."

"Go to hell Marisol."

"Go to hell, after all I've done for you. Allowed you in my home, clothed, you fed you."

"Bitch you also used me as your hitman and your fall guy and your punching bag. Jealous hoe, mad caused he loved my mother."

"He never loved her, as a matter of fact, to prove who he loved more, he made her get on her knees just like you, and executed her trifling ass."

The conversation between the two of them was brutal. No wonder Soraya had a wall up. If this is what I had to contend with all her life I would be constantly on guard. How could you trust anyone if your enemy was in your own home? She looked at her father.

"Is that true?" Soraya stared up at him. "You said it was the cartel. When we were in Texas you said the cartel got her." She shouted at him.

"Soraya, bitch I am the cartel. I'm Griselda, Pablo, and El Chapo all in one. My father's name ring bells and that means that mine does too. If I want you to disappear. You will. Just like your mother. She should have stuck to keeping books, and not fucking my husband."

I cut my eyes back towards the door. There was little we could do in this situation. And where was the fucking backup? No wonder we were never able to catch these assholes. The shit got deeper and deeper every time a layer was peeled back. It was obvious this is deeper than anyone could have known. They hid in plain sight. I closed my eyes and threw back my head, trying to feel my father's presence. This was one of those moments that I needed his knowledge and expertise. The backup wasn't coming in and I didn't know how to get us out of this.

I opened my eyes and looked at all of their faces. Dominique and Trent had looks of pure satisfaction and vindication. Khari and Dro stood towards the back watching but not interacting. Somehow I knew they had to have something to do with this.

"Now I want you to disappear." She pressed the gun to Soraya's head.

EIGHTEEN

THE DOOR BANGED against the wall as a flood of people rushed in. *Finally.* What took them so long? Marisol dropped the gun and smiled. There was absolutely nothing for her to smile about. I stood to my feet. Backup had finally arrived. I felt like my silent prayer to my father had worked.

"FBI, get your hands up." They yelled as they pushed through the room. Everyone's hands went up except the gunmen. They had their guns pointed and ready to shoot.

"You don't want to do that." I looked at Marisol and Tre. "Looks like you were outsmarted. Have your men drop their weapons." She smiled and nodded at them. They lowered their weapons. I walked over to the agents.

"Director Bryant. Man, am I happy to see you." I said.

"What the hell is happening, Mina?" Soraya faced me, her hands still in the air.

"I'm saving us," I said.

"You are double-crossing, us? Again?"

"I told you these people couldn't be trusted. You were right it had to be finished but the way you were trying to do it would only make it worse. I didn't lie to you. What I said I meant. But this way is better."

About a week ago I started getting messages on my cell phone. Vague at first but when I realized it was Director Bryant and he was still working the case I jumped on it. Hiding this from them was one of the hardest things I had to do. Looking at them I could tell they were hurt, but they had to understand. This was a way of getting us what we both wanted. Somebody had to pay for my father and this horrible family would be out of the way. We could live our lives finally in peace after this.

"So just like I said, we have the two families we were after in Texas and Miami, and look we even got bonuses. These two are the head. We finally got the head of the entire organization." I was overwhelmed with excitement it was finally happening. The director just shook his head and turned towards me.

"Cuff her." He said and turned towards me. An officer approached and began to read me my rights.

"You have the right to remain silent and refuse to answer questions. Anything you say may be used against you in a court of law. You have the right to consult an attorney before speaking —"

"Wait, stop. Why the hell are you cuffing me?"

"— to the police and to have an attorney present during questioning now or in the future" He ignored me.

"Them as well." He pointed to Omere and Soraya.

"Wait, Bryant, this isn't what we discussed."

"Viera, I've saved your ass enough times. Get her out of here."

I haven't felt the kiss of cold metal against my wrist since I was undercover the first time. They walked us out of the club all handcuffed. I noticed that we were the only ones being arrested.

I looked over my shoulder, back at the rest of them. Every single one of them looked pleased. We were the only ones confused. How had this all gone so wrong?

"What the fuck is going on?" Omere and Mina looked at me as we were being led out. I shrugged. I had no words because I had no idea what was happening or even why.

When I received the text from Bryant we discussed protection for myself, Omere and Soraya. I would retire from the FBI and we would go on. But none of that looked like it was happening.

Once we were outside they led us to separate cars. I sat in the back of the squad car looking out into the night. My worse nightmare was happening. The door opened and Director Bryant came in.

If looks could kill he would be dead. I was pissed off. I had never been on the receiving end of this situation. I had had guns held to my head. Gone undercover in every dangerous situation imaginable and this dude strolls in and snatches everything that motivates me in life away.

"I know this is a joke right?"

"Do you see me laughing?"

"Sir I don't understand. Why am I cuffed? I pretty much gave you the entire organization on a platter."

"Aiding and abetting, conspiracy to commit murder, the distribution and sale of narcotics, your list is long."

"You know that's bullshit. Why am I really here? The deal was for them to be arrested I was willing to retire. I just asked for protection for them."

"For your girlfriend and boyfriend and y'all twisted love affair. Look Viera, no one gives a shit about any of that. What you and your father never understood is that it all comes down to the bottom line."

"What the hell are you talking about?" I cut my eyes at him. Nothing he said was making sense. Especially because he had been right there with me as I worked the case. He had even helped me relocate to Texas. It was the only way to stay on the case.

"I'm talking about being on the side that pays better. You know how it is. You lived the life, they pay way better than the bureau ever could."

"You telling me you're dirty?"

"I wouldn't call it that, I'm arresting some of the bad guys just not the ones that pay me. And that woman in there, she is connected to one of the largest cartels in Sinaloa. Those pockets are deep, and I got two kids in college."

I sat back in my seat ending the conversation. I had no desire to keep it going. He got out of the car and the officer got in and began to transport me. I rode in silence but I was fuming.

When we arrived at the station, I was booked, had to take a mug shot and was fingerprinted. It wasn't my first time but this time it was for real. I wasn't an undercover agent that could be pulled out at any time. I was an inmate.

"Where are the other two?" I asked the officer that was escorting me to my cell.

"Quiet inmate." He grabbed me by my arm and shoved me through the open door.

"Wait, why the fuck am I being put in segregation?" I stumbled inside from the forceful shove he just gave me.

"Because you're a dirty cop. And cops don't do well in jail." He laughed and slammed the door shut. I looked around the cold gray room. The metal door only had a small slot which was used to deliver my meals.

"Fuuuuuuck!"

"Quiet inmate!" The corrections officer banged his heavy hand against the door to get me to shut up. I slumped to the floor waiting for the door to be opened. Waiting for them to come in and tell me that they only had to arrest me to protect me. I waited in silence for someone to walk in. But no one came in. The doors didn't open and my cavalry wasn't coming.

My eyes watered as I stared at the heavy metal door. It was finally sinking in that my life was completely changing and the door in front of me, the fucking door was never going to open. I leaned back against the bed. The player had just been played.

EPILOGUE

SIX MONTHS. Six months of staring at these steel gray walls. I had no contact with the outside, and no contact with Soraya or Omere. I was alone. I sat in my cell, constantly making notes of things I possibly missed. I was worried about Soraya and Omere but I had no way of knowing what was going on.

I hadn't yet had a court date or anything, it's almost like they had stuck me in here and forgot about me. The guard banged on the door.

"4-5-6-8-2-3, you have a visitor."

I stood and made my way to the door. I didn't know who would be visiting me. I had briefly thought about reaching out to my brother to help me but I didn't want to drag him back into this twisted game. I walked the door and placed my hands through the open slot and allowed the guard to slip the cuffs around my wrist.

I stepped back and waited for the doors to open. I knew the routine, I stood there my hair falling past my shoulders. It was wild, curly and unkept. I'm sure I looked a mess. I felt like a mess. I turned towards the CO.

"Do you know who's here?"

"You'll know when you get there." They never answered any of the questions I asked. When it came to me they rarely did anything. I shuffled slightly behind him until we made it to the room. This was a private room used by lawyers to meet with their clients. I didn't have a meeting today. My lawyer rarely showed up. It was obvious I was stuck in here and the people that put me here seemed to want to make sure I stayed. I was confused but decided not to question it.

The guard opened the door and ushered me in. He removed the restraints and exited the room. I noticed a man in the corner with his back to me. I sat down while rubbing the spot where the handcuffs had roughly rubbed my hands. The man finally turned around.

"Trejo." He took a seat across from me. "I'm surprised to see you here. I am surprised to see anyone from the Bureau."

"I'm surprised I'm here too, but you did save my life. Even if you did slip from my custody and cause an entire shit storm to rain down on me I'm here."

"I'm sorry, I really felt like I had no alternative. You do realize someone was trying to kill me."

"So here's my first question, what the hell happened?"

"I'm still trying to figure that out. I got a message from Bryant, he was my director in New York, he worked the case with me. He double-crossed me."

"I have a question before we continue. What happened to the other two that were arrested with me?"

He paused, staring at me. He shook his head, I guess trying to understand where I was coming from. No one could ever understand what made us work. It just did. He pulled out two manilla folders from his bag and laid them across the table. He opened them and showed me pictures of both Soraya and Omere.

"You talking about these two?" He pointed at their pictures.

"Yes," Duh, damn what was he getting at.

"Both Soraya and Omere Francis were released two weeks after being arrested."

"What?" My chair flew back as I stood. "What do you mean they were released? Why in the fuck would they be released while I'm left here to rot?"Trejo's eyes pitied me. He felt sorry for me. But why? Trejo pulled out more pictures.

"They were spotted in several locations in Miami." He pointed at pictures, of them moving around the city. Free. While I withered away in segregation. By myself fighting not to go crazy.

"How in the hell did this happen?"

"They bonded out as soon as bail was set."

"But my bail was revoked. They are more of a flight risk than me." The more I looked at the pictures the angrier I became. My leg shook chaotically as I attempted to contain my fury. But it was useless, the more I stared at the pictures the more the press built. Every day I worried about them. Every day I wondered if they were okay and they were just fine. They were out before I could even blink an eye. They were living their best lives and I was slowly dying inside.

"Trejo, why are you showing me this?"

"Because Viera, no one knows this case like you do."

"Okay." I was apprehensive.

"Ever since your old director has been here he has been turning the office upside down. Snatching our cases, throwing out evidence and I want him out. And I know you have to know something."

I was silent for a long time. Yes, I knew more than just something that asshole admitted to me that he was on the take.

"What do I get for helping?"

"I'm working on that."

"Get me out of here. I can help, but you gotta find a way to get me out of here. They have locked me away and I don't think they plan on me ever getting out. But if you can do it, Trejo, I will stand with you and will bring Bryant's dirty ass down along with all the rest of them." He sat back in his seat and began to pack up his things.

"I will see what I can do. Guard." He yelled ready to leave the room. I turned to catch him just before he walked out the door. There was no seeing. The only thing I wanted and needed him to focus on was my freedom.

"Don't see, just get it done." It didn't matter to me how he did it just so he did. And then one by one, they were going to pay.

FULL DISCLOSURE: A TALE OF REVELATION AND RESENTMENT

BOOK FOUR SYNOPSIS

Sometimes the end is just the beginning ...

Caught in a bitter fight for survival and barely escaping arrest, the members of the Third Coast Cartel are trapped in a game of cat and mouse.

Under a watchful eye, Dominique has to walk a fine line and prove her worth to the organization. Seeing Khari as a threat, she will stop at nothing to make sure that she is the one that ends up on top.

Khari's quick-witted street smarts has kept her one step ahead of everyone else and landed her favor in the organization, but will the cost of being a boss be at the expense of her life?

With the FBI still hot on their heels, and Amina revealing

their inner workings, they must find a way to put the crumbling pieces of their organization back together.

Will the family come together to rebuild everything, or will the deceit and mistrust be their downfall?

PROLOGUE

7 MONTHS PRIOR

"¿QUIERE hablar conmigo Papí? She shuffled slowly, moving timidly into the dimly lit room. The earthy aroma of the Cuban cigar he smoked filled the small space. She inhaled deeply, the smoky-sweet scent reminded her of her childhood.

"Sí, Marisol we need to talk." Each word he spoke dripped with his Mexican accent. She walked towards her father, standing, awaiting his invitation to have a seat. He had always been a man of discipline and rules, and his presence demanded respect. "Have a seat, mija."

She sank into the plush chocolate leather chair across from him. Her heart raced uncontrollably. If he called her in for a formal meeting she knew things were serious. Whenever she set foot in this room she wasn't his daughter but an employee like anyone else, and she knew when questions were asked, answers would be expected.

Marisol exhaled slowly and waited for him to speak. She fondly looked at her father, even in his seventies he was a man of strength and showed no signs of weakness.

"We have a problem." He spoke.

"What kind of problem?"

"The same problem you sent your husband to handle. I thought you said he could do this," his lips tightened into a straight line as the space between his bushy brows wrinkled in a combination of bewilderment and disappointment.

Marisol didn't know how to respond. To her knowledge, Tre had handled things just as they discussed. Her jaw clenched as she searched for the right words to explain. The chair creaked as her father sat forward. His narrow eyes connected with hers. The balls of fury brewing below caused her to jump. She knew her father would never hurt her, but she couldn't say the same for her husband.

"I handed you the keys to the kingdom and you gave them to him. I told you when I met him, he's not as strong as you. Everything you have learned and endured. The Jamaican and Mexican blood that flows through your veins makes you strong. Stronger than he can ever be. You chose a weak man."

The loathing and hostility dripped from each word he spoke. The man she chose had *never* been enough for his daughter. She overcame adversities that crossed continents, she was smart and beautiful. Her toasted almond skin was like her mother's and her honey colored eyes were his.

His heart swelled with affection at the thought of his late wife. He had hoped his daughter would pick a man like him, instead, she selected a man that wasn't her equal, and her son would be the same if he didn't intervene.

"Papi, I —," he waved his hand to silence her. Marisol closed her mouth, swallowing the words back down before they had ever gotten a chance to be anything more than a thought. Her head fell downward as she succumbed to defeat.

Marisol was always fighting for Tre. After more than thirty years together things were not supposed to be like this. She shook her head, wondering what had Tre hidden from her this time?

"Like I said, we have a problem. This same undercover agent, Amina, that was fucking your husband's daughter and her husband," he spat the words out as if they were poison as he laid out pictures, "your son's whore of a wife Dominique who was never supposed to be his wife in the first place keeps fucking up at every turn, and your son Trent, my grandson, he has no clue what he is doing." She looked over all the information he laid out as he spoke. Her fingers traced across each of the pictures, wondering what was really happening in the states.

"Papi, Tre has done well for the organization. With all the legitimate businesses he has created as a front us and the way he is able to wash all the money, Papi, he's not weak." She was doing it again, defending him and his errors. It was true that he had taken their little Mexican organization international, but she knew, even if she never said it, she was always cleaning up his messes.

"No more excuses, mija. I won't be here forever, and I will kill him before I see your fuck up of a husband as the head of anything I've built." The leather chair creaked as her father sat back again and began to puff on his abandoned cigar. He didn't say anything else, but he didn't have to. Marisol understood loud and clear, and she knew it was not a threat at all, but a promise.

"Don't worry Papi, I will take care of things. I will make sure they are all handled." Marisol stood to her feet as she spoke and made her way to her father. She planted a kiss on his cheek and turned to leave the room. Marisol completely comprehended what was implied, take care of the problem or he will.

ONE

DOMINIQUE

BITCH. I rolled my eyes at Khari. We may have shared blood but she was no sister of mine. I could feel my lip curl as I watched her and her husband, Dro. I didn't even understand how in the hell she could even call him that, how could she marry the same man that tried to kill our mother. Fucking bitch! And here he was sitting on the side of Trent's parents, my in-laws, welcomed into the fold like Marisol birth those assholes.

Seated around the round oval-shaped table in Khari and Dro's club, I watched everyone around me. Soraya and Omere leaned into each other, whispering amongst themselves. Her eyes became tiny slits as she cut her them towards Marisol's direction. Hostility and hatred hovered in the air between them. The bitterness between the two of them was something neither of them tried to conceal.

I reached out and touched Trent's hand, rubbing it back and forth attempting to soothe the frustration I saw in him. From the pulsing vein on the side of his neck, I could tell that his mothers admiration for Khari and Dro irritated him. There was no way in hell they were just going to walk in and take what he worked, what we worked so hard for. There were so many things I did without hesitation. It felt like a slap in the face to have Marisol not see any of it.

I closed my eyes trying to blink away the pounding headache that I felt coming on. I needed to do something, I just didn't know what that something was going to be. Staring at all of them interacting I could tell my sister was sinking her claws into Marisol deeper and deeper. I didn't know what the fuck she was up to but I damn sure was going to find out. When it came to my sister things were never what they seemed. She was a shallow, clout chasing opportunist. If she was helping Marisol she was damn sure getting something out of it.

"I called this meeting for a reason." Marisol stood to speak. Her long black hair moved from side to side as she walked around the table. Her tall slender frame reminded me of Naomi Campbell. Different accent but definitely the same crazy-ass vibe. Trent never talked about his mother and I had only met his father briefly. When I thought about it I didn't know much about the inner workings of the Third Coast Cartel. Trent didn't tell me and I didn't ask unless I had to.

To know that Marisol was just as involved as the rest of them was a shock to me. I cut my eyes at Trent. He was always keeping secrets. I fought off the annoyance that was building, I had kept my share of secrets at the beginning of our relationship. I pursed my lips together and closed my eyes. Trent was miles away from the clean-cut lawyer I thought he was when I met him, and I was no longer the doting wife playing a role. Life and circumstances had revealed both of our true natures.

I watched Trent, mesmerized by his mother. His eyes followed her every move. He looked like a lonely dog begging for attention. His mother seemed to be giving all praises to Khari and I think, no forget that I knew it bothered him. I shifted in my seat and waited for her long ass dramatic pause to end.

"I'm not sure what the fuck you have been doing, but it stops now. Unless you all want us to end up dead or in jail you will do what I say and only what I say." Marisol leaned forward against the table looking me dead in my eyes. What the hell had I done to her? The way she was eyeing me down had me feeling some type of way and I didn't like it.

"We've been holding everything down while you've been chilling in Mexico," Soraya spoke up. Her voice was drenched in resentment. Marisol turned to face Soraya, she looked her up and down. Tre placed his hand softly on hers no doubt in an attempt to calm her. She yanked her hand away from him, never taking her eyes off of Soraya.

"No, what you've been doing is fucking up, again. You are lucky to even be here, cause I should have let your ass rot with your side bitch. For the second time, you let her infiltrate our organization. You let that bitch get way too close to us." Soraya sat up as if she was ready to go to war, but the look on Marisol's face scared even me. Soraya sat back in her seat

"So what chu are going to do? I'm going to tell you what you're going to do. You're going to do what the fuck I tell you! No questions asked. You do what I say and only what I say. Okay." Marisol walked away from the table with her phone in her hand. Khari made eye contact with me and I rolled my eyes at that fake ass bitch. I looked towards my husband and grabbed his hand under the table.

"Is there a way we can fix this baby, look at them," I whispered and nodded towards my sister and that man, "I don't know what exactly happened but I know whatever it was they have persuaded her to buy into their bullshit. I mean Marisol is your mother. You should be the one sitting next to her, I can tell right now she's pissed with you."

Trent sat back in his chair and rolled his tongue around in his mouth. It was as if he was searching for the words to say. I needed him to get on board with me, if we weren't careful Khari just might be the one to cash in on everything we have built for the TCC. My eyes roamed the room. Trent's father, Tre sat there like a damn mute, the same man that I saw order a killing in a dark parking garage was sitting there as if Marisol carried his balls in her purse. I was tired of this. I pushed my chair back and walked towards the back of the room where Marisol was standing.

"Excuse me," I waited for her to acknowledge me. I stood in silence for what seemed like forever staring at the back of her head. I took in all the features I could see, from her height to her long black bone straight hair.

Her form-fitting black pants and sleek sheer blouse revealed she was a woman in charge. For an older woman, a woman who had to be well into her fifties, she was stunning, almost ageless. Realizing I was still being ignored by her, I cleared my throat to get her attention. Marisol finally turned around to face me.

"What do you want?" I stepped back, looking from side to side. She couldn't be talking to me. There was no way a woman who had never met me could be this bothered by me.

"I want to talk to you, on Trent's behalf."

"If my son wants to talk to me he can do it myself." She spat back, her eyes scrutinizing me from head to toe.

"He's not going to admit how he's bothered."

"By?" She looked at me as if I was nothing more than an annoyance. Was she annoyed by my presence? She paused for a moment, what was with her and these dramatic ass pauses?

"By the fact that you seem to be mesmerized by my sister," I cut my eyes towards their direction and caught them both staring at me.

"Khari was the only one that had enough sense to contact me and tell me what was going on. What did you, my son or my step-daughter do besides almost get the entire organization brought down? I'll answer that for you, none of you did anything," Her eyes were ablaze with fury. This was going nothing how I had planned.

"My sister is the reason Amina had so much information on us," I responded. My voice raised. I felt I needed to defend myself. Her lips tightened into a jagged line as she turned to face me head on. Her hip swayed to one side as she crossed her arms, her height giving her the ability to peer down towards me. The look she gave me made me feel as small as an ant, and in any moment she might try to crush the life out of me.

"Do you think I honestly don't know what's going on? I know you don't know me, and as for all, I care we could have kept it that way. I know all about your past. Everything and you were nothing more than a cheap ass whore. My son wasn't supposed to fall in love you were only supposed to take the fall. But we are here now," again with her pause, "so I suggest you walk away before you can never walk again." Marisol turned on her heels, slinging her long black tresses over her shoulders as she walked away from me. I didn't move, I couldn't. She had just threatened me and I didn't take kindly to threats.

At all.

TWO

KHARI

"WHAT THE FUCK is that all about?" Dro barked. My hand instinctively went to the back of his neck. I was wondering the same thing. But Dro was a reactor. He saw something and he reacted but I just simply needed him to keep it together. It was too early to tell which way things were going to go, and one thing I wanted to make sure of is that we came out on top. I wanted us to be good, our business and our money.

"Cálmate," He had to remain calm. I watched my sister talk to Marisol. If I knew Dominique as well as I thought I did, she was up to something. Dominque kept glaring my way, pissed at me I guess because I have the ability to think faster, better, and further than her. She was still playing checkers when this graduated to chess long before she ever saw it coming. From the moment that Dominique and Trent stormed through our club doors, I've been outmaneuvering her, taking her pieces down one by one.

I bit my lip fighting the urge to allow the smile to spread across my face. I didn't believe in premature celebration and I knew things were just getting started. Marisol abruptly walked away, leaving Dominique staring off into space. I don't think that went the way she wanted it to. Marisol walked towards Dro and me.

"Is there somewhere we can talk? Alone." She said as she stopped in front of us.

"We can go to our office downstairs," I responded. I struggled to keep up with her long stride. My heels clicked rapidly against the floor as I moved along side her. With the way she moved through my club, you would swear she knew where she was going and it belonged to her.

I told Marisol she could use our club to get things together while she was here. When I contacted her in Mexico I didn't know what I was going to get, all I knew is that things had to change. Everything blowing up the way it did has not only shut down our nightclub, but the shipments we were bringing in had been shut down too. The port was a no-go right now, so we couldn't make any money, dirty or legit.

"Alright, meeting over get the fuck out!" I could hear Dro yelling as we walked away. He was rough but I loved that about him. We got on the elevator and headed downstairs. I opened the door once we made it and we stepped inside. She stood quietly in our office, looking around the room. I'm not sure what she was looking for. I smiled, if it were me and I walked into anyone's space I would do the same thing.

"¿Qué necessitas?" I cleared my throat and asked. I knew if she was pulling me away from everyone she needed to say something that she didn't want anyone else to overhear. I hadn't known her long but I knew enough about her to know that she wasn't for the bullshit. It had taken me weeks to get contact information on her.

I was looking for Trent's dad but the more I started to dig the more I found that he wasn't really the one in charge. None of the ones that thought they were in charge really had any clout.

When Dominique realized we had the upper hand, she snatched Amina from our club. She thought she was outsmarting me, but all she had done was given her the ability to escape. Her actions put all of us in danger and had she done it my way the problems we were all having wouldn't be happening.

But no, it was always about winning with her, and every single time she to tried to play her games, she ended up creating a bigger mess.

"I need to know I have your complete loyalty." Her heavily accented voice snapped me from my thoughts There were a lot of things about her that reminded me of Dro's mother, who had been more of a mother to me than my own mother ever had. I quickly pushed those thoughts to the back of my mind.

"Totalmente," I responded. "You have my complete trust" I sat down and waited for her to finish speaking.

"Your sister, I don't trust. She's a problem." She tapped her finger against the side of her chin as she spoke, obviously in heavy thought. I didn't trust my sister either.

"She hasn't been my sister for a very long time."

"Either way, I want to keep an eye on her. You told me she was the one that took Amina." She said. When Marisol came into town she demanded answers. She wanted to know when, how and why something happened. I had given her some background information, enough to appease her curiosity.

"Yes, we were going to take care of her. She was nothing but a nuisance. I didn't even know at the time that she had infiltrated before, the only thing I knew was that it was something about her I didn't trust. And no disrespect, but your son played just as much of a role in it as my sister did." I added.

I wasn't trying to turn her against her own son, I knew there was no way I could do that, but I wanted to paint a picture of the effect she seemed to have on him. I didn't know Trent personally, but he seemed to be a strong man, but easily influenced by the women in his life. My sister was the type of person that would latch on to a flaw like that and exploit it. "My sister is impulsive, just doesn't think. Unfortunately, your son follows her influence."

Marisol became uncomfortably quiet. I could tell saying anything about her son hit a nerve. I remember that night, how she came at Soraya saying her son was the only one true heir. She was one of those mothers who absolutely worshiped their son. Her eyes narrowed as she looked at me. She was tall and strikingly gorgeous.

Her long slender limbs should have been awkward but on her they were perfection. She seemed to glide as she moved as if the wind carried her instead of walking. She sat down in the chair across from me and crossed her legs. She didn't speak for a moment. I could tell that with each deliberate pause of hers she was deep in thought. This gave me the impression that nothing left her lips that she didn't mean and wouldn't follow through on.

"Dominique is a problem, and I don't like complications." The ominous tone in her voice gave me pause, but I couldn't deny that she was telling the truth. She was a problem and she created even bigger problems. If Marisol hadn't stepped into save us, Amina would have taken us all down, and it would have all been Dominiques fault. Her impulsive actions could have taken us all down. Thankfully Marisol's connections kept us out of jail.

"I think the bigger problem is Amina Viera. She wants to take you and anyone affiliated with you down." I could tell that Dominique bothered her if I was reading everything right, she blamed Dominique for a lot of what happened and she was probably right.

My sister had that shit storm effect, but if Amina had infiltrated their organization as much as I have heard she knew a lot, probably way too much for her to be putting her focus solely on my sister.

"She's being handled. Ahora, we need to resume our shipments. Since this whole fiasco with the FBI, all of our port connections have been shut down. Can I trust you to handle this?" Marisol reached and grabbed my hand as she spoke.

We were somehow building a bond and I knew that of everyone in that room I would be the first person she came to, to get anything done. That was just the way I wanted it. Once and for all maybe we could put an end to the back and forth bullshit. Trent and Dominique weren't the ones to lead this organization and Omere and Soraya were compromised. I understood the logic behind her thinking. We were the only ones that had no ties to Amina Viera, the only ones who had actually stayed one step ahead of her FBI games and tactics, and the only ones who could see everything for exactly what it was. In other words, Dro and I were the only and obvious choice to put this back together.

"Yes, considered the issue solved. We'll take care of it." I smiled at her, letting her know, unlike her Trent and Soraya, I can be trusted.

THREE
AMINA

"FUCKING BITCH!" Her hand crossed my face with shuddering force. I swung back as hard as I could attempting to get her off of me. Her strength and body weight seemed out matched but I was never one to just take an ass whipping.

"Get the fuck off me!" I screamed to the top of my lungs as I hit and kicked back towards the woman that seemingly came out of nowhere. I had no idea what her issue was. I was just moved into general population and minding my business, but being an agent in lock up was never good for anybody, so there's no telling why this big bitch was coming for me.

She grabbed my hair and pulled my head back while mounting my back. I bucked like a wild horse trying to throw her from my back. This seemed way too personal to be a random attack. I turned my head trying to get a good look at her. I didn't know her but it was evident that she knew me, and more than that she definitely had a problem with me. My limbs swung her direction. I needed to get her off of me. Women gathered around, watching us fight, all of them desperately wanting her to beat my ass.

"Get down! Everybody now!" Corrections officers flooded the room. The woman quickly dismounted me and slipped out of sight. I turned back and forth trying to find the woman in the sea of other women that were now face down against the floor.

"I said down inmate! Now!" I turned to face the officers who rushed in dressed in full riot gear. Their weapons were pointed my way. I placed my hands on the back of my head and fell to the ground, not wanting to get hit with their tasers.

Just as I fell to my knees I felt the jolting pain of the electric current stunning my body into submission. I had no control as my convulsing limbs hit the floor. What the hell was happening? I struggled to maintain consciousness as my body went limp and everything faded to black.

MY EYELIDS FELT heavy as I struggled to open my eyes. I could hear the blaring sound of an ambulance siren. I snapped up, ripping the oxygen mask off of my face and looking around. I didn't know what was happening. The paramedic in the van looked towards me.

"Calm down," She said as she moved closer to me and replaced the mask on my face. I ripped it back off and stared at her.

"What the hell is going on?" I questioned. I needed answers and I needed them right now.

"We'll explain everything but for now I need you to keep this mask on until we get where we are going. Her eyes pleaded with me to cooperate as she slipped the mask back on to my face. I leaned against the gurney and fell silent. I could read between the lines. I looked at each of the people inside the back of the ambulance. There was an armed guard and two paramedics. I couldn't see the driver but I could tell there were two others up front.

I struggled to remember what happened. I remembered being attacked, and fighting, then being tased. What the hell had they tased me for? I was complying. I couldn't believe this was happening.

The last six months had been hell for me. I thought about all the bullshit that landed me here and questioned how in the hell was I going to get out of what was happening to me. It had been weeks since I heard from Trejo and I was starting to get worried that he couldn't figure out a way to get a few steps ahead of Director Bryant.

I was serious when I told him that the only way I would help was to get me out of that place and he still hasn't delivered. The ambulance came to a screeching halt and the doors opened. The paramedics rushed me into the hospital shouting out a lot of medical gibberish I didn't quite understand. I mean other than the aching spot on my back I felt fine. The same paramedic looked at me and nodded, as they rolled me towards a private room.

"Let me get a doctor," She said turning towards the armed guard, "I'm going to need you to wait outside sir. He nodded not questioning the request. Once the door was closed, she pulled off the medical gloves she had on her hands and looked my way.

"Listen, we don't have a lot of time." She turned towards me as her words rushed from her mouth, "I'm Trejo's new partner. We only have about five minutes to execute this entire plan before they are going to realize that you are gone. The guard has to do checks every fifteen minutes until you receive care and are transported back to the prison."

"Ok," I responded. I was all ears.

"Take this," She reached out her hand exposing a key that was concealed under her latex glove. "This will remove the restraints. You have to be fast, this won't work if you don't follow my directions completely. Do you understand?" She said. I shook my head up and down and waited for her to continue with the instructions.

"When I leave out he is going to do a check to make sure your restraints are secure. As soon as he has confirmed it, he will leave and take his post back outside your door. That's when the clock starts. You need to get the restraints off, fast. Once off you will exit out that unlocked door over there. She pointed towards a wall.

"I don't see a door." Clearly, there was only one door in and out. She walked over towards the corner of the room and pushed the panel.

"I brought you to this room for a reason. This room is a new addition that's currently being renovated, the wall panel will remove and allow you to move into the other room, which is empty, change into the clothes waiting for you and exit out of the door. Once you have successfully made it out of the hospital doors, you need to move your ass towards the highway. Stay out of sight. Once you've made it to the highway, go to your left. Don't stop until you make it to the gas station on the left. Go behind the building and there will be a car waiting for you."

I made a mental note of everything she said to me. It was a lot and I wondered if I could pull it off, but then again I wanted out of this and I didn't care how it happened, so hell yeah I was pulling this shit off.

"You got it?"

"Yeah, I got it," I slid the key into my mouth and used my tongue to push it to the side of my cheek. The metal taste of the key was nauseating but I didn't want the guard to search me and find it.

She slipped out of the room, pulling the curtain to semi cover the door before she left. For a moment everything was still. My heart raced as I contemplated if this was going to work or not. It had too. I thought about my father and what he would say to me. I closed my eyes blinking away those tears, he would tell me to handle it and that's exactly what I planned to do.

The door creaked open as the officer entered inside of the room. Just as she had explained he moved towards me checking to make sure my hand was still restrained to the bed. He looked me up and down without saying a word and then left the room again.

As soon as I heard the door latch click I jumped into action. Using my one free hand I grabbed the key out of my mouth and unlocked the restraint. I checked towards the door to make sure it wasn't opening again. Everything was in the clear. I sprung to my feet and raced towards the panel she had shown me.

I pushed it, only opening it enough for me to slip through and then pushed it close again. Just as she said clothes were waiting for me. I threw on the garments as fast as I could and balled up my corrections uniform, tossing it into the medical waste basket. I moved towards the door of the room and peaked out.

I could see the officer yards away staring at his phone. I was sure that was against his rules but it worked in my favor. I slipped out of the door moving as fast as I could. My entire body was on fire with excitement. The closer I got to the hospital exit, the faster my heart beat. I could taste my freedom.

FOUR

DOMINIQUE

MY EYES WIDENED as I stared at Trent, not believing he couldn't understand where I was coming from. I understand it was his mother but at the same time I'm his wife and she threatened me.

But it didn't matter how many times I said it he refused to believe it. I thought his position the organization was bothering him, but it seemed that he was enjoying his vacation. I was having a hard time seeing the man I had married in the man that was standing in front of me now.

"Trent."

"Dominique," He stared back at me with a smirk on his face. I didn't see a damn thing funny about this. We had been going back and forth about this for the past three days. Ever since that dumb ass meeting she called where she paced back and forth, trying to intimidate somebody. *Bitch please.* I rolled my eyes as I thought about her telling me to walk away before I never walked again. Just what the hell did that mean?

"Trent she threatened me. I've never done anything to your mother so I don't understand where all this damn hate is coming from." I stood up and walked towards the kitchen where he was standing. I had done a lot for this family that she obviously didn't know about. It was because of me they didn't get taken out in Texas.

I was the reason they were now in Miami and had made it out with millions transferred into an offshore account that can't be touched by the United States government, no matter how hard they tried. The audacity of this bitch saying I was nothing more than a whore. My pussy had saved us more times than I can count, she should be thankful.

"No, there's nothing to talk about. Just back up. You can't push yourself on her, that's only gonna make it worse." Trent finally responded. Did he think I was supposed to be scared of her? If he knew anything about me he should have known that if you push me in a corner I was going to push back.

"I know you don't like the fact that she's got Dro and Khari sitting at her right hand." He had to hate it as much as I did. I leaned against the kitchen counter and looked up at him.

"They are disposable, it doesn't matter what she uses them for. I know my mother. Once she's done with them they are done. Period. Leave it alone Dominique, the last thing you want to do is start a war with my mother." Trent walked off towards the bathroom.

The door closed and I heard the shower come on. I sat back in my chair, unsatisfied with the conversation. How could I get through to him if he wasn't willing to listen to where I was coming from?

He was way to calm and I was fuming. He didn't seem to see what was happening. I wasn't going to sit back and watch while Khari and Dro climb their way to the top of this organization.

At the end of the day, Trent and I were the next ones up and we deserved to be running shit. We had worked hard to run this shit. Didn't Marisol know how much I had helped her son? Did she even care?

My nerves were in an uproar and I couldn't sit still. I paced back and forth trying to come up with a plan. I could, on one hand, try to get into Marisol's good graces, show her my worth and I was the one to bet on, but that sounded like a hell of a lot of ass kissing and I just wasn't into that.

This entire situation made me feel like I was back in New Orleans, being threatened by Queen. In that situation I had chosen to leave, attempting to outrun my problems, but look where that had gotten me. They still came after me. So now what do I do about my mother-in-law from hell? It was obvious she didn't like me. She had all but told me that to my face, Trent said don't go to war, but sometimes shit just wasn't avoidable.

I didn't know exactly what I was going to do but I know I needed an ally. Someone who was going to be on my side. It would be an uphill battle trying to convince Trent that his mother was an evil bitch that needed to be taught a lesson, so maybe I needed a different approach.

I heard the shower go off right before Trent stepped out soaking wet, water still dripping from his body as he toweled off. I walked towards him. I needed to use a softer hand with him in an attempt to get what I wanted. I wrapped my hands around his neck and pulled his lips towards mine. His lips pressed softly against mine. It seemed like forever since I felt this kind of kiss from him.

His hands roamed my body, pulling me closer into him as he kissed me. I tugged at the towel around his waist and allowed it to fall to the floor. I pulled away from his lips and kissed his chest, running my tongue down his deep brown skin. I dropped down to my knees and slipped the tip of his dick inside my mouth. My tongue went around in circles as I pushed him deeper and deeper inside of my mouth.

"Damn," He moaned. Trent pushed my head down as far as it could go. I could feel him pressing against the back of my throat. I relaxed an allowed him as far as he could go. I bounced my head back and forth, letting my mouth fill with saliva. Wetness dripped from my lips as I slid his thickness out of my mouth and back inside again.

I used my right hand to stroke his shaft as my left hand gently squeezed his balls. I knew just want to do to make him vulnerable to anything I wanted. Trent picked me up the floor and carried me to the bed.

His eyes were on fire with passion, I could tell he wanted more, needed more. With us dealing with all of our problems, we hadn't pleased each other like this, with so much abandon in passion in a minute. Trent grabbed at the pants I wore and ripped them away from my body. He didn't bother to unbutton, unzip or anything. The faster he could get them off the better.

"How do you want me, baby?" I let the words slip from my lips in a seductive whisper. Trent didn't respond, instead, he flipped me over onto my stomach then grabbed me by my thighs and pulled me towards him. He pushed my legs apart and my head down.

He entered me, fast and hard. I could hear my wetness as he pushed deeper and deeper inside of me. Moans of pleasure escaped from my lips as he slammed into me harder and harder. I bounced my ass back towards him, pushing deeper inside of me.

"Yeah you wanna feel this dick deep," Trent grabbed my shoulders and pulled me towards him. I couldn't run I couldn't move, the only thing I could do was take those strokes one after another.

"Fuck me baby, fuck me deep baby," I screamed. Trent grabbed me by my neck and pulled me towards him, our bodies now touching. The strength of his grasp made me even wetter.

He pressed just slightly harder and I struggled for air. The sensation made my walls tighten in ecstasy.

He stroked long and hard as I rubbed my clit. My walls tightened around him. "Baby, I'm about to cum."

His stroke became more intense as he dove deeper into me. Wetness streamed down my thighs as I screamed out in ecstasy. Our bodies collapsed on the bed together. We laid in silence for a moment. Trent wrapped his arm around me and drifted off to sleep. I knew that's exactly what would happen. I eased from under him and walked to his side of the bed. I glanced at him to make sure he was still asleep.

I grabbed his phone and entered in the code he thought I didn't know. I swiftly scrolled through his iPhone looking for Soraya's number. If I asked I know he would never give it to me, and I needed to talk to someone with an objective opinion of Marisol. Trent would never be objective. Judging from our last conversation when it came to his mother, he was not himself.

I sent the number to myself and quickly erased the message before slipping back into bed. If it's one thing that life had taught me, always have a plan B. Initially I thought this was something that my husband and I would handle together but he wasn't trying to hear anything I had to say. So Soraya was going to be my plan B.

FIVE
KHARI

DRO SAT in the living room with his feet up in his favorite part of our sectional, his recliner. I smiled at him as I walked towards him. I fell into the plush leather next to him. I nuzzled against him as he wrapped his arm around me. I loved the feel of his warmth against my skin. He always seemed to run just a little hot, but it was perfect for me. I laid my head on his shoulder and glanced up towards him, I needed to run something by him.

"Baby, I have a question," I spoke softly as I looked up at Dro.

"What's up?" It didn't matter to me how rough Dro was with anyone else. I knew how intimidating he could be, but with me, he was always kind, he treated me differently. I smiled and pulled out my iPad. I gave the screen a few taps and pulled up my notes and started reading through the notes I had made to myself.

"You know Marisol asked us to find some way to allow the shipments back in," I responded.

"Well, as long as you don't lock my ass in that safe room again to do it, I'm cool with it. As long as it is only facilitating the transport, we don't sell no shit, we don't break shit down. We bring it in and they take care of the rest. Got it?"

I shook my head as I moved in closer to him. One of the things that drew me to him was his bold matter of fact attitude. No man was more of an alpha male than my Alejandro, he was the realest man I had ever known and the only one I had ever wanted.

My sister always questioned how I could love him, given how we met, but Dominique didn't know the first thing about love. Our love was untouchable. Part of the reason we worked was because I allowed him to be him, and he allowed me to be me. We had no secrets, no side pieces, and as long as we had each other that's all we ever needed.

"I'm going to ignore that sarcasm," I said. He had every reason to throw a few verbal jabs my way, I really did lock him in our safe room. "What do you know about cocaine, but in liquid form? I have a plan, but I wanted to run it by you before I take it to Marisol.

"Okay but before you start, I mean, how do we know we can trust her?" Dro's eyebrow raised as he waited for me to respond. The truth is, how could you know you could trust anyone?

"Baby, I don't trust anyone but you but I think if we had to take our chances with anyone our best bet would be on her. I've been watching her, how she moves, how she speaks, she's calling the shots, even if Tre and Trent think they are, she's the real boss." Dro shook his head up and down, seemingly agreeing with what I was saying.

He obviously noticed it too. When we first met Trent he stormed into our office, demanding we work for him, when he really was a nobody. Marisol sat at the top, there was no question about it.

"So what about the yayo?" He asked.

"I was thinking, if we can have them turn it into liquid form, we can have it shipped to the club, like liquor. I mean I think it would work and go completely undetected by the Feds or anybody for that matter. I was thinking that we could find some-body like Andre," I paused at the mention of his name.

Dro's entire body tensed but he didn't say anything. I knew it was a touchy subject for him, Andre had been his closest friend, and to find out he was double crossing him all along Dro had no other choice than to handle things the way he did. He didn't say anything because there was nothing to say about it, Andre was gone, the problem had been taking care of.

I continued. "Someone who could set up a web presence and dummy company and make it look legit, maybe even have an actual company that makes tequila. In the shipment the top bottles will be tequila, everything beneath can be the cocaína." I sat back against the sofa and looked at my husband, waiting for his reaction. I really felt like this could work. He nodded his head and turned to face me.

"You're a fucking genius, girl." He grabbed me and pulled me unto his lap, wrapping his arms around my waist and pulling me near him. He held me firmly as he kissed me softly. His tongue slipped inside my mouth, causing a stir below. A smile spread across my face as I pulled back and looked at him.

"Alright, I'm gonna see if we can get a meeting. The sooner we can get this up, maybe the sooner things could go back to normal for us." I kissed him one last time before grabbing my phone and shooting Marisol a text. I kept the contents of the text vague, these types of conversations were better had in person. My phone buzzed with a reply.

"It's a go," I said to Dro. He stood up and followed me to the bedroom where we dressed. He sent a text to Sergio letting him know to get the car ready, and then we were headed to the club.

Once we made it there, I went to the office and waited for Marisol to arrive. I knew she wasn't the type of woman that anyone summoned so I really hoped she thought my plan was as good as I did.

She's here. Sergio sent me a text from upstairs.

Send her down

Dro sat in his chair, and I sat on the arm of it, just as I always did. I waited for her to make the short trip down the elevator. I could hear the click-clack of her heels against the hard floor as she moved towards the office. The closer she got the louder the taps became. The clicking stopped and the door opened.

"Hello, Marisol come in, have a seat," I said, my voice slightly higher than it probably needed to be. I didn't know how she would take my idea. Marisol didn't say how she wanted me to get the shipments back in, just that she did. I knew that the ports were not an option and this seemed like a sure way to get her back in business. Marisol stepped in and then took her seat.

"What is this about?" Straight to the point. She tossed her hair over her shoulders, which she seemed to do a lot, and then wound her finger in a circle. Okay.

"I think I have a solution to your shipping problem," I responded.

I ran down my plan to her just as I had to Dro. Her eyebrows raised as she listened. I could tell the wheels were spinning in her head. I knew I had gotten her attention.

"And you, you think this can work?" She looked at Dro. He had been silent as I spoke.

"Yeah," He huffed.

Marisol turned her attention back to me. "So make it happen. The faster the better."

"Okay, I'm gonna need to find a tech guy that can set up shit fast, make it look legit and then we can get started," I said. Putting this plan together was exciting to me. I got a thrill out of figuring things out.

"Your sister knows someone, back when she was lying her ass off to my son. We tracked her documents to a guy name Berto, we got him set up, upgraded his shit, and all he needed to do was let us know when and if she ever came back to him needing anything. I don't know your sister but I never trusted her." She said the last part through clenched teeth. "We'll get him in here and you get it done, okay."

"Okay. What about your people in Mexico, do you think they can handle what we are about to throw at them?" Marisol let out a long hearty laugh, throwing her head back as if something I said was funny.

"My people are ready for anything, you just do your part." Her tone told me never to question her. I made a mental note. I questioned everything, but in the future, I knew to handle her a tad bit differently.

"Okay, I'm leaving —," Her phone rang just as she was about to leave. "What?" I couldn't hear what the other person was saying on the other end but I knew it was urgent. I stood up, her tone caused me a little bit of alarm. Dro stood behind me.

"Bring that fat fucker to me!" She yelled into her phone before tapping the screen and disconnecting the call. "We have another problem."

"What kind of problem?" Dro stepped forward, pushing me behind him.

"Somehow that bitch has escaped."

"Who?" I questioned.

"Amina, Amina fucking Viera, that's who!" She shouted and then abruptly turned to leave the office.

SIX

AMINA

SHE WAS STILL HERE, why was Marisol still here? Standing in the shadows between two buildings, I watched from across the street as the large black door opened and Marisol exited Dro and Khari's club. She moved swiftly down the sidewalk and jumped into a black car.

I snapped pictures of her and the car, trying to record as much information as possible. Somehow I tricked myself into believing that this was all about surveillance, but secretly, I was hoping to get a glimpse of Soraya and Omere.

I had no idea what made them turn their backs on me, but something inside of me desperately needed to know. I had spent countless days in my cell wondering if there had been any signs and how had I missed them all.

I stared at the tattoo on my arm. It didn't make any sense to me. I know the feeling that we shared was real. The three of us had fought our way back to each other. After all the lies and deceit between us, we had gotten past it. At least I thought we had.

No, I know we had. There was no way that we went through

all of that, our own personal hell, only to find out nothing ever changed. I thought we were solid, I had a plan to protect all of us, take down the TCC and protect the ones I loved. My face flushed with heat as I thought of the betrayal.

The phone Trejo had given me rang. I knew it had to be him because who else would have the number. The phone danced in my hand has his name flashed across the screen. I had only been gone for no more than an hour. I understood he didn't want anyone to see me but he also needed to understand that we needed to get answers.

"Hello," I said. I was annoyed that he was interrupting my surveillance. They weren't doing anything but sitting on their asses and asking me questions, at least I was trying to get information. Good information that could possibly lead to finally bringing these assholes down.

"Where the hell are you?" He was yelling at the top of his lungs.

"Calm down," I said. Why was he getting so worked up?

"Get your ass back here, and don't be seen. I don't think you understand there is a price on your head. I'm sure they know by now about your escape." He said. Trejo was always bitching about something. I agreed to help him and I knew he was trying to help me, but damn he was a pain in my ass sometimes.

"Fine," I said and then disconnected the call. I didn't like being told what to do, but what choice did I really have. I wanted to bring these people down once and for all. They had completely ruined my life.

With each passing year of me trying to vindicate my father's death the deeper I fell into this endless web of deception and this time around, I had found myself on the losing end. I made my way back to the apartment that Trejo had me staying in. I opened the door to find him waiting there for me.

"Viera, you can't just disappear like that. Do you understand just how much everyone has riding on this? This is an investigation that has to be under the radar. This is not just about them, this is also about Bryant and his corruption." He stood up as he talked, his hands flailing left and right, back and forth as he threw a tantrum. I understood he was upset but he was going to have to settle down.

"I don't feel like being lectured." I crossed my arms and stared him directly in the face. I wasn't trying to give him problems, I appreciated that he got me out of that place, but it was only partially finished. I wanted to clear my name, I couldn't be out here looking like some dirty cop when all I was trying to do was my job. Granted my tactics where not always above board but I got shit done. And I would get it done now.

"Well, too fucking bad!" He shouted. We stood staring at each other in complete silence. What I really wanted to do was curse his ass out for yelling at me as if he had lost his mind, but I decided to ignore his anger. I pulled out my cell phone and showed him the pictures that I snapped while I stood in the shadows. Something about her bothered me even from that night, up until now she had never been on anyone's radar.

"This is the woman that showed up the night of the bust. Trejo this thing has deeper roots than we thought. I know that she's Trent's mother and she appeared out of nowhere. I don't know where she has been hiding all this time.

All of our intel showed that Trent and Tre Jamison, along with Soraya and Omere were the ones in charge. We had this shit all wrong all this time, the more we find out the deeper this shit goes." Trejo took my phone from my hand and studied the picture.

"Did you get a name on her?" He quizzed as he studied her picture.

"I overheard Soraya call her Marisol. I remember the mood in the room that night. I remember everything stood still once she walked in. I think she's gotta be the one that has Bryant on the payroll." I said. Trejo tapped on the screen and opened his phone to airdrop himself the picture.

"I will have one of my analysts run it through facial recognition, let's see what else we can find out about her." Trejo handed me back my phone and walked over to the kitchen table and had a seat. "Come sit down." I didn't trust his come sit down, one bit. I walked towards where he sat and took a seat.

"What is it?" I stared at him waiting for him to speak. His light brown eyes glistened with a hint of sadness. Trejo bit his bottom lip. "Just say it," I said. Trejo pulled out an iPad, tapped on the screen a few times and handed it over to me.

"This is your personnel file." He cleared his throat and swallowed. "I know when we got you out the other night the first thing you said is you wanted to clear your name. You wanted your job back. I don't know if that's going to be possible." The words slowly slipped from his lips, low and sorrowful. I could tell he was trying to deliver the news as gently as he possibly could.

"But why?" I had given my life to this job, my father had given his life for it. I knew it wouldn't be easy but I was sure once my name was cleared I should be able to go back to my job. I expected some type of disciplinary action, I mean I did go, rogue, just a little but only for the case. But to not have my job, no I couldn't accept that.

"I took this to another Director, a friend of mine, to look over, see if we could get some help." My eyes almost popped out my head. "Don't worry it's someone who we can trust, who at first tried to help you get released into my custody."

"And what did they have to say?"

"Look at the file Amina," He pointed towards the iPad. "Bryant made sure to make it look like you were complicit. The best we can try to hope for is maybe clear your name, but I can't find anyone willing to help get you reinstated." He sat back in his chair as he finished his sentence. His tone was filled with regret. He really was trying to help me but had done all that he could think of to try to swing things my way.

I looked down at the iPad and scrolled through the digital pages of my file. There were certain words that jumped out at me. ***Insubordinate. Duplicitous. Impulsive.*** There was a list of adjectives that had been used to describe me over the years but the one thing it failed to mention was how hard I worked. It didn't tell how I had lost my father for the job, how my family had been terrorized because of this job. How my mother was now in witness protection after being kidnapped by these people. This file said a lot of things but it didn't mention the sacrifice.

My chest heaved up and down and I thought about how I was taking another loss. I have lost ever fucking thing that I care about now my job too. This job was everything to me and to not have it. That's bullshit.

My entire body was on fire. Somebody was going to pay. One by one those assholes were all coming down, they were going to pay.

SEVEN

DOMINIQUE

I LOOKED at my phone to unlock it. Two days have passed since I took Soraya's number but I had yet to use it. I didn't really know how to take her, but anything had to be better than dealing with Marisol. Ever since she got here she has taken complete control. Even over the bank accounts that I had set up. The fact that she walked into my life feeling that she could control my husband and me angered me. I was a grown ass woman and telling me what to do and putting me on her monetary time out wasn't working for me.

I knew that Trent saw things completely different. He was raised with the money, he knew as long as mommy and daddy were around that he would be taken care of, but me, I didn't grow up like that. I needed every single penny I had and somebody telling me what to do with that money wasn't going to fly. Her threatening me wasn't going to work either.

For a brief moment I felt bad about having to go behind Trent's back, I mean we tried to be honest with one another. Well, as honest as we could be, but sometimes I could see things that Trent couldn't. And when I did I took care of it. That's it, this was happening.

I hadn't worked out my complete plan but the anger I felt behind my mother in law fueled me enough to at least set things in motion. I tapped the text bubble on my phone and sent the message.

Soraya this is Dominique Time seemed to move at a snail's pace as I waited for her to respond.

So

So... I was wondering if we could talk

About

Damn, her and these one word responses. It made it hard to gauge whether or not she was even receptive to a meeting because she wasn't saying much of anything.

Just meet me and we will talk about the rest in person

The tiny bubbles at the bottom of the message popped up at least three times and then went away. Finally, a response came through.

Okay, where?

I'll shoot you a pin with the location

Things had started to move. I grabbed my shoes and bag and walked out the door. In the car, I thought about how this meeting could go one of two ways. It will either go in my favor or I will make another enemy. Either way, something was going to happen.

I decided to meet Soraya outside of the city. I didn't want anyone to see us and I didn't know if Marisol had someone watching us or not. I pulled into the small restaurant parking lot and went inside to wait for her.

I've made it

Pulling in now, she responded.

I sat in the small establishment and took in the scenery. It was a small mom and pop type shop, where I didn't know anyone and no one knew me. It was just the way I wanted. The tables were small and tight so I purposely chose a table in the very back corner. I wanted to be away from anyone who might overhear what I had to say to Soraya.

Daylight peeked into the restaurant as the door opened and two people stepped in. What the fuck was her husband doing here? Soraya stopped in the entry and glanced over the place. I waved my head so she could see me. She tapped Omere and pointed my direction once she spotted me sitting in the corner and made her way towards the table.

"Hello," I spoke. She didn't return the pleasantry, she just took a seat across from me and he sat down next to her. Soraya's stare was ice cold. She didn't blink or look away. Her eyes were deadlocked on me. I shifted in my seat and just decided to jump right into the conversation.

"I wanted to talk to you alone."

"Well, this is what you got, now what is all this about?" This was the first time I had ever even spoken to Soraya. I didn't know anything about her, nothing. I searched for the right words to say, trying to find some common ground that would make her open up to me. She didn't seem like the trusting type.

"I wanted to talk to you."

"You said that already." She stared at me with her eyebrows connected and her lip curled. Omere sat silently next to her seemingly disinterested in the entire conversation.

"I wanted to talk about everything that is going on, you know you weren't the only guys that got caught in Amina's web. She played me too." Maybe we could bond over both being caught up in Amina's twisted games. Even though it seems that they were in way deeper than me.

"Amina never played us." Oooookaaaay. I looked away

because I didn't want her to see me roll my eyes. How could she really sit here and say that Amina didn't play them? Amina played everybody whoever crossed her path. She had to be lying to herself if she believed that Amina hadn't used them the same way she used me, the same way she used Dro's friend Andre. Like I said, Amina played everybody.

"Dominique, I don't have all day. Get to the fucking point and stop wasting my time." Who the fuck was she talking to? I wonder if she realized how much like Marisol she sounded. It was pretty clear to me that there was a lot of bad blood between the two of them, and I'm sure when Soraya found out that Marisol had ordered a hit on her mother that didn't make it any better, but it seemed to me that the very thing that Soraya seemed to hate she was becoming.

"Look, the thing is I feel like Marisol is going to be a problem for me. I don't know how you feel about it but I don't like her stepping in on me."

"What the fuck does that have to do with me?" Her eyes widened as she talked.

"The way I see it, it has everything to do with you. Judging from the things I witness the night of the bust, y'all have a really heated history. She had your mother murdered. She had your little girlfriend arrested. There is no telling what other skeletons are in her closet." I sat back as I finished speaking. Soraya's jaw clenched as she cut her eyes towards Omere. I knew I had struck a nerve with her.

"Check this out," Omere finally spoke up. "You can put all that little shit you talking on mute. I don't care what you think you know cause you don't know shit. Come on baby let's go." Omere stood up abruptly, sending his seat flying backward. The chair tumbled to the floor, causing the few people in the restaurant to turn and look our way.

"Wait, just listen. Aren't you tired of working for her, letting her pull all the strings, and even though he is my husband, I see how he gets the credit for everything." I was now trying to appeal to her ego. "It seems that you guys should both be responsible for some of the things that happened." I finished.

To be honest, I didn't know the whole story and no one was probably ever going to tell me, but the one thing I knew was that there was a lot of animosity between her and Trent and if I had to, I would use that to my advantage. I was going to exploit the shit out of anything I could if that meant I could get her to agree to help me bring that old ass bitch Marisol down.

"I'm done listening to this, you honestly think I would ever team up with you. Look at you, throwing your own husband under the bus in an attempt to have your fucking your way. You ain't loyal to shit but yourself. Naw, we good on that, but here is a word of advice to you Dominique. Chill the fuck out because you have absolutely no idea what Marisol is capable of. You have nothing. No connections, no soldiers on the street, nothing, she would squash you like a bug. Marisol is not the little hustlers you're used to dealing with, she is real cartel, bloodline cartel. With her being Jamaican and Mexican she is able to move freely between both communities and trust me, those niggas would kill on sight for her in a heartbeat. You need to learn when you're outnumbered. Trust me."

Soraya finished her long ass speech and without saying another word turned around and left. She wanted to run down everything about Marisol. I didn't know her, you know what they needed to watch out because they definitely didn't know me and it would be a cold day in hell before I was outsmarted by some old ass bitch.

EIGHT

KHARI

THE HOT, humid, Houston air was suffocating as we exited the plane. I looked around the airport where we landed and spotted the car that was waiting for us. We were only here for two days, long enough to put things in motion.

Marisol had given us her private jet to fly in, once we were done here we would be on our way to Mexico. Dro grabbed me at my waist and pulled me close to him as we walked. I loved the way he always wanted, no the way he needed me near.

I smiled at him as we got in the car. Marisol had taken care of everything for our trips, the jet the cars, the accommodations, she had handled it all. The driver pulled off and we simply waited. I didn't expect any of this to be hard at all. The person we were looking for was already on Marisol's payroll. I scrolled through my phone looking for the guy's contact information.

"You got the guy's info?" Dro asked.

"Yes, I have it." I touched his hand and we rode the rest of the way in silence. Marisol hadn't said much since she hastily left the club. She actually hadn't been in touch at all. Amina being on the loose raised the stakes for everyone. This woman literally never went away. She just kept coming back, no matter how you thought you had taken care of the problem, she kept popping back up.

I hadn't said anything about it but I knew if she got out of prison she had to have help. People don't just break out, she had some kind of help. I made a mental note to make sure that Marisol understood that.

The car slowed in front of a small house in the hood. Looking at the house in front of me there wasn't much to it on the outside. We were obviously in the hood and there were men posted up on the porch.

"Wait, keep going." Dro sat up in his seat and said to the driver. I looked around the area to see what had piqued his interest. There was a van parked about two houses down but the house it was in front of didn't appear to be occupied. Why is there a van at a vacant home? The work truck had darker windows than normal and it just looked a little out of place.

"Don't go back around that block, they will notice the car coming by twice. Instead, pass by to the left and park us two blocks down. Shit looks like a surveillance van." Dro gave commands and the driver complied. My mind raced, what could we do?

There was no way in hell we were going inside of that building with the risk of Feds breaking down the door. But we needed this guy's expertise, if not we would be back at square one with putting our plan into motion and I knew it was a good plan. I could spend months looking for someone who could code like Marisol said he could. I picked up my phone and dialed the number that was given to me.

"Yeah," the voice on the other end rushed almost like it was an inconvenience to answer.

"I don't think you have that much time, this is Khari, Marisol sent me. There's a suspicious van parked two houses down." He was silent on the other end. Was he listening? "Are you listening?" I said.

"I'm here." The tone in his voice had completely changed. I could hear clicking in the background and then the phone went dead. My phone made three beeps. I looked down at it and it was at the home screen again. My nose scrunched in confusion as Dro and I locked eyes.

"What happened?" Dro asked.

"I don't know, he just hung up." What the hell was up with this dude? I stared out the window wondering if I should call back or just forget it and start looking for someone. I wanted to make this work but it couldn't if I couldn't even get him on the phone.

Tap tap tap.

The unexpected sound of someone tapping on the back window surprised everyone in the car. My heart skipped a beat as I turned towards the direction of the sound. Both the driver and Dro instinctively reached for their guns, ready for whatever was about to happen. Everyone looked towards the direction of the sound. A man stood outside, motioning us to unlock the door. Dro rolled the window down.

"Who the fuck are you?" He pointed the gun towards the man at the window. He was short in stature, no more than five feet tall. The man stepped back but didn't look alarmed. A sly smirk spread across his face.

"Chill, it's me, Berto. Let me in, you were right we need to get out of here." Dro and the driver looked at each other with their guns still drawn. I guess we were all thinking the same thing, let him in and if he's not who he says he is, then handle it accordingly. The driver hit the unlock on the door and Berto slipped inside. "Man, we gotta get outta here, let's go!" Dro and I both side eyed him.

"How the fuck did you know where we were parked?" Dro

spat at him. I was wondering the exact same thing, I had not given a location, the only information I had given him was my name. He better start making some sense really soon because none of us in this car was trusting him. He sat down what appeared to be some type of computer drive and smiled.

"Look I don't know how much Marisol told or didn't tell you, but I'm the best at what I do. You called from your cell phone, that's all I needed. I traced the GPS coordinates to this location and shit, I found you. Easy." He smiled as he finished speaking his I sat back in my seat. If he had done all of that in a matter of minutes, what else could he do?

The driver put the car in drive and pulled away from the curb. We headed towards the hotel we would be staying at. I wanted to know more about the man that sat across from me. The way he seemed to so easily track us, the confidence he displayed in his ability and why the government watching him had me intrigued. I began to ask questions.

"How long have the Feds been watching you? You must be into some heavy shit if you're on the government's radar."

"They ain't just watching me," he laughed. "They are trying to recruit me, I have hacked the FBI, the DEA, I can get into anything and out of anything and I only leave a trace if I want to." He laughed, pleased with himself. "But I'm not with it so I'm guessing this is about shutting me down now. They can leave that white hat save the world bullshit to the hackers with bleeding hearts, I wanna get paid. So what kind of job y'all got for me?"

I wasn't sure if I was ready to give that information just yet. This man was crafty and before I divulge too much information I wanted to make sure that I wanted to work with him. I noticed he ran his mouth nonstop about what he could do, I hoped he didn't have a problem keeping it closed.

"So, let me ask you, Marisol tells me you did some work for

someone name Dominique and that's how you met?" He liked bragging on himself so I'm sure he would talk.

"Yes, that turned out better than I hoped. I met this girl, I mean she seemed desperate but she was paying good, I turned into Kyra gave her a business history, funneled money into untraceable bank accounts, I mean made that shit look legit, and then along comes Marisol's people offering to pay me double and fund server and systems upgrades, and all I had to do was give her information. Best of both worlds." He rubbed his hands together as he spoke.

He didn't realize that he gave me more information than he probably meant to when he spoke. I gathered this man was smart, amazingly smart. So smart that governmental agencies were willing to wipe the slate clean just to use him. But his words also told me he talks too much. He likes to talk about how good he was, and if a person comes along with the right price, he would go to the highest bidder. Right now that was us, but I knew I needed to keep an eye on him. I definitely saw the benefit of having him, but I also knew if anybody ever really got to him, he would break like glass and spill all of our secrets.

NINE
AMINA

I HAD a week to sit with my thoughts. The thought of everything being snatched away from me infuriated me. I leaned against the couch and stared at the ceiling. The small, cramped room I was in, inside of the safe house felt suffocating.

Trejo didn't want me to leave but I be damn if I trade one prison for another one. I understood people were looking for me. I understood that many people wanted me dead, but what did that matter if I wasn't living my life beyond these four walls?

I needed to avenge everything that had been done to me and there was no way that was going to happen with me sitting in here. Trejo would just have to deal with it and thank me later. I was never the type to be caged.

Slipping my feet into a pair of shoes I checked the time. What I really needed was a car to move around but I didn't have any way of getting anything. Trejo promised that this would be over soon, but there didn't seem to be anything happening. The way I saw it, Bryant was still free to make me his scapegoat, the TCC was still in business and Soraya and Omere were still out of my life. For me, none of this was over.

If I was going to make things happen I needed help. Help that Trejo or the FBI couldn't provide. They were still bound by the rules of the bureau, but I wasn't. I slowly opened the door and peeked outside, making sure he hadn't left a surveillance detail to watch me. There was no one outside so I slipped out and went down the elevator. I needed a way to get around.

I walked out of the doors and surveyed the street. Parked across the street was a black Suburban with blacked out windows. It was parked heading north so I turned and began to move south. I moved as fast as my legs could carry me without breaking out into a full out run.

I looked over my shoulder. The SUV was now heading towards me with increasing speed. I started running hitting the corner with as much speed as possible. I ran between an ally way trying to get as far away from the SUV as possible. My heart pounded in my chest uncontrollably as I ran. Just as I ran out of the other end of the alley the black car pulled up in front of me and the door flew open, knocking the wind out of me as I fell to the ground.

I rolled over on my hands and knees trying to catch my breath and stand at the same time. The smell of urine and garbage invaded my nostrils as I struggled to breathe. I closed my eyes and then opened them, blinking trying to see what was around me. I moved back on all fours as I saw a pair of black boots coming towards me. I needed to get up and fast.

Finally, I was able to stand. I didn't even bother to turn around to see who the black pair of boots belonged to, the only thing I could think about at this moment was getting away.

Fuck whoever it was, they would have to catch me first. It could have been anyone in that car. They could have been working for many of the many people that wanted me, maybe even needed me to stop breathing. The one and only thought on my mind was putting as much distance between myself and them.

"Mina." I stopped dead in my tracks. His voice. It sounded almost exactly like my father. My lip quivered as I turned to face him.

"Kash." Our eyes locked, the same eyes both just like our father's. Our relationship had always been strained, it had always been hard, there was a lot of blame to pass around between the two of us, but right now, I had never been happier to see him. I ran towards him and hugged my brother. I had so many questions that I wanted to ask him.

"How did you find me?" I asked pulling away to look at him.

"It wasn't that hard," he laughed. "Get in the car we don't need to talk here." We both got into the back of the SUV. Kash looked at me, he was my brother and I knew I could trust him, but I also knew that he blamed me for my father's death. In all actuality, I was starting to blame myself too.

"You've been making a lotta noise Mina." Kash broke the silence.

"What do you mean?" I am pretty sure I knew what he was talking about.

"Word is that you're dirty now, sis."

"Kash you know I would never, I do a lot of things that may be questionable, yeah I'm the by any means type but you know I would never, ever be a fucking dirty cop." I was pissed that all this bullshit had torn apart everything I worked so hard to build.

"I never believed it for a moment. You're too committed to bringing everyone down to ever be dirty." Kash said. "So tell me what really happened?"

"Honestly, I don't know. I've been on this case for so long I'm starting to feel like it's never going to be done."

"It can be, that's why I'm here, we need to get you off the

streets? You're a wanted woman." What did he mean get me off the streets, the streets were where all of my answers were.

"I can't just walk away from this," I responded. There was no way I could just give up. I had to see this through. I had to bring Bryant down, I had to know why Soraya and Omere flipped on me and Marisol and her crew had to be stopped. Nothing else was an option for me.

"I knew you were going to say that." He grinned. "I just merely wanted to make the offer. It's not just you that was affected by this case. Our mother, we can have no contact with her because of this, she's will be in witness protection for the rest of her life as long as they are free."

I didn't say anything. He was right about that, we had both acted irresponsibly when first tried to bring down the TCC. And Soraya and Omere had retaliated against us by abducting our mother. With a hit on her head, the only way we could protect her was to get her into the witness protection program. Neither one of us had any contact with her. I'm sure it cut just as deep for him as it did for me.

The Suburban pulled to a stop in front of a small house. My eyes scanned the surroundings as we walked inside. The house was nothing spectacular, nothing anyone would notice. The area was quiet and the houses sat far enough apart that hearing what was happening here would be difficult.

"What's going on?" I quizzed Kash. Two other agents who hadn't said much of anything stopped at the front door and stood guard. I continued to follow my brother. I stopped dead in my tracks when he opened the door to the backroom. In the middle of the floor, Bryant was strapped to a chair.

"I got you a gift sis. The way I see it, in order to get our mother and us the freedom we want we have to take the problems out at the source. He is the first one up." Kash walked over and removed the gag from his mouth.

"What the fuck is this? Let me go. I am a got damn FBI director, when I'm done with you, you will be under the jail." He screamed as he twisted and turned trying to free himself.

"The jail you put me in? The one that couldn't hold me the first time. You really think that's going to work this time?" I said. Anger was swelling within me. This man had played me. He made me think he was my ally when he was really my enemy.

I remember when I was undercover, how he cautioned me about changing and remembering which side I worked for. Then I remembered how jealous he seemed to be of the things given to me while I was undercover. None of those things mean a damn thing to me.

"You got off easy last time." He spat his words at me in anger. He was very cocky considering he was the one tied up.

"We have all of his bank deposits, this is evidence of him taking kickbacks. He's been up to this for years. That's why they were always one step ahead of us, always seem to know what we were up to, always seemed to somehow get away." Kash said.

"Give me your gun," I said.

"What?"

"Kash, give me your gun!"

"Amina —,"

"Give me the fucking gun." Kash looked at me and hesitantly handed it over. The expression on his face told me not to do anything stupid. I grabbed the gun by the barrel and brought it across Bryant's face. I slammed the gun into his face over and over again, releasing the pent up aggression of months in jail, of having my job taken from me and for everything this fucking rat did to me. I stepped back and cocked the gun, bringing it to his head.

"You're not going to shoot me." He said.

"You willing to bet your life on that?" I pushed the gun into his temple.

TEN

DOMINIQUE

"SO YOU'RE NOT GONNA GO?" Trent asked as sat down on the edge of the bed and slipped his shoes on. I hated being summoned, I don't care who it was, she wasn't just going to snap her fingers and I magically appear.

"For what, like I said your mother has already threatened me, do you actually think I'm just going to walk in and let her finish the job." I sat in a lounge chair in the corner of our bedroom with no intentions of moving. I had no reason to see this woman, she had made it more than clear that she didn't want me around. Fuck her.

"You're going to have to stop acting like this. My mother didn't do shit to you so stop pouting and bring your ass on. You keep going on and on about how it should be us, get off your ass and do something instead of sitting back letting your sister have her way."

My eyes were glued to Trent as he grabbed his keys and walked towards the door. I blew out a long breath as I shook my head. I could feel my lip bend upward. I didn't like how he was acting. Anytime I brought up his mother it was always me that was wrong. Like I was the one that was seeing something that wasn't there. I was baffled as to why he couldn't see the things that I could see.

"Fine, I'm coming," I said before he shut the door. I grabbed my things and followed behind him, stopping briefly to slip my shoes on. We got in our car and started on our way. The car ride was completely silent. I kept noticing that Trent kept cutting his eyes at me like I've done something to him.

"Why do you keep looking at me like that?"

"Why do you keep tripping about my mother?"

"I told you why, haven't you been listening?" I mean we have literally had this conversation every day since she has been here and it seemed like she has been here a long ass time. I just wanted shit to go back to the way it was. Fuck. I told him we would take over the world. He agreed that we were going to be fully honest with one another, full disclosure. But why was I get the feeling this nigga knew way more than he was saying.

"Where are we going anyway?" The only thing he told me is that his mother wanted to meet with us. I couldn't stand the way she was pulling us like puppets on a string. I was used to doing my own thing, I called the shots. This old bitch was going to have to stop. Trent pulled into a parking lot and parked.

"Come on."

"Why are we at a gun range?" I faced Trent. None of this made any sense. It was reminding me of our days when we first got married. Before we agreed to be honest with him. He was making me feel like he was lying to me. Or maybe hiding something from me was a better way of describing it.

Either way, he was being hella secretive and I didn't like it at all. I followed him inside the building. I don't think I had ever set foot inside if a gun range before. The sound of gunshots rang throughout the building.

"She's in the outdoor range. You'll need these to go out there."

The man handed both Trent and I goggles and headphones. We walked outside. From where I was standing I could see Marisol aiming at her target. She held the gun like a trained assassin. One by one she released the bullets into the target, hitting the center each and every time. Who in the hell was this lady?

Once we made it close enough to her she hugged Trent. "Thank you for coming," she said to him. Tre stood in the back shooting at his target. Ever so often his eyes shifted our way but he never said a word.

The look on his face made me uneasy. It was one of those moments where I felt like everyone knew something but me. Marisol finally acknowledged me.

"Hello, Dominique." She said my name slow and deliberate, sounding out each syllable.

"Hey," I waved my hand and stood next to Trent.

"Have you ever shot a gun before?" She asked, holding the gun out towards me. I shook my hands. I didn't want that thing. For all I knew, she just wanted my prints on it or something.

"No, I'm good."

"No?" She turned back around reloaded her gun and began to shoot at another target. She started hitting every target around her. Those in front of her, those to the left of her, even Tre's targets weren't safe. She seemed a little trigger happy to me and now she was just showing off.

Marisol turned to face me again.

"I think you should really learn. Here take it."

"I don't want it," I responded.

"No, take the fucking gun. You're gonna need to know how to use one if you plan on going to war with me." Marisol's eyes narrowed as she turned towards me and thrust the gun into my hands, this time forcing me to take it.

The metal felt heavy in my hands. I didn't shoot guns. I didn't need to, I had always had a man that could handle things if need be.

"What is she talking about?" Trent said, his eyes widen.

"I'm just as lost as you are." I moved my shoulders up and down. I looked around now aware that everyone was gathering around us.

"You're wife is a liar, mijo." She looked me up and down with that same look of disgust she always had when it came to me.

"You having secret meetings, did you think it wouldn't get back to me? Nothing happens in mi familia that I don't know about. Nada"

I stepped back to put some space between the two of us. She was a lot taller than me and I didn't like the way she was towering over me. I hadn't thought Soraya would have gone back and told her.

"What are you talking about?" Trent seemed completely clueless as to what was going on, but I understood what was happening. I was busted. My mind raced. How in the world was I going to explain my way out of this one? *Think think think.* I needed to come up with something and fast.

"Look Marisol, it's not what you think. I only took the meeting with Soraya to see what she wanted from me, I told her I couldn't help her and that was the end of it." I twisted the story around a little bit to make it seem like it was Soraya who had wanted to meet with me. The way I saw it, it was her word against mine. And she wasn't here to dispute any of my lies.

"Mentirosa, you're a liar! Damelo! Lie to me one more time and I'm going to break your fucking legs." Someone handed her a long stick like the officers used to beat the hell out of people. The sleek black stick glistened as the sun bounced off of it. She twirled it back and forth, taunting me with it.

"Trent, what is your mother doing?" My voice cracked just a

bit. I cleared my throat and stared at Trent, my eyes wide, I couldn't believe the shit that was happening.

"Dominique, what did you do?" Trent's voice fell low as he stepped back. This man that I married wasn't even trying to defend me. Wasn't thinking about stopping her from doing whatever she intended to do with this club. My heart beat erratically as I struggled to catch my breath.

"I didn't do anything. I told you the meeting was nothing." My voice caught in my throat again as I struggled to speak. She was kinda scaring the shit out of me. I didn't have anything to defend myself with. What had Trent brought me into? He had to have some idea that this meeting wasn't about pleasantries. Marisol didn't seem like the type to share all information but he knew something. That's what those looks were about.

I began to take several steps away from her. The crazed look in her eyes told me she was ready to back up anything that she said. She raised the stick in her hand and swung it down towards my knee. The force of the stick hit me so hard I toppled to the ground.

"Fuck! I told you it was nothing!" I yelled looking up at her. With the sun behind her back, she looked like a dark figure, a menacing silhouette that was intent on beating the hell out of me.

"I want you to know I have eyes everywhere. And Soraya knows better than to cross me. As soon as I confronted her about it she gave you up. I saw the messages you sent. I know that you were the one that initiated everything. I have had a tail on you since I got here cause I never trusted your conniving, thieving ass. I'm sorry son but you know what has to happen." Marisol softened briefly, laying her hand on Trent's shoulder before turning her attention back to me.

Trent stared down at me. His eyes tighten, he looked at his mother in horror as he shook his head up and down. His face wavered between sorrow and anger.

"She's your fuck up, so you know that means she is your responsibility. You have to deal with this." Marisol caressed the side of Trent's face. I grabbed my knee, I wasn't even sure if I could still walk she had hit me so hard. Marisol looked up towards the guys that brought her the stick.

"Get her out of here, and don't be seen. Take her to the club we've been working out of. We will deal with it there. Have a cleanup crew on standby." Marisol went back to her target practice as her goons dragged me away.

ELEVEN
KHARI

DRO KISSED me as he lifted my dress, slowly caressing my thighs as he moved the garment up towards my waist. His hands greedily grabbed at the lace fabric of my panties and ripped them away from my body. He pressed against me, pulling my shirt above my head to reveal my bare chest.

Dro's eyes connected with mine as his lips found his way to my hardened nipples. He wrapped his lips around the brown mounds and applied just enough pressure. I through my head back in pleasure. Dro's hands explored every bit of my body. He ran them up my back and to the nape of my neck, pulling my hair slightly. My head tilted even more as he ran his tongue down to my collarbone and softly kissed.

His kisses were greedy and I was equally as hungry for him. He found his way back to my lips and firmly pressed. His tongue slipped in and out of my mouth causing waves of satisfaction to surge through my body.

My hands explored him and I found the hem of his shirt and I pulled it off, exposing the lion tattoo across his chest. I ran my tongue over it, pulling myself even closer to him.

I unbuttoned his pants and let them fall to the floor. I wanted him more than ever. Working for Marisol had given us very little time alone, we had been on the go first to Texas and then to Mexico to set everything up for her and there was always someone with us, watching. Now that we were back in the States the few moments we had alone we were going to use to enjoy one another.

Dro's hardness pressed against me. Slowly he slipped between my walls, each stroke causing a surge of wetness. He began to move faster, harder, deeper. Whenever he made love to me I felt it. I placed my hands behind me on the desk for balance and rolled my hips to meet his stroke.

His thickness pushed my walls to its limits, pushing so deep inside of me I could feel the intensity of his thrust throughout every part of my body. My toes curled as I pulled my legs up. I wanted to feel every inch of this man.

"Damn I love you."

"I love you back."

Dro clasped my hips and lifted me from the desk. He stood straight up, holding me suspended in the air as he bounced me up and down on his dick, entering me over and over again, threatening to cause an orgasm at any moment. My hands wrapped around his neck and I tightened my walls as he brought me down, gripping him tighter and tighter as he plunged inside of me.

My hands grasped the back of his head and kissed him, he pulled me even closer to him as he moved us to the small loveseat that was in our office. He laid me down against the soft cushions and glided back inside me. Our bodies moved in unison as we made love. I loved the feel of his hard exterior against my supple skin.

"Let's make a baby," I whispered to him. He looked at me but didn't stop stroking. I wanted all of him inside of me.

"Baby, you ready?" He questioned.

"Yes, cum inside of me, deep. I want to have your son. Dro pounded even harder, pushing so deep within me until he was writhing in pleasure.

"Fuuuuuuck!" He screamed as he poured his seed inside of me.

Dro collapsed against my body, his breath hot with passion.

"Dro," Sergio's voice called from the other side of the door. How long had he been standing out there? "I'm sorry to interrupt you. I been calling, there is a matter that needs your attention upstairs.

"Just a minute Sergio," I yelled loud enough to be heard through the closed door. We stood and I both grabbed our clothes to dress. I glanced at my phone and saw that Sergio had texted several times. Once we were dressed we both made our way upstairs to see what was so important it had brought Sergio downstairs interrupting us.

"Where can we put her?" I watched as they dragged my sister into our club. She looked rough. Her hair was disheveled and she appeared to be limping. She looked my way, and then quickly turned her head away. Even in this position she still refused to ask for help. Although I'm not sure how much I could actually help her.

"Downstairs," I responded. I quickly scanned the surroundings. I didn't know what was happening and was trying to make sense of everything I was seeing. Those were Marisol's people dragging her in. Standing at the entrance of the club was Trent, staring off into space. His jaw clenched and his fist balled as he watched them take his wife downstairs to restrain her.

What happened that would allow the man that supposedly loved you to sit back and watch this happen to you? Dro would never allow this to happen to me, he would burn this building down with all of us inside of it before he let anyone lay a hand on me.

Marisol soon entered and walked towards the bar where we stood. The corners of her lips turned up in a proud grin, as she sauntered across the room. Its was undeniable. By the smug look on her face, she felt victorious.

"I told you she could not be trusted." She said as she stopped in front of us.

"What happened Marisol?" She stared down at me and smiled.

"You don't need to be concerned with these things, you worry about my business. Are things ready." Her words had an icy cold bite to them. Dro stepped behind me. By the way, he was breathing, he didn't like the way she sounded either.

"Things are ready to go. Berto has set up everything and the first shipment is coming in on Friday. Once it is here your people can come in and disburse it however you see fit. The accounts have been set up and Berto has facilitated a thirty percent payout for each shipment we bring in for you." I finished. Marisol paused and looked at me. Her eyes narrowed and shifted from side to side. I understood she liked to call the shots, I understood she liked to be in control, and I hope she understood we want to be paid.

"Who authorize this, this thirty percent?"

"It's the same thirty percent we always charged. The same thirty percent we charged your son to transport through our port connections. Nothing has changed." I smiled as I delivered the news. Marisol gave out a lot of orders but she never mentioned pay, so I handled it. Same deal I offered Trent, same terms.

She stood in front of us in silence for a moment, no doubt contemplating what she was going to say next. I knew she was a thinker, just like I was and I knew that while I was reading her she was reading me.

"Okay fine, good work Khari. The problem with your sister will be handled by tomorrow, ok. If there is anything you have to say to her I suggest you say it now." The left corner of her mouth lifted before she patted me on my shoulder and walked away.

"Shit, that sounded like they are about to murk your sister," Dro said, as we both watched Marisol walk away. I knew that Dominique was meddlesome and conniving, but what the hell had she done this time that signed her death warrant?

TWELVE
AMINA

THE LIGHT TAPPING sound at the front door caught every-one's attention. Kash got up and looked out the peephole.

"Is this him," He turned to face me. I got up and walked over to the door and peer through the tiny hole.

"Yeah that's him," I said moving away from the door and pulling it open.

"Trejo," I spoke. Damn, he looked pissed.

"Amina, I've been looking everywhere for you. I thought we talked about this." I ignored him. I was doing all the work for him and I didn't want to be lectured at all.

"This is my brother, Kash, he's DEA. He has worked this case for years just like me, at one time on a joint task force headed up by Bryant. He's in here." I started walking towards the back of the house where Bryant was and opened the door. Trejo stepped in behind me.

"What the hell happen to his face?" Trejo shouted.

"He fell." I walked towards the desk and grabbed the enve-lope with all of the prepared documents. Bryant looked at both of us, his bruised eye tightly closed but in no way hiding the disdain on his face.

"I am going to have your job next. You let this pyscho persuade you to go against me. I'm your boss." Bryant screamed at him. Trejo stared at him, thoughtfully quiet.

"You're the worse kind of boss, Viera's a pain in the ass but she did her job, and as soon as you got here it seems like any case that came up that had to do with any cartel was squashed. You're a shit boss. I've already reported you to the office of professional responsibility, and now we actually have proof." I handed him the papers that would undoubtedly put Bryant away for good.

"One down, a whole cartel to go. What's the plan, Trejo?" I asked.

"Viera, you're not an agent anymore, you are going to have to stand down and let us handle it, I'm willing to work with your brother but if we want things to stick we have to do everything above board. None of that half cocked off the wall shit you do to get results."

Agents rushed in and took Bryant out in handcuffs. He was getting off easy. My chest heaved up and down as I watched him being escorted out. He had actually been dirty, he had only made me look that way. It took everything in me to stop myself from pulling the trigger the other night when Kash brought me to him.

"Go back to the apartment I got for you, lay low. We wanna make sure you have your day in court at the trial to at least clear your name." Trejo said before he left. I sat down in the empty chair and stared at the walls. My brother hovered in and out of the room but didn't say anything. I guess what could he really say. The door slid open and Kash walked in again.

"Sis, I know you don't wanna hear this," he paused, "but maybe Trejo is right. I know you want revenge, I know you feel like these people completely fucked up your life, but sometimes when we are so hell bent on vengeance we can't see what's right in front of us. We are going to take them down, but he's right. We need to do it the right way." Kash walked over to me and gave me a hug and then left the room again.

Being alone with my thoughts was sometimes unsettling. So many things raced through my head it was sometimes hard to keep track of everything. I had a mental list, of everyone who needed to pay.

Bryant was one of the ones at the top of the list and now he was being dealt with. I wanted to be able to listen, but this was happening to me not them. Next on my list was Omere and Soraya. I needed to know what happens. I was trying to protect us.

We spent so many years thinking we could never be happy together and once I got a taste of what that was like again, I wanted nothing else. Their betrayal cut me deep. Part of me wanted to say fuck it, but more of me needed to know why.

I grabbed my phone and opened the app I downloaded to disguise my number. I dialed the number from memory hoping someone answered. This may have been one of the dumbest ideas I ever had.

Did I really want to open up those flood gates? *Yes.*

I pressed the call button in the app and listened to the ringing on the other end. The phone rang four times and no one answered. Just as I was about to disconnect I heard it.

"Hello." There was a sultriness to his voice that could make waves of wetness form with just a whisper. My heart raced but I said nothing.

"Hello," he called again.

Again I said nothing. The sound of his voice caused tears to pool in the corners of my eyes. Omere had always been the balance between me and Soraya. We were both hot like lava, coming in fast and blazing, but he was the cool earthiness that could temper our fire.

We had worked so well together, I needed to understand how they could just give all that up. I lied about a lot of things, but I never ever lied about the way I felt for both of them.

"Who is this?" He breathed into the phone. His tone lowered some, "Mina is this you?"

My heart thumped faster threatening to leap out of my chest. I hurriedly hit the call end button and stared at my phone. How had he known it was me? Maybe they want answers just as much as I do.

The house was now silent. I walked over to my brother's holster he had left in the room and slipped his gun out of it and tucked it into the back of my pants. I tiptoed to the door and peaked out. Everyone seemed to be passed out in the front. I walked over to the table and slid the keys to the SUV off of the table and moved cautiously towards the door.

Once I was outside I moved hurriedly not wanting anyone to come out and see me. I didn't plan on being gone long but if I was ever going to start letting this go I needed to have the closure I needed to do so. I drove down the highway making my way towards the home we stayed in once we had gotten back to Miami. As I made a left turn down their street I cut the lights. I parked a few houses down the street and got out. It was pitch black outside.

I approached their house, not really having any type of plan. I know I wanted to catch them off guard, that way maybe I would have the upper hand. I made my way to the back of the house, near the glass patio door entrance just off the kitchen. I knew that sometimes Soraya forgot to lock it and I hope this was one of those times.

Grasping the rectangular handle, I pulled softly. *Yes!* It was open. I pushed the heavy glass door just enough for me to slip through its cracked opening. As I walked in I removed my shoes, I didn't think anyone was home but just in case I didn't want to tip them off.

I eased around the corner heading into the living room, my body was hit with such force I fell into the wall. Soraya was on me, her blade out pressing against my neck. Her body weight held me motionless as she peered at me. Her raven colored hair was wild as if it hadn't seen a comb all day, the curls fell in front of her face highlighting her cheekbones. Even in a blind rage, she was beautiful.

"What the fuck are you doing in my house?" She breathed as I stared at her in silence.

THIRTEEN

DOMINIQUE

THIS WAS the same storage room they had held Amina hostage in. I looked around. The room was small and dark, and there were boxes everywhere. I shook my head from side to side. How did Marisol know? I had been careful. I had made sure that I met Soraya outside of the city. I kept hearing her voice over and over in my head. From the very beginning, I told Trent she had a problem with me. I could feel it.

The door squeaked as it was pushed open. The light from the hallway spilled into the room for a moment as Trent stepped inside. My pulse shot up as he walked in. Was he really going to go through with this? He stood at the doorway standing there, staring at me but not saying anything. He grabbed another chair and pulled it in front of me. I panted breathlessly trying to control the erratic thumping of my heart.

"Trent, please," I whispered to him. "You can't do this. Not to me, it's us, remember us against the world."

"Against the world Dominique, not my mother! Just what the hell were you trying to do?" I stared at Trent.

"Your mother Trent, she was fucking everything up *weeeeee*

built." I tilted my head to the side and widen my eyes. Tears slipped from the corners rolling down my face and then dripped from my chin. His facial expression never changed, and that was scaring the shit out of me.

"It's what she built, you just stepped into this, there would be nothing without my mother. She came here to clean up this mess, you were the one that let that agent get close to us, you were the one that let her get away. This is all your fault!" Was he really going to sit here and act like everything was my doing? He was right I did just step into this and all their fucked up family and legal problems too.

"Trent I saved you, her, and everybody! I am the one that came up with the plan, I am the one that funneled the money, I am the one that made sure you got your ass away and someone else took the fall for your ass. Don't sit here and act like this shit is on me, you should have stood up to your mother for me. You were supposed to love me, Trent." I said.

I had loved him, as much as I could love anyone. He couldn't see the cancer that his mother was. "So you are going to kill me? Is that the plan, is that how you have to deal with your problem?"

Trent didn't respond. He stood up and pulled out his gun and screwed in a round cylinder shaped object. I assumed a silencer. I closed my eyes, blinking back the tears that were falling. I hadn't done anything to deserve death. Soraya hadn't even gone along with the plan. Fuck! He raised the gun to my forehead and peered down at me.

"Son, let me talk to you." Tre's voice carried through the closed door. Trent dropped his arm and went to the door.

"Dad, I'm a little busy here."

"Just let me talk to you for a moment, okay." Trent looked back at me and walked outside. I held my breath trying to hear their conversation.

"Trent you don't have to do this." I heard Tre say.

"Yes, I do, you know the rules, to go against our family means death. I brought her into the family, so I have to handle it. The same way you had to take care of Soraya's mom. Sins against blood must be paid with blood."

What the fuck? This was some crazy shit. Soraya told me that Marisol was nuts, I just didn't think she was that crazy. I even knew that Trent got trigger happy. I mean, I had watched him murder Redd right in front of my eyes. I knew what he was capable of, I just never thought I would be on the receiving end of it.

"Your mother is out of control, just hear me out, son."

"She's trying to save our asses," Trent responded.

"Just one conversation, that's all I'm asking."

I didn't hear Trent say anything else, only the shuffle of heavy feet moving away from the room I was in.

Once I could tell no one was in front of the door I flew into full panic mode. My hands were bound and clasped behind my back. I tried to stand. Pain in my knee shot through me sending me falling backward right back into the chair. I had to push through it. It was either that or death. I tried to stand again, this time successfully rising to my feet. I shuffled slowly towards the door, not able to move too fast because of the pain but I wanted, no fuck that, I needed to get out of this room.

I knew the way out of here. If I can just make it to the back door before anyone returns. I turned my back to the door and dipped. The ache in my knee paralyzed me for a moment. I twisted my hands to turn the doorknob and inched the door open as fast as I could. I looked down the hall towards the exit door.

"What the hell are you doing?" I turned to see my Khari standing in the hallway. She stepped to the side and inched down the wall. What the hell was she doing? I looked at her confused for a moment and continued walking towards the exit door that seemed unrealistically far from me. There were miles between me and that door.

"I'm getting the fuck out of here so just let me."

"There are cameras along this hallway, they will know exactly where you went," Khari said.

"So am I just supposed to stay here and let them kill me? No, I'm getting the fuck out of here. I know you are gonna run and tell them, just do me a favor and give me a head start." She stared at me for a moment not saying anything. "Or don't, it doesn't matter, what have you ever really done for me." I started back on my journey to the door.

"A lot. I've done a lot for you. Our mother is the one you should have blamed for all the shit that rolled downhill on us. She was the one responsible, we were the children, and we did the best we could, but I don't expect you to understand that. Because you only see what you want." I rolled my eyes. I just wanted her to stop talking. I didn't have time for this.

"Whatever, I don't know when they are coming back I gotta get out of here. Like I said they are going to kill my ass." I yelled over my shoulder. She blew out a long deep sigh, and then something within her demeanor changed

"You're never gonna get away like that. Not on foot. And not with your hands tied behind your back." She slipped her fingers between the knots and loosened my restraints. I wiggled my hands until they were free. She continued talking. "When you make it outside the door you will see a white delivery truck parked in the back. Under the seat to the left is a key, use that. And get as far as you can. If they catch you and know I helped you they will kill us both."

I didn't have time to process everything that was happening. I think it was possible we might have been having a breakthrough but no one had time for that. I had to get the hell out of here. I moved as fast as I could making it to the door and throwing my body weight into it as hard as possible. I looked back just before leaving. She ducked into her office and that is the last I saw of her before racing outside.

I ran as fast as I could, dragging my foot behind me as I tried to make it to the truck without being seen. I jumped in and slammed the door closed. My fingers fumbled for the key. I felt all around the bottom of the seat. No key, damn.

I decided to check one more time but this time I searched the cushions instead of the floor. I felt a hard metal object between the seat and pushed to release it. I shoved the key into the ignition and started the truck, threw it in reversed and sped off. Damn. I was so tired of always running for my life. Something had to fucking change.

FOURTEEN
KHARI

I SAT down at the computer and logged into our security system. Adrenaline raced through my body, causing my skin to feel as if it were being pricked by tiny needles. I knew I needed to move fast and I needed to make it look good.

I brought up the video clips and scrubbed through them, erasing any of the ones that may have picked up me and our conversations. I noticed the time attached the video code but I hoped they would not notice this when I showed it to them.

Because there were cameras throughout the club I knew there was a chance someone would ask to see them. I planned on getting ahead of the situation. I played it through after I erased everything and once I was satisfied with how it looked I dumped the trash and logged out.

Things had seemed to escalate quickly. I knew that Marisol didn't like Dominique but enough to force her son to kill her? I still hadn't gotten what she had done, but it had to be something big if they were willing to end her life for it. But even though I had been on the receiving end of her games before, I didn't want to see her dead. Maybe, somewhere deep, I still wanted to protect her, even from herself. I grabbed my phone and called Sergio.

"Hey, tell Trent it looks like we have a problem," I said. By we I meant he. His mother didn't seem like the type to accept mistakes or fuck ups. And if she was supposed to be dead and now she is gone this was going to look like a pretty big mistake.

"Okay." He responded and disconnected the call. Moments later Trent and Dro both appeared at the door. Dro pushed past Trent and stood next to me.

"What kind of problem?" Annoyance washed over Trent's face.

"The kind that involves your wife escaping. She's not there. I came here and the door was opened. Looked at the surveillance and this is what I saw.

I turned the computer screen to face him and hit play. What he saw was a video that showed Dominique running out of the room, wiggling her hands to loosen the rope off and then limping out of the back exit door.

"She couldn't have made it very far," I added.

"How the fuck did she get away? You had something to do with this, she is your sister."

"Me? She's your wife and you were the one holding her hostage, why would I be telling —," Dro held his hand up interrupting me.

"Look here motherfucker, you gonna watch how to fuck you talk to my wife. She bringing you this shit as a courtesy, she ain't gotta tell you a motherfuckin thing!" Dro stepped forward, definitely ready to get physical if need be. "I suggest you get to looking for your wife." He spat the words out, then curled his lip up and looked him up and down. Trent eyed him back, both men staring each other down.

"You wanna do something?" Dro stepped from around the desk and came eye to eye with Trent. Trent didn't flinch. He grabbed his phone and turned to walk away, making a call on his way out. Dro and I were in the office alone now. I got up to close the door.

Once I was sure everyone had made it back upstairs I turned to Dro and collapsed in his arms. I was exhausted physically and emotionally. I sat down on the chair in front of the desk and Dro on the corner of the desk.

"What happened?"

"I came downstairs and caught her trying to escape. She was pretty sure they were going to kill her."

"Do you know what she did?"

"No, it wasn't time for that. I told her how to get the delivery truck and helped her. I know we can't trust her, she has done some fucked up shit to everybody, but I just couldn't stand by and do nothing. That ain't feel right." I said.

Dro became silent and we both just looked at each other. At the time I made the call to Marisol it was the right thing to do. It kept all of us out of jail but ever since she has been here things have gotten increasingly worse. It seemed like a better option than working for Trent but the more I worked with her the more I started to see that although Marisol was intelligent, she was also heartless.

I was someone who looked at every option and outcome when weighing a situation and everything inside of me told me as soon as Marisol didn't see a need for us, we were possibly next.

"So what now?" Dro asked.

"We have to find a way to get these crazy assholes out of our club. To get them out of our life. We have made a lot of money, we don't need this life no more baby." I stood up and rubbed Dro's face.

I knew this was the only life that he knew, it was really all we both knew. From his strip clubs to his days of dealing, to us trafficking women and now the drugs, this was the world we knew and we were good at it. But with the shit that's been happening, maybe it was time for us to let it go. Whoever heard of old ass gangstas? They often died by the same rules they lived by.

"You hear me, baby?" I lowered my head to make eye contact with Dro. I promised him the last time I would never just do anything without his knowledge like I had before, no matter if I thought it was in our best interest and we needed to make these decisions together.

"Yes, I hear you, whatever you want to do. I trust you and I got you." I leaned in and kissed him on his cheek. To think when we first met he scared the hell out of me, but he always protected me, and always loved me.

"So, when Berto came here I had him, in addition to the accounts that Marisol knows about, set up an offshore account that all of our accounts dump into. Untouchable, untraceable money! I had an account set up for Sergio too, he's been good to us and when all the shit goes down I want to make sure we take care of him.

The office door burst open and Marisol entered. The door swung open with so much force it banged against the wall. We both turned to look at her.

"What did you do?" Marisol asked.

"I don't know what you're talking about?"

"You know! Did you help your sister escape?"

"Help Dominique? Just like I told your son I was the one that let you know she was gone."

Dro stood to his feet, he would allow her a little more headway because she was a woman, but she wasn't going to have too many times to talk to me like she was losing her mind. Marisol stepped back and looked at me, maybe trying to decide if she could trust what I was saying or not. I decided to change the conversation and redirect her attention.

"Your shipment came in today. Your people should pick it up

as soon as possible so they can get it out and you back in business." Her face lit up. "The pallets are in the very back storage room.

"We will move it out tonight. And we need to find your sister. Dominique's not going to escape her fate one way or the other. She crossed me and my family. Once you do that, you're dead to me. Literally." Her voice was low and ominous, almost as if she was trying to warn me of the same thing.

"Sí, yo entiendo." I understood what she said, even if I didn't agree with it. Marisol stormed out of the room. I turned back to face Dro.

"See what I'm talking about. I don't know what her endgame really is, and if we have to deal with her acting like that, transporting for her is not going to be sustainable." Dro shook his head up and down. He got what I was saying. I wondered how far Dominique had managed to get. It would be all for nothing if she escaped only to be recaptured.

I went to the computer and pulled up the spreadsheet of all of our vehicles. That delivery truck was the only one we had in that size, I quickly looked for the make and model and found the license plate number. I grabbed my phone, in total shock of what I was about to do. I searched for the number and dialed.

"Miami-Dade County non-emergency, how can I help you." Her voice sang on the other end.

"Yes, I would like to report a stolen vehicle. I have the license plate." I responded. I would rather Dominique take her chances with the police than with Marisol and Trent hot on her trail.

At least this way she might make it out alive.

FIFTEEN

AMINA

"WHAT ARE YOU DOING HERE?" Soraya asked. "I thought you were in jail." She genuinely looked confused. She pushed the blade of her knife back in and slipped into the pocket of the robe she wore. I looked her up and down. She had some nerve. I was in jail meanwhile they were out, living life as if I or nothing we had ever mattered.

"I thought you were too, but it looks like I'm the only one that had to do actual time." Soraya stared at me. I could hear Omere's heavy steps coming down the stairs. I could feel him before he even made it down the stairs. His presence had always been big, I could always feel his energy before I ever saw him.

"Amina," his voice went up a few octaves, his surprise evident. "So it was you that called me." I have no idea why I made the call, I believed I needed some sort of connection with them, no matter how small.

"Called you when?" Soraya shouted his direction. "Why didn't you tell me she called you? Do you ask her to come here?"

"Today, and no she didn't say anything just breathed on the line like a stalker." Omere stared at me, then corners of his mouth lifted. His eyes were warm. He was happy to see me. Soraya on the other hand, didn't seem like she gave a shit about seeing me.

"I'm not going to keep asking, what are you doing here?"

I swallowed hard. *Was I ready for the conversation we were about to have?* I've had months to wonder what happened. Why did it happen? Everything from that night was a blur and honestly, if Trejo hadn't shown up to help me I would probably still be rotting in that cell all alone, going crazy.

"Do you know how many sacrifices I made for you guys?" I asked. My eyes connected with them both. Seeing them made me want to put it all back together, but how? How could things go back? We had attempted to pick up the pieces before and look how that all worked out. It hadn't worked out. I felt we were on the cusp of something great, but we could never make it, each and every time reality slapped the hell out of us.

"You ain't the only one that made sacrifices Amina!" Soraya said as she slapped her hand against the arm of the chair that she sat in. "Everybody sacrificed something, Amina."

"I had a plan and you betrayed me, how could you just let me set up in that jail and rot?"

"You were the one that turned on us, you called the FBI in." She stood up her arms flailing back and forth as she talked.

"I was working out a plan to protect us, I only wanted to take down them, not you. I didn't know that Bryant was dirty." I wasn't sure why this was so hard for her to believe. Every decision I made was to make sure we were okay, to make sure that we were protected.

"Bullshit."

"Soraya, it's not bullshit. If I was really setting you up why the fuck would I be here trying to get answers from you?"

"Because that's what the fuck you do!" She shouted back at me, aggressively getting in my face. "Always with the fucking games. You told us you weren't an agent anymore, you told us you were done with that. But those were nothing but lies. Fuck, sometimes I hate I ever let you get this close to us."

Her words cut like a knife into my heart. I couldn't understand how she could even allow those words to come out of her mouth. No matter what we had been through, I never wished that we never happened. Us happening was what showed me I could love someone, maybe even love someone more than I loved myself.

"I was just trying to do what I needed to do to protect us, to avenge everything that has been done. You of all people should understand that, Soraya. You gonna sit here and tell me you never believed none of it was real?"

"It was real for us, Mina, but for you..." Omere voice trailed off. I was surprised to find out that he questioned me too. He had always been the one that could sway Soraya in my favor, but now it seems that he was starting to have his own questions about how I felt.

"Omere, Soraya, I have given up every fucking thing. I am not an agent, I stole a government vehicle, broke into your house! Why would I do that if it wasn't real? If I didn't want what we had?"

"Marisol told us you set us up. And we are paying dearly for letting you back in. Basically reduced to runners and lucky to still be alive."

"How could you believe anything that woman had to tell you about me? She's been working with Bryant the entire time, they finally got him. It's just a matter of time before they are on to her."

"They will never catch her, and if you keep showing up she's going to eventually kill you too."

"Well, I'm gonna keep showing up, because I fucking love you." I grabbed her by her neck and pulled her in and kissed her, no longer able to control myself. I wanted this, I wanted them and somehow I was going to find a way to have it.

Her soft lips kissed me back with so much intensity I almost lost my balance. She tasted like fruit flavored lip balm. Our tongues danced, gently tapping against each other, slipping between our lips as I lips press gently against once another. I savored her taste, I inhaled her scent, I tried to soak up her entire essence as I held her in my arms. I wrapped my hands around her waist and tugged at the loose nightie she wore.

"I want you" I breathed. Her kiss said she wanted me to. Omere stepped behind me, the scent of him intoxicating me. I turned to face him. He brought his head down to me and pressed his lips against mine. My hands moved downward as I began to run my hands up and down his solid six-pack. My fingers traveled to his belt and began to unbuckle and then unbutton his pants.

Soraya kissed my neck and back as Omere explored my hardened chocolate nipples. Her hands slipped across my thighs and pulled at the soft fabric that covered me. The pants slipped off my hips and exposed my panties. She pulled at those as well and then slowly pushed her fingers to my middle.

Wetness began to pour from me. Their touch, the both of them touching me, loving me did it for me completely. Her fingers slipped inside of me and then out making small circles before gliding them back inside of me.

"I want this forever." I didn't mean to say it aloud but before I knew it the words had slipped from my lips.

"I missed you," Omere whispered in my ear. Omere couldn't wait a moment longer he grabbed me and cradled my body in his arms. He took me to the sofa and laid down on his back. I climbed on top of him and guided him inside of me. I bounced up and down, feeling each and every stroke long and deep. My tongue greedily searched for Soraya's mouth as Omere dove deep inside of me.

"Let me taste you," he said to Soraya. She got on top of his face. Her head rolled and her eyes closed as his tongue slipped in and out of her. I leaned forward taking her breast into my mouth as I bounced up and down, plunging him further inside of me with each movement. Passion overtook me as I rode Omere while suckling Soraya's nipple. I pressed my thumb against her clit and began to make movements back and forth.

Her hips rolled as her eyes glowed with desire. The tension coiled inside of me causing a wave heat and excitement to surge through my body. We teased and touched and fucked each other to orgasm. Each of our bodies shuddered in ecstasy as our bodies collided on the sofa. Without our moans echoing throughout the room, everything became silent. My phone rang disrupting the euphoric quiet.

"Hello,"

"Mina, get your ass back here," Kash yelled through the phone.

DOMINIQUE

"GET OUT THE CAR NOW! Hands up!" I squinted trying to see the clock on the dashboard. I had been sleeping for hours. An officer tapped on the window. I was surrounded by officers, guns drawn and pointed directly at me. I was scared to even blink.

"Get out now!"

I jumped at the sound of his second command. Feeling as if I had no other choice, I opened the door and moved my leg to try to step out of the truck. The pain shot through my body, I was really starting to think something in my knee was broken and I would never walk the same again. I finally wiggled my legs towards the open door and pushed myself forward. My body hit the ground with a thud. I was unable to keep my balance with my leg in so much pain.

"What's your name?" The officer handcuffing me asked as he slipped on the metal bracelets. My mind raced, should I give him my name? Fuck it, it was either the police or Marisol.

"Dominique, my name is Dominique Simoneax also known as Kyra Jamison." I gave them my name and my alias. I felt safer in police custody than with my husband and his crazy ass family. The officer put me in the back of the car. The only thing audible was the clicking of the keys on the computer in his patrol car. I knew he was running the name I had given him.

"Shit! Harris, we got ourselves a real live wire here, look at this rap sheet! Looks like you are on the FBI's most wanted list." The officers rejoiced as they radioed in a bunch of gibberish I didn't understand. The car rolled forward and I was taken to the station and placed in a holding cell.

I sat down on the cold metal bench inside the cell. I took in all the surroundings of the cold brick room. It was gray, void of any color and reeked of despair, but I knew that I would rather be here than anywhere near Trent and his family.

I passed the hours in silence. I couldn't believe he was going to kill me. In those moments it's as if my entire world was shattered completely. Trent should have known to be careful with me, cause now I was going to do whatever I needed to do to fuck up his entire world.

"Simoneaux." A guard called my name. I stood as they came to the cell door and opened it. He reached for my arms and pulled them up to put the handcuffs on.

"Where are you taking me?"

"You're being transferred to federal custody." The guard said without even looking my direction. He walked me down a corridor leading me back to the same area I came in through.

"Here's your prisoner," He said as he shoved me towards the pudgy man that stood before me. My mind raced, how could I know this wasn't just another one of Marisol's games? What if they had found me? Didn't she have dirty cops working for her everywhere?

"How do I know he's really FBI?" I asked the guard stepping back so far I bumped into his rounded belly.

"You're just gonna have to take my word for it." He spat the words out quickly and grabbed the cuffs and led me out the door. My legs were like jello as he walked me outside.

I was sure as soon as I got in the black SUV that waited for me I was going to be shot on sight. Maybe this idea to hide within the confines of the police was misguided. I started to wonder just how long Marisol's reach really was.

"Get in," He said. I stepped back and he pushed me forward. "Get in." He nudged me to the door and I got in the car. When I sat down is when I noticed her.

"Amina." It was weird calling her that, I had known her by a completely different name and my sister knew her as something different as well.

"Hi, Dominique," she smiled smugly as she stared back at me. I thought about the first time she put me in custody, wanting to protect me, and I had outsmarted her and disappeared giving her only the information I wanted. Part of that had been done to save Trent's ass.

"I want a deal."

"Really?"

"Yes, Amina help me. Please. We have history." The way I saw it we had both crossed and double crossed each other for our own reasons but what I saw was something mutually beneficial.

"I can't give you anything anymore, because of your fucked up family I lost my job, so you better hope and pray whatever you can give my friends here is worth giving you a deal, or you might as well get ready for a life in jail." She finished.

I partly felt that she was enjoying what was happening way too much. I didn't say another word. I didn't feel as if I had any room to do so. I needed this to work and I didn't have any space for fucking up based on my ego. Maybe I was learning, or maybe I was just desperate enough to kiss a little ass. I looked towards the two agents and decided to pucker up.

"I will give you whatever you want, whatever information. I

will go on the record. I've seen things, I know things, where the money is and where the bodies are buried. But if I talk I need y'all to protect me. Because these crazy motherfuckers will kill my ass. I need y'all to help a bitch out." I was practically begging for their help.

It was important for them to see that I knew a lot, I had seen a lot and this time I planned on doing it for real. I planned on making sure that I could put them away so that maybe I could live in peace. The agents looked at each other and laughed just a little. I didn't see anything funny.

"Okay, start talking."

"I need to know you're going to protect me first. The only power I have is what I know. I need it in writing and then I will spill everything. Every name I know, every contact, how they get money and drugs in and out. I will give it all to you. But you gotta give me that guarantee first and not just your word."

"Oh, Viera you're right. She's smart." One of them smirked.

"Trejo, I don't know if it's smart or just conniving as hell, either way, if she is willing to help finally put away the TCC for good I say give it to her. But make sure she earns that deal, cause Dominique is sneaky." Amina's cold stare peered into me as she spoke. I could tell by the look on her face she felt like she was winning something. I was the one that was winning. They say there is nothing worse than a woman scorned, and I was going to bring hell to that family if it was the last thing I did.

SEVENTEEN
KHARI

"DID YOU BOOK THE PJ?" I asked Sergio as he entered our home. He rushed inside the house and took a seat. We asked him to book a private flight out. We were leaving life as we know it, and a commercial airline wasn't an option. This was very sensitive and we needed to be able to control as much of the situation as we could.

"Sí, everything is a go, we don't have much time to get you to the airport." He said. "Where are your bags?" He looked around for our luggage. All of these material things weren't worth a thing to us. New lives, new stuff.

"We aren't taking any." Dro appeared from the kitchen and chimed in. After our last conversation, we decided it was time. Time to walk away from the bullshit. They can have it. We had more than enough money, and having Marisol in our club day in and day out was overwhelming.

Our club had basically been hijacked by her and her people. She walked in and out of our doors whenever she felt like it, she never asked permission, she just took or expected everything to be given. That club wasn't ours anymore and it was never our intent to be apart of her organization.

We talked about going legit before but Dro was never really with it. I felt like to keep him happy we needed to bring in enough money. But I wanted the money with the least amount of risk, and doing business with Marisol showed me the stakes were too high.

"Sergio you're coming with us. I'm not leaving you here." He looked surprised. There is no way I was going to leave him here. I walked over to Berto. I needed his help in order to make this happen. It wasn't as easy as people may think to disappear without a trace and I wanted to make sure that we would never be found.

After working with Marisol I realized that she had a huge organization. Marisol probably a full network of people that she could put on her payroll at any time to find us. If she ever decided to do that I didn't want to make it easy for her.

"Do you have the account info I had you setup for him?" I knew when meeting Berto he would be useful.

"Yep," Berto reached over to his stack of papers and handed me the envelope. "I suggest y'all memorize the accounts and then destroy all of this." He had previously given us the same instructions for our account. With the money that we already had plus what we made from Marisol's first shipment, we had more than enough money to make sure that everyone was taken care of. If I eat then my family eats, and Sergio was definitely family. I walked towards Sergio and handed him the paper.

"This is for you. No amount can ever repay your loyalty, but this should be enough to make sure you don't want for anything. Gracias, por todo." I hugged him. There was no way I could thank him for everything. This man had helped to protect us, he had killed for us and he was loyal.

No amount of money or shine from anyone else could ever

deter him and for that, I would always appreciate him. He unfolded the paper and stared at me. His eyes widened in disbelief.

"Fifteen million dollars?"

"Yes," I smiled and shook my head. This is for you. I patted my hands against his shoulders, you can do whatever you want with it. Like he said, learn the account number, once we get to Cape Verde we will have access to the accounts and after that, you can go and do whatever you want."

"Cape Verde?" Sergio asked.

"No extradition." I winked at him and a smile spread across his face. I turned my attention towards Berto.

"Is everything almost done?" I asked Berto.

"Just about," His fingers clicked away on the keyboard. "I just have to hack our flight manifest and change around some things. It will be a wild goose chase for them if they ever tried to find us." He was undoubtedly a genius.

The only way I had gotten him to agree to do this was first with money, and then painting the very clear picture that it was only a matter of time before the Feds or Marisol got him caught up in something that would get him killed. Working with the government against the TCC would get him killed and working with Marisol also left a trail of bodies. Either way rolling with us had to be his very best option. My phone danced across the table as it rang. I reached over and looked at the caller id.

"It's Marisol," I said, unsure of if I should answer the phone. I decided I need to make things seem as normal as possible.

"Why are you not here?" She asked.

"We just decided to stay in today. Everything's good at the club, your people are there."

"I know but you are supposed to be here to watch my shipments. So why are you not here?" Was she going to keep asking me the same question? What else did she want from me? I saved her shipments, I had just given her the damn club, what else could she want? This is exactly what I was talking about when I said we needed to get away from this insanity.

"Everything is good Marisol. The shipment is in the back, just like I said the other day." There was no need for me to babysit pallets of liquid cocaine. So why was she so irked by it? I could only guess it was part of the controlling issues I had started to see. I knew I always had to be careful with my answers to Marisol. Because even though she was bat shit crazy she was still very intelligent. That's why disappearing had to be done on the low. I just hoped once we were gone she would leave it at that.

"Okay fine." She said when I didn't respond and then disconnected the phone. I shook my head. I thought about how fast Berto had found us when I called him and jumped into action.

"Okay, it's time to go. Give me your phones. We don't need anything that we can be tracked through. I handed them to Berto please wipe these clean and then destroy them."

Berto did as I asked and then we all headed out the door. It was so close I could taste the freedom. We got into the car and headed towards the airport.

I briefly thought of Dominique and hoped she got away. I hoped that at some point she would grow up, I knew I would never see her again and that was fine with me too.

When we were younger we had been close, I would have done anything to protect her. What I did to help her escape was my final act to protect my sister. Hopefully, she could make it out. It was time to let our old life go, and that included any thoughts of Dominique.

I leaned against Dro and he wrapped his arm around my waist. I loved this man and I couldn't wait to start our new life together.

EIGHTEEN
AMINA

"WHAT DO YOU THINK?" Trejo asked me. It was funny how they kept telling me I wasn't an agent but they kept needing my help. After getting Dominique to agree to a plea deal and testify they were feeling a little ambitious. They had my testimony as well as hers but wanted to make the case even stronger if they could.

"I think it's possible but they will never talk to you guys," I responded to him. He scrunched his nose and scratched his temple as he tilted his head in deep thought.

"What about you? I mean if we can get multiple testimonies it will make the case so much stronger. Dominique has info on Trent but Soraya and Omere, they have seen way more." He was trying to convince me that this was a good idea. I hadn't decided if it was or not. I would have to talk to them about this and with this subject things could get a little testy between us.

I sat back in my seat. I don't know if I could persuade them to do this. So much has happened and I wasn't sure if the last time we were together meant what I thought it did or was it our final goodbye. I hoped it wasn't. We hadn't had a chance to talk about it. As bad as I wanted to, I was afraid if I brought it up I might hear an answer I don't like.

"If they said yes, what type of deal you talking? Full immunity?" If we were going to make this happen we needed to be on point. The offer couldn't be bullshit.

"I don't know if we can swing that, they may have to do some jail time," Trejo rubbed the back of his head. I know he was trying to figure out how in the hell he could make full immunity happen.

I knew from experience making it happen would not be easy, but I also knew if I could pull this off, anything they had to say would be worth it. They probably had enough on all of them to put Trent and his family under the jail.

"Trejo, if I go to them it's gotta be something good. They ain't gonna wanna do no jail time when you are coming to them." I pointed out his error in logic. It's not like they had been arrested. They probably had enough cash on standby to disappear and live off of for a few years.

"Okay, okay. Take it to them and if they will talk to me I will get it done,"

"And for me?" I asked. I had a few thoughts tumbling in my mind, thoughts that had honestly been there a while and I finally saw an opportunity to perhaps make it happen.

"You don't need immunity, we are clearing your charges based on the charges that have been brought against Bryant." Trejo raised his hands and shoulders up, waiting for me to explain what I meant.

"I know, but," I paused. "But I will have to go into WITSEC and if they decided to do this I want to be placed into witness protection with them." This was my opportunity. If the other night meant what I thought it did, this was my chance maybe to find some happiness.

Kash looked my way. The expression on his face was

complete horror. He never understood any of this. I honestly didn't expect him to. I didn't go out looking for this type of relationship. I didn't want to fall in love with the couple I was targeting undercover, it just happened. And now that it has, I felt a need to see it through.

"Kash, I appreciate you so much. Cause you know our relationship was hella rocky. Don't look so shocked. I wanna be happy. I wanna have the feeling that our dad gave mom." I tried to explain to him why I needed to be with them. Without the Bureau, without them I was desolate, I needed them. Kash shook his head in silence. I could tell he still disagreed but perhaps he was saving that argument for another day.

"Fine," Trejo said snapping me back to our conversation. "I'll give you whatever you want if you can make this happen." He walked away towards the couch to the left of me, rubbing his forehead as he took a seat.

"Okay somebody I need a car." I looked around the room. Trejo handed me his keys.

"Thank you, let's see if I can work my magic." I got up and headed out of the door.

On the entire drive over I thought about what our life could be like. I didn't know how I was going to be able to convince them of this but I had to try. I practiced over and over what I could say. How do you open up a conversation like this?

I know how I would do it if I was still an FBI agent, but to say it to people I wanted to spend my life with, I didn't know. I pulled into the driveway and noticed a car I didn't recognize. I hesitated, questioning whether I should go in. Fuck it, it was now or never.

I stepped out of the car and went to the door, ringing the doorbell and then softly knocking on the door. I stood at the door for a moment but no one came. I tapped again on the door and rang the bell twice.

"It's me, Mina, I said through the door. I could hear people talking although I was unable to make out what was being said. Finally, Omere opened the door.

"Mina, what are you doing here?" He asked standing in the door. A smile spread across his handsome face. I didn't have time to get distracted, I pushed my way past him and into the house.

"Where is Soraya, I need to talk to you guys about something?" I rounded the corner towards the kitchen searching for her. I stopped in my tracks when I saw her sitting at the table with her dad. That was totally unexpected. After everything that she found out about her mother and what really happened, I was surprised to see they were talking.

"What are you doing here?" She questioned.

"I need to talk to you about something. In private," My eyes darted his direction. Why was he here and if he was, did that mean that Marisol was somewhere on the premises?

"You can speak freely," He said. "I have no beef with you." His voice sounded tired as if he was carrying the weight of the world on his shoulders alone. He sounded exhausted. Given the way he was responding, Marisol couldn't have been here. I know she wanted me dead, and I had a feeling for her that hadn't changed. If she was here, she would have been on me by now.

"I don't. . ."

"Amina, just talk."

"I, well..." I was having a hard time finding the words. No matter how many times I practiced in the car, the words were still difficult. This was a big moment. "I received an offer today, from the FBI," I said. Soraya eyes became tiny slits as she peered at me. Omere stood behind me, his presence calming me.

"I really think that you, Omere and I should have this conversation elsewhere," I said. I really didn't want to have this conversation in front of Tre.

"We can have the conversation right here. I thought you said you were done with the FBI bullshit." Soraya spat. I needed her to listen. She was always expecting the worse from me, but how could I blame her? "I suggest you start making some sense real fast." She stepped forward towards me.

"Soraya, let's hear her out," Omere spoke, calming the fire that was building in her.

"The offer I received is for the case against Bryant and everything that I know about the TCC," I couldn't believe I was saying this in front of one of the very people I've always wanted to bring down. "They want to offer you guys a deal too. Full immunity, in writing to testify against Marisol." I cut my eyes towards Trent's father. I have no idea what I was getting myself into saying this in front of him. I understood there was a strong possibility that I could not walk out of here alive.

"Hell no, why the fuck would I do that?" She asked. Omere was quiet. I know he wasn't a snitch but I felt like he could see the bigger picture, at least I hoped he could.

"It would mean a way out. It would mean a fresh start, it would mean we could move forward. Together."

"By snitching?" She said.

"Not snitching, surviving. Honestly, it's just a matter of time before something happens she deems her final straw and she tries to kill you. I damn near thought that was about to happen the last time. This is a way that we can live, be protected and be happy." I turned towards Omere, pleading with him with my eyes. He looked down at me. His expression much kinder than Soraya's but he still hadn't spoken.

"I think you should do it, at least see what they are talking about," Tre spoke up. Up until this point he had been quiet. Everyone turned to face him. He walked towards his daughter and cupped her face.

"Baby girl, you've lost so much, endured so much for me, and for this family. Growing up I knew Marisol treated you differently, I fought for you as hard as I could, but not hard enough. Your stepmother lost her mind a long time ago, she forced me to kill either your mother or you, I had to choose, now she's forcing your brother to kill his wife. This has gone far enough. If you have a way to get out then take it. Take it." I hadn't expected that. "If I had the same chance, I would take it." He hugged his daughter. It had always seemed that he chose Trent over Soraya, maybe this had just been his way of protecting Soraya all along.

"Maybe you can, have the same deal. Do you know what it would mean if you turned state's evidence, I'm sure they would want to hear you out." My pulse quickened as I spoke. I had come here wanting to make a life with the two people I loved, it was a bonus to be able to take him back to Trejo. Having Tre testify against his own wife was like the nail in the coffin for Marisol and the TCC.

"Let me make a call," I said stepping away to call Trejo and let him know we were all coming in. I didn't say too much on the phone but I was certain we were on our way to happier days.

NINETEEN
DOMINIQUE

THE DOOR to the room I was in creaked open. It was one of the armed agents that had been tasked with my safety for the past two weeks, I was being kept in an undisclosed location, as they put it, until my transfer to witness protection was complete. These had been the calmest two weeks I had in a long time.

"It's time to go." He said.

"Where?" I asked. I hadn't seen much of the outside lately. They kept me heavily guarded, and confined, like jail with all the comforts of home. In comparison to the dirty storage room I had been kept in, this was a five star suite.

"To start your new life." He smiled. I stood, my knee still slightly aching from the beating that Marisol had given me and walked with him to the car that awaited us outside. Luckily she hadn't broken anything, it was only swollen,

A wave of relief washed over me. Even though I was being kept at a safe house I didn't know how much I could trust that. I knew how to get out of one of these houses, who's to say people don't know how to get in? I couldn't wait to get away from this city, the further away from Miami, the better. I wasn't sure how everything was going to work, but I'm sure all of that would be explained in due time.

We got into the car and started on our way. They didn't tell me much of anything so I didn't know where we were going, only that we were going. It seemed that it took us no time to reach our destination. The car rolled to a stop. The door was opened and I was lead inside of a building. As we walked multiple agents surrounded me. I could see in the distance the man Trejo, from the FBI and a woman that I didn't know.

"Good morning Dominique, you ready?" He smiled and reached out his hand. I shook it.

"More than ready," I responded. And I was. These last few years had been rough. Trying to stay one step ahead, trying to stay alive, chasing the bag. Damn a bitch was tired. Hell yeah, I'm more than ready to get this new life popping. I had done it before, I was certain I could do it again. I followed the two inside the building and was escorted to a small room.

"Have a seat," She said. I took a seat at the table and she did on the other side. She pulled out a file.

"I'm Marshall Jackson. My team will be facilitating your transfer into your new identity. We have a few rules we need to go over. These rules are for your safety. Please adhere to them." She paused for a moment.

"Okay," I responded.

"Firstly, once you are officially transferred into the witness security program there will be no contact with your former world. This is to keep your location a secret and to keep you alive. Do you understand?"

"Yes, I understand." If it's one thing I knew it was to how to keep a secret. I had no intention of trying to contact anyone from my past. Trent was the one that wanted me dead, I had no ties to Marisol and I doubted I would ever see Khari again. I was just fine with disappearing without a trace.

"Your WITSEC id will be, Andrea Walters." Ugh.

"That's so blah." She laughed at me.

"It's supposed to be, there isn't any reason why it needs to be otherwise. Remember there is someone who wants you dead. Let's not make it easy for them to do so. Got it, Andrea?" She smiled.

"Got it," I responded.

"Here is your new identification, and your new social security number and birth certificate. Once you leave here you will be transferred to our witness safe house where you will have orientation, then you will be given your location and your new life begins.

"How long do I have to stay in witness protection?" I asked.

"As long as someone out there wants you dead."

"So I basically have to live the rest of my life hiding?"

"Many people go on to build healthy happy lives in the program. You can too. We will get you set up with a new location, you have your new identity and soon this life will be nothing more than a distant memory." The agent finished speaking.

I briefly wondered just how safe they could really keep me. Could they keep Trent and Marisol from coming after me? I really hoped that they could. Trejo entered back into the room with his own set of paperwork. He laid it down before me.

"This is your immunity agreement. This is in exchange for your testimony, which you provided via video deposition. Please review and sign the agreement." He slid the papers towards me. This reminded me of when this same thing happened with Amina. This time I didn't have any thoughts of running. I honestly needed the protection this time around.

I glanced over the document and signed my name on the dotted line. It was done. My life was about to change and everything I knew in it. I was starting over. *Again.*

The first time I ran, I had the funds to help me start over, now all I had was me. There were no bundles of cash. No fancy were jobs waiting for me. That part of it was a little scary for me.

I didn't know anything but the hustle. I didn't know anything but the game, but the thought of actually living a life where I maybe didn't have to worry about any of the bullshit that came along with the street life might be what I needed. It could possibly be the one thing that finally allows me to be free. I looked up at both of them.

"I'm ready, let's do this!"

TWENTY

KHARI

THE WAVES CRASHED against the sandy white beach as I laid in our hammock underneath the shade of two palm trees. I never thought that this could ever be my life. The world Dro and I came from things sometimes got hard, and when they did, the only thing we knew to do was go even harder, but the pace of this small island town had given us something we desperately needed, peace.

Until now I didn't realize that it was even missing in my life. I was always trying to save everything around me. I saved my mother, my sister, our business, but now it was time that I saved myself. It was time to give my family a chance to grow.

I watched as Dro plowed through the water, causing the crystal blue waters to splash and stir as he whirled around on his jet ski. He loved the water and he loved his water toys. It had been almost a month since we made it here. As soon as our plane landed Berto disappeared into the wind.

I didn't worry about him, he was a tech genius, had he not chosen a life of crime he probably could have been a Steve Jobs or Bill Gates. I knew that he probably wasn't going to stay and that was best. Too many of us in one place may really call too much attention to us all. He served his purpose and now he has moved on. I hoped he could find the same happiness and peace that we had stumbled upon.

Life for all of us was crazy good. All this time working with Sergio, who knew all this man wanted to do was fish. He spent his days fishing and selling his goods at the dock market. He bought a small house not too far from ours and I loved having him near. I was happy he decided to stay. Like I told him, he was family. It was and would always be his choice to stay, and I'm glad he chose to do so.

A smile spread across my face as I thought of how many times I had to remind Sergio that we were all equals here, he didn't have to protect us anymore, his service was done. But he just couldn't help it. Sergio's protective watchful eyes were always watching over us.

I stood up and watched Dro tie the jet ski to the dock. I walked into our small bungalow style beach house. It was cozy and quaint and I loved every bit of it. It was just enough for us, we woke to the sunrise and the sound of the water and fell asleep under the stars and staring at the night sky. Our life was like a romantic movie.

I opened the fridge to grab the dough I had chilling and some beef. I started to roll out the dough stuffing it with beef. Dro loved empanadas. I made them just the way his mother, Gabriela had shown me. I thought about her often. I think she would be proud of who we have become.

I wanted to give him something that reminded him of home and the home that we were building. I grabbed the rectangular gift box I had for him. He was outside in the outdoor shower rinsing the salt water from his body.

"Baby, lunch," I called towards him. Dro walked over and took a seat next to me on my hammock.

"Thank you mi amor," He took the pastry and greedily took a bite out it. He always seemed to work up an appetite when he played in the water. I enjoyed seeing him enjoying himself. Just letting go and having fun. He was never one to just hang out or party but we all deserved to let go, especially with everything we had endured.

"So have you thought about what you want to do?" Dro kept telling me he still needed to do something, even though we didn't have to. He wanted to find something that made him happy. Just like Sergio had found fishing.

"Yeah," He said between taking bites of his empanada. "I've been thinking I want to open a little beach bar. I've always had clubs, but this time just a small club serve some island drinks good music, no trafficking, no drugs." He laughed. It was funny but then again it wasn't. We had almost given our life for the life-style, his mother had died because of it. I'm glad we both didn't want that life anymore.

"That sounds like a wonderful idea." I leaned into him and kissed him on his cheek. I nuzzled my head into his neck and inhaled his scent. Feelings, deep emotional waves rippled through me causing my heart to swell. I was lucky to have this man, no matter what we had been through. I don't want to go through it with anyone else but him. I reached for the box next to me.

"You're going to be really busy. I have another job for you," I handed him the box and waited for him to open it.

"What's this?" He sat the plate down next to him and grabbed the box.

"Open it." I nudged. Excitement swelled within me as I waited for him to untie the small ribbon and remove the top. He slipped the box top off and peered inside. He picked up the long stick that forecasted our future.

"Wait, is this? You're, you're pregnant." He jumped up. I shook my head up and down.

"Yes, I was late. I took a test. We're having a baby!"

Dro jumped up and wrapped his arms around me. Our family was growing, a baby. I was going to be a mother. I wanted to give my child everything that I didn't have. My child would have a mother, my child would be loved.

"The best decision we ever made was leaving, baby," I told Dro. He shook his head in agreement. It truly was. We didn't need the speed of the streets to be happy, and even though we had a lot of it, it wasn't the money that was fueling joy in our lives, it was us having each other and now we would have an extension of us, a tiny little reflection of our image.

"You're going to be a great mother." Dro kissed me on my lips and placed his hands on my belly. "My seed is growing inside of you." He beamed with happiness.

"Yeah, I'm gonna have your baby!" I smiled and pulled him down on top of me, kissing him as the cool wind breezed over us. At this moment everything was perfect and I wouldn't have it any other way.

TWENTY-ONE
AMINA

WE WERE NOW OFFICIALLY, Angela, James, and Sonya. Light crept in through the tiny cracks of the blinds as I rolled over and kissed Soraya, well Sonya and James. That would take some getting used to. I was used to answering to different names, becoming who I needed to be in any given situation. But this wasn't one of those situations. This was something completely different.

"Today's the day, huh," Soraya asked groggily as she sat up in bed.

"Yep, today is the day." I was excited.

We had just completed our mandatory WITSEC orientation. We received all the dos and don'ts of our new identities and today we would receive our location. We all had given testimony a recorded testimony. Hopefully, this would be the end of it. But I knew how this went. If she didn't take a plea deal, and I felt like she would with all the testimony against her, we may be called back to testify if this thing goes to trial.

I got up and started to get myself together. I never would have thought all those years ago things would go like this. If someone had asked me a year ago, I would have definitely said that victory would consist of arresting the TCC. I would have thought the only thing that could make me happy would be that and of course maybe a promotion in the Bureau.

"So I'll never see my father again," Soraya asked.

I had been so lost in my thoughts that I hadn't heard her walk up behind me. She didn't realize it but I know exactly how she felt. To save my mother she had to disappear into witness protection and despite all of our difference, knowing the possibility of seeing her was slim to none cut very deep.

I turned to face Soraya. Her eyes were heavy with sadness. I was excited for this day but I could tell she was nervous as hell.

"Hey, it's going to be okay. Just like us, your father was giving a new identity, a new life, and a clean start. He will be okay, maybe now he will have a chance to find some true happiness."

We had been at the orientation center. This facility could house up to six families. Tre Jamison was here, and even though contact was kept to a minimum she had gotten a chance to see him. I guess it was hitting home that after today, that will be it.

"So you have any idea where we are going?" Soraya asked.

"No, they won't tell us anything until it is almost time to go. We won't know where your father is going, and vice versa."

"I don't understand why we all just couldn't be relocated together." The uncertainty of what was happening was something that completely threw Soraya for a loop. She was used to having control in her world and the things that she couldn't control, like Marisol, she at least knew how to maneuver, this was uncharted territory.

"We couldn't all be placed together, that increases the chances of someone finding us. It's already three of us, and I had to fight for this to happen. It will be okay, he understood what he was signing up for. Think about this. It gives us a chance to finally be free. We can finally start our life." Running out of words to say, I stepped in and wrapped my arms around her. My lips found my way to hers. The only thing I could do was let her know that I was here for her.

Omere was moving quietly in the background. He had already gotten dressed. His eyes darted towards us ever so often but he didn't jump in, he had an amazing ability to know when to interject and when to fall back. In our relationship there was no them and me or us and him, we were we, and I loved it. There was a soft tapping on the door before one of the US Marshalls stuck their head inside.

"It's time,"

"Okay," All three of us said in unison. I briefly wondered how many times had they placed a polyamorous couple in protection, maybe we were the first. It didn't matter to me if we were the first last, or the only. The one and only thing I was concerned about was that we were finally together. We would finally be able to live our lives in peace.

We followed the Marshalls down the corridor towards the exit door. Everything was coordinated. I heard other groups being moved but we were being shuffled past each other so fast we barely got a look at one another. I glimpsed to see Dominique walking by. She looked happy, good for her. I don't know what kind of deal she got, or where she was going. And I didn't care.

Once we made it outside I saw three different cars lined up along the street. We were all taken three different directions. We were taken to the third and final vehicle. It was all black, the windows were heavily tinted, completely blacked out on the small SUV.

We slid inside and sat in silence. I sank back into the leather seat and I looked around the car. The agents in the front speak but their faces said what their mouths did not, this was crazy. It still didn't matter. People didn't have to understand us, as long as we understood one another, I was good.

Our handler slid inside the car, snapping me out of my thoughts.

"Anyone want to guess where you're going?" The WITSEC Marshall asked.

"Just as long as it's not somewhere in the middle of nowhere and it has a decent coffee shop I don't care where." I laughed as I spoke. I knew it was a toss up when it came to where would be sent, but I was praying for somewhere nice, somewhere decent. I wanted us to be in a place that we could get used to. We were all originally from New York, and I just didn't think a slow country pace was for any of us.

"Well, if it's coffee you're interested in you're gonna love this place. You guys are being relocated to Seattle," the US Marshall replied.

"What in the world are we going to do in Seattle?" Omere asked. I hadn't considered just how hard this had to be for him. I reached my hand over and caressed his palm. He looked at me and weakly smiled.

"Baby, we are going to do whatever we want to do, but most of all we will be free to do it. No constraints, no Bureau, no family ties and no cartel. We get to just be free." I leaned in and kissed him on the cheek and then Soraya on hers. I was full of hope and optimism, our new life was going to be well worth every peace of pain we endured.

EPILOGUE

SITTING in the back of the cell, she slipped her hands inside the elastic band of her panties and pulled out the cell phone that had been smuggled in just for her. There was nothing she wanted that she could not have, even behind bars. Even still, this is not somewhere she wanted to be. She was not free and that lack of freedom infuriated her. She looked at the time on the phone. It was almost three. They said they would call at three.

During her time in the United States, her father's health had taken a drastic turn for the worse. When she left he had been the picture of health, but what she could not see was the lung cancer that had started to ravage his body.

Her plan when she heard the news had been to handle the spiraling shit storm in the US and then make her way back to Mexico. She had thought she had time to say her goodbyes but her unexpected arrest had thrown a wrench into her plans.

She looked around the cell. In all these years she had managed not to do time. They could never touch her. She had always stayed one step ahead, her hands were always clean. This is how the organization had worked so well. This is how she stayed squeaky clean. Soraya had taken many cases for her, but this time the Feds came in and they had information. Information that you could only get if someone talked. The cell phone buzzed. She looked at her bunkie, giving her the signal to be her lookout.

"Bueno," She answered.

"Senora, it is not looking good." The nurse spoke on the other end. "He has been in an out of consciousness, the doctors don't believe he will make it through tonight."

Tears slowly trickled down her cheeks. Her father had taught her everything she knew, the only thing she ever wanted to do in life was make him proud, his final wish was that she repair the broken pieces of the mighty cartel he built. She felt as if she had failed.

"Can I talk to him?"

"Sí,"

"Mija," his voice was scratchy and low, but the sound of it elated her just the same. Marisol's heart ached at the thought of not being able to be there with him on his death bed.

"I'm so sorry Papí, so sorry," Marisol said. The tears were now torrents streaming down her face.

"You have nothing to be sorry for, mija, you make me proud. I know you will avenge our family name. I know that you will make sure that someone pays for the transgressions against us. Sangre por sangre." He fell silent on the other end. She could still hear the rise and fall of his breath. He was still hanging on.

"Te amo papí," He didn't respond back to her but she knew that he loved her just as much. Sangre por sangre, blood for blood, an eye for an eye, that was the way they had lived. Any sins against the family would be avenged with blood.

She disconnected the call and kept the cell phone out. Marisol expected another call. Everyone had seemed to disappear on her, the only person she had any contact with was her son. Tre hadn't been answering his calls, Soraya and Omere hadn't been answering theirs, and she hadn't spoken to Khari since the shipment came in. Things were more than fishy, she had smelled a rat from the beginning. The phone buzzed again.

"Hello,"

"I have eyes on them," Trent said.

It didn't take long for her lawyer to find out the state had a witness list a mile long, consisting of Dominique, Omere, Soraya and most surprisingly of all, Tre. The man that she had given everything to. The man her father had told her wasn't worthy of her. She had made him. Given him a chance at excellence and this is how he had repaid her? Her mood had gone from solemn to enraged.

"And is everything a go?" She asked. Her son was the only one that she could ever trust.

"Aniko and her girls are on it." He said as he watched from a hill behind the secured facility. His binoculars gave him the advantage of seeing exactly what was happening. He watched as his father, his wife, and his sister were led outside along with the agent who sank her claws into his way of life and hadn't released her grip until she had ripped everything apart.

As the group walked towards their designated transport team, he noticed they all looked happy. They looked as if their lives were about to take off. He swelled with hatred at the thought, they were getting second chances while everything he knew was falling apart.

The agents stopped them right before entering the cars. The agents then inspected the vehicles. He watched as each of them took one of the cars, checking the hood, underneath and inside. They kneeled down and ran their hands along the bottom of the car and then all three gave a thumbs up and allowed the group to get inside. Each of them entered into different cars.

"Ma, are you there?"

"I'm here son." She said, her voice slightly jittery from the adrenaline that surged through her.

"We have to get off the phone now. When you are ready, dial the number that I gave you." Trent wanted to make sure his mother understood how this worked. Once she did her part the rest would be taken care of.

"I understand." She said. Technology had come such a long way. Before, if someone had wronged her she would put a bullet in them.

This had all started with her family, her father's legacy and her family name were both on the line and just as she had required of both Trent and Tre when they fucked up, she needed to be the one to do this.

She had been the one to allow Tre into her life, even after her father told her he was no good, which led to him having his bastard daughter that he begged her to allow to live. Because it all had started with her, it all had to end with her.

Trent watched and waited. The three agents that had checked the car were not noticed when they slipped away, stepping out of the baggy uniforms they had stolen, they ran off through an old underground tunnel that hadn't been in use for years. After they had pried the door open, they shut it and disappeared into then air.

The three black Suburbans started and slowly advanced down the long paved pathway that led to the exit. Marisol's fingers shook slightly as she tapped her phone. She opened the message her son had sent her and pressed firmly on the number. The phone rang.

Trent continued to watch from his perch on the hill. He knew that his mom should be making the call about now. He whipped out his cell phone and began to video the cars pulling off. With the amount of time the had passed, he wondered if his mother had somehow changed her mind. He quickly dismissed the thought and continued to record with his phone.

The gate opened and the cars pulled through one by one, and then with a loud clattering boom that shook the earth, each car exploded one by one. Trent's heart raced as he saw the cars engulfed in a blazing flame, almost his entire family had been in those cars and now they were gone.

For a split second, Trent felt the tinge of sadness but just as quick as it came, it was gone. He ended the video and sent it to his mother.

It's done

Marisol opened the message and watched the video in silence. Even though she couldn't play the sound without alerting one of the guards, watching it happen in silence was still tremendously satisfying. She replayed the video over and over again, content that she had properly avenged her family. She laid down against her hard bottom bunk and closed her eyes. Thoughts of her freedom filled her head. She knew her lawyer could get her out, and now that she had every cancerous person out of her organization, she and her son would rebuild what her father had once put together, and again own the streets.

REMEMEBER TO LEAVE A REVIEW

Did you enjoy the series, remember to leave a review! Let me know what you think.

THE GAMES WE PLAY

AVAILABLE NOW

Two friends and one man, when it comes to matters of the heart nothing ever goes to plan.

Khia Bradford and Danica Deveaux work together and play together. Khia confides her inner most desires and to her surprise Danica is ready to play. Developing a twisted game of tag, the women conquer men taking what they want but protecting their hearts.

When Khia sets her sights on the sexy and successful Kaulin Alexander, all bets are off. Both women can't deny the man's attraction and soon their twisted love games turn in to a web of secrets, and things quickly spin out of control.

What happens when two friends seeking a thrill cross the

point of no return? Will one woman's desire become another woman's obsession?

THE GAMES WE PLAY

EXCERPT

Prologue

"Dig!" The voice roared through the crisp night air, breaking the calm summer silence. Just as quick as the sound came it went. The thick quiet resettled and the only thing audible was the soft rustling of the trees in the Texas wind.

The shovel hit the ground with a loud thud, breaking through the soil, creating a tiny hole that grew larger and larger with each thrust.

"Did you really think you could get away with what you did to me? Did you think I would allow that?" There was a long pause, it wasn't a rhetorical question but answers never came.

"Answer me dammit!"

Each question was again met with silence. There was only defiance and defeat as they watched each other, both questioning how they had gotten here. How had things gotten so out of hand?

She took deep deliberate breaths as she attempted to calm herself. With her heart racing a mile a minute, she struggled to keep her composure. Chills formed tiny goosebumps up and down her arms, causing the fine hairs to stand at attention. The digging abruptly stopped.

"I'm not doing this shit!"

"Oh, now you want to talk?" The shovel fell with a thud to the ground. They faced each other, eyes locked in determination.

"Pick it up and dig!"

"You want the hole, dig that shit yourself."

"I'm the one holding the fucking gun, now finish digging your grave! You are gonna regret the day you fucked over me."

"Fucking you and fucking over you are two different things. It's not my fault you got shit fucked up!"

"Fucked up? I got shit fucked up? I don't have a damn thing fucked up." The gun bounced forward with each word spoken, threatening to release its anger at any moment. "Now I said to dig the hole! Now!" The gun thrust forward releasing a loud bang that echoed through the dark woods.

"Pick up the shovel! Now!"

"Or what? You gonna shoot me? We both know you ain't gone do shit!" The gun exploded with a loud bang that gave both of them pause. The two stared at each other, both contemplating their next move, neither of them knowing what to expect from the other.

"You have lost your mind. Crazy ass bitch!"

"Put that shovel down! No! Get Back!"

The shovel swung with paralyzing force, hitting the gun so hard it flew feet from where they were standing. They looked at each other, then as if on cue, both shot towards the gun. In a struggle for life or death, they both knew that the person that reached the gun first would be the only one leaving alive. Fury fueled them as they raced towards the tossed weapon. With it being just within reach they both dove for the gun, reaching it at the same time.

Pulling back and forth each tried to gain control. She

wrapped her hands around the handle trying to pull it away but losing the struggle, neither of them was willing to give an inch.

BOOM

The last and final bullet ejected from the chamber, causing both bodies to fall to the ground, one desperately clinging to life, the other teetering on the edge of death.

Download your copy today

ABOUT THE AUTHOR

DeiIra Smith-Collard is an author from Houston, Texas. With a creative writing style that intertwines fact with fiction, love and lust, and moral dilemmas, her books are thought to challenge the mind and question the lines of relationships, love and life.

DeiIra's first novel, Love Lust & a Whole Lotta Distrust was self-published in 2008 and met with great reviews. After the success of the first novel, DeiIra went on to write for Anexander Books, publishing her next 2 full length novels, Secrets, Sins and Shameful Lies and Role Play. In addition to her full length novels, she has also published a short story, My Extra and was also featured in 3 anthologies, Bedtime Stories ,Coffee Confessions and Love Never Fails.

In addition to writing DeiIra Smith-Collard is also the Founder and Editor-In-Chief for Le Charme Magazine and a freelance photographer/graphic and web designer.

Text GETLIT to 66866 for updates, giveaways and more!
www.deiirasmithcollard.com
info@deiirasmithcollard.com

ALSO BY DEIIRA SMITH-COLLARD

LOVE & LUST SERIES

Love Lust and A Whole Lotta Distrust

Secrets Sins & Shameful Lies

UNDISCLOSED SERIES

Undisclosed: A Tale of Love And Deceit

Undisclosed 2: A Tale of Obsession and Revenge

Undisclosed 3: A Tale of Passion and Betrayal

Full Disclosure: A Tale of Revelation And Resentment:

STAND ALONES

The Games We Play

My Extra: Short Story (Free Read)

www.ingramcontent.com/pod-product-compliance
Lightning Source LLC
Chambersburg PA
CBHW031018030726
47497CB00004B/913